# Alex Huntsman

Copyright ©2025 Line By Lion Publications
www.pixelandpen.studio
ISBN  978-1-948807-56-2
Cover Design by Thomas Lamkin Jr.
Editing by Dani J. Caile



For more information, email www.linebylionpublications.com

*For Jay, my first and truest fan*

# Prologue

AHSHA'S mind was beginning to drift just as her ship fell out of the Fastlane. The slowing of the craft was imperceptible at first, long enough for her to scramble to prevent some of the myriad of papers from being thrown off the central console. She grumbled as the deceleration grew more rapid, throwing her carefully sorted piles of seismic recordings around the already cramped cockpit. She gripped the side of her worn leather pilot's chair, feeling the familiar crackle of the aged synthetic skin. She'd flown this ship for so long, dropped into and out of so many different Fastlanes, that she knew the feel of the armrest like the back of her hand. She noticed another seam had popped loose, and a bit of support foam was beginning to push through. She made a mental note as the ship went through a final jolt and stopped.

Her craft had been designed to come to a full stop once it left a Fastlane. It was an old safety standard, one from the early days of expansion when the Fastlanes hadn't been mapped and a majority of the universe's asteroids were still floating freely through the vacuum. Nowadays, with almost every inch of the cosmos mapped and all but the important, habitable rocks blown to dust, ships could leave a Fastlane with barely so much as a pause. Still, Ahsha was a woman of habit, and she refused to replace her ship with a newer model. It wasn't out of any sense of attachment, however. Ahsha Reindare was a pragmatic woman to the core. If the ship still functioned, she saw no reason to throw it to the wayside in favor of some sleek, fancy model that would empty out her research funds.

She took her usual survey of the ship. Cabin, sleeping quarters, storage, cold storage, and the lab. In each one, she made sure nothing particularly important had shifted during the exit. As always, there wasn't a single item out of place. The whole survey took the same amount of time it always did: two minutes and sixteen seconds. It was easy to inspect your ship when you didn't waste time decorating or cleaning up old packets of research.

Her onboard AI chimed a low chord, indicating that they had arrived in the system as intended. Ahsha settled back into her pilot's chair and gazed out at the wide curved glass that lined the front of her ship. Technical readouts and planetary specifications hovered in the display near the edges, but her eyes were fixed solely on the object in the center of the screen.

*     *     *

CYGNUS-4 was a simple looking planet, one Ahsha had seen hundreds of times. It had a temperate, slightly varied climate that grew colder near its properly aligned northern and southern poles. It orbited the system's star at a reasonable distance, at a speed similar to the galactic average of 400 days in a single revolution. Ahsha knew all of this because she had studied this boring little planet with every waking moment over the last three days. Everything about it was so...ordinary. So unassuming. It was an out of the way, simple little world with a modest population and no major importance on a universal scale. Ahsha couldn't understand, then, why every being on that planet was going to die that day. She aimed to find out.

"Al, did you send out those files as I requested?" she asked aloud, breaking the silence that had permeated the ship for the entire journey.

"Of course, ma'am," a computerized voice responded in a stiff, monotone Universal Standard. "Your messages have been sent successfully."

Ahsha nodded, knowing better than to ask if there had been any response. "Keep the ship right here. Run low power systems and prioritize data preservation above all other systems."

"Understood," it chirped. "Would you like me to continue the data broadcast?"

Ahsha leaned back in the chair, allowing herself a few precious seconds to think. "No," she said finally. "Just make sure the files and the message go through, and back up the recordings every 2.3 seconds. And prep the skimmer, I'm going planetside."

"Are you sure that is advis-" She pressed a button on the center console, a personal modification she'd made years ago that overwrote the system's danger assessment systems. She had a lot to worry about today and wasn't about to waste time arguing with a computer.

"Have a safe journey and return soon, Captain." The automated response was annoyingly trite, but at least her ship wasn't talking back to her.

*　　　*　　　*

WITHIN a few minutes, Ahsha was gripping the flight stick of the skimmer, piloting the cramped craft away from her vessel and down towards Cygnus-4. She didn't take time to glance back at the ugly gray box she used to conduct her research. Lesser scientists saw their ships as secondary, or even primary, homes. To Ahsha, it was a ship. A simple tool to take her place to place. Her home was wherever there was something to study.

Cygnus-4's atmosphere was thinner than some of the industrialized worlds she'd been to; Ahsha barely had to watch the readout of her heat shield as the landscape below filled her viewport. A tired sounding voice requested a clearance code, which she transmitted with a roll of her eyes. As she guided the ship towards the single intersystem telescope array on the entire planet, Ahsha kept an eye on the sky.

The sky here was a dark blue. Not as pale as the ancient skies of Sol-3, but far removed from the dark purple of her homeworld, a colony known simply as Horizon's Edge. It was refreshing to look up and see a Sun in the sky, rather than the distant swirling white dwarf that her homeworld orbited. Try as she might, she found nothing unsettling in the sky. There were no dark, looming clouds promising a storm so violent it might disrupt the tectonic stability of the planet. The Sun, a single star that was younger than average for a system of this size, showed no signs of implosion or going into a spontaneous supernova. The ground below was even and unbothered, just a vast array of green, rolling plains occasionally pockmarked by brown fields of grain.

"It makes no sense," she muttered to herself, sending every reading back up to the ship as she began the landing process. "No sense at all."

Cygnus-4's telescope "array," if it could be called that, was about as ramshackle as Ahsha had ever seen. A single dish, about 200 standard meters long, hung over a modest assortment of computing towers and transmitters that barely fit in the shade of the dish. As Ahsha lifted the cockpit of her skimmer and stepped out onto the nearly empty tarmac, she made note of at least 23 components of the telescope that were vastly outdated and several more that could stand to be replaced. "Unbelievable," she spat to no one in particular as she strode across the walkway. A sign planted in the grass announced that this poor excuse for a scientific institute would be hosting a potluck and game night within the month. She tried to scoff, but the idea that the event would almost certainly never happen now made her keep walking.

The entrance was guarded by nothing but a human-sized conical machine with a tinny voice that requested a genescan before allowing entry. Ahsha pressed her thumb against the green glass embedded in the droid's outstretched arms three times before the scanner recognized her and printed out a visitor's name tag that read "Ms. Ashah Reindare, Visitor." It made Ahsha pause and rub her thumb across the laminated paper, before she clenched her teeth and made her way inside.

The doors slid open to reveal what looked more like the lobby of a seedy Rest-and-Refuel than a genuine data storehouse. Dark synthwood panels lined the wall, adorned with several framed paintings of sunsets and oceans. All of the chairs, thin black metal frames with cracked leather seats, were empty, save for the one behind a high desk in the corner of the room. Behind it sat a young man, Ahsha estimated he was in his forties, with glasses and short, neat hair. He was utterly plain, and gave her an utterly plain greeting.

She sighed as loudly as she could and crossed the room in four long steps. "My name is *Doctor* Ahsha Reindare," she explained, unhappy to be wasting time. "Your system misspelled my name. It also forgot several of my credentials and titles, as well."

The man looked taken aback for a few seconds before collecting himself. "Oh, I am so sorry about that, Dr. Reindare. We haven't gotten a genuine system upgrade or data package in ages. I'll get that fixed right away." He held out his hand for her card, which she slapped into his waiting palm.

"See that you do," she said matter-of-factly.

She waited in silence as he typed nervously at his station. After a moment, he handed her a new card with her correct name. "So, what brings a big shot Sol graduate all the way out here to Cygnus?"

Ahsha despised small talk. "A hypothesis," she answered simply.

"Oh, I see," the man said, raising his eyebrows. "Keep everything under your hat until the publishers have got their hands on it, totally understandable. So, what can I do to help?"

Ahsha chuckled. As if she was afraid of a backwater array staffer stealing months of her research and making sense of it, let alone craft a sensible enough article on it to be published. "I need to send a dataset of all seismological, meteorological, and solar readings you've gathered across the planet for the past six months. Also, I'll need a separate file containing every issue of the most popular news publication on the planet, as well as an archive of posts made by citizens to the Universal Web Union."

"Whoa," the receptionist said, acting like he was catching a breath. "Want me to send up my grocery list and the local holovision schedule for tonight too?"

"That won't be necessary."

"Right," he said slowly, giving her a side-eye that people on more urban planets had learned to do discreetly. Ahsha didn't mind. In fact, she barely noticed the way people so often tended to react to her blunt, pragmatic speech. "That's a pretty hefty set of data. We've got it all in the archive, sure, but it might be a few minutes before it can transfer up to orbit. Why don't you just make yourself comfortable while I send it up."

"I'll be outside, actually," she said. "Get it there as soon as possible; it's drastically important." She put as much emphasis into her words as possible, and as the man's typing grew faster she knew her words had the desired effect. If her calculations had been correct, and if Cygnus' satellite network was strong enough, all of the data would make its way to her ship before what happened next. Ahsha, satisfied with her work, went outside to stand in the grass and observe like any good scientist. She took a small pad of paper and a pen from the pocket of her coat and began scribbling furiously as she waited for the end of the world.

Five minutes later, her ship received a data package containing several petabytes of information on the planet below. Five minutes after that, Cygnus-4 was gone, and the ship hung there in space, completely still and pointed towards a planet that might as well have never been there in the first place.

# Chapter 1
## The Drunken Duck

IT wasn't until Tristan raised the glass to her lips that she realized it was empty. She'd been lost in thought, possibly for several minutes, staring blankly at the strip of pink light that lined the bar's baseboard as some horrid song droned over the speakers placed around the low building. She leaned forward as she set the glass down, and a stray curl of jet black hair fell into her face as she did so. She blew it back and made a note to take a knife to it as soon as she didn't have to focus to set down a glass the right way.

She slid out of the corner booth she'd claimed for the night and began unsteadily making her way to the U-shaped bar top along the wall. She made an effort to hold her hand still as she passed the bartender her charge card, on the off chance he decided to cut her off. "Whatcha need, Tris?" he said affably, setting down an opaque black cup that smelled of strong chemicals and stronger liquor.

Her voice came out gravelly and strained, a side effect of remaining silent since she'd arrived. "Let me get another one of whatever I was having." She turned her back to the bar and scanned the Drunken Duck. The bar was smaller than average compared to the other bars around the Belt, which she liked. It was tacky and dingy and overpriced, but it was the perfect place to vanish into a crowd without being smothered. It took a few passes for her to make up her mind. "And while you're at it, send a shot of spicelick to that lady in the red dress, a signorian cherry margarita to the brunette at the end of the bar...and a Fastlane to the lady sitting at that table over there."

The bartender raised an eyebrow, his bushy moustache curling into a smirk. "Nothing for me?" he asked while he began grabbing glasses.

"You know what, Ry? I'm feeling generous tonight. Pour yourself a tonic and put it on my tab." She knew he'd do it, too. He laughed and handed her drink to her.

"I've got 'em all charged. Take your drink and sit down, I'll get these all delivered and see which one comes up to you first."

"If you had to guess, which one will it be?" Tristan asked, taking a sip. He'd clearly taken most of the actual spirits out of the recipe, but she didn't mind. She was here to drink, not get drunk. Ry took a moment to watch each of the girls Tristan had pointed out and shrugged.

"Couldn't tell ya, Tris," he admitted, "but I'm willing to bet you won't be taking any of 'em back to that dock of yours."

Tristan leaned forward, her eyes alight. "Watch and learn, Ry." She was sweeping her drink off the counter when she saw the figure that had taken her table. For a moment, she thought it was just some patron who didn't know any better. Then she saw the dark hood drawn closely over their face, and the gloved hand tapping on the sticky barroom table impatiently. They had sat down on the opposite side of the table that Tristan had originally been in. Had they been watching her? For how long? How had she zoned out for so long that someone so obvious had followed her? Ry caught her staring and leaned closer over the bar. He pointed at the figure with his chin.

"Trouble?" he asked, all the joking gone out of his voice.

"I'm not sure," Tristan answered. "Don't bother Belt-Sec yet; I'll figure this out." She grabbed her drink a little tighter and made her way to the booth. The figure cocked their head just slightly to the side as she approached, but otherwise made no move towards her.

Tristan took a wide arc around the figure to the other side of the booth and slid down onto the hard plastic seat. The figure didn't have to remove their hood for Tristan to know exactly who it was.

"How the hell did you find me?" she asked bluntly. The woman across the table tilted her head back and revealed her face. It was a face Tristan hadn't seen in years, but still remembered clearly. She was all harsh angles: a jawline that may have been chiseled from bedrock, a steady, firm brow over wide, glimmering eyes, and a large nose that had a slight leftward bend to it, a feature Tristan had contributed to. Her dirty blonde hair was short; the straightened but unstyled strands falling just below her chin and dancing just above the bronze skin of her neck.

"You're not a hard woman to find, Tris," she said, her pale blue eyes just as piercing as ever.

"You *are* a hard woman to get rid of, Cordelle," she fired back. "And my name is Tristan, to you. My friends call me Tris. You are the furthest thing I have from a friend."

Joane Cordelle nodded bitterly. "Good to know you haven't changed, Ninomae. Still as cuddly as a gray bear."

"I just said my name is Tristan," she said, crossing her arms pointedly. "I know you remember how hard I can punch, and I promise you I've been practicing. So unless you want another broken nose, start telling me why you're here and what you want."

Joane eyed her for a minute, then let out a sigh. "Ahsha's gone."

"I know."

"You know?"

Tristan finished a long sip of her drink and nodded casually. "Yeah, I got her message a few days ago. I was trying to delete it but my holoscanner wasn't calculated right so it played anyway. Sounds like a crazy load of shit she's shoveled herself into. Doesn't explain why you're here."

A look of surprise flashed across Joane's face. Tristan felt a bit of satisfaction from it, like she'd slapped her without having to reach across the table. "I'm going to find her," she finally said after collecting herself.

It was Tristan's turn to be shocked. She, however, didn't bother collecting herself before responding. "Why?" she half-shouted. Several of the people in the bar glanced over at the table, and she glared back at each of them until they turned back around. "No, seriously, why?" she said, quieter this time.

"Did you listen to the message? All of it?" Joane asked, lowering her voice.

Tristan chewed her lip, trying not to look Joane in those piercing blue eyes of hers. She had always been good at prying. She didn't want Joane knowing that she had, in fact, read the entire message twice, just to be sure she wasn't imagining it. "I was only sort of paying attention," she said, "like I said, sounds crazy. I'm not about to risk my neck or any other part of my body going on a wild duck chase."

"Tristan, she could be dead!" Joane said quickly, struggling to stay quiet.

Tristan cut her off before she could keep talking. "Cordelle, Ahsha could've died any day in the past three years, and I wouldn't have known. You know why? Because I don't talk to her anymore. Because I left the damn galaxy to get away from her. Because she's a bitch."

"But she still sent you that message," Joane pointed out.

Tristan paused. Admittedly, she'd given that some thought. Ahsha had sent what may well have been her final words to her and Joane, who she hadn't spoken to in years. "I imagine she hasn't gotten any better at making friends since we all split up, simple as that. She felt the need to drag someone down with her, and we were the last people to waste our time on her."

"Whatever the reason," Joane continued, ignoring her just like Tristan remembered, "you saw what she was after, right?"

"Her absolutely insane hunches about the planets, yes, I gave them a quick look before flushing them from my ship's computer."

"They were some of the best guesses I've seen anywhere about what's been happening," Joane countered. Tristan gave her a look that made Joane frown. "Planets don't just vanish, Tristan."

"Apparently they do," she responded, taking another sip of her drink. "The universe is a big place, you know. They say that even though every known planet and star system has been colonized, only about three percent of space is really mapped out. Who knows what could be out there, just eating planets left and right?"

"How do you explain the fact that Ahsha sent her theory from Cygnus-4, the same day that planet disappeared off the map?" Tristan fell silent as Joane watched, expectantly. Finally, Tristan leaned back as far as she could into her seat.

"Luck," she said.

"Bullshit," Joane countered, putting her elbows on the table and pointing a finger at Tristan. "You do not believe that, and I know it."

"So what if I do?" Tristan snapped. "What do you want me to do? Help you find however many planets are gone now?"

"Twenty-seven. Twenty-eight now that Cygnus is gone," Joane added quickly. Tristan slumped into the uncomfortable seat and rubbed her eyelids.

"Tell me you didn't read through all of those files." Tristan had read the letter, yes. It was a terse, harshly-worded collection of requests that was nowhere near apologetic enough for her tastes. The mountains of files had nearly crashed her shipboard computer when the data package arrived. She wouldn't have known where to start even if she had bothered to open them.

"I've been keeping an eye on the Vanishings already. I thought that Ahsha may have found something helpful." Joane produced a few slips of hard paper from within her dark cloak. "Look at this: Ahsha's latest readings included six of the last ten planets to disappear. Clearly, that means she's on to something."

Tristan stared at the paper, glancing at a few lines of data that Joane must have picked out of millions. "Do you remember Ahsha?" she asked, flipping the card back onto the table. "Like, how she was?"

"I try not to, but yes, I do." The comment was so unexpected that Tristan couldn't help but laugh. Joane chuckled a bit with her before her face grew stony again. "What's your point?"

"My point is this: Ahsha is certifiably insane. I don't know if she smelled the wrong test tubes in her lab, or if she peeked through the blinders in a Fastlane, but her mind is gone. She nearly flew our ship into a black hole because she was convinced she could reverse the supernova process. She once ignited half of the Cartesian nebula on a hunch. She dragged us across the universe making one stupid mistake after another."

Joane was quiet for a long time. She began tapping her finger on the table, chewing the inside of her lip as she searched for a response. Tristan took the momentary rest to inspect the woman's face. She hadn't aged in the three years since they'd spoken, which wasn't surprising. There was more brown in her hair, and it was swept towards the right of her head instead of the left. She wasn't sure if it looked better or not that way. Her hazel skin had gone a bit pale, most likely from being off-planet for too long, but it still betrayed her Solan ancestry. Unlike most of the patrons of the bar, Tristan included, Joane Cordelle could trace her family line all the way back to Sol-3, the ancient homeworld of the race that had spread across the universe and eventually evolved out of existence, replaced by the millions of intermediate species they'd created as they spread across the stars.

Tristan was more Solan than most, with a traditional face shape of two eyes and a single mouth. However, her ash gray skin denoted her connection to one of the Hollow Worlds of the Dimmed Galaxy and the early years she spent entirely underground. It wasn't until she'd been hired by Ahsha that she ever thought she'd leave those tunnels…

"Tristan," Joane said forcefully, jolting her out of her stupor. "You weren't listening, were you?"

"Uh, no," she said truthfully. "I spaced out, what were you saying?"

Joane sighed heavily. "I'm going to Cygnus-4. I'm going to find whatever information I can, and then I'm going after Ahsha."

"It'll never happen. The Fastlanes near all the missing planets get too unstable to travel through, and the Consortium is too busy patrolling the sectors already; they aren't going to just let you through."

"Of course they aren't," Joane agreed. She reached a hand out across the table and snatched Tristan's glass. "That's why I found you. If you come with me, we have a better chance of-"

Tristan was already walking away. She'd humored her this long, but she refused to be dragged into another one of Ahsha's ridiculous schemes.

Joane caught up to her on the street outside. "Where are you going?" she yelled.

"Away!" Tristan shouted back, taking long steps into the narrow street. "You want to follow Ahsha headfirst into hell? Be my guest, but don't drag me down with you." By now, the Sun-Disc overheard had been switched off for the next several hours, and the streetlamps that peppered the city had taken over the job of illuminating the path. It was the closest thing they got to day and night here in the Belt, the line of asteroids so far from the system's sun that it was the same size in the sky as any other star. "You want to go chasing after her coattails, fine by me. I couldn't care less how you waste your time, as long as you don't waste mine with it."

"Come on, Tristan!" Joane said, still following her. "We aren't just talking about Ahsha. We are talking about countless lives, dozens of worlds, the safety of the entire Consortium. We have a chance here to do a lot of good, which might be a nice change of pace for you."

Tristan whirled around on one foot. Joane stopped mid-step when she saw the look in the woman's pale green eyes. "You...pretend to have any idea of what I've done since we split up? You act like you had the monopoly on all the morals in our happy little group? I've done a lot of good without you, and I can sure as hell do a lot more without killing myself for a wild tunnel-snake chase." Without realizing it, she had stepped over to Joane and was staring daggers directly into her eyes. The drinks had affected more than she'd previously thought.

"Are you saying no because it's Ahsha, or because it's me?" Joane asked. Her voice was calm; clearly she had no idea how close Tristan was to punching her. Still, the softness and vulnerability in her voice made Tristan take a half step back.

"Yes," she said, trying to slip as much malice into the word as she could. She knew she was lying, but Joane clearly didn't. Her face dropped into a deep frown and her eyes fell to the floor.

"Alright then," she said. "I'll leave you alone, I guess." She turned around and quickly made her way down the street.

"Where the hell are you going?" Tristan couldn't stop herself from calling after her.

Joane put her hood up as she walked, but she never turned as she answered. "I'm going after her. With or without you." Tristan instantly knew it was a fool's errand. Joane was a lot of things: dedicated, stubborn, clever, yes. She wasn't a good pilot, though. And she didn't know how to navigate an unstable hyperlane or run a blockade like she did.

Every part of her sensible brain yelled at her to let her walk away. They weren't friends, they weren't even colleagues anymore. Just seeing her had ruined Tristan's night. So why then, she wondered, did she know she couldn't let her go alone? She reached down to her side and yanked something from her belt. There was a soft click of thin metallic springs, followed by the quiet whistle of a thin silver bolt that streaked across the dimly lit street. Joane started as the bolt tore into her cloak and planted itself in the wall next to her head, pinning the black cloth there. She began frantically grabbing at the tiny bolt as Tristan approached, displaying her wrist crossbow openly and non-threateningly. There was a brief flicker of fear in Joane's eyes, even as she pulled a large knife from her belt with her free hand.

"If I'd wanted to hit you, I would've," Tristan assured her. She returned the crossbow to her thigh holster and clasped her hand around the bolt. "I've got a few conditions." Joane nodded slowly. "First, we take my ship. Secondly, you're gonna pay for fuel there and back, plus an extra spare tank for my trouble. And third, you're going to pay for all the supplies we need for this stupid little trip, which I will be picking out myself."

Joane straightened and stepped away from the wall as Tristan easily ripped the bolt free. "Anything else?" she asked sarcastically, "Are you sure you don't want to just take my wallet while you're at it?"

"Oh, don't worry, I did," Tristan said, holding up her hands. In one, she held the crossbow bolt. In the other, she was holding a small metal wallet. "You need to learn to watch both hands, Cordelle."

Joane reached forward and snatched the wallet back. "If we're going to do this, you might as well call me Joane, Tristan. There's no reason we can't be respectful."

Tristan chuckled. "*If* we're going to do this, you need to start packing. I'm gonna finish my drink and head down to the docks. Meet me at H-23. If you're not there by the time I get there, I'm leaving without you. And I promise, it won't be as easy to find me again. You get me?"

Joane rolled her eyes. "I get you. H-23. How do I know you're giving me the right dock number?" Tristan shrugged. "Right. This is going to be fun, I can already tell."

Tristan watched her walk away for a few moments. "Hey, Joane?" she said.

The woman turned, her eyebrows knit in confusion. "What is it?"

"When this is done, you'll leave me alone?"

Joane frowned, angrily this time. "Yes, Tristan. Help me try to save some lives and then I'll leave you alone. Will that make you happy?" She turned on her heel and walked off into the darkness, leaving Tristan wondering if she'd gone too far.

# Chapter 2
## The Docks

TRISTAN made her way inside, thrusting her hands into her pockets. As she stepped up to the door, the blue lights lining the entry panel lit up and the door began sliding open. She reached out, wrapped her fingers around the edge of the door, and shoved it open against the hydraulic system.

The Drunken Duck was already completely silent, broken only by the groan of the door trying to correct itself. Everyone was staring blatantly at Tristan. She stood there for a few seconds, glaring at each person in turn. When everyone had been sufficiently threatened into minding their business, she stomped to the back of the room and approached the bar.

"So, that was fun," Ry said, leaning against the counter. Tristan glared at him.

"You couldn't have...cranked the music, or something?" she asked. "You just had to let everyone listen in?"

Ry shrugged. "You didn't have to yell so much. I don't think I've ever heard you get that loud."

Tristan slapped her charge card on the counter as loudly as she could. "Your mother would disagree, asshole." Ry held up his hands placatingly and plucked the card off the counter.

"Relax, relax," he chuckled. "I'm just having a bit of fun. Seriously though, that sounded like...a lot. Guessing you want something pretty strong now?"

Tristan shook her head. "Nothing else for tonight, Ry. I'm going away for a bit. A while, actually. So I think I'm gonna close out my tab, just 'til I get back."

Ry nearly dropped the card from his hand. "Tris, I- What the hell are you talking about?" he said, halfway laughing. "You never close out your tab. Ever! It's extremely frustrating."

Tristan smiled at him, warmer than he'd ever seen her smile. "Thanks for the drinks, Ry."

He closed out the tab in bewildered silence while Tristan took one last look around the bar. She'd spent a lot of nights here since she came to the Belt almost two years ago. She'd found work, dates, and most of all drinks in the Drunken Duck. As Ry handed her card back, she couldn't help but feel like this might be the last time she set foot in here.

"You're coming back, right?" he asked. "Place feels a bit emptier when I lose a regular."

Tristan couldn't bring herself to say anything. She'd learned never to promise anyone she'd come back.

*    *    *

JOANE was at the docks five minutes after she left Tristan. Everything in the Belt, she learned, was packed as close together as possible. When you were forced to carve out a city on a network of asteroids lashed together with thick metal bridges and tunnels, you learned to be pretty efficient about your space. She gave the number to the Consortium guard manning the login desk, a bored looking man who didn't comfortably fit into his uniform. He tapped something on his keyboard, and gave her a long list of turns and landmarks to follow to get to the dock. Joane committed each turn to memory and thanked the man before taking off into the network of stone hallways. The worked stone arched high over Joane's head, echoing each of her quick footsteps as she made her way through the empty space. A sign on the wall said the docks had been designed to mimic ancient Solan transportation systems. Joane thought it was a nice touch to the decor, but it was unsettling to walk through alone. In all honesty, she didn't need the directions she'd been given as much as she did. There were several signs hanging over each archway pointing her to dozens of different levels. The network was more complicated than it needed to be, but it gave Joane time to think about Ahsha's message and what Tristan had said. It had occurred to her that Ahsha may have been wrong, or just plain lying about her hunch. Still, she had sent her message from Cygnus-4, and then the planet had vanished. Joane had run with Ahsha and Tristan long enough to know when something was seriously wrong, and when Ahsha was being...extravagant. The letter Ahsha had written had been addressed to *her*. Apparently, she'd sent it to Tristan too, but that was still more personal than Ahsha had ever gotten with her.

Ahsha had only ever treated her and Tristan like employees. To be fair, they'd started that way. Ahsha had been a young researcher needing protection for a field research opportunity out in some badlands near the Dimmed Galaxy. Joane had signed up, needing the money after her last muscle job had fallen through. They picked up Tristan from her homeworld not long into the mission, after the other man Ahsha hired had been eaten by a giant glowbug.

Joane chuckled humorlessly as she thought about that first trip. It hadn't been the first time she'd watched someone die, and it certainly wasn't the last. A few years into their five-year employment, when Ahsha had accidentally ordered an alcohol far stronger than she normally drank, she had admitted to Joane that it had been the first death she'd watched. Years after that conversation, Joane still thought about it from time to time. She'd thought about it a lot in the few days since she'd read that message. It was full of the same forced, uncomfortable vulnerability that she'd seen in Ahsha that night. She knew that it hadn't been easy to write that message, partially because Ahsha had said no more than five times in the letter, "this is hard for me to write."

Joane suddenly found herself standing at the entrance to dock H-23. The intricate, vintage-looking stonework gave way to genuine meteorite metal panels and advanced screens and readouts being displayed on the holo-walls. As she stepped through into the dark space, lights flared up in the floor and the ceiling, bathing the ship in a pale yellow light. The sight nearly made Joane step back into the hallway.

All the way here, she wasn't certain one way or another whether Tristan had given her the actual dock number. In all their time together, Joane had learned to read Ahsha, but she never fully figured out Tristan Ninomae. They'd become fast friends after she joined the small crew, mostly bonding over complaining about Ahsha. Regardless, when things fell apart, Tristan had turned on Joane as soon as possible and disappeared out into the universe. She was surprised Tristan had even spoken to her, let alone agreed to come with her. She hadn't wanted to believe it was true, but here it was. "Hello, Darling," Joane whispered to the vessel parked in front of her.

Their old ship wasn't the most beautiful thing in the cosmos. Tristan and Joane had tried to spice it up, but Ahsha had stonewalled them at every possible turn, claiming it to be a waste of time and resources. It hadn't stopped them from hijacking it one night when they came into port and giving it the most garish, ridiculous red and white paint job. Ahsha had been furious for a few days, but looking at the deep crimson paint and twin strips of white paint that ran the length of the ship made Joane crack a smile.

"I was kind of hoping you wouldn't show up," a voice behind her piped up. Joane had trained herself not to jump at sudden noises after years running merc jobs, so she didn't flinch as she turned to see Tristan approaching.

"I wasn't expecting you to," she answered plainly. Joane turned towards the ship and waved a hand towards it. "You kept it."

Tristan looked up at the ship, trying to appear nonchalant. "It's a good ship," she muttered, hands in her pockets. "I don't like her, but Ahsha had taste. And money. I see you packed light."

Joane looked down at her simple black cloak she'd worn to hide her reinforced outfit. The brown jacket and blue shirt was just visible under the folds of simple dark cloth. "I...don't have any other clothes." she said. Tristan fixed her with a glance.

"Alright then, well," Tristan said slowly, making her way to the ship. "Just don't sit too close in the cockpit, yeah?"

She pounded a fist against a random panel, which popped open to reveal a few hastily wired buttons. She pushed one, which sparked violently as the ramp began to lower out of the back of the ship.

"It's self-cleaning," Joane stammered, scrambling to follow Tristan, who vaulted up onto the ramp as it was still settling into position.

If the outside had felt comfortably familiar, the inside was completely alien. Crates and boxes of all sorts lined the already narrow hallways. A few of them were sealed closed with keypad locks, while a few were overflowing with random pieces of junk. Several of the panels had been replaced, repainted, or removed entirely, revealing the solid silver hull underneath. Temperature regulators blasted alternating waves of hot and cold air from their empty circular frames. Tristan was halfway around a stack of boxes when she turned to glance at Joane. "I don't want to hear a word of it. I move around a lot, so I don't have anywhere else to put this stuff. And this is good stuff, too, so I'm not gonna trust some storage barge out in the middle of the void to keep it safe."

Joane shrugged. "I can't blame you. It's just...do you bring people back here?" Tristan raised an eyebrow. "I saw you buying drinks for half the bar back there, don't be coy."

The pilot shook her head, making the long strands of black curls form a sort of wave around her face as she scowled. "Let's get one thing straight, Joane. You are not my friend. I am not your friend. You are the person buying my fuel and my supplies, and I'm your pilot. That means we do not need to talk about personal lives at all. Got it?"

Joane sighed. "Fine. Might get a bit boring, but fine." Without thinking, she slid around a row of boxes bristling with climbing equipment and made her way towards her old room. Even three years later, it was almost automatic. She made a note of everything Tristan had changed. Monitors she'd removed, scientific stations that had been repurposed into shelves, all of it felt wrong, like walking through a familiar place in a dream. Just enough details were different that it didn't feel right, but it was still undeniably the ship that had been her home for years. Most notably, Tristan had taken down any small hint towards their past together. Pictures, memos, even the deed of ownership with all their names on it; they'd all been torn down. Joane imagined they'd been jettisoned out into a Fastlane not long after they all fell apart. It was all the same, though. Joane wished she could throw her memories of that time out the airlock, sometimes, too.

The door to her room was wiped clean of her nameplate. Instead, the thin strip of silver embedded in the synthwood simply read "Cloth Goods and Papers." She hesitantly tapped a few numbers on the keypad: the galactic latitude and longitude of Sol-3. To her shock, the door chimed and slid open, revealing a darkened room a bit larger than a sizable closet. The floor was invisible under a mass of random lengths of fabric, soft and sturdy, brightly colored or plain, massive blankets and tiny handkerchiefs.

"I had a problem with some mites that got onboard a while ago," Tristan explained, suddenly behind her. "Your room was the only place that stayed sealed, so I kept all the important paper and stuff in here."

"You kept the lock the same," Joane said, smiling a bit as she stepped onto the nearest pile of shirts.

Tristan shrugged it off. "I figured out the code the week I moved in. I didn't want to mess with resetting it." Joane wanted to say something about all the trouble she'd gone to scrubbing the rest of the ship clean, but decided to let it lie. "We're going to be hitting the Fastlane pretty soon, so uh, don't move around too much."

"You need any help getting the ship ready?" Joane offered. She thought she heard Tristan laugh for a second.

"Absolutely not. When you're on my ship, you don't touch anything that controls *anything*. I've done a lot of work on this ship; I think I might be the only person who *can* fly it. Just...stay here. Move everything if you want, but just be...careful with it, because I need a lot of this stuff," Tristan said, gesturing around the room. "I left everything in here alone, just piled stuff on top of it." She nodded quickly and left without another word.

Joane listened to the sound of heavy footfalls on the semi-hollow floor panels as Tristan made her way to the front of the ship. She reached blindly for the lightswitch, placing her palm flat against the wall before finally finding the control wheel. She clicked it in, feeling the satisfying click of the button that she thought she'd completely forgotten, then spun the wheel towards her. The lights flared up around the baseboard, the same orangish-yellow light she had set up ages ago. It didn't feel like home again, but it was something.

# Chapter 3
## Pre-Flight Checks

TRISTAN dropped herself into the cockpit chair, picking her feet up off the floor so she could gently spin with the momentum. She laid her head against the high plush back, closing her eyes hard and trying to figure out what exactly she was doing here. She'd spent three years trying to put Ahsha and Joane behind her, and all it took was one night for them to both come crashing back into her life.

She tried to put it out of her mind by putting herself to work. She spent very little of the pre-flight prep in the pilot's chair. Ahsha's ship had always been designed to be crewed by several people. With Tristan as the only person onboard for the past few years, she'd had to learn the ship in and out to be able to perform every role simultaneously. She'd wired most of the ship's power controls, defense mechanisms, and scanning capabilities to the steering console, but it was easier just to walk around and activate each station individually.

One by one, she made her way between stations. One by one, each one gave green reports like they always did. Tristan took good care of Darling. She treated it well, and in return, it did the same to her, unlike her old crew. The other two had always looked down on Tristan. It went unsaid, but she could tell they both thought she was less than them. She wasn't educated, strong, or even particularly good with people. The one thing she was good at, though, was flying.

It took about fifteen minutes to get the ship ready for launch, an impressive speed for one person piloting a sizable research vessel. Tristan finally plopped back into her personally modified pilot's chair, cracked her knuckles, and drummed her fingers across the dashboard.

"Good morning, Darling," she said aloud, and the bridge flared fully to life. Pale blue overhead lights clicked on, picking out every detail of the bridge, which was the one place on the ship Tristan made sure to keep completely spotless. There was the distant thrum, about 40 meters behind her, of the engines flaring with the same blue light. She took a brief look at the rear-facing cameras, looking at the short white wings that ended in long bulbous repulsor engines. She counted the power rings on each engine: eight a piece, all full with rotating blue plasma that was ready to lift the arrow-shaped ship off the ground. She turned away from the cameras and activated the exhaust vents, clearing any dust or debris that may have found its way into the flight system's inner workings.

With the roar of air escaping the vent at the back of the ship, she deployed the control sphere from within the console. Suspended on a vent of grav-pulses, Darling was piloted by a many-sided control "sphere" that allowed the ship to move in most directions without wasting time turning or course-correcting. It had taken Tristan months to learn how to operate the finicky, ultra-responsive system. Growing up, she'd flown the more common models of joystick and steering wheel-based ships, but she doubted she'd ever go back to those clunky systems.

She slowly brought her hand up under the sphere, feeling the grav-pulse tingling across the back of her hand. The gray sphere lit up white wherever her hand cupped it, letting out a slight hum of acknowledgement.

With a slow curve of her wrist, she brought her palm around to the top of the sphere, and the ship slowly pulled itself off the landing locks. She put her second hand to the left side of the sphere, and the ship began turning towards the left, rotating in the cramped garage space. Flashing yellow lights directed her towards the gaping hole in the far side wall, through which Tristan could see the infinite expanse of stars and planets before her. She put her right hand against the back of the sphere and pushed forward, urging the ship into the tunnel. She had promised herself when she left her homeworld that she would never, ever take this view for granted. As Darling burst out of the smooth stone tunnel into the expanse of void between the asteroids, Tristan let her eyes widen with the same wonder they had when she first left the Hollow Worlds on this very same ship.

She maneuvered the ship to be exactly halfway between the asteroid they'd just left and one of the other nearby rocks. She enjoyed drifting between the two cities, with the larger buildings on each side reaching towards each other. When she flew between them, she felt like they were reaching out for her, trying to grab a hold of her ship and keep her there for just a bit longer. It was immature and stupid, but it made her feel better about leaving. It was nice to imagine herself being missed by someone for once. She gradually curved her hands around the control sphere, angling Darling up and away from the Belt and towards the cloud of ships waiting for Fastlanes a few dozen kilometers away.

The Consortium Wayfaring Station at the Belt was, oddly, one of the most well-kept businesses in the entire region. The Consortium, as far as governments went, was pretty effective considering how much territory they covered. Still, the Wayfaring Stations where they generated and connected Fastlanes often fell into disrepair and mismanagement. With the amount of traffic, legitimate or otherwise, that came through the Belt, it was obvious the Consortium wanted to put their best foot forward. The massive circular station was made of bright, gleaming silver, with powerful gold lights that dotted the edge shining like a second Sun-Disc. Tristan groaned as she brought Darling up into the cloud, pulling the ship to a halt a few dozen meters away from a boxy green thing that looked barely held together and an odd blue craft that Tristan wasn't familiar with. She tapped at her console, already exasperated at what promised to be several hours of waiting. Finally, she successfully pinged the station staff, and the winged seal of the Consortium appeared on her comm-screen.

Tristan sat in silence for what felt like hours, but might have really been about ten minutes. She was in the middle of kicking the floor, pushing her chair around in circles, when a sickly sweet voice filled the cockpit. "Hello, welcome to the Consortium of Worlds' Wayfaring Station Number 867328. My name is Riedelle, how can I help you sail the stars today?"

"I need supplies for 3 universal standard weeks, fuel for three times that, and a Fastlane to the Waning Crescent system," Tristan said bluntly.

The woman, Riedelle, barely suppressed her sigh. "Understood...Darling. We'll have some of our automated supply drones fuel and supply your vessel while we begin calibrating the warpblades for your journey. Please make sure your airlock is unobscured and available for docking with Consortium standard procedure. Also, I have to let you know that this calculation might take longer than our usual lead time, because of the distortion caused by the recent vanishing of Cygnus-4."

Tristan had expected this. Thankfully, the Waning Crescent nebula was just far enough away that the Consortium was still allowing civilians to travel there. It would mean a week of standard travel through the void, which Tristan hated, but it was better than having to deal with questions from the Consortium bureaucrats on the other end of the call. "Yeah, yeah, just tell me how long."

Dealing with the Consortium officers was tiring, but Tristan wasn't really as exasperated as she acted. She'd learned plenty of times that people don't like interacting with assholes. She always tried to be as standoffish as possible to anyone in those stupid blue coveralls so they would do what she asked and then move along without too many questions. Today, she hoped  she'd be proven right again.

"About three hours," the woman on the other end said, the cheeriness gone from her voice. "You'll be pinged when the Fastlane is ready for you. Fly safe and true with the wings of the Consortium." Tristan groaned after the connection ended with a sharp click. Three hours. Three hours of waiting for a Fastlane, in a cloud of similarly bored pilots, with a passenger she definitely did not want onboard. She quickly set the ship to hover mode, dimmed the cabin lights, and kicked her chair back into a reclining position where she could lay back and stare at the stars through the window. There were too many ships in the way to draw constellations in her mind, her tried-and-true time killer, so she simply watched the distant twinkling until her eyes began to feel heavy.

*     *     *

"TRISTAN!"

She shot back to consciousness. Her vision blurred as she fought the sleep out of her eyes.

"Tristan!" Joane shouted again from the entryway. "Are you planning to answer that?"

Tristan sat up, leaning forward onto her knees. She didn't remember falling asleep, but her hair felt tangled and untidy and her tongue was heavy in her mouth. The ringing in her ears, she quickly discovered, wasn't just a product of being woken up so quickly. The screen on her console was lit up blue, and the Consortium wings were flapping away on it. Tristan swore repeatedly at herself while she adjusted the captain's chair back to its normal position.

She slapped the comm-screen, and an annoyed sounding voice filled the cabin. "Vessel Darling, are you there?" It was a different officer this time, sounding a touch more gruff than the one Tristan had checked in with.

"Uh, yes, yes," Tristan said, forgetting to be rude in her stupor. "We were just- uh, having a bit of trouble with the comm array. Are we all set?"

"No worries, Darling," the officer said, "We're just pinging you to let you know that your requested Fastlane to the Waning Crescent Nebula has finished plotting and we are ready to generate it the moment you are ready."

Tristan slapped herself across the face and deployed the control sphere. "All good on my end, Wayfaring Station," she responded, waking up the ship's engines in the process. She could feel Joane standing behind her, watching the entire show.

"Excellent, please proceed to the runway coordinates we've marked on your navigation system and prepare for Fastlane generation. Fly safe and true with the wings of the Consortium!"

"Rest secure in its nest," she answered like a reflex. She may have imagined it, but she thought Joane laughed. The channel clicked off, and Tristan began nudging Darling through the thinner cloud of ships waiting their turn for the gate. As she drifted carefully around a box carrier waiting to return to a storage barge somewhere, she turned her head slightly towards the back of the cockpit.

"It's not a good idea to be walking around when we take a Fastlane," she said. Now that she was more awake, she was back to being annoyed at her passenger. "Or have you finally gotten your space legs?"

"If it's all the same to you, I think I'll stay in here until we're on autopilot. I'd hate for my pilot to fall asleep at the controls again."

"Whatever," Tristan muttered. "How long was I out?"

Joane shrugged and took her old seat near the recon station. "I'm not sure. They were pinging us for a good five minutes, though." Tristan sighed and pushed her hair back from her face. "I guess you never stopped napping wherever you could, huh?"

Tristan wanted to say something snarky in return, but simply rolled her eyes at the woman. "And you never stopped barging into places, huh?"

Joane smiled and shook her head. It was that same shit-eating grin she'd grown to either love or hate depending on the day. Tristan twisted her hand sharply to rotate the ship into position, forcing Joane to grab the edges of her chair to steady herself. Tristan chuckled slightly to herself.

They both fell silent as the Wayfarer's Gate filled the viewport. A hollow circle the size of a small city, the lights around the edge highlighted the intricate power systems and relays that covered the ring's surface. In a motion that would've been unbearably loud in an atmosphere, seven massive silver warp-blades deployed from around the inside edge of the circle. The edge of each curved blade began to glow, dimly at first, then brighter and brighter until they outshone the stars twinkling in the void beyond. Then, they began to spin. It took a monumental amount of power to activate and use the warp-blades, a drain offset only by the output of the millions of power production planets scattered across the Consortium. Every time she watched them spin, she thought of the sprawling worlds covered in wind turbines, hydro-dams, and solar absorption screens. Worlds ten times larger than her homeworld with a population of only a few thousand. She tried not to think about it, compared to how little habitable space there was on the Hollow Worlds. The blades kept spinning, consuming a small star's worth of power as the lights began to become thin lines of white, then a solid ring that glowed brighter and brighter as the blades spun faster, tearing a thin sheet through the pure emptiness of the void.

The blades speed picked up as they began extending towards the center of the ring, the light following close behind. Soon, the blades would meet, the gate would be finalized, and the Fastlane would be open. Tristan watched the dancing, racing white light for as long as she thought her eyes could take it. Joane squinted her eyes almost completely closed, then put a hand up to shield her face, then turned away entirely. When Tristan was just beginning to feel the edges of her vision go dark, she slammed the button and closed the shutters on the viewport. Darling's curved glass immediately disappeared behind an unyielding wall of gray metal that cast the cockpit into near-darkness. There was silence for a moment, during which Tristan held her breath and moved the palm of her hand to the back of the control sphere.

Then, the all-clear chime rang out, and she pushed as hard as the ship's engines would allow her. Darling lurched forward, the pulsing engines roaring throughout the ship. They shot forward like a dart towards a gate they couldn't see, the shields flashed their usual warning, and for a moment, every system on the ship crashed at once. It felt like the ship, and everything in it, was drifting weightlessly.

And then, with the only sound that could be heard in space, they entered the Fastlane.

# Chapter 4
## Life in the Fastlane(s)

JOANE had always considered herself an adventurous person. She had refused a cushy job in the Consortium, sought out the dingiest, most backwater planets to travel to, and only took the jobs that sounded like they might be interesting, regardless of how much they paid. She was always eager to seek out new experiences; the riskier the better.

All that said, she *hated* Fastlanes. On paper, they were phenomenal. They took space travel from a slow, arduous process of warp drives and void hopping to near-instantaneous jumps through brief, controlled rips through space itself. The Wayfaring Stations were the crown jewel of the Consortium. In fact, they were the only reason something like the Consortium existed. No government could have dreamed of spanning the entire universe without making travel so fast and efficient.

Still, did it have to be so loud? The boom of entering a Fastlane defied physics just by existing, much like the rest of the concept. It always sounded a bit too much like an airlock decompressing for Joane's liking. And no matter how many times they were proven to be entirely safe, she could never get over the feeling of the ship shaking and groaning as it rocketed across millions of light years a second. She found herself staring at the shutters while vibrating in her seat, praying they would stay closed. No one talked about what staring at the inside of a Fastlane could do, because no one knew. The ship was traveling through a hole in reality. Whatever nonexistence surrounded their ship right now, Joane's eyes were not meant to see it.

Tristan's voice was somehow audible over the groan of the hull around them. "Hanging in there?" she said, sounding bored. Joane frowned to herself.

"I'm fine." Joane could hear herself gritting her teeth. Tristan tilted her head towards her.

"Well, if you say so. Just know it'll probably be a few hours. Even by Fastlane standards, we've got a ways to go, so I can't blame you if you wanna get some shuteye." That was the thing about Tristan. It was so hard to tell when she was being genuine and when she was trying to get something out of you.

"You just want me out of your way," Joane guessed. She was shocked when a moment of hurt passed across her former friend's eyes.

"No," she said slowly, "I just- I thought you always hated this part, so you'd want to...Whatever, do what you want."

The cockpit fell silent for a long while, broken only by the horrible sounds of the ship. Finally, Joane couldn't stand it. "I'm sorry," she groaned, unsure if she meant it or if she just needed something to drown out the awful noise. "It's been a while, and I just got defensive. Thank you for offering."

Tristan nodded, but said nothing. They lapsed into silence again for a while. Joane began to feel nauseous. "I think I am going to lay down, though," she said, holding her stomach as she got up. "Can you come get me when we get to the Nebula?"

"Yeah," Tristan said, checking some internal data that Joane had no hope of deciphering. "Don't puke all over my ship, if you can help it, or you're paying for cleaning when the job's done."

"I don't have enough credits to my name to have this ship cleaned properly," Joane called over her shoulder as she maneuvered around a pile of what she recognized as temperature control units. Her leg hit something that fell over with a resounding clatter, but she could barely see what it was. She cursed as she stumbled out into the hall, the noise cut off by the hissing of the cockpit door.

*  *  *

TRISTAN chuckled to herself. "Probably not," she whispered. She pretended to be checking the system for a bit longer, just until she was sure her passenger was gone, then threw her head back against the seat and sighed.

It was just like old times, both of them looking for any reason, real or imagined, to start a fight. If only Ahsha had been there, it could've devolved into a screaming match that ended with something being thrown and knocking something important off a shelf, which would have kept Ahsha mad until the next fight started, and on and on again. And for what? Tristan had been trying to be friendly, for whatever reason. She didn't want Joane to sit and suffer through one of her greatest fears if she didn't have to, and that made Tristan the bad guy? She should've just let the woman struggle through however many hours the trip would take.

She sat and steamed for a long while, glaring at the shutters so hard she worried her eyes might burn a hole through them. Finally, she decided it would be easier just to kick her seat back and finish her nap from earlier.

*     *     *

JOANE stumbled her way through the ship, grumbling every time she bumped into something. She managed to make it to her room without vomiting all over any of Tristan's precious garbage, and made sure to close the door behind her.

During the wait for the Fastlane, Joane had set about turning her room back into a somewhat livable space by shoving the mass of scarves, blankets, and tapestries off to either side, making a narrow path through to her bed. It was all she really needed; she hadn't intended the trip to be comfortable by any means. The fact that Tristan had only shot at her once so far was actually pretty encouraging in her mind. It didn't make anything she said sting any less, though.

She collapsed face first onto her bed, letting her body sink into the heavy foam mattress before rolling onto her side. She reached out to the small shelving unit that sat next to her bed and rested her hand on the dusty synthwood. When this was her home, there had been a framed holopic of the three of them sitting there. It was some random still from an afterparty to a scientific conference Joane couldn't remember. Ahsha had been recognized for some data they'd helped her gather and credited them on the paper. The details had always been fuzzy to Joane, mostly because of the amount of champagne the three of them drank that night. She would never forget that picture, though. It was the one picture she had where all three of them were smiling. She tapped her finger against the empty shelf.

"I thought you might've missed this, too," she said to no one, her voice strained. Darling groaned like she might tear herself in half in response. Joane closed her eyes hard and tried to scream over the noise. When it died down a bit, she opened her eyes and realized she'd pushed out the tears she'd been holding back.

Swearing at herself, she grabbed a random fabric, a scarf made of crimson plastifiber, and wiped her face. There was no way she was getting through this Fastlane. A thought crossed her mind, and she reached into the drawer of her nightstand. It took her a second to find the slot she carved, but eventually she managed to pull the false bottom out. Originally, she'd kept the sleeping supplements out in the open, but Ahsha had let her know that Tristan would swipe them occasionally, so Joane had to start hiding them. She sighed with relief when she found the compartment still full of the small blue capsules. She popped one in her mouth and bit down, and the familiar bitter taste of sleep hormones and depressants took over her mind in a matter of seconds. She wondered if, after three years, the medicine's effects may have dulled.

That was the last thought she had before sleep took her.

# Chapter 5
## The Waning Crescent

THERE was a hand on her shoulder. For a moment, she thought the ship was still shaking, then she realized it was just her. Her head felt like it was underwater, still swimming from the sleeping capsule. Someone was calling to her and shaking her harder than before.

"Cordelle!" the voice came through the fog in her mind, sounding more worried than exasperated. Joane moaned in protest as her eyes began to open. "Finally. Stars above, I thought I was gonna have to pitch you out of the airlock. One more condition for the rest of this trip, you don't scare me like that again, yeah?"

Joane pulled herself away from the mattress reluctantly and turned towards the voice. When she saw Tristan standing over her, she was consciously thankful she had fallen asleep in her jacket. "Whahappen?" she mumbled.

"We're here, Joane," Tristan said loudly. "Thought you'd wanna see."

"Right, right, yeah," she responded, untangling herself from the thin sheets. Tristan looked her over and left the room without another word.

Joane made her way into the cockpit a few minutes later, trying to smooth down her short auburn hair into something that looked partially presentable. Tristan glanced over her shoulder from the captain's chair. "You good?" she asked hesitantly.

"I'm fine," she mumbled, striding over to her spot. "It's been a while since I've had a sleep capsule, that's all."

"Those things are rough," Tristan mumbled. "Didn't think you'd mess around with that kind of junk. Anyway, I thought you'd wanna take a look before we got underway." Joane followed Tristan's finger to the viewport, which was angled towards a sprawling nebula a few thousand kilometers away. It was roughly the shape of an oval, glowing from within with a dim red light. From this distance, it was difficult to pick out the individual stations peppered throughout the gas cloud, mining the scattered elements of the nebula.

More than anything, Joane was happy not to be staring at the shutters anymore. "It's been a while since I've been to a nebula, you know," she said, making sure there was no edge to her voice.

Tristan answered with the same careful, friendly tone. "Me too, actually. Not a lot ever goes on around these-"

As if the universe had heard her, there was a roar somewhere in the distance. Tristan glanced down at her console and saw only green lights. There was nothing wrong with the ship, which could only mean the roar was coming from the void outside, which could only mean-

"There's a Fastlane opening, right on top of us!" Joane yelled, her eyes glued to the recon station now. Tristan wasted no time wondering how or why two Fastlanes had been plotted to the exact same location. She palmed the control sphere and nearly threw it towards the viewport. Darling rocketed forward, her engines screeching with the sudden acceleration.

With her other hand, she brushed the front of the sphere, pivoting the ship around as it continued to rocket up and away from the exit point. Mere seconds later, what looked like a crack almost a kilometer long appeared in the void, and a cube nearly two hundred meters long cascaded through. The unstable Fastlane flickered and vanished, leaving only the giant orange vessel careening towards the nebula. Tristan and Joane both recognized it as a storage carrier. The four small engines located on the bottom corners of the craft were completely inert, but the leftover inertia from the Fastlane meant the cube was flying impossibly fast.

Tristan muttered a curse under her breath and pressed both hands to the back of the control sphere. Darling's engines soaked up every ounce of power they could hold and jettisoned it as soon as possible. The arrow-like ship shot through the vacuum, tracing lines of pale blue behind it as they chased the massive object. "Try and raise the pilot!" Tristan shouted at Joane, who nodded gravely and began scanning the available wavelengths.

Joane's eyes rapidly scanned the radiowave frequencies that were functional in this sector, selecting each one as she went. "Off course storage carrier, this is Darling, can you hear us? Are you in control of the vehicle?"

"Joane!"

"What?"

"Don't bother, it's a waste of time."

"How do you know that?" she shouted, spinning to face the pilot, whose eyes had gone wild with intensity.

"Because their comms array just bounced off our starboard shield."

Joane turned and scanned the ship. It was hard to tell because of how fast it was moving and spinning, but Joane definitely didn't see the narrow tower of a comms array anywhere. "Look, we have to slow this thing down before it gets to the nebula, or we're gonna have a bigger problem. The place is chock full of monitoring stations, gas mining, and stabilizers. If this thing hits any of them, there's a pretty good chance it could ignite the fuel in the engines and take a good part of the nebula with it."

"So what do we do?" Joane felt like the response took ages to come.

"Well, easy answer is to blow it up now, and hope everyone on board is already dead. Or, we could do something really stupid," Tristan said, her voice unreadable. Joane met her gaze. Her light gray skin had darkened under the stress, turning the same slate gray as the ship's interior panels. That same intensity was focused on her, asking a simple question: *I trusted you enough to come on this trip, do you trust me?* Joane hesitated, but she nodded. "Alright then," Tristan said, her voice hissing through the grin spreading across her face, "Let's open her up."

Joane's neck flew back with the force of Darling's acceleration. She had no idea what Tristan had done, but they were gaining on the carrier now and the ship was shaking harder than it had in the Fastlane. "Joane!" the pilot called, "I need you on the weapons station; get as many Jumpstart Charges in that thing as you can, see if you can get the engines up."

Joane hadn't fired a starship's weapons in ages, but knew better than to argue. At the moment, she was the only real option. By the time she had brushed the dust off the station and devoted the smallest amount of power possible to the weapons, the carrier was nearly filling the viewport. She shifted her eyes to the screen, where the ship's tiny forward-facing weapons transmitted their targeting vectors. The Jumpstart Charges hopefully wouldn't damage the freighter; they would simply provide an electrical charge to the ship in order to try and restart its systems. She waited until the gun-mounted cameras lined up perfectly with the carrier and fired. On either side of the cockpit, she heard the crackle of electricity charging and releasing from the turrets.

The lines coursed the void, dissipating rapidly as the energy dispersed into the emptiness. They might have reached the ship, but both lines of blue-white energy went wide. Both women swore. Tristan glanced down at her master console and checked the map display.

"We're coming up on the nebula fast, Joane. We can't afford to be missing right now."

"I know!" she hissed back, "Just hold us steady."

"We're perfectly level! Just hit the thing! It's bigger than our ship! You know the whole saying 'oh, you can't hit the broad side of a storage barge?' Because that's you, now!" Joane gritted her teeth and pulled the trigger, harder this time. The shots landed on the carrier, but dissipated uselessly across the scratched orange storage unit.

Joane stared daggers back at Tristan. "There, I hit it. It didn't work."

"I noticed, Joane, thank you so much!" Joane shrunk back into her chair. Not because of Tristan's words, or the fear that they might get swallowed up in the fireball that destroyed the nebula if this ship went. No, the thing that scared Joane the most was the fact that in the middle of everything, Tristan was *smiling at her*. Not a malicious or mocking smile, either. She looked genuinely happy at that moment. "Charge it up again, I'll get us closer." She shoved the control sphere harder and the ship rocked with the force of the engines.

The carrier grew even larger in the viewport, and it fully filled Joane's camera view. She yelped and released the charge, but the impact was lost as the two ship's shields crashed into one another, sending Darling careening off to the side. Tristan reoriented the ship as quickly as she could turn her head. The engines were still completely inert.

"We're only going to get one more shot at this before they hit the nebula," she reported, watching the map as she blindly set the ship back on course. "If we can...uh, blast the couplings? We can separate the carrier from the ship, maybe try and divert some of the momentum?"

"No," Joane called back. She flexed her fingers against the control stick. "This can work. Get us back in, but not so close this time. You don't have to land on the damn thing."

Tristan nearly dropped the control sphere. "What'd you say?"

"I said you don't need to get so close to the giant crashing ship! I remember you being a good enough pilot to know that!"

There was a plan formulating in Tristan's mind. It was ridiculous, more than likely to fail, and would probably get them killed in the process. Either that, or it would work perfectly. "Joane, get back on the recon station, try and raise any of the nearby stations. Tell them that if they have any sort of gravity generators, they need to turn them on and point them at that crate."

"Tris, I can't even begin to know what you're thinking." Despite her words, Joane darted across the cockpit towards the recon desk. Tristan barely registered the sight of her jacket flying out behind her shoulders as she half-slid into the chair. Joane began saying something to the computer, but the blood rushing in Tristan's head drowned her out. It took a lot of manual overrides, but she finally managed to lower and prime the ship's assisted landing systems. Darling had three landing gear pylons, each one shaped like a small sled lined with a strip of ridiculously powerful electromagnets. She'd had them installed after some pirates had tried to make off with Darling during a resupply run. With the magnets engaged, nothing short of a singularity could move the ship from wherever it docked to.

The red cloud of the nebula was beginning to envelop them. Thin strands of minerals and vapors hung around them like the mossy vines that occasionally dangled from the cave ceilings back on Tristan's home. Soon, they'd be completely inside the nebula, surrounded by the fuel that might one day ignite a newborn star. If they weren't careful, that day would be today.

She brought Darling up as close as they had been to the carrier before Joane's final shot. Right before the nose of the ship was about to slam into the crate, Tristan gripped the bottom of the sphere and twisted upwards. Darling immediately turned its belly towards the craft, and Tristan slammed her hand on the dock button so hard that her knuckles popped. Invisible magnetic waves reached out from the ship, and for a brief moment, nothing happened. And then, there was a final boost of speed as Darling was pulled in and latched onto the side of the crate.

Tristan's mouth dropped open. The fact that they weren't dead yet was astounding, but there was still plenty of time for something to go wrong. She pulled back hard on the control sphere, noticing that her skin had darkened almost to the color of graphite. The engines fired in reverse, the blue lights shining like twin stars near the back of Darling's hull.

The inertia of the crate still pushed them forward into the nebula, but their speed was definitely dropping. Tristan didn't dare loosen her death grip on the control sphere as she nearly yanked it out of the gravity suspension column. She was leaning her entire body back, putting every ounce of strength and leverage into trying to coax more power out of the engines.

She wasn't sure how long they were latched to the craft. It could've been hours or maybe only a few standard seconds. Eventually, though, there was the satisfying thrum of a gravity beam latching onto the conjoined ships. Darling fought the pull for a moment before Tristan mercifully dropped the sphere, which simply bounced back into place.

Tristan fell back into her chair; she didn't remember standing up. Her legs had gone gelatinous. She looked over at Joane, whose hair was plastered to her forehead with sweat, something that was impossible for a Hollow Worlder like Tristan.

"That," Joane said, her voice unsteady, "was insane. It was dangerous, irresponsible, and downright stupid." Tristan crossed her arms and prepared herself for the verbal assault. It never came. "But it was damned cool, Tristan. I'll give you that."

*     *     *

IT took a few minutes to reel them in. Joane discovered through a brief radio conversation that the crew she'd reached was one of the mining stations planted here to pull minerals and important elements from the cloud. As such, the gravity beam hadn't been calibrated to pull in much more than single atoms of raw hydrogen. Thankfully, they managed to get both Darling and the crate pulled into the pressurized atmosphere dome without any further incident. There was a crowd waiting at the docks as Tristan and Joane stepped unsteadily down the ramp.

Mechanics swarmed the ship, tools already whirring as they began to inspect the crafts for damage. A few official-looking people stepped forward holding datapads, brows furrowed as they tried to raise their voices over the throng of civilians and workers hurling their own questions. Somewhere in the madness, a camera flashed, causing Joane to blink stars out of her eyes. Tristan stepped forward, trying to answer as many questions as she could. "We're just passing through. No, I don't know what happened. Yes, my landing gear is busted. Yes, I *am* an amazing pilot, thank you."

Joane, meanwhile, slipped through the crowd and towards the freighter. There was smoke rising from the ship now and a second, larger crowd was forming around it. She tried wiping the sweat from her bronze forehead, but quickly realized it was pointless. Instead, she simply pushed her short hair back and blinked hard.

She muscled her way through the crowd as quickly and silently as possible. She had learned a long time ago that the easiest way to move through people was to act like they weren't there. If you asked someone to move, you opened yourself up to being stopped. The smoke, she discovered, was from a plasma drill one of the workers had taken to the carrier portion of the ship. Now it was her turn to ask questions.

"No sign of any crew?" she asked, raising her voice over the loud buzz of the drill. A man behind the worker turned to her and shook his masked face. He offered one to Joane, a simple sheet of orange metal with a nearly opaque black visor. She accepted it with a nod and fastened it around her head. The light of the plasma torch became much more bearable to look at, and there was a slight suction as the inside of the mask formed a vacuum seal around her mouth and nose.

"As soon as we get this thing open, we're going to go find out what happened. If you want to tag along, you'll need that. Odds are the cabin's depressurized, so there won't be much crew to talk to. Best we can hope for is some intact logs and trajectory reports," he said, his voice sounding tinny and muffled by the mask suctioned to his own face. Joane nodded grimly. It wouldn't be the first time she'd picked through the bones of a ghost craft. Joane craned her neck towards Darling, where Tristan was still surrounded by the crowd. She'd probably still be there talking after they finished sweeping the ship, so she felt no need to tell her where she was going. Joane stepped through first, keeping a hand on the hilt of her pulse dagger as she moved inside. The ship was bathed in dark red light, which was a good sign for the state of the ship's life support system. For the time, though, Joane was content to breathe the stale, dusty air the mask was feeding her.

"Bridge is this way," one of the workers said, pointing a glowpod down a corridor. "I used to fly these things."

"Must be a bit creepy then, huh, Teves?" another one of the workers asked. Teves' response was cut off by the soft groan of the giant orange storage bay latched to the top of the flat ship.

"Keep your voice down, Moht," the man in the lead whispered. "You'll bring the whole ship down on us if you keep yapping." Joane tried to drown them out. With the eye shield lowered, she could just make out enough of the wall in front of her to make her way to the bridge. The door, predictably, had auto-sealed itself when the ship's main power went offline.

"This isn't gonna be easy to splice into," one of the men said as he began inspecting the access panel. "Nine digits, looks like a standard five digit code lock. We'll need to get one of the computing droids down here to-"

Joane pulled her knife and shoved it at the thin seam between the doors. The workers all took a shocked step back as Joane pressed all of her weight against the flat hilt of the dagger and wedged it further into the door. Her feet were beginning to slip across the floor backwards when she clicked the small button at the tip of the handle. There was a flash of purple light between the door, and it violently jerked open. Joane kept the dagger out and activated as she motioned for the others to follow her.

The bridge was completely dark. Joane flicked the trigger of her knife again, sending out a pulse of purple electricity. In the brief moment of light, Joane saw the lines of completely burnt out monitors, computers, and the collapsed bodies of the ship's crew slumped over in their chairs.

She sucked in a breath before steadying herself. It was impossible to tell if they were alive or dead. If the bridge door had sealed before the ship decompressed…it was possible. "Let's get them out of here. Is there a medical center on this station?"

"Yeah, not too far from here," the leader said, ushering his men into the room. "Traumatic decompression is…it's a hell of a thing, ma'am."

"I know, I've seen it," Joane said back, lifting one of the bodies onto her shoulders. "but I'm not in the business of leaving folks behind. Are you?"

*     *     *

TRISTAN was desperately trying to get the station crew to leave her alone. There were already a few people on top of Darling, applying energy siphons to the twin cannons to recharge them, while another crew had jacked up the landing gear and was sliding off the now deactivated magnetic sealing strips. There was the pale blue light of a holoscan flashing across her face, which she turned and glared at. At the moment, though, there were more important things to worry about than someone taking her picture.

There was a commotion to her left, and people began peeling off from her ship to make a path for a group of men carrying bodies out of the carrier. On the backs of five of the men moving through the crowd were the brown-uniformed crew of the cargo ship. The last person out of the ship stumbled, and the limp body on their back shifted just enough to dislodge her protective mask. Tristan involuntarily sucked in a breath; it was Joane. She was done taking questions. Without a word, she slid off Darling's ramp, ducked past the crowd, and sprinted over to where Joane was struggling with the unconscious person draped over her shoulders.

"You ran into a disabled ship without waiting to see if it would blow or not?" Tristan asked as she bent to take some of the man's weight.

"You're really gonna question me, after what you just pulled?" Joane responded, almost laughing at the ridiculousness.

Tristan laughed despite herself. "Alright alright, wanna just call it even?"

"Works for me." They continued in silence for a while, with the ragged breaths of the body between them the only sound in the corridors. They followed the other crew members hauling the bodies, unwilling to wait for stretchers to be delivered to the hangar. It was a miracle they had survived this long; much more waiting around would kill them for sure.

"You're thinking about something," Tristan said, more of a statement than a question. "Your eyes are going all cloudy."

Joane blinked hard. "It just seems...weird, doesn't it? Planet vanishes, and not a few days later the first Fastlane incident in centuries happens half a system over? That can't be a coincidence."

Tristan cocked her head to the side. "It's weird, I'll admit it. Not sure there's a connection, though."

"How can there not be a connection? Fastlane double-ups only used to happen because of gravitational anomalies, just like what they think is taking the planets," Joane prodded.

"First of all, gravitational anomalies *do* just happen. That's why they call them 'anomalies,'" Tristan interjected. Joane continued without pause.

"Cygnus-4 would've left a huge gravitational vacuum after it vanished. If we can track the ship's trajectory, it could give us another lead, and it might make it that much easier to find out where the planets are going."

"But it could take ages to crack the ship's data stores," Tristan countered. "Do you want to chance waiting around for that, just for it to be a dead end?"

"I…" Joane closed her mouth and stared at the floor for a moment. "I don't know. I'm worried we'll get there and it'll just be void for millions of kilometers in every direction. I'm trying to ask myself what Ahsha would do."

"That's the mistake you're making," Tristan grunted, shifting the weight of the unconscious person higher on her shoulder. "Ahsha only ever thinks like Ahsha, and she's missing because of that. If you try to think like Ahsha, you're going to do something insane and wind up in a worse position. You're smart, you're clever, and you're a good tracker. Did Ahsha find me on the Belt, or did Joane? Start thinking like Joane, even if that means doing something brash and thoughtless."

Joane fell silent for a long while. Tristan wondered if she'd said the wrong thing, or if Joane was just trying to think of a clever enough comeback. When she finally did speak, her voice was softer than usual. "That was...thank you."

"Don't trip over yourself," Tristan said, smiling sarcastically at her. "'Not Ahsha' is maybe the lowest bar there is for me." By now they'd made it to the medbay. A woman in a Solansky-blue outfit helped them guide the body onto a stretcher. The others were already lying in heavily monitored med-pods with fluids and oxygen pumping in and out. "How many made it?" Tristan asked the woman.

"So far, all of them," she responded, the disbelief palpable in her voice. "We found no signs of any decompression. It looks like they just got a bit knocked around when they left the Fastlane. With any luck, they'll be awake and ready to tell us what happened in a few hours, tomorrow morning at the latest."

The three exchanged thanks, Joane asked the doctor to contact her personal call-band if there were any developments, and the two left the med-bay. "Overnight," Joane said. "I think we can afford to wait that long."

"I agree," Tristan said back, not eager to begin the long journey to Cygnus. Artificial atmosphere was still far preferable compared to being cooped up in Darling for a week. "In that case, I'm going to go grab some dinner before it's nothing but flavored nutrient dust for the rest of the trip."

"Oh, alright, sounds good," Joane said, her voice trailing off. Tristan paused and looked over her shoulder. Silence hung in the air.

"Yes, come on, sick little pebble puppy," she laughed. Joane scowled at her but followed along a few steps behind. For a moment, Tristan felt a flutter in her heart, a twinge of nostalgia for old times. She sighed inwardly and strode off, looking for the nearest food court.

# Chapter 6
## Answers and Questions

STATIONS the size of the one they had landed at usually had one or two simple food courts stationed around. While the bulk of the city-sized disc was devoted to the hollow tube-like mining facilities in the middle, the workers still needed somewhere to live, relax, and eat. Consortium regulations required a great deal of care be taken to make sure these areas were fully locked off from the working zones, so the workers could fully disconnect themselves from the job and enjoy planetside living without having to take a Fastlane every night. For Joane and Tristan, this meant the food was surprisingly appetizing, and the food court was in an open, grassy courtyard with no hint of minerals or nebula byproducts in the air.

With Fastlanes making the universe so much smaller than before, the universal time zones had largely been made obsolete. Two ships could jump to the same location within five minutes of one another, but one might have just begun their day while the other was ready to turn in for the night. According to a large silver tower with a holo-display above it, it was mid-morning in the Waning Crescent Nebula. Tristan did the math in her head. She had slept for three hours while waiting for the Wayfarer Gate, but that had been late into her day. Then the Fastlane had taken them another few hours, and then another thirty minutes or so of chaos once they'd reached the nebula. All in all, it should be time for a hearty breakfast. Tristan ordered a burger.

She was leaving the stall with her plate when she felt someone approaching her. It was a simple tingling on the back of her neck, a survival instinct that had kept her alive in the tunnels throughout her childhood. She whirled around to see a woman in dark brown coveralls standing there, hands in her pockets. There was something vaguely familiar about her: the way her jet black hair curled unnaturally around her neck and the vertical slit-pupils in her bright pink eyes.

"Hey there, I'm Marj," Marj said, inclining her head in greeting. "I work maintenance down at the hangar." Tristan remembered the woman now; she had caught a glimpse of her prying the electromagnets from her landing gear.

"Morning, Marj. I'm Tris," she said casually, setting her tray down at a nearby table. "Everything okay with the ship?" Tristan really did not want to be stuck here for weeks waiting on repairs.

"No, no, the ship's fine!" Marj said earnestly. "That's kind of what I wanted to talk to you about. That ship of yours; it's beautiful. I don't think I've ever worked on a vessel like it before."

Tristan felt a surge of pride. She'd spent a lot of time and Lux credits making Darling the best ship this side of the universe; it was nice to have her hard work recognized. "Well, I try to take good care of her, and she pays me back. I suppose I owe her an apology and a fresh coat of paint after that stunt today, yeah?"

Marj laughed, a breezy, sing-song laugh that was just practiced enough to not sound forced. "That was sure something. You're a hell of a pilot, Tris. You saved a lot of lives today. Mine included."

Tristan shrugged. She wished they had kept talking about her awesome spaceship, and not her. She laughed awkwardly. "All in a day's work."

"Well," Marj continued, glancing downward. "I just wanted to say I'm really thankful for that. And you have an amazing ship. If you need any extra maintenance or just a…thorough check-up on the internals, I'd be happy to lend a hand."

*Ah.* Tristan could handle this. She shifted her weight and began to think of a fake wiring issue to make a double-entendre about, but then caught sight of Joane halfway across the courtyard. She was hunched over a tray, at a table by herself, scrolling across a datapad. She stopped for a moment to scan the room, then slowly lowered her head back to the datapad.

Tristan sighed and cocked her head to the side. "Listen, Marj, I'm only gonna be in the system for a few more hours. As much as I'd love to have you take a peek under my hood, I'm on a bit of a time crunch. But, once I get done with this job, I'm sure my ship is gonna need a lot of work. I'll, uh, look you up."

Marj raised an eyebrow, then nodded and pursed her lips tightly before walking away without another word. Tristan watched her go, unsure why in the world she had just turned her down. Then, she looked back at Joane sitting by herself. "Damn it all," she muttered, already walking across the courtyard. She tossed her tray down with a hefty sigh and slumped into the chair opposite Joane. Joane looked up, chewing a spoonful of rice thoughtfully as she tried to read Tristan's face.

They both got halfway through their meals before either woman thought about talking. It had been nearly a day since the meeting at the Drunken Duck, and neither of them had eaten since then. The two of them inhaled the food quickly and efficiently, the way they always had during brief lunch breaks while on data gathering trips. After a while, Joane tossed her spoon into the empty bowl and said, "She was pretty; what was her name?"

It took Tristan a moment to even understand what she was talking about. "Oh, uh, Marj. She wanted to thank me for saving her life."

"I bet," Joane said. "Should I bunk in one of the spare cabins tonight, or will I have the ship to myself?"

Tristan scoffed and rolled her eyes. "I'm here on business, not pleasure, Cordelle. It wouldn't do for me to have too much fun while chasing after Ahsha's coattails again. I might get a taste for it."

Joane stared at her for a long time, her expression blank. "You really don't like Ahsha, don't you?"

Tristan almost choked on the last bite of her burger. "Not particularly. Why do you ask, was I sending vague signals?"

Joane brushed the snide remark off. "No, you made it quite obvious. I just have to know, if you hate her so much, why'd you come?" They met each other's eyes. Tristan looked away first, unable to stand Joane's soul-piercing blue eyes staring back at her.

"Ahsha is a manipulative, lying, selfish, awful person," she explained, "but, you said you were going after her. I learned a long time ago that once you've set your mind to something, there's really no stopping you. I figured you'd get yourself killed without me around and thought I'd keep you alive for old times' sake."

"How sweet of you," Joane said as she rolled her eyes. "You're not wrong though. That was all you, back there. You saved me and everyone on board that ship. Probably quite a few people in the Crescent, too."

Tristan waved a hand dismissively. "What can I say, I'm good at what I do. I told you I was out doing good for the past few years. It wasn't always this intense, but...yeah." There was a pause, and Tristan fixed her with a glare. "You look like you don't believe me."

"It's not that I don't believe you; I'm just surprised, is all. I figured after you cleared out the grant account, you'd decide to just post up shop somewhere and retire," Joane said honestly. "That much money could've set you up for life."

Tristan's face darkened to a slate gray. She scrunched her eyebrows together tightly and didn't let go of Joane's gaze. "What are you talking about? The grant account?"

"Yeah, you know, when things were starting to get...bad. Ahsha said the grant accounts got emptied out and that, ya know, you had them." Tristan slowly shook her head as Joane spoke. "I'm not mad anymore, Tristan. I'm alive right now because of you; you can basically admit to whatever you want."

"I...didn't take that money," Tristan said, her voice hushed. "In fact, I have no clue what you're talking about."

Joane shook her head, glancing around the courtyard as if looking for the answer. "That...huh. Maybe I'm remembering wrong, but- No...I don't know. Whatever, I forget a lot of things. It's nice to hear you've been doing good out there, Tristan."

Tristan glared at her, trying to read the woman. Joane wasn't the type of person who just "forgot" things. She was meticulous and clever. Not like Ahsha's pretentious book smarts, either. No, Joane remembered people, not points of data. "What about you?" she asked, eager to change the subject. "What have you been up to?"

Joane sighed. "Trying to keep my end below ozone," she replied simply. "When things fell apart, I didn't have a ship or the money to get one. Did some odd jobs on a few planets, hitchhiked across a few galaxies, but I never really got back to the way things were. Last night was the first time I've taken a private Fastlane since we split up." Her eyes fell to the table and her brown cheeks began to grow red. Tristan wanted to say something, but she knew an apology wouldn't be genuine.

"You've still got it, though," she said, forcing a smile. Joane smiled back, though weakly. "Y'know, eating like this with Ahsha nowhere to be found...it kinda feels like old times, doesn't it?"

"It's a little different," Joane said. "Ahsha isn't in the next room having her dinner without us."

Tristan chuckled at the memory. Her and Joane in the crew lounge, while Ahsha took her carefully constructed dinner back to her room, pounding her fist against the wall if their conversation ever got too loud. She remembered the nights spent laughing and pulling from the ship's small liquor supply. Joane's hair had been a bit longer then, which had hidden her shining blue eyes and the soft angle of her cheekbones. The jacket was new, too. Tristan thought she missed her old clothes better, with the simple white short-sleeved shirt that just barely showed the tattoo on her upper-arm.

"You okay?" Tristan jolted out of her daydream. She could feel her own cheeks darkening into an intense graphite.

"I spaced," she explained quickly. "Thinking about how things were back then. I miss a lot of it."

"But there's a lot more you don't miss," Joane guessed. There was a brief silence. "It's okay. I feel the exact same. Things could be good, but they could also get really, *really* bad."

"Yeah. I guess I'm just trying to figure out what happens after all this is said and done."

Joane shrugged in response. "I figured you'd drop me off back at the Belt and move on with your life. After you take all my money, of course."

Tristan was about to be snarky when she saw the grin on the woman's face. "Oh, don't worry," she said, "I already took all your money; that part's been taken care of." Joane laughed, and Tristan laughed with her. "But, ya know...first we have to survive this mess. Flying into an obstructed gravity well, even at voidpace, it's risky. Not to mention the Consortium patrols. If they catch us trespassing in a restricted region, we're toast. And then, even if we figure out where Ahsha went, we have to get there and back with her."

Joane put the knuckle of her pointer finger in between her teeth and began chewing. It was an old nervous habit, one Tristan had forgotten. "So, not easy," she said.

"No, I listed all of those things because they're very simple tasks." Joane rolled her eyes and smiled at the same time.

"We've done crazier things before. Do you remember the volcano planet?"

"I still can't believe the shields held up that whole time," Tristan said, instantly recalling the memory. "Was it you who had the idea to dive *under* the melting continent?"

Joane jokingly flipped her hair behind her ear. "That was all me. And it worked, too. We managed to destabilize the vent and save most of that continent."

"Ahsha was looking at the atmospheric readings for a week," Tristan recalled. "Said she was trying to figure out a way to shut down every volcano in the universe."

"I remember that!" Joane said, leaning back and laughing. "It took us ages to talk her out of it."

"I wonder if she ever finished that design she was working on. What'd she call it?"

Joane was trying to remember when a man in orange work pants and a black shirt came up to their table. "Excuse me?" he asked, "Doctor Rahsam said you two wanted to be contacted when one of the crew woke up. Well, they're starting to come around, so you might want to head over there." Joane's smile dropped into an eerily intense expression.

"Thanks," she said flatly, turning to Tristan. "You ready to figure this out?"

"As I'll ever be," she answered, though she couldn't shake the feeling that something was off, or that she could feel a slight tingle on the back of her neck. They made their way out of the lush courtyard, pausing to throw away their half-eaten meals.

*     *     *

RETURNING to the stark industrial hallways of the station felt like a shock after the food court. Joane tried to read signs posted outside of offices and workrooms, looking for information on how or if the station had seen any effects due to the nearby disappearance. She found nothing of note, save for a few mentions of new workers coming on, people fleeing the Cygnus system afraid that their planet might be next. They passed a few people milling about in the halls, taking breaks from their shift to discuss the events of the day or their normal lives. A few people watched the pair as they made their way to the medical center. Word traveled fast, apparently, which surprised Joane a bit. She remembered Tristan's insistence that they keep a low profile, which had already gone out the airlock.

Thankfully, it didn't take long to reach the medbay. Outside the door, Joane paused and grabbed Tristan's arm. The heavy black fabric felt cold in her grasp. "Before we go in there, Tris, I think you should ask the questions."

Tristan didn't point out the way Joane said her name but did look confused. "Why? This is your whole thing, I thought."

"Yes, but," she stammered, "I'm not great at talking…to people. You were always the social chromafly."

Tristan didn't correct her. "You're the one who knows the situation, though. I didn't read all the documents, because I'm not insane. You, on the other hand, know what to ask."

Joane groaned. "Will you help me, at least?" she begged.

"Yes, I will help you talk to people," Tristan said dramatically, sliding open the thin semi-translucent door. "By the singularity, this really is like old times."

The medbay was more controlled than they had left it. In the half hour or so since they'd dropped the body off, beds had been shifted and equipment reallocated to provide the best care for the victims. Across the room, there were only a few other beds with the station's normal workers occupying them. Doctors were scurrying between the beds, taking every measurement they could. A few of the crew from the carrier ship were beginning to rouse, but most of them were still unconscious. One, however, was sitting up in his bed, picking at a bandage wrapped around one side of his face. Tristan and Joane shared a look, nodded, and approached the man's bed.

He was obviously from one of the aquatic worlds somewhere, with blue-ish purple skin that glowed faintly from within, like a light shining behind frosted glass. His hair was a pale purple that had been combed to one side to make room for the bandage. His eyes looked glazed over, as if he wasn't entirely back to consciousness yet. Joane glanced down at his hands clasped together in his lap and saw dark blood pouring from a now sealed cut. The minty smell of skin sealant filled the room, reminding her of bad times.

"Excuse me, sir," she tried, approaching slowly. "We wanted to ask you some questions about what happened earlier." The man shrank away from her.

"L-look, officer, I'm just a nav officer who-"

"Hey, buddy," Tristan piped up. "No Consortium wings here. Just two people who wanna know why your ship almost *ate* ours, y'know? No one's blaming you or anyone; I just want to know if you know why it might have happened." The man's shoulders fell a bit and his eyes focused. Joane turned to look at Tristan and nodded encouragingly.

"You're the ones from the ship?" he asked, "The ones who...who stopped us?"

"That's right, buddy, my name's Darya Mulcouth, and yours is?"

"F-Frederic," he said with a lisp, "Frederic Leshtad."

Tristan- Darya- smiled warmly at him. "Frederic, it's a pleasure," she said. "So, what brought your crew out to the Waning Crescent?" The man paused and stared at his hands. "It's alright, take your time. You've had a hell of a day."

He finally spoke up. "Standard job, really. We were going to pick up some of the product from one of the nebula mines and take it back to the Ara region, around the Westerlund graveyard."

"So what went wrong?" Tristan prodded gently. Frederic closed his eyes hard and shook slightly.

"I...I don't know," he managed. "Our Fastlane trajectory was perfectly normal for most of the trip. Right before we were about to go back to voidpace, though, something in the engines went wild and said there was a gravity signature *inside* the Lane. The automatic response took over and started flying us in circles, so we were still going top speed when the Fastlane spit us out."

"Do you remember anything after that?" Tristan tried.

"I blacked out the moment we appeared," he said, "We all did. The force of a sudden stop like that...we're lucky we aren't painted all over the inside of the cockpit."

"This gravity signature," Joane piped up. "It would've been cataloged in the ship's trajectory history?" Frederic nodded. "Is there any way we could copy your ship's data to take a closer look at it?"

"I...guess," he answered. "I don't think you'll find much, though. It's just normal readouts for however many hours, then a bit of weird glitched readings for a few picoseconds and then boom."

Tristan looked at Joane as if trying to read her mind. Joane gave her a look that said *I'll explain later*. Frederic reached into his pocket, wincing as he moved his arm, and produced a small transmission cylinder.

"That's our login key," he explained. "It lets us access the ship's database from our terminals. If you've got the right port on your ship, you should be able to pull all the data you need, no problem." Joane took it and slid it into a side pocket of her jacket.

"Thank you," she said, trying to match Tristan's smile.

"I should be thanking you two," he said back. "You saved all our lives back there."

Joane patted her pocket. "Let's call it even, yeah?" Frederic looked more confused than before, but nodded vacantly. "You just rest up, okay? Give it a standard day or two and you'll all be right as rain and laughing about this."

*        *        *

"'RIGHT as rain?'" Tristan said as the medbay door slid shut with a chime. "You were right, you do need my help."

"It's something I heard in a holoflick once, lay off," Joane said. "Thank you, though, seriously. He called me a cop! Can you believe that?"

"Absolutely," Tristan answered, not turning to look at Joane. Joane scrunched up her nose and scowled, but was interrupted before she could say anything. Tristan quickly slid an arm around the shorter woman and pulled her in closer. Joane's heart skipped a beat as she felt Tristan's fingers brush against the sleeve of her jacket. Something in her stomach moved in a way it wasn't supposed to, and her next words died on her lips. "Listen, let's get back to Darling and rest up for a bit. I know you're upset we didn't get anything out of the crew, but we'll find some other lead, yeah?" Joane looked up at the woman, her eyes wide. She was trying to formulate words when Tristan whispered as quietly as possible, *"Play along."*

Joane immediately closed her mouth and leaned into Tristan. The two fell into a rhythmic pace and made their way back to the ship, making idle chatter about lunch and the station as they went. At one point, a man bumped into Joane so hard she nearly fell, but Tristan's arm held her steady. The entire way through the city-sized facility, Tristan's arm never left Joane. It was either on her arm, her shoulder, or around her hip. Something was clearly happening, but Joane was too busy panicking to have any ideas. It was hard to scan an environment for threats without being obvious about it. She didn't let go of her until they made it into the ship and the latch closed behind her. As soon as the seal hissed closed, Tristan's hand slipped away and the gray-skinned woman fell back against a countertop.

"Uh," Joane managed to say, "What was that?" Tristan looked around, her eyes glancing at the ceiling and the walls around them.

She quickly held up a hand and said, in universal signals: *Followed.*

*By who?* Joane responded in kind. Tristan shrugged and shook her head, reaching into her own pocket and producing Frederic's login key. *How?* Joane signed forcefully.

Tristan smirked and wiggled her fingers before signing, *Watch both hands.* Joane quickly gave her an unofficial sign with a universally understood meaning. Tristan smirked and gestured towards Joane's waist. *Knife,* she motioned with the other hand.

She handed the knife over without question, mostly because her universal signal was a bit too rusty to argue. Tristan tested the weight of the dagger in her hand and began making her way through the ship. Wordlessly, Joane followed. They took a twisting route around empty tables and random towers of boxes until, finally, they stumbled into Tristan's room. Joane watched the woman fumble around in a heavy orange crate, eventually producing a large object that looked like a cross between a kitchen scale and a void torpedo. She jammed the knife into a socket on the top and flicked the trigger, causing lights all over the device to hum worryingly.

"There we go," Tristan said, sighing in relief. "If they bugged the ship, they won't be able to hear us now, at least not in this room."

"Who the hell are you talking about?" Joane said, her voice coming out as a squeak. Tristan shrugged, glancing around the room.

"Honestly? I don't know. Could've just been some random pickpockets, or it could've been something else. I have no idea, but I do know one thing: Freddy back there was lying to us."

"What? Why didn't you say something?"

"Gee, Joane, I didn't think of that. If I'd just let him know we were on to him, he would've told us everything and we'd be halfway to the lost planets already! I don't know who, or how, or why, but *someone* is tailing us. Someone planted a fake crew member in that medbay to feed us a bunch of nonsense and give us *this*," she said, brandishing the login key. "Which, I want to add, I am not plugging into my ship. It could be a virus, or an EMP, or worse."

"Tristan," Joane said, narrowing her eyes, "you sound paranoid."

"And? You're the one who asked me to become a conspiracy hunting super spy! Don't blame me when I start finding clues. The fact of the matter is, there were people tailing us there and back. If I had to hazard a guess, they've been tailing us since we got here. Maybe even earlier." The look on Joane's face was a mix of bewilderment and concern, as if she was saying *I don't believe you, and also, you're scaring me.*

"How do you know they were following us?" Joane said, even as Tristan brushed past her shoulder and began moving as fast as she could towards the cockpit. Joane darted to stay close to her, staying within a few feet of the device in her arms. "Aren't you always going on about coincidences?"

"They were trailing us since we left the medbay," Tristan explained. "I caught one of them watching us and talking to his friends. Then the one that bumped into you tried to get that login key off of you. That's why my arm was there. He made a move for your pocket, but got my hand instead. Amateur."

"Oh, right, gotcha," Joane said. "That doesn't explain why you think the ship is bugged or that they're going to follow us."

Tristan whirled around to face her. The lights on the device pulsed with each word they spoke. "Think about it, Joane. Let's say for a second I bought into your conspiracy thing with Ahsha and the planets. In that universe, that means someone somewhere somehow knows something about what's happening and doesn't want us to find anything. Anyone who knows how to make a planet vanish probably knows who's looking for them, and they could probably make those people disappear, too."

"You're saying those people might know where Ahsha is, where all the planets went?" Joane asked. Tristan haphazardly shoved open the cockpit door. Within a second, she was in the pilot's chair and punching buttons.

"No," she said, "I'm saying those people may have been hired by someone who knows where the planets went. I'm willing to bet they have no plan to tell us anything about it, either."

"So, what do we do?"

Tristan slammed down a lever, feeling the satisfying thunk of the metal against the console followed by a hum from the engines. "I don't know yet; I'm working on the plan right now. At the moment, we leave and hope they don't kill us."

"Wonderful," Joane deadpanned.

"I can get us out of this," Tristan said, the emotion gone out of her voice as she set to work powering up the ship. She meant every word of it: they were not dying in this nebula. "Things might get a bit dicey, though." Joane nodded in understanding and made her way to the weapon's station.

# Chapter 7
## Followed

TRISTAN set a new record for the pre-flight checklist, although her mind was racing too fast to notice. The moment she got all the all-clear from the ship's onboard computing assistant, she lifted Darling's new landing gear, pivoted in a half-circle, and launched the ship out of the station's atmosphere. They passed through the thin artificial ozone and out into the pure vacuum of voidspace. Without the force of oxygen weighing them down, Tristan was able to dump power into the engines and take off, leaving the station behind almost instantly.

"The plan is still the same," she explained to Joane, who was busily checking every available camera for signs of pursuit. "We go at voidpace towards Cygnus, which could take us close to a month. If anyone follows, we keep out of their range, fire a few warning shots, and see if they turn back."

"And what if we can't outrun them?" Joane asked, tapping a finger against the gray countertop nervously.

Tristan laughed. "Oh, don't you worry, we can outrun them. Darling and I will take care of that."

Joane didn't seem fully convinced. "I- oh no," she said, her eyes darting towards one of the rear screens. "You're right. There are ships launching from the station." Tristan cursed. Why was she always right about the bad things? She shook her head and pressed one palm hard against the control sphere.

She rested the other at her side, ready to bring up to help the ship turn sharply, if needed.

"How many?" she asked over the rumbling of the engines.

Joane leaned forward, almost completely out of her chair, to try and decipher the horribly pixelated screen. "It's hard to tell," she said. "I think I saw three? But it could be one big one, or nine really small ones."

Tristan wasn't sure which option was worse. "Are they gaining?" she asked. Joane shook her head. Of course they weren't, Tristan knew that was virtually impossible after all the modifications she'd installed to Darling's engines. She thought about it for a moment longer, then relaxed her handle on the sphere. The ship began to move noticeably slower, and Joane started in her seat.

"What's going on?" she asked, "Do they have us in a grav-lock?"

"No," Tristan said evenly, "but I want to know who's after us. And sometimes you have to let someone come just a little bit closer so you can figure them out." The ships began growing larger in Joane's camera view. It wasn't long before she knew for sure that there were three squat, rectangular ships approaching at what appeared to be their fastest possible speed.

"I don't think we can fight them," Joane said loudly.

"We aren't going to fight them," Tristan responded coolly. "Not much, anyways."

The ships closed on them quickly, two of them breaking off to either side to take up a flanking position. Tristan rhythmically tapped her fingers across the console, her other hand resting easily on the control sphere. She glanced at one of her personal modifications, a screen that she'd soldered to the console and wired in to give a constant scan of nearby ships. As Tristan watched, the readout changed to indicate that the ships were powering up their weapon systems. She sighed and tightened her grip on the control sphere. She'd hoped these were people planning on taking them in peacefully. She flicked her eyes up at Joane. "I don't plan on killing these people if we don't have to," Tristan said grimly, "but...we might have to. Are you okay with that?"

Joane was already leaned forward, intently staring at the screens. Somehow, her shoulders tightened even further. "I'm used to doing what I have to do," she said, her voice clipped. "That didn't change while you were gone."

Tristan nodded. There had only been a few times in their travels together that things ever got that bad. Once it had been pirates that ambushed them outside a Fastlane. Another time, a hivemind virus took over a small colony world and the three of them had to fight their way out. Another time, a rival scientist sent hit squads after them for months on end. Tristan could pull the trigger if she had to; she'd done it before. It weighed on her though in a way that copious amounts of alcohol only barely helped. Joane, it seemed, didn't have the same hangups.

Tristan was pondering the woman for so long that she almost missed her window. The ships were closing, three glowing pylons visible on each one of them. Afraid of missing her chance, Tristan immediately ripped the control sphere towards herself. Darling rocketed backwards, the blue lines appearing in the viewport in front of them. Six bolts of red light buzzed through the void where Darling had been moments before. Tristan slammed a button on the console, and Darling fired a wide line of blue light as it scanned the vessel they were sliding underneath. Tristan waited until she saw that the scan had been completed, then gunned Darling ahead.

Before they could clear the ship above them, however, Joane pulled the trigger on her station. Darling jolted downwards from the blast as a series of lasers tore through the ship above them.

Weapons had never been the strongest part of Darling's design. The ship was, after all, originally a research craft. The forward mounted cannons were simple defense weapons, primarily built for electric blasts that could disable advancing ships. The top of the ship's hull, however, had six dual-barrel laser cannons. Joane had insisted on the upgrade after the pirates.

Even still, the cannons weren't exactly the strongest things on the market. Only a few of the shots made it past the ship's energy shield, and those seemed to rip through only a few layers of the heavy hull plating.

Tristan grunted as the light of the explosions filled the viewport, but carried on regardless. "Did you get what you needed?" Joane yelled, twisting the joystick toward the other ships.

"Yeah, now we just need to get out of here alive to do something with it," Tristan muttered, definitely not audible over the loud hum of the engines. "Here's the plan, alright? We're going to Cygnus. I've got a feeling whoever's flying those ships knows that. I'm not going to waste any time trying to shake them. We're setting a course for Cygnus, and we're going. The only hope we have is that they can't keep pace with us and give up. If that fails, we blow their engines and leave them behind. Anything to add?"

Joane shook her head, never turning away from the screen. Tristan nodded and turned back to the viewport. An alarm blared from either side of the cockpit, letting her know that the flanking ships were too close to Darling for comfort. Tristan pushed the sphere down towards the console, fighting the gravity beam as hard as she could. Darling dropped as if a gravity well had appeared below the ship. The ships all shifted to follow her, but they were obviously not built to be as nimble or quick as Darling. Joane squeezed the trigger. There was a series of dull thuds as the cannons unleashed a volley at their pursuers. Tristan checked the canopy camera view and saw shields flickering, but not breaking.

"At this rate, they'll be tailing us all the way to Cygnus, Tris," Joane yelled, squeezing the trigger until the weapons automatically cycled off to cool down the firing coils.

"Would you like to get out and push?!" Tristan shouted, both of her hands pressed firmly against the control sphere. "I'm working on it, okay? Give me a picosecond."

Another volley of red lines burst across the viewport as the ships behind them unleashed their arsenal. Most of them went wide, but the ones that found their mark bounced harmlessly off Darling's bright blue shield.

No matter how fast Darling was, the ships could obviously keep up well enough to put shots in on them. And if they really could follow them all the way to Cygnus, it would only be a matter of time before they got a lucky volley and broke through the shields. Their weapons weren't strong enough to take on the three in a straight fight, either. They had already left the station far behind, so going back wasn't much of an option either. "I'm pulling a bit of an Apollo," she said, her voice shutting down to hide her nerves.

"You're going to do something insanely half-baked and get us all killed?" Joane asked.

Tristan nodded and began flipping switches with her free hand. "That, or I'm going to do something extremely clever and fix everything." There was a sudden, deep groan from the ship as Tristan pulled a lever towards her.

"I just lost the weapons," Joane said, uselessly pulling the trigger. "Did they hit us?"

"No, I did," Tristan explained. "I'm going to need a lot of power for this. You might want to strap in."

"I really thought that docking with a moving ship would be the stupidest thing we did today," Joane complained, wrapping a loose band around her stomach.

"Yeah, well, that's really a problem with your expectations more than anything," Tristan said as she pulled another lever and the shields powered off. As if on cue, a laser blast tore a burning strip across Darling's left wing.

"Tris!"

Tristan flipped up a small glass panel, uncovering a now-glowing blue button. She didn't have time to consider what might happen next, so she balled up her fist and punched the button.

Outside the ship, two dorsal wings began unfurling from Darling, forming a cross with the two voidpace wings positioned on the sides of the ship. The upper and lower wings curved outwards, coming to sharp points behind Darling. Each wing carried a bulkier, heavier engine filled with pulsing orange light. The two began to pulse in rhythm, like the steady thrum of a heartbeat, and Darling picked up speed. The ships behind them began to fire faster than before, as if knowing they were on the edge of losing the ship.

"Joane?" Tristan said, feeling the ship rock. The woman turned to her, her face expectant. For a moment, Tristan hesitated, trying to find the right words. "I used to steal your conditioner so I wouldn't have to buy my own."

Joane's face twisted into a look of confusion, then indignation. "That was you! I knew I didn't use that mu-" Tristan scrunched up her face and punched the control sphere as hard as she could. The hard metal cut into her fingers with the force, but that was nothing compared to the impact that came after that.

Faster-Than-Light travel was an ancient method of transportation that had basically disappeared with the advent of the Consortium's Fastlanes. For the most part, it was because it was slow, inaccurate, and extremely resource-intensive. The fuel needed for a single FTL jump was rivaled only by the tremendous energy cost of a Fastlane, but only covered a fraction of the distance at a hilariously slow speed, by comparison. Nowadays, it was uncommon for a ship to even have a functioning FTL drive, especially one as small and slight as Darling. Fastlanes could make a ship travel at such incomprehensible speeds because the ship itself wasn't accelerating; it was simply being catapulted through reality itself. FTL meant the ship itself was traveling through actual space. The speed and force of such a method used to rip apart huge colony city-ships after the slightest miscalculation. Tristan had no idea how FTL had become the best option in this situation, but it was. Darling's Redshift drive was outdated, untested, and not entirely legal. Still, she'd kind of always wanted to test it out. As she slammed the button, there was a brief, imperceptible moment where all four engines did nothing.

And then, everything went dark. Moving faster than light meant that light couldn't reach the ship. The stars turned red and vanished. The void became just a bit darker, and only the roar of blood in Tristan's ears told her the drive had worked. She saw Joane thrashing with momentum in her seat, the belt barely hanging on. She only had a moment to think about her own restraints before the force of inertia carried off her feet, and the back of the cockpit raced to meet her. The roar of blood in her ears was drowned out by the loudest snap she'd ever heard, and then everything went *really* dark.

# Chapter 8
## Redshift

DARLING'S inertial dampeners took what felt like ages to activate. For a minute, Joane's body endured the purest, most powerful forces in the universe tearing at her. She gripped the seat beneath her so hard her fingers grew numb and pierced the plastileather. Her teeth were gritted so hard she began to taste blood, but wasn't sure from where. She thought she might have screamed, but couldn't entirely be sure. It felt like her conscious mind had been left behind when the ship jumped. Somehow, she managed to turn her head towards the viewport to see the starlight turn a deep, sinister red and then vanish as Darling outran the visual light spectrum. In an instant, Joane realized she'd given Fastlanes an unfair break. Compared to this, they were a luxury hover carriage ride through a park. The edges of her vision began to go blurry. Joane had no idea if the forces were pushing her to unconsciousness, or if she was simply moving so fast that she was going to lose the ability to see anything, inside or outside of the ship. Part of her wanted to simply let go and let luck decide her fate.

Just as the darkness was about to overtake her, bright white lights flashed on overheard, forcing the darkness back immediately. The viewport was still dark and empty, but something inside the ship was generating a field that kept them from being ripped apart. Joane collapsed in her seat, unsure if she had pissed herself or was just sweating all over. She didn't care, because she was, for the moment, alive. Still, Tristan needed to be yelled at for that stunt.

Joane slowly, carefully rotated her chair, careful not to move too much at once. She expected to give the gray woman an earful, but when she finally turned, Tristan wasn't at the pilot's console. "Tris?" Joane asked the empty space. She unsteadily pushed herself to her feet, and then saw her pilot crumpled into a pile right next to the cockpit entryway. Joane cursed under her breath and began struggling toward her body. She took a step, fell, and pushed herself up over and over again as she tried to cross the room. It felt like it took an hour to force her legs to carry herself the five meters to the unconscious woman.

She put two fingers to Tristan's neck and sighed with relief when she felt the slow, even pulse underneath the skin. She pressed her ear against the woman's chest, waiting to feel the motion of breathing. It came, slowly, but there. Satisfied that Tristan wasn't in any immediate danger — no more than either of them were, at least — Joane began looking at the wound itself.

The cockpit door frame itself had dented from the impact. Joane quickly and carefully pulled Tristan's jacket off before slicing the back of her shirt open to inspect the wound. Any impact that could dent metal had to have done a number on her. Joane wasn't surprised by what she found, but she still wasn't happy about it.

A spot of skin on her back nearly the size of a sheet of paper had already bruised to an extremely dark and angry purple. Her left leg wasn't bent incorrectly, but her calf bone was clearly snapped like a bundle of empty fuel pylons. Blood trickled down across her forehead, the wound hidden under her dark hair.

"Tris?" Joane tried. "Tris!" It was no use; the woman was out cold. For the moment, Joane was alone on a ship she couldn't fly, hurtling through the void at a speed that threatened to rip Darling apart the moment the inertial dampeners failed. She wanted nothing more than to lean her head back against the door frame and scream, but it wasn't time for that just yet.

She slapped her knee and scrambled to her feet, hooking her arms under Tristan's as she did so. Tristan was taller and more muscular than Joane, so it wasn't an easy task to heave her up into a sitting position. Still, Joane was strong enough to haul her upright and began slowly dragging her limp form through the ship.

The lights flickered off and on as she went, carefully steering around Tristan's endless stacks of garbage strewn about the cabin. Joane cringed each time she noticed Tristan's back drag across an uneven surface, or her leg bumped into a stray crate. It was almost a blessing that she was unconscious, because the pain would have knocked her out by now. "I'm sorry, I'm sorry, I'm sorry," she muttered as they went. Joane remembered their "medical bay" being nothing more than a small storage closet with a few sealant packs and assorted pills, so she made her way toward Tristan's room instead. Joane imagined it would be the only clean room on the ship, or at least cleaner than the rest of the place. Joane faintly remembered that her room had been down the opposite side of the ship from her, along the right wing of the ship. She found the first room with an active passcode lock and assumed that meant it was Tristan's. Joane had never tried to break into anyone else's room, so she didn't know the passcode for the door. Instead, she tapped the tip of her knife against the keypad and clicked the trigger. There was a faint wave of energy that spread across the device, and the screen went dark as the door hissed. Joane gingerly rested the unconscious woman against the wall. She turned back to the door and pressed her fingers as far as they could go into the crack between the door and the wall. It took a minute without any sort of leverage to pry the door open, but it scraped and screeched along until there was room enough for Joane to pull Tristan inside. The lights clicked on in response to the sudden motion, bathing them in a low red light as sensual music began to play.

"Classy, Tris," she said, smiling despite the situation. The room itself was messier than Joane expected. There were scattered nutrient dust packs and bowls full of half-eaten meals across the floor. What may have an even stack of touch-tomes had slowly spilled into a pile as each one was read and haphazardly replaced. The edge of the bed was filled with a mound of clothes, mostly reds and blacks with a few colorful scarves thrown into the mix. To Joane's surprise, there was a clothes washer in one corner of the room with a heaping basket next to it. She'd expected Tristan to prefer the ease of self-cleaning clothes like she did. There were dark red curtains over a long viewport behind the bed, which dominated most of the room. The fitted sheet remained on the bed, but the pillows and loose sheets had been tossed randomly across the room, most likely due to the Redshift. As she approached the side of the bed, she noticed a large amount of dust hanging in the air, kicked up by the commotion. It took her a few attempts, and more than a few deep breaths, to lift Tristan up and deposit her onto the bed.

The mattress sank under the weight in a way that made Joane miss sleeping in a bed so comfortable. She made sure to stuff one of the sturdier pillows under Tristan's side so that she wasn't lying on her bruise or the broken leg, then tried to arrange her clothes so that they covered as much of her as possible. Joane, even in crisis-mode, took a moment to pull her eyes away from the smooth, soft gray skin of her back and shoulder blades. She quickly jogged out of the room, stumbling through the hallways as the lights continued to flicker. The medkit was where it had always been, shoved on the top shelf alongside some spare light rods and long-expired nutrient dust. Joane pulled it down and pulled open the light metal lid, revealing a modest assortment of pain suppressants, sealant gel, adjustment bandages, and vital sensors. It was less than what Tristan needed, but it would have to do. She made her way back to the room to find Tristan exactly where she'd left her.

It occurred to Joane that there was a chance the ship still needed a pilot, even while whatever Tristan had done was active. First aid wouldn't do either of them much good if they smacked into a planet at several times the speed of light. Joane shook her head and crouched down beside the bed. Even if that were true, Joane had almost no experience flying an integrated control ship. If she were to put a hand on the control sphere, she'd probably put them in more danger than if she left it alone. Right now, her friend was hurt, and she could do something about that.

Her friend. Was that what they were? They had been for five years, but that hadn't ended spectacularly. They'd been traveling for what, a day and a half now? Time was hard when Fastlanes became involved. It hadn't been long, Joane knew that much. Still, they were joking, having lunch together, and remembering old times like they weren't that bad. She'd let her call her Tris a few times, even. She wasn't really sure. Remembering some of the things they'd said to each other...it was going to be a hard warpgate to rebuild.

"Whatever we are, you're about to like me a little less," Joane whispered to the body and began wrapping the adjustment bandage around her splintered leg. The white fabric was flexible enough, but the interior skeleton rigidly latched into place as Joane finished covering Tristan's calf. With a series of rapid clicks, the brace locked into place and twisted, sensing and setting the broken bone with a horrible crunch.

That was enough, Tristan awoke with what was, for a moment, a groggy moan of discomfort. As her senses returned to her, she bolted upright faster than Joane could register and screamed as loud as she could for a solid ten seconds. When she finally ran out of air in her lungs, she began heaving with heavy breaths interspersed with shaky sobs of agony. It took Joane a moment to realize that she had her hand in a death grip. Joane reached out with her free hand and grabbed Tristan's shoulder as the woman thrashed.

"Wh-What- WHAT DID YOU DO?" Tristan yelled, her voice screeching. Her face had gone so dark that Joane could barely make out the tears streaming down her face in the glint of the red light.

Joane held her for a moment longer, not grabbing her shoulder too tight for fear of hurting her more. "Tris, breathe, okay?" she said, trying to keep the panic out of her voice. "You're hurt, and I'm just trying to help."

The shock had seemed to fade from Tristan's mind, and her eyes lost their wild look. She collapsed onto the pillows, her forehead slick with sweat. "Did it work?" she asked weakly.

"As far as I know," Joane confirmed. "As far as I can tell, we lost them. You took a hell of a hit, though."

"Yeah," Tristan groaned, "I noticed. Did you cut my leg off or something?"

"I almost wish I had," Joane said, forcing a smile onto her face. Tristan tried to laugh, but when her chest rose too quickly, her back seized up and she let out a guttural howl of pain.

After nearly a minute of short, hissing breaths, she managed to say, "I hurt my back."

"Yeah, I'm not done, lay on your side," Joane ordered. Tristan complied, whining as she did so. She steadied her with a hand on her upper back, and Tristan gave a short yelp. "What's wrong?" Joane asked, withdrawing her hand.

"Your hands are cold," Tristan said. Joane rolled her eyes and put her hand back. There was no broken skin on the back, so sealant would do no good. It took a bit of digging in the kit, but she found a small tube of anti-inflammatory and numbing gel. Joane placed a large blob of the bright blue gel onto the bruise and began rubbing against the hardened skin. As the pain began to subside, Tristan leaned into Joane's hand and let out a noise that Joane tried to ignore. The gel sank into her skin, taking some of the dark purple along with it. The skin still felt tough, but the worst of it seemed to be fading.

"Okay, uh, that's taken care of," Joane said, wiping her hand hastily on the comforter. "Let me take a look at your head."

Tristan slowly raised a hand to her forehead, pulled it away, and grunted at the blood on her fingers. "Ow," she muttered as she turned to look Joane in the eyes.

"Yes, we'd hate for you to have brain damage." Joane said, reaching for the sealant. "You might start doing stupid things like catapulting us into FTL travel." To her surprise, Tristan didn't have a snarky comment to offer. She simply tilted her head towards Joane. She'd been joking, but now Joane worried for a brief moment that something had actually messed up the woman's head. She held the sealant with one hand and began brushing through Tristan's hair with the other. "You weren't kidding about my conditioner," she remarked. "It's not made for hair like yours, and it'll really mess up your scalp."

"I think the blunt trauma messed up my scalp."

"That too," Joane said, finally finding the origin of the blood. There was a long cut hidden far back on the left side of her scalp, with bloodsoaked hair matted into the wound. "You'll need to wash this later, but I'm going to try and close the wound now so you don't bleed out. Now hold still." Tristan complied in silence as Joane pressed a small amount of mint-green sealant against the wound. It flattened into a sheet across her scalp, sticking a bit to her hair as it did so. As the blood reacted with the foam, it puffed up into what looked like a slightly green marshmallow taped to Tristan's head. Joane shaped it a bit more into place then let it rest. Tristan fell back into the bed, tilting her head up to keep the sealant foam off the pillow. She stared up at the ceiling for a bit, then turned her gaze towards Joane.

"Thanks, doc," she said, her voice thin. "Listen, you used to have some, uh, sleeping pills right? You got them for when we took Fastlanes. I don't know if you took them with you when you left, but if you didn't, do you think I could borrow one? I could use a nap."

Joane frowned and crossed her arms, shifting her weight back and forth. "I don't...I don't think that's a good idea, Tristan."

Tristan looked genuinely heartbroken. "I- why?"

"Because, you know, you used to have a problem with that. I don't want to risk you getting back on those."

Tristan looked like she had no idea what Joane was saying, but was in too much pain to think about it. "I have no idea what you're saying, but I'm in way too much pain to think about it right now. Can you just... give me some suppressants?"

"That I can do," Joane said, pulling a syringe out of the kit. "Give me your arm." Tristan practically ripped her shirt even more as she pulled the sleeve up. Joane looked for a moment at the old tattoo of Darling on her upper arm, then carefully injected the numbing serum right into the crook of her elbow. Tristan's eyelids fluttered as Joane injected the medicine.

"Thank you," Tristan breathed, relaxing more into the pillow. A strand of hair fell into her face, which Joane brushed away without thinking. Her forehead was burning hot and wet with sweat. "The ship's computer will take care of the flying for the next few days. Can you...will you stay with me? Please?"

Joane sucked in a breath. "You need to rest, Tris."

"I'm going to," she promised, pulling her knees up to her chest. She was beginning to shake, and the effort of moving her leg was clearly almost too much for her. "It hurts, Joane. It hurts really bad." Her voice was quivering in a way she'd never heard in all the years they'd traveled together.

"Hey, hey," Joane said. "I'll stay. I'll stay with you, Tris. I promise." Tristan smiled shakily and pointed towards the other side of the bed with her chin, the only part of her body that didn't seem to ache when she moved. Joane nodded and stood back. Her mind was simultaneously racing and completely blank as she walked around the huge bed. *She's in pain, she just needs someone there with her,* she told herself. She kicked off her boots instinctively and crawled under the comforter. Her earlier guess had been correct. The bed was the most comfortable one she'd lain in for as long as she could remember. Tristan tried to roll towards her, but winced as her leg shifted. "No, no, don't move," Joane said.

"Hold," Tristan slurred, the medicine beginning to take effect. Joane began to protest, but instead let out a sigh and obliged, shifting over and putting an arm around Tristan's shoulder. It was the closest she had been to anyone who wasn't throwing a punch at her in...a long time. Tris hummed with contentment and nestled her head against her shoulder, and within a few seconds she was unconscious and snoring. Joane tried to pull away but found there was no way to untangle herself without exacerbating Tris's injuries. She huffed, settling in for a long night. There were worse places to be, she supposed. She *was* tired, after all, and the bed was comfortable. Joane didn't see anything wrong with resting her eyes for a few minutes, just long enough for her to clear her head and get back to work.

# Chapter 9
## A One-Way Trip

TRISTAN dreamed.

She only ever had the one dream, and she only had it when things were really dicey. She was standing in pure darkness, but she could see the walls around her clearly. After all, that's the way things were back on her homeworld. When you lived in the Hollow Worlds, eking out a life underground in uniform 20-foot tunnels, your eyes learned to see through the constant, crushing darkness. She was in the middle of a tunnel now. She was pretty sure it was the same tunnel every time, because some nights she'd dream of the tunnel, and the features would be the same as when she'd last had the dream. Certain scratches on the wall or a pebble in the floor that were too familiar to be a different tunnel. And always, in the distance, the sound of starship engines priming. It was electrifying. The promise of freedom, escape, of starlight to bask in. An escape from the horrible monotony that plagued her entire childhood. So, like every other time she had the dream, Tristan ran.

She took the first step, and collapsed. There was a shooting pain in her left leg. She tried to scream, but when her mouth opened, it filled with a thick foam, and the horribly clean scent of it made her gag. The scent of it filled her nose until she recognized it as sealant foam. She looked down to inspect her leg, only to see hooked fangs growing out of her leg. They pierced through the skin, growing and growing before turning back on themselves and sinking back into her flesh. There was no blood, just more teeth rising up out of the wounds and back down to what remained of her leg. She tried to pull away, but her clothes began to shred across the broken rocks under her feet. She tried to make a noise, any noise, to call for help or just remind herself that she could.

But nothing came. Instead, the foam grew up and over her eyes. In an instant, Tristan's view went from her own eyes to above her body, thrashing and shaking on the rocks. With each movement, a piece of her fell away. There was never any blood, just pieces flaking off like a rock being chipped away. She was turning herself to dust. She wanted to stop, to keep her arms still and to stop kicking her legs, but she'd left her body behind. It moved on its own, bashing itself over and over against the hard, unyielding rocks below. Unable to look, Tristan tore her view away to look down the tunnel. Someone would come from the ship, she thought, someone who would help her, and then they would take her away from this place. That's how it happened, she told herself, Ahsha and Joane took her away. Instead, a sickening feeling washed over her. Because it was her dream, she knew what would happen next. The engines would depart, and a wall of blue flame from the backdraft would fill the tunnel and burn her already ruined body away. She begged for some kind of miracle to save her, but in the next five seconds, she heard the engines grow fainter and fainter as a different roar filled her ears. The wall of flame materialized in the middle of the tunnel and raced towards her. Right before it hit her, Tristan was finally able to choke out a hoarse scream.

*　　　*　　　*

TRISTAN'S eyes flew open. Her body tensed, which she immediately regretted. However, she managed to keep the rising scream in her throat as the nightmare faded. She tried to breathe out slowly, a technique she'd picked up ages ago when she'd first learned to fly at high speeds. The blood pumping in her ears gradually subsided and she managed to come back to her senses. That was unusual, she thought. The dream was never a comfortable one, but it usually meant she woke up with sore calves and, depending on the night, an angry woman next to her. She quickly discovered the reason when she realized her pain suppressants had worn off and her leg felt like it might actually be eating itself. She nodded to herself. This was probably the worst shape she'd found herself in for years, maybe in her entire life. She didn't remember anything hurting this bad before.

Maybe, she thought, she could sleep it off for just a bit longer if she ignored the pain and let the adjustment bandage do its job. It was fruitless, she knew, but worth a shot. She pulled herself, gingerly, closer to Joane and-

*Joane.* Tristan froze. The impact of redshifting was still fresh in her mind, but everything that had happened since then was foggy. Had she actually, like a sick child, asked Joane to crawl into bed with her? Her heartbeat quickened again. How in the name of the Singularity had she let herself do that? It must have been the suppressants messing with her head, or the sealant pressing on her skull, or the way Joane's hand had felt against the bare skin of her back as her short auburn hair, glowing just a bit under the dim red light, fell past her eyes. Those bright, shining, focused eyes like sunlight shimmering on the oceans Tristan had never been lucky enough to see in person.

No, she thought, it wasn't that last one. Probably the drugs. Definitely the drugs, actually. Tristan tried to pull away, gingerly again, hoping that she might not wake the woman next to her. "Mmph," Joane mumbled through her barely-open lips. Tristan closed her eyes and willed the inertial dampeners to fail. Let Darling crumble apart into sheet metal and the void crush them both.

She had no such luck. Joane's eyes began to flutter open as she rolled onto her back. She looked over at Tristan, who was half-sitting up, obviously trying to crawl away. Joane's eyes darted open, now. "Uhm, hey?" she tried, her voice low and husky from sleep.

"Hello," Tristan answered, unable to think of anything else.

"How are you feeling?" Joane asked, the words stilted and awkward.

"I am in so much pain!" Tristan said, her voice far more chipper than she expected it to be.

That seemed to stir Joane fully, and she began to stumble out from the covers. At some point, she must've shrugged off her jacket to sleep comfortably, revealing the fitted blue shirt underneath. "Right, right," she stammered, getting to her feet and racing to the medkit. "I'm...so sorry; I blanked for a second. I should've been doing more doses while you rested but, uhm, I got tired, and it's a really nice bed and, well-"

"Please just shut up and give me the drugs," Tristan begged. Joane handed it over, then quickly looked away. Tristan smiled in return and jabbed it into her thigh, where the cloth had been cut away to check for injuries. Immediately she felt the muscles in her leg relax, and even her back felt a bit looser. Her head was still throbbing, however. "We should get to the cockpit," she muttered, picking up her leg and maneuvering it over the side of the bed.

Joane's face went from stunned horror to stunned confusion. "Tris, what the hell are you talking about? You took a door to the back at near-lightspeed. You're going to lay back down and sleep."

"Joane, I appreciate it, I do," Tristan murmured, getting to her feet unsteadily. She wavered for a moment, trying to balance on one foot and a hand against the nightstand. "But I'm fine. You're a fine medic; I feel great. But I'm *not* going to feel great if the ship crashes or we get to Cygnus and there's a pirate barge waiting there for us."

"I don't agree with this," Joane said indignantly while helping Tristan to her feet. She refused to say it, but she was happy for the help.

"What a shock that is," Tristan said in an attempt at humor, but it came out harsher than expected.

They made their way into the hall, trading low light for brief flashes of bright blue. It was disorienting to say the least, and it made shuffling towards the cockpit even harder. Several times over, Tristan caught her bad foot against a wall or some scattered object and yelped as sharp pain overwhelmed her.

After the third hit, Joane spoke up. "Tris, why do you have all this stuff? I don't remember you being a hoarder."

Tristan grunted and waved a hand. "I'm not a hoarder. It's just...stuff I might need. I don't like asking for money when I help people. But something has to keep Darling fueled up. So if someone offers me a gift, I take that, and I sell it later."

"I don't know if that's all that different."

"I don't either," Tristan sighed, "It makes me feel better, though." Almost on cue, she clipped her toe on a sound-boosting system and yelped. She whipped her head around to glare at Joane before the woman could even open her mouth. Joane quickly quieted, settling for an "I told you so," glance.

Eventually, they made their way into the cockpit, where Tristan tipped forward into the pilot's seat. Joane tried to help as much as possible before returning to her radar station. "Listen, Tris, about-"

"Nope," Tristan interjected, cutting her off. "No. Nothing to talk about here, and I will not let you force an issue when there isn't one. I was half-conscious and jacked up on those pain suppressants, nothing I said meant anything. Which is exactly why I never messed around with stuff like that, thank you very much."

Joane frowned deeply. "I just- Hold on. Never?"

Tristan nodded without looking at Joane. She was focusing on adjusting her seat to hold her closer to the console. "Nothing. Void-dust, Sparkjoy, not even Solan Crack. That's not me."

"But then, what about..." Joane was obviously grappling with something, so Tristan turned back to her console. Her scans of their friends back in the Nebula were still waiting for her to examine. Just as she thought, Darling had detected several pings being sent to some far-off destination.

Whoever was after them had backup, and that backup would be waiting at Cygnus once they calculated their FTL trajectory. Tristan took a quick visual scan of the ship, trying to find any identifiable features that might give her a hint to who wanted them dead. If she knew who, she might be able to guess why.

After a minute of searching, she found it, and it took her breath away. "Joane. Come take a look at this. Now." Joane was still mumbling to herself across the room, but stood at the sound of her name. She crossed the cockpit and examined Tristan's now extended screen.

"I don't...what am I looking at?" Joane asked. Tristan sighed and tapped a portion of the screen.

"This..." Tristan motioned to a list of hull components, "...is an alloy called Core Steel. It's one of the strongest alloys in the universe, and is only made at the core of collapsing stars and massive terran planets. As such, it's heavily regulated for the use of inter-asteroid connection pylons and the construction of vessels for one group." Joane waited patiently, staring blankly at the picture. Again, Tristan sighed loudly. "The Consortium. Joane. The ships that followed us were Consortium ships."

Realization began to dawn across Joane's face. Somehow the two of them had managed to piss off the first and only government capable of maintaining control and peace across the entire universe.

"No chance the scan was...wrong?"

Tristan gasped and put a hand on the control console. "You would dare question Darling?" she mocked. "In all seriousness, there's no chance, no. Core Steel is extremely unique in composition, it would take a monumentally bad scan to get results like that."

Joane cursed and walked a few paces away from the console. "This is bad," she stated.

"Insightful," Tristan deadpanned. Joane looked like she wanted to yell at her, but decided against it. "I'm not going to pretend like it'll help, but we should make some kind of a plan."

"I don't think we have many options, except maybe running."

Tristan gave a short sad laugh. "We actually don't have that option." Joane spun around on her heels and glared at Tristan, a concerned look plastered to her face. "See, the Redshift drive is a one-way trip. I'm not steering the ship right now, because once I fire the drive, the ship basically rides the initial blast until the slow-down element fires. And once we get there, the drive is going to be too spent to fire again for hours, maybe even days."

"So they know where we're going."

"Yes."

"And when we'll get there."

"Most likely."

"And we can't do anything to change course?"

"Not a bit."

"We're screwed."

"Severely."

Joane sighed and put her hands on her hips. "How long until we get there?" she asked, her voice clipped.

Tristan turned and checked Darling's onboard clock. "About six and a half standard days. Plenty of time to write up a will."

"Or grab a drink," Joane grumbled. She turned and left the cabin, leaving Tristan in silence. She stared out the completely darkened viewport, trying and failing not to think about the way her head fit against Joane's shoulder.

Eventually, Tristan decided to stop staring at the empty viewport and leave the cockpit. There was nothing she could do to change their course now. That would be like firing her crossbow, then reaching out and plucking the dart from the air before it could hit its target. They were on a one-way trip, in more ways than one. Part of her wanted to ponder why the Consortium wanted to bring them in. They must have been involved with the disappearances, somehow. Ahsha was getting too close to the truth, but decided to put her faith in two idiots who chased blindly after her, right over the edge of a cliff. Tristan hated when Ahsha was right about something, which sucked because the woman so often was. She wanted to ask herself why they were taking planets. There had to be some purpose.

Another part of her brain won out though. That part of her brain wanted to get drunk before she died. Drinking alone always made her miserable, so she thought she might share an awkward shot or maybe six with Joane. She wanted to avoid talking about her pathetic display last night, but assumed it was inevitable.

She hated that word. Inevitable. She'd spent her life trying to avoid inevitable things. The unfortunate thing about them was that inevitable things tended to be...inevitable.

Tristan was surprised when she found the small dining area empty. Her first, morbid, thought was that Joane may have taken matters into her own hands and jumped out of the airlock. Immediately, a dozen other alternatives jumped to her mind,

Tristan shook her head and decided maybe it was best to drink alone. She ripped a cheap bottle of Liquid Plasma from the cupboard and limped to her room. Last night had been the first time she'd actually slept in that bed for ages, and she'd forgotten how comfortable it was. At the moment, she needed that.

The door lock was still disabled. Tristan looked at the dangling wires and sighed. Joane must've brute forced her way through the lock without thinking of the one number the code could've been: the universal standard date of the day she left the Hollow World with them. She wrapped her fingers around the partially open door and pulled it open. Tristan was halfway inside when she nearly jumped out of her skin.

There was Joane, sitting on the side of the bed, a bottle of wine clasped firmly in her hand. She looked just as surprised as Tristan felt. They looked at each for a while, both of them unsure of what to say. "What's up?" Tristan finally asked.

Joane gestured down to the bed. "It's...a really comfortable bed. I thought I'd rather sit here for a bit instead of those awful plastic chairs in the dining room or on a pile of scarves.

Tristan nodded, biting her lip a bit as she did so. "Alright. Don't spill wine on my sheets." She moved across the room and sat down at the head of the bed. Joane, at the foot of the bed, waited for a moment.

"I can stay?" she asked. There was something in Tristan's voice she couldn't exactly pick out.

"I'm not in the mood to drink alone," Tristan mumbled lamely, trying to sound relaxed. "Just, don't flip out about it, okay?" Joane nodded, and Tristan pointedly pulled the top off her own bottle.

"What do we talk about?" Joane asked after a few minutes of completely silent drinking. Tristan was in the middle of taking a sip from the awful blue liquor. The taste lived up to the name, but it was already slowing her racing thoughts.

"I have no idea," she said truthfully, looking at the bottle for a moment. "How's your family doing?"

Joane shook her head. "No idea," she said bluntly. "Never really checked up on them after I left home, 'cause I didn't have a reason to. Yours?"

Tristan shook her head as well. "I only lived this long because I got off that death trap of a planet. Dad died in a tunnel collapse a while ago, and Mom got picked off by the crawlers."

"I'm sorry."

"Thanks." They both fell quiet for a while. Conversation clearly wasn't going to be easy. Tristan wasn't sure if it was solely because of their impending death, or the events of last night. A passing thought grabbed Tristan's mind, so she followed it. Anything would be better than the oppressive silence. "Let me ask something, why didn't you want to give me those sleeping pills?"

Joane took a deep breath, her shoulders moving up and then down like a cresting wave. "Alright, fine, Ahsha told me about your problem back in the day."

"My problem?"

"With the pills. She said you would sneak them from my supplies, so I had to hide them in the drawer," Joane explained. "I'm sorry I never talked to you or tried to help you get over it. I just know how headstrong you can be and things were already getting worse so I thought it would be better to just-" Joane caught Tristan's green eyes glaring at her in the dark, their intensity evident even with the low light. "Why are you looking at me like that?"

"Because I've never touched those things. I *found* them when I was cleaning up that room, but I left them there. I don't take sleep aids, let alone for kicks. You said Ahsha told you that?"

Joane looked aghast. "Y-yeah, she saw you...She told me to be careful about it and helped me...hide them."

Tristan threw up her arms and took a violent drink from her bottle. The fire in her throat was nothing compared to the seething rage in her stomach. "Unbelievable. The lying little..." she drew in a long, shaking breath. "I'm guessing there's nothing I can say to make you doubt your bestest friend Ahsha, the super scientist."

Joane hesitated for a moment, a few choked noises emanating from her mouth. "I...I've learned a lot about all of us recently. I don't know if I even remember the way things were before we all split up."

Tristan's rage dissipated slowly, but it did. She watched Joane's face shift from confusion to sadness to fear and knew the realization was weighing on her. "Hey, hey, it's okay." It wasn't, but Joane needed to hear it.

"And you didn't take the money," Joane guessed. Tristan shook her head. "And you didn't sell us out that one time the board of ethics impounded the ship." She shook her head again. "And you didn't put pigment in my shampoo to turn my hair black that one time?"

Tristan cringed. "That one was me, actually." She met Joane's gaze. "What? I wanted to know what it would look like. That was like four years ago."

The woman sighed, brushing a stray strand of longer hair with a finger. "I actually liked it, kind of."

Tristan laughed. "I did too, actually. It suited you."

"You liked it?" Joane asked. "I mean-no-the other stuff. I mean...Ahsha told me everything, I thought."

"Look, Joane..." Tristan sighed. "I really don't know what to tell you. Maybe she saw something, and thought it was one thing when it wasn't."

"No." Joane's voice was like stone. There was no budging, no uncertainty, only a solid rage. "Ahsha doesn't just *see* things wrong. She's a smart woman." Tristan wanted to say something, but Joane had already half-stumbled to her feet and barged out of the door.

She sat alone under the tacky red lights, trying to think of what to do. Ahsha had always been manipulative and controlling, but it was clear she'd messed with Joane's head in ways Tristan didn't fully understand. If she tried to help, she might break the poor woman entirely. She drank for a few minutes, hating the acrid taste of the liquor. Finally, she couldn't stand the silence anymore and pushed herself to her feet.

She grunted as her foot hit the floor. The adjustment bandage was doing its job of setting the bone, but the healing itself would be slow and painful. It made the trip across the ship slow and awful, but she made it to Joane's door with sweat dripping down her face. There was the soft sound of muffled sobs behind the thin metal door.

"Joane?" Tristan leaned her head against the door. "Look, you don't have to believe me. Hate me, think all the awful things you want about me, whatever you want. I'm not trying to change the way things-" The door chimed and slid open rapidly, causing Tristan to fall forward with a start. Joane's hand reached out and caught her shoulder, holding her up. Tristan caught herself and found her footing before looking down at the woman, who had tears freely running down her face.

"But I *do* believe you!" Joane shouted, gesturing wildly with her arms. The bottle sloshed, but Tristan noted there was not much left in it. "You're kind and selfless and you won't take money for saving lives and you can't handle a light-dose sleep aid because it makes you pass out and say things you don't mean."

Tristan gave her a smile. Something in that last sentence made her hurt deep inside, but she wasn't sure why. Still, it felt good to have Joane sticking up for her, even if they were the only people on the ship. She kept going. "And I told her that. I said that things weren't going missing like she said. I counted my pills, I kept watch over the money, everything. But she insisted and I just...believed her. Why would she say those things? Why would she even do that?"

It took Tristan a minute to realize Joane was expecting an answer. "I-I'm sorry, Joane," she said, her voice catching. "I don't know." It hurt her to have to say, but she didn't. She never could read Ahsha. She never had the need or want to figure her out. Tristan was the people person in their little group, but Ahsha was more like a particularly rude computer system than a person. Tristan knew Joane, though. She was sturdy, resolute, and confident. She was never rattled. To see Joane like this...Tristan wanted nothing more than to take that pain and confusion away.

She was silent for a moment, then downed the rest of her bottle. Her shoulders twitched, but only the slightest hint of a sob escaped her lips. She turned and walked deeper into her mess of a room. Tristan was about to say something, but she was cut off when Joane hurled the empty bottle at the wall. The glass shattered instantly, sending shards spinning into the sea of cloth across the floor. Tristan sighed but said nothing. Whatever Joane was feeling, she needed to feel it alone for a moment. Neither of them moved for a long moment. "I hated you," Joane's voice eventually came out in a series of short, hitched syllables. Tristan nodded solemnly, staring at the back of the woman's head. "I hated you because of a bunch of lies. You...were my best friend."

"Joane-"

"And we threw that away. All of us did." Joane's voice was quaking. "And then I dragged you back trying to rescue the person who drove the wedge between us in the first place. And now we're going to die for her."

"We're not going to die," Tristan said, unsure if she believed herself. "We...we'll find a way, like we always used to."

"It's the *Consortium*, Tris," Joane said, almost laughing as she turned her head to look at her. "That's more over our head than we ever were." She kicked one of Tristan's nicer jackets across the room.

Tristan shrugged, trying to seem relaxed. "It wouldn't be a trip on Darling if it were easy, you know that."

"How are you so calm right now?" Joane asked, shaking her head back and forth in disbelief. Her hair had gone a bit wild in the past few minutes, but Tristan liked it that way. It felt like she was talking to the real Joane, not the illusion of control she always used to put on.

"I do my best thinking in a crisis, you know that. I'm sure one of us will come up with some insane half-baked idea that ends up saving all our asses and we'll laugh over drinks and bad nutri-supps. Do you remember when we got knocked out of that Fastlane past an event horizon of a black hole? I thought we were dead then, too, but you and Ahsha did *something* that I still can't pronounce and we nearly restarted the star on the way out of the system."

Joane sniffled. "Anti-spaghettification gravity ordinance," she recalled. "That's still pretty small scale compared to this, Tris."

Tristan shook her head and waved a hand dismissively. "Come on, we all love trying to outdo ourselves. I don't know how we'll top this, but I'm sure we will someday."

Joane wiped her eyes with the back of her hand. "It really does feel like old times, doesn't it?" Tristan nodded, happy just to see a faint smile on her face. "Do you think...at least, until we get out of this mess, that we can just pretend like it is old times? Like none of that ever happened?"

"Just two friends getting into trouble?" Tristan suggested, her smile widening.

"Yeah," Joane said with a slight nod. "Whatever happens afterwards happens, but we've got some time before the Redshift ends, right? For now, why can't we just be friends again?"

"Cordelle," Tristan said. "You've got a deal. If we're gonna do things the way we used to, though, you're gonna need another bottle."

"I should probably stay out of your bedroom, too," Joane noted, chuckling a bit as she crossed her room carefully, watching for glass. Tristan paused for a moment, chewing the inside of her mouth.

"Well, it *is* more comfortable than that old kitchen," Tristan's voice trailed off. She felt her face growing hot. Her painkillers were fading; why had she said that?

"You're not wrong," Joane answered carefully, turning the empty bottle in her hands. "It's a weird place to drink."

"There's no normal place to drink in a Redshift," Tristan countered.

"If I didn't know any better, Tris-"

"I'm just saying! The invitation is there. You want to go drink bad wine in that awful chair, you go right ahead. I, however, will spend my last days as a non-fugitive drinking bad liquor in my extremely comfortable bed." She stopped at the end of the hallway towards her room while Joane stood in the middle, preparing to head for the liquor cabinet.

The two looked at each other for a long while, both trying to read one another. "I'll be there in a minute," Joane said finally, grinning as she darted out of sight. Tristan walked quickly to her room and threw herself across the bed. She took a long drink and waited, screaming internally the entire time.

She had no time to make any coherent thoughts out of the jumble of ideas in her brain before Joane returned, holding two bottles in each hand and several more under her arms. The smile on her face was contagious.

It wasn't long before they both lost track of time, talking and laughing about nothing serious or remotely important. For that night, while Darling redshifted across millions of kilometers, Joane and Tristan were content to drink and talk like the old friends they were, and it was the happiest either of them had been in a long time.

# Chapter 9
## The Best Laid Plans

JOANE woke up before Tristan this time, with a pounding headache and the urge to vomit. Yep, it was just like old times. They only ever drank so much when they got *out* of a terrible situation. She supposed neither of them expected they'd have a chance to celebrate getting out of this one, so they decided to party early. As send-offs went, it had been fun.

Now though, she felt sluggish and ill, like she might sleep until the Redshift ended and the Consortium blew them into dust. She looked around to take in where she was. When she opened her eyes and saw no awful red lights above her, she figured she'd returned to her own room at some point. When she saw Tristan lying maybe a foot away, she realized she hadn't. Her friend must've turned off the lights before falling asleep, which meant Joane had fallen asleep first, and Tristan hadn't thought to kick her out or sleep somewhere else. It made her stomach do a flip, especially when her eyes began to adjust to the dark and she started picking out tiny details of her face as sleep cleared from her eyes. Her hair, for instance, was a wreck, something Joane could never get used to seeing. Even when they'd first met, and Tris had been some random urchin who'd spent her entire life underground, her hair had been in perfect waves. To see it draped haphazardly and split across her face made Joane smile. Her face was still and relaxed; all the hardness gone out of her expression. It was like looking at a different person, and Joane couldn't take her eyes away. She tried to, screaming at herself to stop, but the way her shoulders rose and fell in a smooth rhythm was mesmerizing. After a while of looking into a woman whose face she couldn't stand a few days before, Joane finally woke up enough to realize what she was doing and tore her eyes away. She shook her head to clear it and climbed out of the bed, stepping over empty bottles as she did so. A few of them clinked harshly as they rolled into one another, and Joane froze. She pivoted and looked back at the bed, but Tristan didn't stir.

Joane breathed a sigh of relief and pulled out her knife, using the soft glow of the power pack to light her way through the mess to the door. She pushed it open as slowly as possible, trying not to make any noise as she exited the room. The lights outside were immediately abrasive, but Joane remembered where the control panels for the overheads were, so she made her way there and dimmed them to a warm orangish-yellow. She sighed and rubbed her eyes, trying to force the hangover away as she pushed into the kitchen. The kitchen was, predictably, a mess. Most of the food packs Joane found were expired, empty, or made for atmospheric conditions only. They'd been pulverized by the force of launch and landing so many times they were unrecognizable.

Joane tossed everything that wasn't usable into the garbage disposal unit, hoping Tristan wasn't saving any of it for some hoarder reason. Finally she found a set of void-frozen rolls spiced with cinnamon and culaska, and blocks of powder that could be melted into a sweet glaze.

Joane was by no means an excellent cook, nor did she care much about food. Most of the time, even when she was under atmosphere somewhere, she simply went to one of the Consortium sponsored locations and got their simple free meals rather than spending her credits getting specialty food anywhere. Food, to her, was food. It kept her running and that was all she needed.

This morning, though, she thought it might be nice to have an enjoyable breakfast. So, she followed the instructions of the sturdy metal package as closely as possible and ended up with a surprisingly acceptable plate of warm rolls.

She poured a few packs of flavor-gel into two glasses of water, creating the closest thing one could get to sowfruit juice in the middle of the void, and began lugging breakfast back to Tristan's room.

The room was still dark, and Tristan hadn't moved an inch from earlier. Joane shouldered her way inside, taking in the sight of her friend passed out in the thin strip of soft light coming in from the hallway. She hung there for a moment, not wanting to shatter the peaceful expression on her face. Joane had always known Tristan was a beautiful woman. Hell, Ahsha was too. Nothing ever happened between any of them, though. They were always too busy fighting or running from some disaster or going on a wild adventure. Why did something feel different now? Was it the time they'd spent away from one another? Was it the fact that Joane's entire view of Tristan had been thrown out the airlock? Was Ahsha's intervention what kept them from growing closer? Joane doubted it. Still, she wasn't an idiot or a teenager. She knew what she felt when she traced the line of Tris's jaw down her face and her gaze landed on the gentle curve of her soft gray lips.

She had no idea why this was happening *now*, when they were on a one-way trip to what would most likely be a quick execution to cover-up some conspiracy they had no business even beginning to unravel. She was going to die with no answers. The missing planets, Ahsha, how the Consortium was involved. All of it would gnaw at her mind as the ship exploded around them. If they were lucky, the officers might board the ship and shoot them there. That bothered her, but what she really wanted to know was why, suddenly, waking up in Tristan's bed felt more like home than anything ever had. She couldn't bear to dwell on it anymore and cleared her throat loudly.

Tristan started and rolled onto her back, looking out at the light with unfocused eyes. "Gah," she said, her voice slow and rumbling. "Oh, hey. Does your entire body hurt, too?"

Joane nodded and crossed the room, carefully balancing the tray and the glasses. "Yes, but probably not as bad as yours does. How's your leg, Tris?"

Tristan looked down at the bandage and shook her leg. "It's getting there, should be back to normal in a few days. Maybe a week." Neither of them wanted to say that they probably didn't have that long. "What's this?"

Joane placed the tray on the comforter between the two of them as she sat at the far end of the bed. She wanted to climb back into the warm divot her body had made in the mattress while she slept, but she thought that might be presumptuous. "I found some usable food in the kitchen, and I thought that after last night, we both deserve a decent breakfast."

Tristan took a deep sniff of the rolls and grinned widely. "I haven't had culaska rolls in forever," she said, "I forgot I even had these!" She grabbed one, ignoring the steam rising off the glaze, and took a bite out of the side. "Even you couldn't mess these up, Joane, I mean it."

Joane took one, enjoying the distantly familiar scent of cinnamon. It reminded her of something from her home planet, a lifetime ago. She couldn't place it, but pushed it out of her mind. "When was the last time we had these?" she asked, trying to pick a different memory. "I remember it being cold."

"Eternity's Spire," Tristan said immediately around a mouthful of dough. "That mountain on Charonus, in the Centaur system, right?

"Yes!" Joane exclaimed, leaning back as the memory came to her. "Ahsha wanted to do what again?"

"Who cares?" Tristan answered. "All I remember is she dragged us up that mountain for two weeks up and two weeks down. Freezing winds, icicles raining out of the sky, just the absolute worst climb I've ever been on."

"And when we got to the top-"

"And Ahsha saw that we brought the rolls!" they said in unison, howling with laughter. It took them a few moments to collect themselves.

"The look on her face," Tristan finally managed to get out. "She was so red, I thought the snow was going to melt under our feet, I did. She went on and on about 'packing efficiently' and 'pragmatic economy of rations,' but those were the best rolls I've ever had."

Joane nodded. "But the best meal has to be the diner at Mariana's Station, right?"

Tristan glared at her. "Did you forget? I got food poisoning at Mariana's. That fish they'd brought over from half a galaxy away almost killed me." She watched Joane break into a smile. "You *do* remember, you little bitch. Just like I remember the time you tried to pet that rodent on Raxtalon-6 and it nearly pulled your hand off."

"I still have the scar!" Joane said excitedly, holding her arm up. She expected to pull down her jacket sleeve, but remembered that she wasn't wearing it. She self-consciously tilted her chest forward, hoping it wasn't obvious that she wasn't wearing any kind of support under her shirt.

"Of course you have the scar!" Tristan said back. "*I* have scars from that thing! None that you can see, mind you."

"Did we ever find out what species that was?"

"No, we didn't." Tristan sighed happily and pulled a piece of her roll apart. "We had some wild times, didn't we?"

"We did," Joane said, stifling a yawn. "I wish we could have some of that time back."

Tristan nodded solemnly, but she was frowning at her. "Don't go and get sentimental on me, Cordelle. I'm getting us out of this mess, one way or another."

Joane set her mostly-eaten roll down on the tray gently, trying to smile despite the immediate turn the conversation had taken. "Have you figured anything out yet?"

"Not yet," Tristan said, sipping her flavored water. "I keep having ideas that just about work, but there's always some sort of catch. Like, for example, I thought we might be able to tamper with the slowdown drive and make it fire earlier than the system would normally let it. But then I think that doing that would fry the dampeners, and we'd get turned to paste before the Redshift finishes."

"Which isn't the goal," Joane surmised.

"I don't know why Ahsha is the one with all the degrees," Tristan continued, her voice dripping with sarcasm. "Then I think about trying to Redshift out of Cygnus the second we leave, but the drive can't handle multiple firings in such a short amount of time."

"What about a cloak?" Joane suggested. "Like when we had to run that blockade around the hurricane nebula? Remember, Ahsha did something to the shield generator that made Darling invisible to basically any type of scanning equipment? We could come out of the shift, hide, then jump away while we make a better plan."

Tristan stared down at the plate, reaching for another roll as she thought it over. "That would work really well," she said, "if we had a super genius on board who could do that. I could give it a shot, but if Ahsha left any instructions on how to do it, I would have found them by now. More likely than not, we'd just break the shields and be in a worse spot than before."

"There aren't many worse spots than the one we're in now," Joane pointed out. "The Consortium is the first government to ever unite the entire universe under one banner. And they did it peacefully, too. Millions of years of respected, legitimate, equal rule unchallenged by any major uprisings. We're two women with a theory that they *might* be stealing planets for a reason we don't know. They don't even need to kill us, because no one would ever believe it."

"I always thought it might happen," Tristan said. "You read the old docs, you watch the ancient holo-flicks, and they all tell the same story: people in power get too much and it goes to their head."

"And they decide to steal planets."

"Hey, I've read books that made less sense than this did. There's an answer to what's going on somewhere out there, and I am not dying without finding it." Tristan's intensity made it easier to ignore the crumbs on the sides of her mouth, which she brushed away in frustration.

"Then we might want to start with a sure thing," Joane said, reaching into her pocket. She kept the messages from Ahsha saved on her personal device, which she activated with a slide of her finger across the thin glass screen. "Ahsha sent us the coordinates of her ship. She said that there's data on there she didn't have the ability to send us, because it's sensitive. I can't make heads, tails, or sides of the files in her message, but there might be a missing piece in the data vault on the ship."

"If the ship is still there."

"If," Joane agreed. "I know, it's a long shot. A planet is a big area, though. The gravitational anomaly they leave behind affects entire systems. There's a good chance they just haven't found the ship, especially if it was left inactive somewhere. But we have something they don't, the exact last location."

"It's a starting point," Tristan agreed, "but we need to think about what happens immediately when we get there. Odds are there will be a fleet and a half of Consortium craft there waiting to blow us out of the void. We won't have time to lock in to Ahsha's ship, board, and sift around for the files we want."

"Not there," Joane said with a nod. "But we don't have to do it there." The Solan stood up and began pacing excitedly. "I was thinking about what you did back at the Waning Crescent with the landing pylons and the carrier ship. The seal is strong enough to slow down a ship moving at near redshift speed, right?"

"Yes..." Tristan said hesitantly, obviously not following her.

"So, here's my plan. We drop into the system, dodge whatever chaos is waiting there until we find Ahsha's ship. When we find it, kick on the landing gear and attach ourselves to the craft. All the while, the Redshift engine is powering back up, and once it's ready, we take off on some random vector and hope it buys us enough time to find a desolate corner of the universe to pick through the data."

It took Joane a moment after she finished talking to notice that Tristan had been watching her walk the entire time. She straightened her back a bit when she noticed. Tristan's green eyes narrowed and focused, but not on her. She was running a simulation in her head, Joane realized, trying to figure out how many ways the plan could or would go wrong and how spectacularly they would do so. She had to admit it was a rough plan which didn't account for that many variables or have much of a backup. She didn't know if any part of Darling could handle the strain. Finally, Tristan spoke up.

"It's better than any idea I have," she conceded. "That doesn't mean it's safe, smart, or likely to work. For one, the magnetic seals need to be calibrated and boosted for the fastest, most secure seal possible. If it breaks while we're redshifting, it could take half the craft off with it and tear through a star at hyperlight speeds. Next, the drive would be completely fried after, even if I optimized the heat sinks. We'd need to pick a good place to wait, because we'd be completely disabled once we get there. And lastly, you're assuming that I could manage to dodge however many Consortium Wingships *and* dock with an inert hunk of metal somewhere in a solar system being ripped apart by gravitational anomalies."

"Can you?"

"Of course I can, don't be ridiculous," Tristan chided. "It's just going to take a lot of upgrades on Darling, and we only have another day or two before we get to Cygnus."

"We might as well work on that while we think of other ideas," Joane said. "It couldn't hurt."

"It could, actually," Tristan noted, "but no more than anything else." She shoved the last bit of the roll into her mouth and brushed her fingers off on the comforter. "Let's get to work," she mumbled around the cinnamon-culaska roll. "We've got our own lives to save."

*     *     *

REDSHIFTING was far from an exact science, which was the main reason no one bothered with it anymore. It risked too much human error, like the ancient highways of Sol-3. Millions, even billions of people piloted their own rudimentary shuttles across paved lanes dug into the ground by hand for hours on end every day. Eventually, standardized, rapid public transportation replaced the archaic system, the same way Fastlanes had taken over the dangerous and destructive redshifts. Because of the uncertainty involved, Tristan had to constantly check the pilot's console while she and Joane began modifying Darling. Every few minutes she would steal away from a project to go check their estimated distance and time to Cygnus. Sometimes the clock said it would take another three days. Sometimes it said as little as eight hours. Tristan had no idea if they were slowing down periodically or if the navigation tracker was malfunctioning due to the rapid speed they were traveling at. Every time she checked, she would run a system diagnostic on the engines, shields, redshift drive, and nearly every other functioning part of the ship. She did her best to tune everything up to its best possible condition. It would be embarrassing for a flap to jam as they made their mad dash toward Ahsha's ship and careen into a passing comet.

Nearly every moment of their time was spent preparing the ship. Tristan managed to retract the gear into the ship's cabin, so they didn't have to do any voidwalks at multiple times the speed of light. They went through several power storage coils, but eventually managed to connect enough and wire them correctly into the pylons to where the magnets were insanely powerful. If they didn't smash the two ships into one another, they would definitely form a seal so tight it would withstand a short redshift.

The drive itself was an easier task. It was made to be accessible from inside the ship, thanks to a small hatch in the ceiling of the kitchen. Tristan and Joane spent about three hours in the crawl space, unavoidably pressed against one another while they worked on different parts of the machine. Removing the melted and frayed machine parts was almost trivial compared to the awkward tangle of limbs as they tried situating themselves in the tiny area.

It was uncomfortably warm work, mostly due to the immense heat given off by the active redshift drive. Tristan hated it, but they had to work slowly and carefully so as to not accidentally damage the drive as they worked. Almost every movement she made, she felt Joane staring at her intently. In the past, she would've made a sly comment to tick her off and send her away, but for some reason she didn't mind it this time. Maybe she had missed having friends on the ship for the past few years. Maybe it felt nice to know she was seeing her as she really was and not the twisted image Ahsha had created in her mind. Maybe it was because in the dark, cramped space they were in, it would take almost no effort to put her hands around the smaller woman's waist and pull her in close enough-

Tristan jabbed her finger into a live current and yelped, pulling it back so fast she nearly punched Joane in the face. A small curl of smoke rose off her now blackened fingertip. "Are we gonna die now?" Joane asked, half-joking. Neither of them wanted to admit how little they knew about the machine in front of them.

"Yes," Tristan said, pretending to sound grim and resigned. "Even now, our bodies are being torn apart by the void, but our brains are moving too slowly to comprehend it."

Joane chuckled. "There's worse ways to go, I guess. Makes for a nice story at least." She grunted in effort as she tightened a bolt, then slammed a cover shut on it. "That's all my stuff done, I think. Are you good?"

Tristan licked her fingertip and set the wire properly in place this time, forcing her mind not to return to the image it had conjured moments before. When she turned to nod at the woman next to her, it sprang back into her mind without warning. "Drive is all set," she said. "Now we just hope it holds up when the time is right."

Joane let out a long, slow breath and glanced around the crawl space. "This better work," she whispered, running a hand along the ceiling only a few inches above her face. Tristan watched her fingers move lazily across the metal, softly illuminated by the red glow of the drive's heat sinks.

"It will," she assured her. "I'm the best pilot this side of the universal equator, you're one of the best planners I've ever known, and we make a hell of a repair crew. I'm pretty sure that makes us unstoppable."

Joane let her head fall to the side and looked at Tristan. "We do make a pretty good team," she said, almost staring past her. "Can you imagine what Ahsha will say if we find her? Seeing us work together again, even better than before."

"I can see her smirk now," Tristan said, "and she'll take all the credit for getting us back working together."

"You're so right," Joane said, reaching out an arm and playfully slapping Tristan's arm. "I just hope...she doesn't try to change things. I'm already mad at her enough; she's got a lot of explaining to do. If she tries to put that wedge back between us, I'll wring her pretentious little neck."

"I'd love to see that, actually," Tristan said. "I wanted to do that for years. You're right, though, we make a pretty good pair." She immediately regretted her choice of words and felt herself blushing. She hardly ever blushed at people. Joane went quiet. The two women were frozen in place, staring into one another's eyes, daring the other to say something else. The tight space felt like it was closing in around them, pushing them closer to one another.

Tristan felt her hand moving across the dust covered panel. Her inner voice was screaming at her. *What are you doing? There's no time for this! There will never be time for this!* But what, she thought, is this? Joane had always been beautiful, Tristan knew that, but they never quite worked together well enough for her to think about her friend that way. Now they were working together, and it felt perfect. Did she really want to jeopardize that? Then again, they would probably be dead in a day's time. What would it matter if she grabbed Joane by the front of her blue shirt and pulled her in? She wondered what it would feel like. She'd kissed a lot of women in her time, but not many who she cared about, none she was close enough to call a friend. Was Joane just her friend, if she couldn't get the image of them together out of her mind?

She didn't have time to question anything further, because her hand had found the edge of Joane's jacket. The brown synthleather was bunched up in her fist, which she was clenching so tight she thought she might tear the fabric apart. Her eyes refocused and found Joane's again. The woman looked like she was facing down a rampaging Sunderbull, but with a twinge of something else behind the nervous energy in her lovely blue eyes.

"Tris," Joane whispered breathlessly. Her mouth had fallen open just slightly, to where Tristan could just see her teeth behind Joane's soft pink lips, curled into the perfect shape at that moment. Tristan felt her own mouth hanging open. She imagined she looked ridiculous, but she didn't care anymore. She tugged on the jacket. Joane didn't resist. In fact, Tristan thought she might have been moving herself in. In the darkness of the cramped space, Tristan tried to bring her other hand up to cup the side of Joane's face.

That was the moment it clicked. She didn't just want to kiss her. She didn't just want to know the way her lips tasted or the way she moved in bed or the way her hands would feel on her. No, Tristan wanted to know everything. She wanted to hold her tight, to fall asleep next to her and go skywatching and-

*Fuck*, she thought, *this wasn't the plan.* They were only a few inches away from each other. By the orange glow of the light, all Tristan could see were Joane's eyes. She was transfixed by them so completely that she almost forgot to close her eyes when she tilted her head and moved in.

Sparks flew. Literally. With the worst possible timing in the universe, a coil sprung loose from the drive and unleashed a shower of burning white points of light in the crawl space. Both women screamed as the machine clanked and whirred and hissing sparks bit at their faces. Tristan tried to pull Joane into her and shield her face, but the solan had already ripped her jacket up over her face to shield it. Over the course of a very loud and chaotic minute, the coil began to lose its stored charge and began to lose its glow.

When the sparks stopped, Tristan smelled nothing but ozone and burnt hair. She coughed out a plume of acrid smoke, and Joane did the same. It was difficult to wave the smoke away with hardly any space to move in, but eventually their weak motions and the fire repellent system in the ship's inner workings managed to clear the smoke.

Tristan and Joane lied there for a while, coughing out the last bits of dust and smoke. "Maybe we're not the best mechanics in the universe," Joane said finally, her voice tight and constricted.

"No, we're not," Tristan muttered. She was enraged. Enraged that the coil was now useless. That their drive wouldn't have range or power they'd planned on. Enraged that she wasn't rolling around this crawl space with Joane in her arms right now. She wanted to punch something, but there wasn't enough room in the space to move her arm. "Damn it."

"What's the next step?" Joane asked. Her meek tone indicated she knew just how serious of a problem this could be. If the drive wasn't at full strength, a redshift wouldn't take them as far away from Cygnus. It made them easier to follow. Worse still, it made the chances of a misfire even higher. They could be shot into the surface of a star, the hull could implode, or the engine might not work at all, leaving them stranded with an angry super-government at their airlock.

"I've got more coils," Tristan said with a sigh. "I'll install one real quick; it shouldn't take me more than fifteen standard minutes. You can go shower off and get yourself cleaned up." *Please leave,* she begged silently, *before I do something stupid again.*

Joane twisted to look down at herself. There were a few burns on her face and hands, but most of the damage had been done to her brown jacket, which was now pitted with holes and scorch marks. She looked heartbroken. "This was my favorite-this was my *only* jacket," she said weakly.

Tristan almost laughed, though she didn't really find anything about the situation funny. If anything, the sheer unfairness of it all gave her no other choice. Still, she held back her laughter as best as she could. "Hey, don't beat yourself up. I've got plenty of spare clothes you can borrow. They're all in your room, obviously. And when this is all over, we'll go shopping and buy you more than one boring, dreadful outfit, alright?"

Joane scoffed. "Excuse me, Tris, but all I see you wear are black coats and gray shirts, and *maybe* a scarf with some color in it." She was inching her way towards the ladder down into the ship's interior.

"Hey," Tristan said, reaching out to help Joane through the hole. "Just because I don't dress fashionably doesn't mean I don't know how to. I'm perfectly capable of dressing up, but I choose not to so people ignore me."

Joane laughed, clearly not believing her. She began to lower her back half through the hole and onto the flimsy deployable ladder they'd positioned below the hatch. It wobbled a bit when Joane touched it, and she gasped a bit before Tristan reached out and grabbed both of her hands. It shocked Tristan that a woman so warm could have such freezing hands, but she was still happy to be holding them at all.

After a bit of unsteady lowering, Joane made it to the floor and walked out of Tristan's sight. A few minutes later, she heard the onboard water system activate and began cycling water towards the washroom. Tristan immediately poured her focus into replacing the spent coil, blocking any other thoughts completely out of her mind as she carefully plucked the wires from the connection ports. It took her even less time than she thought it would, even though she caught a few jolts to her fingers as she did so. Eventually, the work ran out, and Tristan stared blankly at the connection she had triple-checked. It was on securely this time, with no chance of it dislodging again. She sighed and exited the crawl space, a difficult task with a broken leg and no hands to guide her down. Joane's shower was still running, and Tristan didn't know what she might do if she went to the same washroom to use one of the other showers. She decided it would be best to wait for Joane to finish cleaning up, then wash the soot and sweat off.

Tristan headed for the cockpit. Over the years, it had become more of a room to her than the actual bedroom, which she hardly used save for when she had visitors onboard. The pilot's chair was far less comfortable than the bed, but she'd grown used to the stiff material and the way it held her. She kicked the bar under the chair as hard as she could, flattening out the seat into a somewhat curved pseudo-bed. Tristan flopped onto it, listening to the groan of the springs from the sudden weight and covered her eyes.

"What did you do?" she asked herself. As much as she wanted to ignore what had just happened, it was impossible. The realization, the epiphany, the way Joane's lips had curled and whispered her name, they all sat at the forefront of her mind. She wanted to scream. No, she wanted to walk down to the washroom, grab Joane by her shoulders, and shake her until the woman told her what she'd done to make her feel this way so suddenly. No, actually, she wanted to walk down to the washroom, grab Joane by the hips, and push her against the wall-

Tristan slammed her head against the back of the chair a few times. She didn't want this. She didn't have time to feel these feelings. She needed her head clear and present so that maybe they could survive the shitstorm they were flying into. How would she feel if her pathetic teenage pining got them both killed? The thought was unbearable. The thought of them dying, now, was unbearable. Tristan had simply accepted it a few days ago as a regrettable fact. But now, as she felt herself falling for the insufferable, amazing woman down the hallway, she knew she had to do *something* to get them out of this.

She grabbed her small crossbow out of its side holster. The arms of the weapon clicked into place and tilted back, their grav-strings pulling a bolt into place. She turned the tiny defense weapon around in the cockpit lighting. "I'll tear the whole thing down if I have to," she promised no one in particular.

# Chapter 10
## Shower Thoughts

JOANE pressed her back against the stark white tiles of the bathroom. The cold made her suck in her breath, but she needed something holding her up right now. Joane had dimmed the lights to almost complete darkness, the way she always preferred to shower. The clothes she'd picked out in a daze from her room were sitting and waiting on the countertop next to the line of sinks. Her own ruined outfit was piled into a sad, gently smoking heap on the floor. Joane had showered off the dust, soot, and sweat in a matter of minutes, then spent the next twenty under the barrage of warm water, letting her hair get plastered to her face as her mind stood frozen in place.

Ahsha had hired Joane because she thought the woman had a knack for analysis. Which was true, Joane was a fast-thinker. She could feel out a situation and come up with a solution to most problems within a few seconds. Now, though, it was like all of that practice was gone out the airlock. All she could think about was Tristan's hand in her jacket and the way she felt when she pulled her in. How badly she'd wanted what she thought was happening to happen. How she felt herself move into Tris's arms as if on instinct. It had felt so natural, so right, only to have the moment shattered. Did that mean the moment was gone? She'd seemed perfectly eager to get rid of her afterwards. Besides all that, Joane was probably reading into it. Tristan probably saw the coil loosen and was just trying to protect her. Joane had never known much about Tristan, but she knew one thing: she wasn't an emotional woman. She didn't catch feelings for people the same way Joane did, especially not the feelings she was having now.

Even if she had been pulling her in, Joane knew there wouldn't have been any meaning in it. She thought back to The Drunken Duck, watching her buy drinks for half the women in the place. Joane was just another woman at the bar. She was the warm body that was there in a tight space to take the edge off before everything hit the ventilation fan.

Joane sighed and tilted her head back, feeling the water splashing against her chest. The heat and pressure were almost painful, but Joane liked the intensity. It matched the flutter of her heartbeat. If she closed her eyes, she was back in that tiny compartment, and Tristan's arms were around her, and she felt safe and excited and nervous all at the same time. She pressed her thighs together and bit down on her lip, the pain sharpening her focus and pulling her out of her fantasies. She yanked the shower knob to the left with all the strength she could muster in her state, cutting off the water and giving her no more time to think about the way Tris's breath had felt against her face.

*     *     *

JOANE didn't meet Tristan's eyes as she walked into the cockpit. Despite her efforts, Tristan spun around in her chair, adjusting the back as she did so. "Were you planning on leaving any hot water for me?" she asked, a hint of a joke in her tone. Joane flinched, too on edge to hear the sarcasm. "You were in there for like, half an hour."

Joane rubbed the back of her neck, looking for imperfections in the floor paneling. "Sorry, it's been a while since I had a warm shower, is all."

"And it'll be a while before I have one," Tristan mumbled. She glanced up and down at Joane, taking a few moments to take in her outfit. "You know, I think there are some clothes in there that might actually fit you."

Joane raised her arms up and gave the outfit a look. The shirt was a dark orange fabric stamped with an intricate pattern of planetary orbits, a souvenir from a solar-system sized concert Tristan had attended a few years back. The collar had become loose after years of wear, so it was close to sliding off her shoulder. The shirt was much too long for Joane, reaching halfway down the woman's thighs and covering up most of the paradoxically short shorts she'd found. Every other pair of leggings she'd seen dragged across the floor as she walked, so this had been her best option. "I don't see anything wrong with it," she said, "especially since you blew up my nice jacket."

Tristan's eyes fell to Joane's thighs and stayed there. "You're free to borrow some pants, if you like. It gets cold here." Joane rolled her eyes and lifted up the shirt a few inches.

"I'm wearing pants, you child," she said. "Yes, you're taller than all of us, we established that. I hesitate to think about what these look like when you wear them." That was a lie, Joane knew. She had thought about it the moment she picked them out of a pile of longer pants.

"Well," Tris began, her eyes glued to the shorts. "I think those actually belong to a girl out in the dorsal arm of Alexandria. They look good on you, though." Joane's eyes widened and she dropped the edge of her shirt, hiding the shorts.

"Tris, why do you keep other women's clothes onboard? Are you taking trophies?"

"I forget they're here!" she said with a shrug, then corrected herself when Joane glared at her. "The clothes, not the women, obviously. Things get left and, ya know, if they're comfortable, I might sleep in them from time to time. Get off my back, alright? You're welcome for the clothes, let's start with that."

Joane sighed and pulled herself into a chair, still not meeting Tristan's eyes. How was she so calm? Joane could feel her pulse in her neck, yet Tris seemed to be her usual snarky self. It was infuriating. Joane swallowed hard as her mouth went dry and began pouring over the recon station's data cache. She heard Tristan working on something at her own console, muttering obscenities to herself. That was fine by her. They could work in silence, focus on their own tasks, and maybe get some work done instead of wasting time staring at one another. Of course, there wasn't a lot of data in the computer system that could help them. Joane spent most of her time reading up on shield generator maintenance, making sure they'd done everything they needed to take as many hits as possible.

After nearly an hour of unbearable silence, Tristan spoke up, nearly making Joane jump out of her skin.

"Water should be hot enough now," she said, climbing out of her seat. "I'll be back in a few minutes." She left without another word, and Joane couldn't stumble through a decent response before Tristan had left the cockpit. She sat alone on the small bridge, tapping her finger against the gray metal device in front of her and trying to make sense of how she'd gotten here.

*  *  *

TRISTAN returned not too long after, carrying a few bowls of soup made from simple nutrient dust. Joane took one of the bowls with a small smile and nod, then returned to her chair to eat. She found herself mostly pushing her spoon around in the bowl, watching the hot brown liquid slosh around in silence.

"You should eat," Tristan said after a while. Joane looked over her shoulder to see Tristan hunched over her bowl, staring at her. "We need to be alert tomorrow."

"Tomorrow?" Joane said, surprised. The engine data had been all over the place for so long; she'd fooled herself into thinking they might have more time.

"Yeah." Tristan gave the console a grim look. "Whatever we did to the drive worked really well. All the projections say we're going to reach Cygnus by late morning tomorrow." Joane fell silent for a bit, and the small appetite she had left vanished.

"So this is our last meal?" she asked. Tristan set her bowl down, the ceramic scraping unpleasantly against the metal console.

"*No,*" she said pointedly. "We'll have breakfast."

Joane dropped her spoon into the bowl with a heavy sigh. "I appreciate your optimism, Tris. Truly, you've really turned yourself around from glowering all the time."

Tristan looked a bit taken aback by the sudden rise of Joane's voice. She leaned back in her chair and fixed Joane with a look that she'd come to recognize over the years they'd spent together. It was half anger, half a challenge. Any time an argument began to spiral into a shouting match, she'd give that look as if to say *Try it, I dare you.* "I think I've earned a bit of a pessimistic streak, Cordelle," she answered. Then her face switched into a scowl. "You've been to the Hollow Worlds: you know where I grew up. How are you going to be on my back about hopelessness and moping when that's all I had growing up, and then the moment I try to be a little bit optimistic, you shoot me down?"

Joane, like she always did, took the challenge. "Because it isn't fair!" she yelled. "You ran away from us, Tris, from *me*! Now here we are, three years later, Ahsha is missing and I'm nothing more than hired muscle, but you're doing just fine. You're a traveling hero rescuing people in every corner of the universe, you fixed all your attitude problems, everything about you is so damn perfect now, isn't it?"

Tris's eyes flashed with pain for a moment, but it quickly solidified into anger. "You think *this* is perfect?" she gestured wildly around the cockpit. "That says more about you than it does about me. I live in a ship crammed full of junk I have to keep so I can keep the engine running, I'm risking my life every other month because someone needs me to, and I haven't had an actual place to rest my head in years!"

"And what about me?" Joane shouted. "I don't even have a ship to call home! I'm out here risking my life for money because it's all I can do."

"Why not just get set up in a Consortium block, then?" Tris countered. "Get a nice house on some backwater, take an odd job and live a nice peaceful life on their dime?"

"Oh please," Joane said with a roll of her eyes. "You and I both know I'd never be happy that way. I had a taste of that life as a kid, and I'm never going back to that."

"See, that's your problem." Tristan pushed herself to her feet and jammed a finger in Joane's direction. "You know what I had to look forward to when I was a little girl? Cave-ins. Giant spiders. Dying alone and afraid in a dark tunnel because our world was 'technically habitable' enough that the Consortium never sponsored an evacuation. So yes, I'm so sorry that you think a quiet life with a sun over your head is the worst thing imaginable, but it isn't."

"You," Joane hissed, rising to her own feet. She held her eyes open for fear she might start crying if she dared blinked, "have no idea what my life was like. You had a family that loved you; I remember the way they told you to go with us so you could have a better life. You weren't there at the start, Tris. My father sent mercenary crews after Ahsha and I for almost a year, because he couldn't stand the idea of one of his daughters disgracing the family name to be some traveling scientist's assistant."

"Maybe he was right." Tristan's words cut through Joane like a knife. She froze, but Tristan either didn't notice or didn't care how deeply those four words had struck. "Look at where we are! Tell me right now you wouldn't be happier back in your cushy home sipping wine and playing politics, or whatever it was you did." Joane was across the room before she knew it, her finger inches away from Tristan's face and her other hand on her dagger.

"That wasn't life," she hissed at the woman, who was too taken aback to step away. "I was a decoration, a tool of power, nothing else. My parents were just waiting for the right time to use me as a bargaining tool, to marry me off to some other family for a bit more money in their pocketbooks. My social life was rented out my entire life. People would pay for the young Cordelle girl to swing by whatever party they were throwing that night, and I'd sit there and smile and be proper so that my family would let me step outside the house the next day. You and Ahsha were the first people I met who ever bothered to use my first name. You two are the most difficult, frustrating, infuriating women I have ever had the displeasure of knowing. But I wouldn't trade our time together for anything. Would you?"

Tris's face softened. She clearly knew something had struck a nerve with Joane, and she'd gone too far. That's how those fights always ended: with regret. "No," she said, too dumbstruck to say anything but the honest truth. "I-I wouldn't. I'm sorry, Joane. I didn't know."

"No, you didn't," Joane sighed, pushing hair back out of her face. "You can see why I never told you. It's just...you aren't the only person that Ahsha helped escape from something, Tris. She took us on because she knew we were broken and desperate and easy to manipulate. But I would stare down the entire Consortium before I went back home, I mean that."

"But you don't have to," Tristan said. Her voice was full of promises she didn't have the breath to say out loud. Joane flinched when her gray hand reached out and grabbed her arm, but the grip was gentle and comforting. "We don't have to fight. We...we can get out of this. I'm not going to let you die here, Joane. I'm not giving up yet."

"I thought you already had," Joane choked out. "What changed your mind?" Tristan's face fell into an almost imperceptible smile. Her eyes were sparkling with the faintest hint of tears. She shook her head and blew her black wavy hair out of her face. Tris's other arm found its way to the side of Joane's face, resting along her gently curved jawline. Joane was paralyzed, staring up into her eyes.

"You did," was all Tristan could say. And then she kissed her. Joane let out a surprised gasp that was immediately stifled by her lips against hers. It was so sudden and shocking that it took her a second to close her eyes and kiss back, leaning up and into Tristan. Her hand fell away from the dagger's hilt and grabbed at Tris's cloak, trying in vain to hold her steady as her legs turned to jelly.

The warmth of Tristan's lips filled her body, like she was back under the near-scalding water in the shower. Like the shower, it was painful in a delightful sort of way that made Joane want to feel it all the more. She gave in, letting Tristan's hands hold her in place as she opened her mouth to let her push further. Tris's hand let go of Joane's arm and found her waist, grabbing it so tightly Joane thought she might bruise. Her other hand continued to hold her face, a few of the fingers brushing up and down Joane's cheeks while Tris kissed her with enough passion to make up for all the times she suddenly realized she should've kissed her before.

Joane tried to meet that passion, reaching and pulling at Tristan to bring her even closer as their bodies pressed harder and harder against one another. Both women shuffled their feet, trying to stay on their feet as they swayed, their lips locked firmly together as they threatened to tip over with each motion. Joane knew she was whimpering at each kiss, each time their tongues met and twisted into each other's mouths. She didn't care, though. All her brain could focus on was the gentle lavender scent of Tris's hair and the way her mouth tasted like cinnamon and sweet herbs. It was nothing like she'd imagined. When she'd grabbed her in the crawl space, she'd prepared herself for a forceful, domineering feeling from Tris.

The reality was far from the case. Even in all the passion, Joane could tell Tristan was trying to be gentle and slow. She waited a second each time they parted to take a breath, and her hands would be lax as if to offer Joane a chance to back away. Those moments were agony to Joane, who urged back with a tug of her cloak. Tristan held her like a glass statue, tight enough to keep steady, but not too hard that Joane might break. Joane, however, grabbed at Tris with the urgency and desperation of a rock climber losing their grip. Her hands scrambled across Tristan's body, searching for somewhere to hold on to to keep from falling. At one point, she grabbed at the spot where Tristan's back was bruised, and even through the layers of clothes, the sudden pressure made Tris grunt in shock and pain into Joane's mouth.

Joane was horrified that she had broken the spell of the moment, that Tris might pull away and realize what they were doing, but her kisses grew even more fervent and the hand on Joane's face fell to her bare shoulder. She shrugged, trying to push the shirt further down on her arm.

Tristan stopped again, pulling her mouth away from Joane's and pressing their foreheads together. They were both breathing shakily, unable to catch their breath in the middle of their embrace. Their eyes locked, both of them lost in the moment and not daring to speak.

"We're not going to die tomorrow," Tris said, her voice filled with so much conviction that Joane believed her. Joane nodded, biting down her lip as she did so. *Kiss me again*, she begged silently. She didn't want to think about tomorrow. In fact, she wasn't sure she could. All she wanted to focus on right now was the way their chests rose and fell in perfect sync and the way they fit perfectly in each other's arms.

"But just in case we do," Joane stammered, the words barely making it out of her mouth.

"But just in case we do," Tristan echoed with a smile and a nod.

# Chapter 11
## The End of the Road

TRISTAN had the dream again that night. After hours of ecstasy, she and Joane finally collapsed into each other's arms and fell asleep, blushing and smiling like idiots. Tristan was confused, then, when her peaceful sleep was interrupted with her waking up on the floor of the tunnel. She groaned and stumbled to her feet, peering into the darkness. "Why?" she asked the walls around her. Her voice echoed in the empty space for what felt like several minutes. "Why am I here? I...I'm happy."

The walls answered her with her own voice, growing gradually more distant and distorted. She sighed. Her father had told her the legend of tunnels speaking to lost miners when the Hollow Worlds had first been dug out, offering them directions back to their camps. Apparently in the millenia they'd been digging into the world, seeking some inner pocket of paradise, the walls had decided to stop being helpful.

She waited for a while, listening. Eventually, there it was: the roar of engines in the far distance. She hung her head and took a step forward. Her leg still hurt, but it was nowhere near the pain she felt the first night. "Let's get going," she said reluctantly.

"Yeah, we should," someone said. Tristan yelped, then the walls repeated the noise a few times. Tristan whipped around, reaching for the crossbow that was never there in these dreams. She stopped when she saw the woman standing there, in the brown jacket and blue shirt she'd burned into her memory. "Hey, Tris," Joane said with a relaxed smile. "You gonna shoot me, or are we gonna get moving?"

Tristan stood completely still, her mouth open. There had never been anyone else in the dream with her. She was always alone in the dark, racing to find someone who could take her away. Joane walked up and kissed her, but it wasn't like any of the fast kisses that had left her tingling all over. No, Joane kissed her like she'd been kissing her for years and knew exactly how to do it. It was comforting and soft and warm, and it made the tunnel feel just a little bit brighter. Tristan took Joane's hand in hers and intertwined their fingers.

"I'm happy too," Joane said as they walked. Tristan turned to the side and smiled at her. Joane smiled back, and the engines sounded closer for the first time Tristan could remember.

*　　*　　*

TRISTAN came to consciousness slowly, her eyes opening one at a time. The dream was fresh in her mind, and for a moment she feared that all of last night had been part of a wishful dream. That faded when she felt the slight ache in her thighs, the tight pain in her jaw, and the naked woman in her arms. Joane was still fast asleep, so tightly enveloped in her arms that Tristan could barely move her head downwards to look at her. Joane's hair was tousled and rough, and it still smelled faintly of the lemon shampoo she'd left in the showers all those years ago. Tristan bent her neck just barely to place a soft kiss on the top of her head, and her stomach immediately did a flip.

Why did I just do that, she thought. She had no idea what last night meant for her and Joane, but it wasn't her place to be getting sappy right now. She knew how she felt, and as much as she wanted to deny it, she had fallen hard for Joane. Kissing her had felt like the numbing gel on her bruise. The instant her lips met Joane's, the hard pain locked inside her had melted away into blissful warmth, and she would have stayed in that moment forever if she could've. But what did it mean? Did Joane care about her like she did? Had it been a moment of passion, or a simple desire for a last night of pleasure before reaching Cygnus? They'd been screaming in each other's faces moments before, Tristan remembered. The way Joane had looked at her when she mentioned her home...it made her heart hurt. She wished she'd known earlier, because she never would have said the things she did if she had. She ran a hand along Joane's bare back, feeling the smooth curves of her shoulders down to the small of her back, and then up again. She had no idea what time it was. Maybe she'd been asleep for an hour. Maybe they'd slept into the morning, been vaporized by the Consortium, and this was Tristan's afterlife. She'd be fine with that, she decided.

Unfortunately, reality made itself known. A pleasant chime played over the ship's speakers. Tristan let out a sad sigh when she felt Joane stirring. "Attention, Redshift ending in thirty minutes. Slowdown engine activation beginning in fifteen minutes," an accented voice chirped at them. The message repeated a few times, then the chime played again, and Tristan was left in silence.

"So much for breakfast," Joane muttered, pulling herself away from Tristan's arms. She looked over as Joane pulled herself into a sitting position on the side of the bed, watching her silhouette in the low light. "We...we should get ready." Tristan nodded at the woman's bare shoulders and turned away, unable to hide the disappointment in her face. They threw on the clothes that had been haphazardly strewn across Tristan's room last night in utter silence. Tristan tried to keep a timer running in her head, but all she could count were memories from the night before, a scattered collage of images she could not afford to focus on right now. Joane had gotten ready and was out the door while Tristan was still slipping her bra on. She wasted a precious moment staring at the blank door, wondering if she'd ruined everything just in time for the world to end.

She sighed and pulled on a black shirt, threw on a black cloak that was just enough of a different shade to clash horribly, and didn't bother with a scarf for today. When she made it to the bridge, trying to brush her hair into something semi-manageable with her hands, Joane was already there, drumming her fingers against the weapon's console. Tristan released the latch anchoring her pilot's chair to the floor and pushed it back along a groove. She felt like standing for the next few hours.

She checked the readouts as Darling gave them to her. The slowdown engine was working fine, and their speed was already dropping rapidly. The inertial dampeners were holding steady, and no sections of the hull reported any undue stress. She ran her fingers along a series of controls and deployed the grav-tube and control sphere. As soon as the redshift was over, she'd have complete control again. And she'd need it.

"Joane?" she said to the woman. Joane didn't take her eyes off the monitor, but tilted her head in acknowledgement. "This isn't going to come down to a fight. If anything, I need you on the power shunting controls to keep the engines and the shields running. Even then, I can do that alone."

"What are you saying?" Joane asked, still not meeting her eyes as she walked briskly to the monitors a few meters away. Her voice was all business.

Tristan chewed her lip. "I'm saying, you don't have to be a part of this if you don't want to. I can get us out of this mess and you can go back to sleep."

Joane shook her head and slid into the power control station. She ran a hand over the screens, brushing dust off the dim displays. "Absolutely not." she sounded offended. "I'm the one who dragged you into this, and you think I'm letting you do this alone? Besides, I'm not dying in my sleep, Tris."

Tristan again nodded at the woman's back. "Alright then, let's do this."

The computer chimed as the redshift began to end. The deceleration of the ship became painfully clear as the inertial dampeners groaned and readjusted to the rapid change of speed. Tristan dug the heels of her boots into the metal and gritted her teeth. She had one hand in a vice grip on the console, the other held under the waiting control sphere. In the viewport, the endless black void became pockmarked with lines of dim yellow light, then more of them grew brighter as the ship slowed and the traveling light of the universe began to catch their ship again.

As Tristan watched, her heart thudding in her ears, the lines shortened and became dots, which clarified into recognizable stars and constellations. She forced herself to breathe regularly as the computer counted down to full deceleration. "3, 2, 1- Transferring control to-"

Tristan grabbed the control sphere as soon as the faint circles of light appeared on the edges and shoved it forward with as much force as she could muster. Then, before she even got her bearings, she twisted her wrist violently and threw Darling into a corkscrew spiral through the void. She ripped her arm towards the console, and Darling pivoted and fired downwards. Tristan grunted and put both hands on the sphere, drawing more power into the engines and sending Darling rocketing through the empty void. With every twist and rapid spin, she expected a silver and blue laser to streak into the viewport and end the spastic dance she'd thrown the ship into. None ever came. In fact, she caught a brief glimpse of a console showing no nearby active vessels. She pulled the sphere toward her body and spun the ship around rapidly, bringing it to a halt as she switched her view between the recon monitor and the viewport itself. She couldn't believe either of them.

Her navigational records indicated that she should have been in a satellite orbit around Cygnus-4, a lush green planet with a few sparse oceans and a spattering of modest mountain ranges. The planet, obviously, wasn't there, but Darling was still orbiting around the gravitational forces left behind in Cygnus's wake. It was eerie and peculiar, for the computer to begin orbit trajectories around an empty space. Tristan felt a shiver run down her spine. It hadn't been a large or particularly important planet, but for it to just disappear without warning or reason… it didn't sit right with her. The missing planet was, ironically, the less surprising thing she saw in her viewport. Instead of a waiting swarm of angry Consortium wingships, Tristan saw nothing.

Joane was half out of her chair, looking in disbelief at the sight. "I don't…"

Tristan cut her off. "I don't either, but we don't have to worry about it. Tell me where Ahsha's ship is so we can get the hell out of here." Joane raced across the bridge, practically throwing herself into the recon station in the process.

"Coordinates are coming for you- to you," Joane quickly amended. She still hadn't looked Tristan in the face. It upset her. Tristan had hoped to look Joane in the eyes at least one more time, but business came before pleasure, she supposed.

Tristan glanced at the coordinates, swept her left hand across the monitor displaying them, and pushed Darling as fast as she could go towards them. Her redshift had been surprisingly accurate; it only took them about five minutes of full throttle flying to reach the ship.

Tristan noted immediately that the ship appeared intact and undamaged, but completely inert. It was a heavy looking vessel, vaguely shaped like some sort of bird, with five engines mounted on the back of a five sided body covered in burnt out signal lights. If she had wanted to wait around and see, she could've watched the ship lazily orbiting a planet that didn't exist anymore. Tristan, however, knew they were far from out of the woods. She gunned Darling towards the empty gray ship as fast as she could muster while the engines shifted back to a normal voidpace drive.

"Come on, Darling," she urged, twisting the vessel over and around until it was oriented the same way as Ahsha's ship. All the while, she was checking the nearby scans, just waiting for the Consortium to arrive. They never did.

For a brief, stupid moment, Tris thought they might just make it out scott-free. Then, something strange happened. Darling...jolted. Her engines were still oriented towards Ahsha's ship, but something yanked it a few hundred kilometers away to starboard. The two women grunted in shock as Darling was pulled along by something they couldn't see.

"Grav-lock?" Joane guessed, pulling herself upright in her chair. Tristan's eyes ran down all the monitors. There was nothing.

"No," she said. "No ship could generate a gravity wave this big. It must be-" There was another pulse that rocked the ship even further towards whatever was pulling it along. Tristan had to fight to stay on her feet, and a tinge of nausea passed through her. "It must be the anomaly that Cygnus left behind. Planets don't usually just disappear, right? So the void takes a bit of time to catch up with it."

"Which is probably why they aren't opening Fastlanes to this system," Joane surmised as Tristan struggled to regain control. "You know, I'm kind of surprised the Consortium wasn't lying about that part. Ever since they tried to kill us, I've been rethinking a lot of stuff."

Tristan finally managed to wrench Darling away from the horrible draw of Cygnus's ghost and turned Darling back toward Ahsha's ship. Thankfully, it had been pulled along with them, so they were actually closer than they had been when the pulses began. "I don't care what the Consortium is telling the truth about," Tristan said through gritted teeth as she slammed the landing pylon release switch. "I'm getting out of this system as fast as I can." A loud buzz answered her.

Joane's eyebrow went up in concerned confusion. Tristan stared down at the monitor and nearly broke the control sphere in her grasp. *LANDING PYLONS DAMAGED, DEPLOYMENT BLOCKED* read the blaring red screen. "By the Singularity," she muttered, following it with a string of curses from almost every planet she'd visited while Joane looked aghast. Tristan finally yelled in frustration and looked at Joane. "The mag-seals aren't working," she explained. "We won't be able to drag the ship with us. We've got two options: we get the hell out of here *now*, or we dock with that ship, rip anything useful out, and take it with us. What's the play?"

Joane stammered. "I-I-, Tris, we- we can't just leave! We've come this far!"

Tristan muttered another curse. "Yeah, that's what I thought you'd say." She nearly dislocated her shoulder with the force she used to spin Darling around on a dime. "Go grab an atmo-suit and something to fight with."

Tristan hardly registered Joane running out of the bridge towards the EVA storeroom as she sped through the docking process. Darling's airlock was rudimentary but automated, so Tris didn't have to worry about her shaking hands causing a catastrophic depressurization. She typed out a hurried command to patch any and all scans, alerts, or alarms directly into the pilot's earpiece, which she yanked out of the console and pushed into her right ear. It beeped an affirmative once it had locked on, and Tris followed Joane out of the bridge.

The airlock lights were glowing orange, signifying an acceptable but not perfect connection with the other side. It would have to do. Joane wordlessly offered a small black disc the size of a dinner plate to her, which Tristan took and fastened the steel-cord straps around her torso. The disc hummed faintly, and the air around Tristan began to distort slightly before clearing. She watched Joane activate her own atmo-suit. It would keep them alive in case Ahsha's ship had lost atmosphere, but it wouldn't do much under actual void conditions. Worse still, if the Consortium blasted open the ship, the suits would just keep them alive to suffer for a few more minutes. Joane was holding a simple rifle, a synth-wood paneled weapon a farmer had offered her for helping evacuate his livestock from a solar storm. It was nothing special and would be utterly useless in a vacuum, but something was better than nothing.

"Are we expecting them to board us?" Joane asked as Tristan began typing in access codes to open the airlock. She shook her head. "We'll be in and out, ten minutes."

"Exactly," Tristan agreed as the first door unsealed and they stepped into the buffer compartment. A few agonizing moments later, the green light chimed and the tunnel opened before them. Joane sprinted ahead, the rapping of her boots against the metal muffled slightly by the thicker atmosphere surrounding her. She jammed her knife into the far doors and released a pulse of electricity. The door shuddered and groaned as the mechanisms flared to life and pulled the door open. There was no rush of void into the tunnel, which Tristan took as a good sign. If the ship hadn't depressurized, it was all the more likely that something valuable had survived.

Tristan watched Joane repeat the trick with the buffer doors, and just like that, they walked into Ahsha's ship. Everything about the ship's interior made sense to Tristan. The walls were blank, lined with a coarse white plaster material. There were no windows to be seen, and most of the dividing walls had been torn down. This was Ahsha's ship and no one else's. There was a measly bed off to one corner and a small but well-stocked kitchen area a few feet away. A square of plaster walls marked the washroom location, which Ahsha had decided to leave separate from the rest of the ship. Everywhere else that wasn't necessary for survival had been turned into a workplace. Papers and apparatuses littered every inch of the floor, the tables, and the shelves welded poorly to the walls. Despite the fact that Tristan felt like she'd been shrunk down on top of a mad scientist's workbench, she couldn't call the ship a mess by any means. Darling was a mess, she knew that. This was organized chaos. Each stack of papers was neatly arranged and labeled with protruding blue plastic markers. The equipment was clean and orderly, and most of it looked to be in decent shape, too. It was simultaneously tidy and wild.

"Start looking," Joane urged. "We need anything remotely related to gravity, the planets that have vanished, the Consortium, anything." She shoved past Tristan and began thumbing through a pile of papers almost as tall as she was. Tristan knew there was hardly any chance of Joane understanding all the scientific jargon Ahsha stuffed her papers with to make her seem that much more important to her rivals, and absolutely no chance for her. What she did understand, however, was piloting. She danced around the stacks and breakable vials towards the front of the ship, where a simple chair sat bolted in front of three measly monitors and a small viewport. After all her time spent flying Darling, the stark difference made Tristan pause as she sank into the chair. She had to remind herself how to operate a simple transport ship. It was clunky and slow to boot up after how long it had been sitting still in the void. Ahsha had thought to set the ship to enter low-power mode, which was smart. It meant Tristan could get into the files, most importantly the nav data, without too much fuss.

One of the monitors finally lit up, displaying a list of Ahsha's recent coordinate logs. Tristan immediately grabbed a data drive from a pocket of her cloak and connected it to the ship. *Anything and everything,* she told herself as she began transferring as many of the files as she could. The nav data didn't seem like anything special. Ahsha had apparently visited the anomalies where the last few planets had vanished, refueled a few times, but nothing special. Still, Tristan knew you couldn't build an engine without every screw.

She was scrolling through other lists of recon and shield flare data when the silence became unbearable. Joane had hardly said a word to her since they woke up. There was a chance it was her nerves, but Tristan had never known Joane to lose her head in a crisis. It was usually in the calm moments when she went wild. "Joane, I just wanted to say about last night-"

"Busy," Joane blurted out, making Tris stop in her tracks. "Ten minutes, remember?"

Tristan turned her chair halfway around and glanced at Joane, who was rapidly sifting through an endless mountain of papers and digital file holders, sorting the ones that seemed important into a separate pile. She wanted to say something, but she knew Joane was right. Tristan was acting needy and immature, she knew that, but it didn't make her feel any better. They were on borrowed time now, and every moment since the kiss made Tristan regret not saying anything more and more. She slammed her fingers against the console keyboard rapidly and loudly, setting up a transfer of all recently updated or accessed files on the ship's computer. She had no idea what good it would do. Ahsha seemed to prefer hard copies of her papers, but hopefully there were a few gems hidden in the onboard drive.

Not wanting to sit and watch a download, Tristan was about to go help Joane search and force a conversation when her earpiece emitted a high-pitched chime that made her chirp, followed by the monotonous voice she had never thought to reprogram. "Attention, incoming hail."

Tristan cocked her head to the side. That wasn't what she'd expected. "Repeat?" she asked. Joane's head lifted from a datapad and looked at her quizzically.

"Incoming hail," it said again. "Contact: Consortium Sentinel Designation 83.672.40."

Tristan paused for a while, then spoke hesitantly. "Put it through." Joane mouthed something at her that Tristan couldn't understand. She responded by pulling the crossbow from her pouch. Joane's face hardened as she scrambled to gather what she'd found.

The transmission connected, warbling oddly as another gravitational wave passed over the ships. Thankfully, Ahsha's inertial dampeners held them firmly in place while the ship was moving. After a moment, it cleared up and Tristan could hear a vague voice calling out to her. "Errant vessels! This is Ensign Riscell Marlain of the Cygnus Consortium fleet, if you can hear me, please sound off with the number and names of your surviving crew!"

Again, Tristan felt confused. The crossbow dipped in her hand ever so slightly, but she wasn't sure if this was some sort of trick just yet. The panic in the voice sounded genuine, but so much of the Consortium had up until a few days ago. She decided it was best to stay quiet. Riscell repeated the urgent call. "Please, sound off! We have relief craft and medical professionals inbound to your location.. Just hold on a bit longer in there!" Sure enough, a small contingent of crafts were entering the vicinity. Tristan swore as the alert came through the earpiece, drowning out the already warped speech.

"We're about to have company," she whispered to Joane, who nodded solemnly.

"Do we run?" she asked. Tristan turned to check the monitor. The download had finished, so she pulled the data drive out and stuffed it into her shirt. She didn't think it would be any more hidden there than if it was in her pocket, but holding it closer made it feel more secure somehow. She nodded and began briskly heading for the airlock. The sound of their feet racing across the floor was cut off by a series of deep, hollow thuds that made Tristan's heart drop. Something had just landed on Ahsha's ship.

"Errant vessels," Riscell chimed in, sounding out of breath. "Please, I repeat, sound off. We have evac pods docked with the hulls of both of your ships ready to breach your hulls and initiate rescue, but we can save a lot of damage if you can undock your ships and allow us in that way. Do not be alarmed, we have atmosphere generators active in a hundred kilometer area around the ship, you're perfectly safe."

"They want to dock with us," Tristan reported. Joane's face scrunched up in confusion. "The airlock, freak." The woman's face soured over the pile of paper she was carrying. Obviously she hadn't missed Tris's coping methods.

"I know that, Tris! Why, though?" Joane demanded. Tristan shrugged and kept the crossbow at the ready.

"They've docked with our hulls," she said, pointing at the general point of the ceiling where she heard the clank of metal. "They're going to cut through and come in that way. Be ready." Joane immediately dropped her stack of papers and pulled the launcher from her back. It wouldn't do much in tight quarters like this, but it was something.

"We're going to slice into your ships now," Riscell called, "The Consortium deeply apologizes for the inconvenience and a full repair and refund will be granted once medical attention has been administered." There was a sound like a hundred steel cables snapping in unison as the pods latched to the ships fired slicing lasers into the hulls. Each one cut a perfectly pressurized circle through the hull, maintaining the inner atmosphere but allowing the Consortium in. A hunk of sizzling metal fell from the ceiling three meters away from Joane and Tris, while another tumbled off the far wall.

Joane didn't waste a second. She fired her launcher into the wall entrance, unleashing a dark gray sharpened bolt that disappeared into the dark. She whirled up to the other hole and fired the second of three loaded bolts upward. There was the sound of metal puncturing metal and a soft yelp.

Tristan heard boots thundering around in Darling, toppling her crates and searching through her rooms. The thought made her quake with rage and fear at the same time. She gripped the handle of the crossbow, but didn't fire. Joane didn't share any of Tris's hesitation. She had pulled two more bolts out of the small quiver on her back and stuffed them into the barrels of her launcher. All three were pointed at the airlock, and Joane's fingers rested easily under the weapon. The sight of her so calm while preparing to take however many lives made Tristan uneasy.

"Stand down!" a voice yelled from the wall. "We mean you no harm! We're medical professionals, please just lower your weapons!"

A figure in a white uniform stumbled out, clutching their shoulder. Joane's bolt was sticking out of it, and the blood was quickly turning their uniform dark red. They were holding out what looked like a small case in their free hand, but then stumbled and fell to the ground. Two more figures emerged behind them. Joane fired at the first, but they just managed to duck out of the way as the bolt slammed into the plaster. "Please, no!" she yelped, her blonde hair twisting around her neck as she spun to look at the projectile a few inches from her face. "Just let me help him!"

She dove for the man on the ground and pulled open his case. Tristan could just make out a set of bandages and assorted medications inside. She began tending to the wound, glancing up occasionally at the women pointing weapons at her. The third officer, a rounder man with gray hair and deep blue skin, seemed to have pressed himself against the wall and held his hands up in terror.

"If I see any sudden movements," Joane said in a low growl, "I will stick all of you to the wall, do you understand?" Tristan tried to muster her courage and straightened her back, aiming at the woman kneeling next to the man. She didn't want to have to take any lives today, but things were apparently heading that way.

"Ma'am," the blue man said. "We-we're just here to help. Your ship- we don't know how you managed to end up so off course. They sent us out to see if there were any survivors that we could-"

"Finish off?" Tristan interrupted, moving the crossbow towards him. He whimpered and cowered against the wall even harder than before. She felt a twinge of guilt before remembering that this man was probably here to kill her before she could reveal anything to the public.

"No!" the woman cried out. "We have a medical station a few parsecs away. Not top of the line, but we're taking any survivors from Cygnus or people who were affected by the anomaly there for treatment."

"Treatment of what, exactly?" Joane asked.

"I don't know yet!" she exclaimed, "No one is supposed to be able to make it through the shield ships! There could be any number of untreated symptoms, like gravity sickness, inverted organs, Fastlane blindless-"

"We're fine," Tristan said forcefully. "So why don't you just let us go?"

"We will, of course," the blue man said uneasily. "We just need to repair your ship and give you a check-up. I understand you're probably busy women who don't want to be trapped in a vanished world's gravity well, and I apologize. It won't take more than a few hours if you cooperate."

The thundering footsteps grew louder as a few more figures emerged out of the airlock. The two medics tried to usher them back, but three of them poured into the room before Joane squeezed off another bolt. The shot went wide and the three screamed as they ducked. The clank of metal made it impossible to hear the flurry of panicked shouts that broke out in the cramped ship. Tristan caught a glimpse out of the corner of her eye of one of the figures reaching to their belt. She tried to urge herself to move, to break out of the frozen stupor she found herself in. She saw the woman drawing a small white object from her waist, saw it charge with a pale blue light, and saw Joane turn towards her. All the while, Tristan was screaming at herself to do something. To aim, to pull the trigger, to do something to stop what was going on. But just like a dream, she saw what happened a few seconds before it did, and was powerless to stop it.

The woman unleashed a fuzzy beam of dazzling light towards the pair. It lit the ship up as it hurtled through the air and caught Joane right in the stomach. She made a soft sound as the air escaped her lungs and she fell, slamming into the floor with a hollow thud. Tristan watched her fall, watched her face go lax and vacant. She thought she screamed, because she wanted to, but no sound came out. Instead, she pulled her wrist up and pulled the trigger. It was suddenly a lot easier than before. For a moment, there was only the sound of the bolt pushing air aside as it streaked through the air, then the wet thunk of it hitting the woman's chest. She coughed and stumbled backwards, dropping the weapon. Her two compatriots caught her and lowered her to the ground while Tristan threw herself to her knees.

Joane's body felt wrong in her hands, even as she got a hand under her stomach and pulled her into her lap. She looked for the wound on her stomach, but there wasn't one. There was blood running down the side of her face, however, and a small pool of it on the floor where she'd fallen. Tris brushed the hair out of the woman's face and searched it for any movement, any signs of life. The woman from earlier shouted something at her compatriots, and an instant later she came into Tristan's view. Tristan snarled like a cornered animal, pulled Joane away, and tried to pull the pulse knife from Joane's side.

Something about the way the woman held out her hands and gazed at her made her pause. For a moment, she was able to hear again as she spoke to her. "Listen," she implored, the fear barely contained in her stark white eyes. "She's okay, that was just a quick-release sleep aid to help with the panic. We aren't here to hurt you, miss, you have my word. Please just come with us, we'll get her stitched up, and then we can all try and figure out what's going on here."

"I'm not letting you take her," Tristan said, her voice tiny and frightened. She was clutching her so hard she was afraid one of them might break. "I-I-I can't, I made a promise. I'm not leaving her again."

"I understand; it's going to be okay," she said earnestly. Tristan never saw her pull the stunner from her belt. There was a flash, and then darkness so complete she couldn't even dream of the tunnels.

# Chapter 12
## Empty Orbits

TRISTAN saw white when she finally opened her eyes. She thought she might have been staring at the unnaturally pale woman who'd shot her, but her vision quickly cleared. She was on her back, staring up at a spotless tile ceiling, with overhead lights glaring a few feet away. She tasted iron and salt in her mouth, and her entire body ached. She wasn't dead, she hoped, because she hadn't imagined the afterlife being so uncomfortable. She tried to raise her arms to push the annoying strands of black hair out of her eye, but quickly discovered her wrists and ankles were strapped to the tough, thin mattress she was on.

That's when she panicked. She lurched in the bed. No waist or neck restraint, that was good. It gave her some, if any leverage. She began thrashing around, trying to pull and test the tightness of the white cloth bindings. The scratch of velcro began to irritate her skin, but she kept pulling. All the while, she was scanning the room. It reminded her of the medical bay on board the mining station, but more ramshackle. The empty beds she could see weren't connected to the floor, but simple mattresses balanced on flimsy, collapsible stands. The monitors and equipment all seemed state-of-the-art, but none of it looked used or permanent. It was all clinical and brand new, and the thoughts racing through Tris's mind made her pull even harder. The worst part was that she saw no one. No guards, no torturers hiding behind surgical masks and goggles, no man in a dark suit stroking a Scampcat taunting her. Most importantly, there was no Joane.

That's when she really panicked. Joane was gone. She'd been unconscious and hurt the last time Tris had seen her. Defenseless, alone, lost. "Joane," she hissed in a hoarse whisper. "Joane!" There was no response except for a rapid beeping from a monitor that had been wheeled up next to her bed. Tristan finally noticed the series of tubes and needles connected to her left arm and practically shrieked. She had no idea what sort of cocktail the sick freaks running this place had already pumped into her, but she guessed it could make her eyes melt out of her head if someone pushed a button. The beeping grew faster and faster as Tristan tried to flex her arms and push the needles out to no avail.

She was in the process of tilting her head down, frantically attempting to bite into her own arm and yank them out when she heard the sound of a door sliding open. Her movements became more frantic as she heard boots racing towards her. "Ma'am, ma'am! By the Singularity, what are you trying to do?" a soft voice rose in pitch as a figure rounded the thin blue sheet blocking her off from the rest of the room.

Tristan pulled back against the pillows, her eyes wild with terror. She was tied down, alone, and out of options. She'd failed. It took her a few seconds to recognize the woman from Ahsha's ship: Same pallid white skin, almost invisible irises, and white hair that blended into her white Consortium uniform. Her mouth was wide open in shock. "I've had patients yank out their IVs before," she said as she approached the bed, "but trying to chew through your own arm to get to it? You must have had quite a day."

"Go fuck yourself," she spat in defiance. The woman nodded as if she'd expected that answer.

"I see the sedative has worn off," she muttered, turning the monitor to face her. "You might want to try and steady your breathing. I haven't met many Hollow Folk, but I know a heart rate of one-hundred and eighty isn't healthy for most humanoids. So, why don't you take a deep breath, lay back, and tell me your name?"

"Surprised you don't already know it you silver-feathered pencil-pushing bureaucrat," Tris said with as much anger as she could muster. The woman pinched the bridge of her nose and sighed.

"Okay," she said finally. "How about this? *My name* is Dr. Daniella Toscana. I specialize in neurotrauma as a result of gravity and outside-atmosphere related events. My doctorate comes from the Institute of Supervoid Study and Shrinkage in Andromeda, but I have been on retainer for the Consortium for the past few months, trying to treat those affected by the anomalies the vanished planets have left behind. There, that's my story. What's yours?" Tristan only half-listened to the story, but by the time the doctor had finished talking, the "cornered animal" part of her brain had given way to reasonable thoughts.

"You...you aren't one of them, then?" Tristan asked, "They just brought you on?"

"A conspiracy theorist?" Dr. Toscana let a smile creep onto her lips. "That's a rare thing these days, but we've run into a few of you since the vanishings began. Back in my college days I enjoyed a bit of speculation here and there, too. I still don't think the Kennedy they found on the Moon was the real one, honestly."

"What?" Tristan said, narrowing her eyes. "No, I'm not talking about some crackpot theory, this is something I have genuine, certifiable proof of, alright? The Consortium tried to kill us when they found us investigating it, and now that you know, they'll kill you too." Toscana raised an eyebrow and smirked, but Tristan continued. "Look, that ship we were on has data and valuable information that can explain everything, we need to make sure no one gets into the computers to wipe them, and you need to get these cuffs off of me right now, understood?"

Daniella's smile never faltered, except for a brief moment of concern. She didn't believe her. Tristan felt like she was being stunned again. "Look, you've had a harrowing day. You and your partner are lucky to be alive after flying into a blank orbit like that."

"Joane," Tristan whispered before she could stop herself. "Joane, where is she?"

Dr. Toscana saw her starting to panic and put a gentle hand on her shoulder. "She's fine, she's fine. It's taking her a bit longer to sleep off the sedative than you did, partially due to the mild concussion she got. If you were wondering, the woman you shot is recovering and stable."

Tristan tried not to show her relief. She had hurt Joane; she was about to hurt her. Tristan hadn't wanted to pull the trigger, but it had been her only choice. "Where is she?" she demanded.

"Your friend is fine," Toscana said with a roll of her all-white eyes, "Your ship is fine. You are fine." She turned and grabbed the plastic sheet, pulling it aside to reveal an identical bed. Joane was lying there, unconscious but clearly breathing easily. There was a soft-looking bandage taped to her forehead with just a hint of a bloodstain visible. Tristan flicked her eyes to the tubes embedded in Joane's arm, then up at the monitor they connected to. There was a steady rise and fall of a heartbeat, and a few other similar readings that Tristan recognized from the hospitals she'd been in, but had no idea what they actually represented. Tristan's breathing began to slow, and the rage faded into a dull, quiet fury.

"There's still a chance for us to get out of here, you just need to let-"

"Dr. Toscana!" another voice called. With the curtain pulled back, Tristan could see them entering the room. The one who had spoken had their arms open wide, giving Tristan a clear view of a well-made gray and black suit that lengthened at the ends into a slightly billowy skirt of sorts. The ends trailed behind them as they entered. They had a slender, average height and build, with no obvious strength or weakness about them. They had bronze, tanned skin that almost seemed Solan, but the slightly longer arms and faint forehead ridges proved that they weren't. Their hair was a dark, almost black, brown that fell in a long straight curtain down their back, and they had a thin but noticeable amount of stubble across their chin. They seemed relaxed, even cheerful, but their black eyes gave off a nervous energy that even Tristan could sense. "I heard you had a bit of a run-in earlier and wanted to come by and express my concern in person."

Dr. Toscana glanced down at Tristan, then back at the new arrival. "Senator," she said, "I had no idea you were even in the system."

"My place is with my people, Doctor," they said as casually as possible. "As many of them as possible."

"The research teams are making every effort," she said assuringly. "Wherever Cygnus-4 is, they'll be the first to know." Tristan grumbled under her breath, causing the senator to notice her.

"Ah, forgive me," they said, turning to smile at her. It was a smile that was meant to be disarming, but immediately put Tristan on guard. "Senator Orion Masenna, Consortium representative for the system of Cygnus and its outlying bodies, it's a pleasure." They crossed the room in short, quick steps and held out a hand to her. Tristan gave a short wave with her fingers. Orion looked down, noticed the restraints, and turned on Dr. Toscana. "Doctor, surely this isn't necessary."

"She nearly killed one of the medics," Daniella explained. "She nearly killed *me*."

"I read the incident report," the senator responded. "I know what happened. These two women have had a very taxing day. In fact, you all have. Keeping them strapped to a bed isn't going to help anyone relax, is it?" The doctor looked like she was about to argue, but decided against it and began loosening the straps. Orion turned to Tristan next. "Alright, I'm trusting you by having those taken off. I hope that means you can trust me enough not to try and hurt any of the good people working here."

"I'll consider it," Tristan hissed as the restraints came loose. She began rubbing each wrist until her circulation came back. Orion's phony smile never faltered.

"I'll take it," they said. "Now then, I don't believe I caught your name."

Tris sighed. She was so far in the deep end, she saw no reason in keeping up a facade now. "Tristan Ninomae. My friends call me Tris."

"May I call you Tris?"

"Absolutely not."

"Understood," they said, trying to remain upbeat. "Tristan, I can't imagine how stressful today has been for you, and I have to express my sincerest regret that such an incident occurred. The shield ships are supposed to form a complete gravitational shield around the system until the gravity well Cygnus-4 left behind disperses. I genuinely have no idea how or why your ships made it through, but I have my top minds trying to figure that out right now so we can prevent something like this happening again."

Tristan was confused. For a politician, especially a member of the government trying to kill her, this person seemed almost genuine. "This wasn't an accident," she said, curiosity stringing her along. Orion raised an eyebrow. They gestured for her to go on, so she did. "We were trying to get to Cygnus, but you already knew that, didn't you?" Orion shook their head, and Tristan laughed out loud. "Look, Senator, we've come this far. I know when I'm cornered. You win, whatever. Can we please just stop pretending like you don't know what's going on so we can get on with this?"

The senator glanced up at Dr. Toscana, who shrugged noncommittally. "That's...quite an accusation, Ms. Ninomae. As much as I would like to know what's going on, I'm afraid I do not. Just like I don't know why you're in this system or why you seem so threatened by one senator and a few relief workers."

"We're going to figure this out," Tristan saw no reason not to try it. "We've got the data from the other ship. In just a few days, we can know what you're doing with those planets, where they are, and how to get them back." This gave Orion pause. They shifted their weight and looked down at Tristan with a look that made her feel very exposed.

"Interesting," they said thoughtfully. "You...believe you know something about the vanishings?"

"I'm working on it," she admitted. "And the ships the Consortium sent after me in the Waning Crescent lead me to believe I'm on the right track." Orion and Toscana shared another look, and she saw the senator frown for the first time.

"I beg your pardon?" they asked. Tristan said nothing, but stared at them so hard she thought she might burn through their black eyes. "Look, I have no idea what you're saying, but if you truly have a theory...I want to hear it. I have some other matters that need my immediate attention. You and your friend rest, and Dr. Toscana will let me know when you are both ready to speak with me. Then, the three of us will sit down together, have a nice lunch, and you can tell me who you think made a planet with almost a third of this system's populace on it disappear in an instant."

Tristan nodded slowly, almost fully convinced that whoever this was wasn't connected to the ships that had tried to kill her. It made sense, actually, that maybe not the entire universe-spanning government could be in on the same conspiracy. That still didn't mean she trusted them, however. She'd played all the cards in her hand in the hopes of getting some information out of the Senator, and had succeeded only in revealing how much she knew. Orion definitely expected something from her now, and if Tristan couldn't give it to them, it could be a long time before they left this room.

# Chapter 13
## An Average Political Lunch

JOANE began stirring after a few minutes. Tristan watched her eyes flutter open as she struggled against her own restraints, which Dr. Toscana had refused to open for Tristan. She watched helplessly as Joane fought through the same initial wave of panic that she'd gone through, which finally subsided when she looked over and saw Tristan sitting on the edge of the other bed, her legs dangling over the side.

"Tris- what, what's happening?" she panted, her eyes wide and unfocused. They darted around the room, scanning over the walls and the doctor waiting halfway across the floor. "Who- why, Tris?"

"It's okay," Tristan whispered, trying to sound comforting. Joane turned to face her, her chest heaving with rapid breaths. "Joane, look at me and breathe, okay?" Joane tried to do so, closing her eyes and counting the seconds as she inhaled and exhaled. When she opened them, Tristan was still watching her. "As for what's happening...it's a bit of a mess. All I know right now is that we're safer than I thought we'd be."

"Where are we?"

"We're, uh, that's a good question. Dr. Toscana?" The woman glanced over at the pair of beds, exhaustion evident in the way her shoulders slumped. She clearly didn't want to waste any more time on them, but had no other choice.

"This is a temporary evacuation and medical treatment center set in distant satellite orbit around Cygnus-4's gravity well," Daniella said with boredom as she approached Joane's bed. The woman shrank back, and the doctor sighed in exasperation. "This again. Ma'am, I am a doctor. I'm trying to read your pulse and vital signs, not put a chip in your brain or turn your lungs into eyeballs."

Tristan held up a hand. "It's okay," she repeated. "I don't think the people here know."

"Oh yes, we're all in the dark here," Dr. Toscana grumbled as she pressed her fingers to Joane's wrist. "All of us woolworms hiding away from the nasty truth of the evil power hungry elite running everything behind the scenes."

Tristan stared daggers at the doctor. "You know, maybe you should at least consider the idea that there's someone who knows something about this, since you all clearly know nothing, and planets don't just disappear on their own." She caught a glimpse of Joane staring at her and immediately remembered being on the other side of this argument a week ago.

Dr. Toscana sighed. "Look, you're not trying to convince me. That's good news for you two, because Senator Masenna has been scrambling for answers since Cygnus vanished. They'll listen to just about anything if it helps them find their people." She leaned back from Joane's bed and made a note on a small paper pad. "Alright, your vitals seem fine," she said, "I will go check on some of the other rooms and give you both time to clear your heads and think about-"

"Oh good!" a voice sounded as Orion strutted into the room. "Sounds like I'm right on time. Senator Orion Masenna, pleasure to meet you, miss…?"

Joane looked over at Tristan as the person trotted up to her bed and stuck out a hand. Tris gave her a gentle nod as if to say, *I know, just play along.* Joane slowly shook their hand, not returning their wide smile. "Joane," she said. Her last name might have carried some weight here, but she wasn't sure dropping it would lead to anything good.

"Miss Joane Ninomae," Orion said back. "I want to take this opportunity to apologize for that mess earlier onboard your ship."

"Oh, no," Joane said reflexively. "We're…we're friends." She glared at Tristan, trying to silently ask why she had given this person her real full name. Instead, Tristan had averted her gaze and was staring at her hands.

"My apologies," they said with a nod. "I can imagine the two of you would like to dispense with the pleasantries and get down to business. I can assure you that the two of you will be free to go as soon as possible, but before that I would ask that you do me the courtesy of…contributing to the investigation. Joane, I've already spoken with your friend Tristan. She says the two of you may have information regarding Cygnus-4 and its current whereabouts."

"She told you that, did she?" Joane said, narrowing her eyes at the woman next to her. How long had she been out for? Long enough for Tristan to give the Consortium everything they knew? Tristan still wasn't looking at her. Joane had to pull her gaze away from a familiar bruise on Tristan's neck to look back at Orion.

"Yes, she did," they said warmly. They were about to continue when Dr. Toscana began making her way out of the room. "Oh, doctor? Would you mind staying for just a few moments? I know this isn't your area of expertise, but I wouldn't mind having a scientifically minded person here with us to discuss things." Daniella looked like she wanted nothing more than to keep walking but didn't want to upset the senator. She pivoted on her ankle and returned to her seat.

"I'll tell you if something sounds insanely inaccurate or implausible," she relented, raising her voice from across the room. Orion's smile faltered, but they turned back to the two women.

"Now, I apologize," Orion said. Joane was already tired of hearing it. "I know I promised you we'd discuss this over lunch, but circumstances are so...demanding right now that I can barely make time to eat, let alone sit down for a full conversation. Instead, if you could just tell me everything you think I should know, I will pass it along to my scientists and we can all help one another."

Tristan opened her mouth to speak, but Joane cut her off. "You'll have to forgive us, Senator," she said, putting as much venom into the last word as possible. "We aren't exactly trusting a lot of authority figures right now." Orion nodded and grimaced.

"Yes, you had mentioned a run-in with what you believed were Consortium ships," they said, turning to Tristan.

"That's what my scan showed me," she responded carefully. "There were three ships all trying to blow us out of the void, and all of my scans showed their hulls were made of Core steel."

"Ships can be stolen," Dr. Toscana piped up. Joane watched Tristan look up for the first time in minutes to glare at the woman.

"Not Consortium ships," Orion countered, leaning back. "There are failsafe commands in each ship, so they can't be flown without Consortium credentials. And Core steel is almost impossible to, uh, steal." They gave a small chuckle that none of the women in the room returned.

"Exactly," Joane said. "They may as well have come at us in wingships with silver wing holos on full brightness."

"But they didn't," Orion guessed. "Which could mean several things. The scans could have been inaccurate, and you all were attacked by random pirates. However, it could also mean this is a separate faction of the Consortium not wishing to draw attention to themselves. Regardless, it begs the question, why would they be trying to stop you, and what exactly are you two trying to do?"

"Don't answer that," Joane hissed before Tristan could open her mouth. She knew enough to know when she was being interrogated. She wasn't about to give every last bit of information to this person just because of a smile and a handshake. Orion looked disappointed, and for a moment, Joane could see through the thick veneer of relaxed positivity. She saw bags under their eyes, a downward curve to their lips, and wild hairs that most senators wouldn't be seen dead with.

"I see," they muttered, taking a step closer to Joane's bed. She pulled back as far as her restraints would allow. "Let me make this clear. If I were part of some intergalactic scandal to...steal planets, I suppose you think, I don't think either of you would have woken up in such comfortable beds. Except of course for these straps, which I *asked* you to remove, Doctor." The edge in their voice was new, but not surprising. Dr. Toscana said nothing, but rapidly made her way across the room and removed the straps on Joane's hands. The thought hung in her mind that it would be extremely easy to reach out and choke both the senator and the doctor at the same time, but she still felt the sluggishness in her body from the stun and the fall. She finally noticed the heavy pounding in her forehead and the dull whine in her ears. She decided it would only complicate things even further if she attacked now, so she pulled her arms close to her sides. She noted that she was still wearing her normal clothes, but that didn't mean they hadn't been searched while unconscious. "I understand this is a difficult time for you both," Orion continued, "but there are three billion people missing right now. It's my responsibility, as their representative, to find them or at least to know what happened. You have to understand why I'm so eager to speak with you both."

Joane nodded slowly as she watched intensity fill the senator's face. Innocent or guilty, there was only one way Orion could help her right now: by letting her go. And the only way that was going to happen, was if she told them something helpful. The problem, of course, was that Joane knew nothing about *where* the planets were or *how* they were vanishing.

"I'd love to find the planets, Senator," she said honestly. "I really would. The problem is, we weren't given the chance to decode all of the data we've recorded. Data, of course, that only we can access." She was starting to lie, but carefully. The more truths she told, the less likely she was to get caught with what lies she peppered in. "Where are our ships?"

"Your ships were towed to the docks a few floors down," Orion replied calmly, barely containing the excitement in their eyes. "I instructed the technicians not to tamper with any of your ship's onboard systems, because I figured you might have some important data that I didn't want to risk losing somehow. Now I'm very glad I said that."

"How do you know you can trust them?" Tristan said. Orion turned around, looking bewildered. "You just said, there's a chance that there's a faction in the Consortium trying to stop people from looking into this stuff."

"Yes, I said it's possible," Orion admitted, "but far from a likely outcome. I mean, the Consortium is an organization of such scale that I will probably never interact with more than a fraction of my colleagues. At the same time, though, the process of joining the government is punishingly intense. The people vote, of course, but even then, there's a much larger process of examinations, morality tests, and all sorts of other grillings that rule out any chance of corruption, power-chasing, anything of the sort. The idea that a group large enough to pull off such a massive conspiracy could slip through the cracks of that is just not feasible."

"You've got a lot of faith in your colleagues, senator," Joane muttered, crossing her arms. "Are you new to this?"

"Well," Orion blushed slightly. "Yes, as a matter of fact. This is my first term. Most likely my last. It's hard to keep your approval rating up if half the people you work for can just disappear."

"That's rough," Joane deadpanned. Orion sighed.

"I shouldn't focus on myself, obviously," they added. "It's just...I wanted to do right by this system, not lose the biggest planet in it. I didn't think something like this would happen here. Obviously we've heard about the vanishings, but all of our precautions put in place were working just fine until one day when...poof."

"And there were no signs beforehand?" Tristan asked, earning yet another glance from Joane. "No strange gravity fluxes? Solar storms, dark matter waves, anything?"

"Nothing our monitoring satellites picked up," Orion said with a sad shrug.

"Maybe the 'how' isn't as important as the 'where' or the 'why,'" Joane said begrudgingly. She didn't want to help this politician, but Tristan was making it difficult to withhold anything. "Senator Masenna, you want your planet back, right? We all know complete teleportation is impossible. Even Fastlanes have to move through something, they can't just take matter from one place and put it in another. So that means, unless the planet was completely vaporized, which would've left some sort of trace, it was *moved* somewhere."

"Yes, obviously," Orion said, following her logic. "Go on."

"Well, when something is moved, it leaves behind a trail. You all probably haven't found it because you don't know what you're looking for. And neither do we. But the information on those ships might tell us what to look for. Once we know that, we can find it, and then we find your planet." It wasn't her worst idea yet, but it made more sense to check than anything else. Ahsha's gravity readings hadn't seemed abnormal, but that didn't matter. If it got them out of this room and onto the ship, they'd be halfway across the supercluster before Orion could blink.

"Alright," the senator said. "It's as good a lead as we've had so far. Crazy? Yes, but these are crazy times. Once you two are ready to get on your feet — which I'll let Dr. Toscana decide when that is — you two will be free to return to your ships, which I will personally make sure are kept under careful lock and key until that time, and will be given access to any tools or information you need within reason."

They were turning to leave when a thought seemed to strike them and they turned back. "I'm trusting both of you a lot here. I hope you'll extend that trust, if not to everyone here, than to me, for the sake of all those people out there." Joane was already turning to yell at Tris for giving up so much information when she heard Orion talking with someone. Something drew her eyes to the doorway with the way Orion's voice sounded surprised and confused. She couldn't see who they were talking to through the angle of the doorway, but the hushed tones were starting to draw her attention. Dr. Toscana apparently shared her curiosity, because the pale woman made her way over towards Orion's shoulder and peered into the hall. Joane watched a look of shock pass over the doctor's face, and then there was a dull thud of an air canister firing, and a black dart hurtled past Orion's shoulder and into Toscana's chest.

The woman let out a gasp as she stumbled back. Joane and Tristan both sucked in breaths of horror as Orion yelled out in protest. Something promptly slammed into them, and Orion's hair blew out wildly as they sailed across the room. Before Orion's back hit the wall and Toscana slumped to the floor, Joane was already on her feet and pulling at Tristan's ankle straps.

Joane was too busy trying to free Tristan to see the figures squeezing into the doorway until she saw the look of fear flash across her friend's face. She turned, reaching for a knife she knew would've been confiscated. The first two were huge figures with no visible skin, only heavy gray armor that looked like the hull of a spacecraft. Their blank spherical helmets stared impassively as they made their way inside and took up positions on either side of the door. One of them was pushing a small black dart into the barrel of a unique looking crossbow, and the other was holding a large flat hammer glowing from within with some sort of orange light. Following them was an older man with sleek, well-groomed gray hair and a seemingly-kind face with no visible lines or wrinkles. He was wearing a black version of the suit jacket Orion had been wearing. His skin had a sallow green tint to it, like someone becoming slightly starsick. The skin of his mouth was drawn and thin, revealing tiny chapped lips that stretched into a welcoming smile as he strode in.

"Hello, ladies," the man said, his voice a thin rasp. "Sorry to barge in."

Joane sighed and nodded to herself. "You look more like the planet-stealing type," she said, keeping her eyes on the two people flanking the man.

The man dropped his smile and drew his shoulders up. He seemed to grow taller and more imposing as he did so. "Now, Ms. Cordelle, that's quite presumptuous. I believe, in fact, you'll find your ancestors were much more predisposed to planetary relocation than my semi-aquatic progenitors from New Europa."

"Well, good on you for breaking stereotypes," Joane answered back. Whoever this man was, she wasn't going to let him rattle her with something as simple as her last name.

"Once again, we're rushing things," the man said, looking down at his boots. The blood pouring out from Dr. Toscana's stomach had spilled over and was beginning to touch the edge of his shiny black shoes. He gave a brief sigh. "Oh well," he said. "In my line of work, one learns to accept a bit of dirty work from time to time."

A pained sigh echoed across the room, drawing every pair of eyes over to the source. Orion was stumbling to their feet, clutching their stomach as they tried to rise. "Senator Regille," they said, forcing the words out in a breathless wheeze. "What are you doing?"

The man, Senator Regille, apparently, turned on his heel to face the struggling, wounded senator. He clicked his tongue in discomfort. "Oh, Orion, try not to take it so personally, youngblood. You're new to the game, and maybe you would've understood eventually. Unfortunately, you just got too close." He gave an overexaggerated shrug and then motioned towards the beds. "You have these two women to thank for that. Sticking their noses into things bigger than any one person could ever imagine. The gall of it is...astounding. Truly I would love to explain it all in detail, so we could all leave understanding why the planets are gone and why they *need* to be so that the others can live on. However, since I'm going to have to kill all three of you, I don't see much point in wasting each other's time. Gentlemen, if you would."

Senator Regille gestured to the guards at his sides. The two stepped forward as the senator clapped his hands together as if concluding a successful meeting. He immediately spun on his heels, ignoring the bloody footprints he left in his wake as he exited the room. Joane immediately turned to the guards. Tristan had finished undoing her restraints, so she could easily get up if she chose. Tristan herself had stepped back, trying to form a wall between Joane and the guards. It wouldn't do much good, but Joane expected Tris wasn't thinking through anything logically. Whenever things got bad in the past, Tristan had always shut down, acting more like a cornered animal than a rational woman. At times that had been helpful, but Joane couldn't imagine this was one of those times. She needed a plan, and fast. She looked around the room. The guard with the hammer was approaching them slowly and deliberately. There was nothing she could reach in time to defend herself in any meaningful way. The only exit she saw was past the other guard, who stood completely still with his gun at the ready. Orion was draped over a low cabinet, breathing heavily. Dr. Toscana wasn't moving, and the pool of blood around her body was no longer growing.

Running through all the information she had, Joane came to one conclusion: she was going to die in this room.

Then, Tristan did what any cornered animal would do. She lashed out. Joane hadn't noticed Tristan slipping the scalpel off a nearby rolling stand and into her hand, but she saw the flash of silver as the gray woman roared and brought it forward with a rapid, decisive stab. The guard, in the process of raising the massive black metal hammer, turned his head towards the motion but was unable to pivot and block the strike. Tris slipped the knife right into the gap between the thick armor and the guard's shoulder, eliciting a low grunt from the faceless figure. Almost immediately, though, he brought his right arm up and over Tristan's, trapping it between the handle and his massive arm. She grunted as she tried to pull it loose, but he didn't budge as he began to force the handle of the hammer against her elbow.

As Tristan began to scream, Joane pulled herself out of her stupor and rolled forward on the bed until she was crouched right next to the pair. She glared at the expressionless mask with a fire in her eyes, drew the scalpel out of the armor, and plunged it into a similar gap on the man's arm. It did no good to loosen the grip, but Joane had no time to worry as the other guard raised his gun. She was preparing to kick backwards off the man's massive torso until she realized the shot wasn't meant for her. Tristan, in the throes of madness and pain, didn't see the boltgun turn towards her.

Joane roared and planted her feet against the man, bracing her arms around the edge of the hospital bed. It wasn't the sturdiest point of leverage, but it would have to do in the moment. Joane threw every bit of strength into her legs and kicked into the guard's side, trying to twist him as she did so.

To her utter surprise, it worked and sent the guard tumbling down into an awkward spin just as the boltgun fired. The guard fell right into the path of the dart, which slammed into his shoulder blade as he fell and hit the floor with a loud crash. Tristan made a strangled noise as the man collapsed on her, but Joane needed to handle the other guard before she dared check on her. She threw herself out of the bed, landing in a crouch next to the guard on the floor. She ripped the bolt out of his shoulder, unleashing a stream of dark red blood. With it clutched firmly in her hand, she rolled out from between the beds. Then, she was in the middle of the room with no cover and a small thin weapon. The guard was maybe two meters away, hurriedly trying to reload the now empty gun. Joane sprinted for him, her breath coming in quick gasps each time her foot struck the floor. The guard was just sliding the bolt home into the barrel when Joane reached him and jumped. The guard had been expecting this, so Joane wasn't shocked when he braced and took the impact without moving. Instead, she transferred her forward momentum into a quick scrambling climb onto the man's back and locked her legs into place around his waist. Her left arm quickly formed a deathgrip on his firing arm and held the gun down, while her right hand came up with the bolt clutched like a knife. Joane brought it down, straight into the base of the man's neck. He groaned slightly under the mask, a noise that rose in pitch when Joane pulled the bolt back, twisted it to the side, and plunged it into the man's throat. He let out a choked gurgle and brought his hands up to the mask as he fell to his knees. Joane removed the bolt and stepped back, her hands shaking with adrenaline as she watched the empty helmet hit the floor. The blood pouring from his neck eventually met with Dr. Toscana's.

The rush of combat faded from Joane's mind, and immediately she looked for Tristan. She let out a sigh of relief when she saw the woman picking herself up slowly, pushing the guard's limp arm off her shoulder as she did so.

"There'll be more," Joane insisted, crouching down to retrieve the now-loaded boltgun. "We need to find our things, find our ship, and get the hell out."

"I couldn't agree more," Tristan said, a faraway look in her eyes as she took in the scene. "We don't know where they are, though."

"I do," a voice choked out. The two looked over to see Orion, now sitting on the floor with their back pressed against the wall. Sweat was pouring down their face, and Joane could tell from the way their chest was moving that several of their ribs were broken. "Low-lower level," they mumbled. "Need...access."

"Shit," Joane muttered. "They'll have locked down the ship and our weapons. We don't have time to try and hack a Consortium lockdown command."

"We don't need to," Tristan pointed out, raising a finger to Orion. Joane looked over at the senator, surprised they were even still alive.

"They'll slow us down," Joane said, shaking her head. Orion made a weak pleading noise. "We can't be sure they aren't actually in on this, either."

"Joane, we've worked together long enough that I know you don't hit your partners with hammers," Tristan countered. "They're just as much a target as we are now. Having a senator on our side might not be something we want to pass up."

Joane met Tristan's gaze, something she found herself struggling to do. She looked over at Orion, who had tears streaming down their face. *Please*, they mouthed, in too much pain to force words. She threw her head back. "Fine!" she relented. "You carry them, I'll try to keep us alive." She reached down and pulled a small bundle from the guard's belt and rifled through it, finding several more bolts for the gun. She only hoped she could figure out the air propulsion mechanism. She watched Tristan reach down and pull the hammer up, her back tilting from the weight. She groaned and dropped it back down with a resounding clank that made Joane's shoulders twitch. She didn't want to be mad at Tristan right now; she couldn't afford to waste precious time on something like that. She wasn't making it easy, however.

"Come on," she urged, pressing her back against the doorframe. Tristan nodded and hopped over to Orion, gingerly putting their arm over her shoulder and helping them to their feet. Orion made a high-pitched noise like a teapot boiling, but even Joane couldn't fault the senator for that. She'd broken ribs before, and she imagined it was the first time they'd felt such a burning, inescapable pain.

Still, though, they managed to pull Tristan to a halt in the middle of the room and look down. "Help...doctor," they breathed out, pointing at Toscana. Joane took one glance at the pool of blood, the way Toscana was lying, and the completely limp stillness of her body. She simply shook her head once, and Orion's expression went from one of pain to despair. "She...helped," they strained.

"We don't have time for this," Joane sighed, pointing her gun at the door as she kicked one foot up and slammed the control panel. The door chimed and slid open, revealing an empty hallway behind it. She took a step into the hall and didn't die immediately. Good, she thought, one step closer to actually making it off this station. As she heard distant shouting, she imagined that would be the easier step she took. She pushed the thought out of her mind and kept going.

The hallways through the station were barren and unadorned, the monotony of the flimsy white walls was broken only by occasional holo-displays haphazardly bolted on, showing a rolling screen of information about gravity waves, wounded, and missing person counts. Joane led the group while Tristan hauled Orion a few paces behind. They were moving too slow for Joane's liking, but Tristan was right about needing Orion around.

"Which way to the lower level?" she hissed, tilting her head to the side but not daring to look away from the dark hall stretching in front of her. She never lowered the gun, nor did she take her finger off the trigger guard.

Orion raised a weak finger, drawing a raspy breath that sounded more and more like a death rattle. "Stairs," they whimpered, pointing. Tristan shifted them, trying to give them a bit of comfort.

"We should try to pick up the pace; they need medical attention, quick," Tris said, following Joane towards a door nestled in a side pocket of the hall. Joane didn't stop, she couldn't allow herself to waste even a moment in this situation.

"I would love to," she said matter-of-factly, throwing open the door and aiming her weapon in the stairway. "But unless you want to leave the dead weight behind, we're already going as fast as possible." The senator whimpered behind Joane, and she rolled her eyes at the sound. The first few flights of stairs she could see were empty, but she heard pounding footsteps coming up. She cursed and leaned over the solid waist-high wall, looking down at the lined metal stairs stretching countless levels underneath her. The first attacker came into view, another massive figure in that same featureless black armor. They didn't have time to raise their weapon before Joane put a bolt through the top of their helmet. "Wait here a moment," she asked. Then, she vaulted over the wall and plummeted ten feet down. The wind rushed past her face as she fell and twisted her body to land on the shoulders of the next soldier she saw. This one was more slender than the earlier ones, which made Joane brace for a harder impact than she'd planned for. Sure enough, when she smacked onto the figure's shoulders, they both dropped to the stairs. Joane managed to roll off the body, softening the blow and preventing any major injuries. She felt a slight knock in her head, which was still sore from earlier, but she had enough presence of mind to reach back, yank the bolt from the first soldier's head, and plunge it into a third guard's neck before they could even raise a shout. "All clear," she called gently, sliding the bolt back into her gun.

Tristan and Orion came into view, limping slowly down the first flight of stairs. Tris took in the sight of Joane standing over three dead bodies and gave her a look that Joane couldn't quite describe. She didn't know what Tris was trying to say with her eyes, but it pulsed with pain like the concussion she felt. She pushed it to the back of her mind. They were still in immediate danger. She didn't have time for guilt, regret, or mercy. She reached down, pulled the gun from one of the guards, and kept moving.

There were only two flights of stairs down to the next level, which Orion wordlessly signalled the door to with a limp motion of their arm. The look in their eyes concerned Joane. They were risking a lot trying to get this senator to safety. If they succumbed to blunt force trauma on the way back to the ship, it would be of no use to anyone. The door was unguarded and unlocked, thankfully. It made Joane think that maybe these guards hadn't taken over the entire station. When Joane pushed open the door slightly, she saw a single figure with their back to her. She silently tilted the gun upwards and sent the bolt into the back of the soldier's neck. They dropped without a sound, and Joane kept moving forward.

Thankfully, she no longer needed Orion's directions. A few occasional signs broke up the monotony of the walls, with arrows pointing down different hallways. She followed the signs pointing towards "Hangar and Unloading," trying to usher Tristan forward faster as she did so. Oddly, they met no resistance on the way there. No barricades had been set up, no ambushes were sprung, and no patrols had stumbled across them. It made Joane queasy, but she simply held her stolen weapon tighter.

She eventually found herself standing in front of a thick heavy metal door with a keypad situated next to it. She tried the handle, but wasn't surprised when it didn't budge. Of course she didn't have her pulse knife to override the mechanisms. She looked over at Orion, whose head was now hanging down weakly. "Senator," she said forcefully, causing them to stir. "We're almost out of here, just get us into the hangar and onto our ship."

Orion nodded and pulled themselves off of Tristan's shoulders, nearly collapsing into the wall as they fell against it. With a great deal of effort, they pulled a sleek black card from their pocket and pressed it against the side of the keypad. The tiny screen lit up blue with a small picture of the Consortium seal in the middle, and the door clicked heavily as the locks disengaged. Orion groaned and raised the card towards Joane, who nodded and pulled the card into the palm of her hand. "Let's go," she told Tristan as she shouldered the senator again.

Joane twisted the handle and put her shoulder against it, grunting as the heavy door struggled to swing open. The metal scraped loudly as the hinges swung out, and Joane cringed to herself. With the door open, she dropped into a low roll for a few feet, came up onto one knee, and swept the barrel of the gun across the hangar, ready to pull the trigger the second she saw a threat. Once again, the hangar was empty. It was even more unsettling here, with the high rectangular ceiling only distantly illuminated by heavy industrial rods of silver light and rows upon rows of thin metal scaffolding creating makeshift docks for all manner of spacecraft. Joane saw medical carriers, small but quick skimships, heavy shieldships with their protection projection pylons recharging, and there, about a hundred meters away on the floor level, was Darling. Her hull seemed mostly intact, though Joane could just barely make out a few hastily applied charcoal gray sheets of metal covering the holes the Consortium medics had drilled into her. Still, the ship was there, intact, and not being surrounded by guards.

Joane wanted to be suspicious of it. She wanted to keep her guard up and take a slow route around the edge of the hangar. She also knew that any second wasted onboard this station meant another second that more soldiers could be arriving. "Run," she whispered, and took off in a mad dash for Darling. She heard Tristan struggling and Orion yelping with each step as the injured pair tried to keep up with her. With each step, Joane prepared herself for the sound of a bolt being loosed, or a gravity projector activating somewhere near her, or even a concussive blast of a grenade.

It didn't come. There was nothing but the sound of her feet pounding against the gray metal underfoot and the occasional shifting of tools as she sprinted across an abandoned mechanic's tarp. She was only a few meters away from the safety of Darling's ramp when the shoe finally dropped. It was almost completely silent, but Joane heard it and knew their luck had well and truly run out. The soft hiss was hard to identify at first, but when she felt the cold slash of steel across the back of her leg followed by a rush of blood, she knew she'd been shot. As the momentum spun her around but failed to knock her to the floor, she saw Tristan and Orion stumbling along several meters back, completely exposed. The sound of bolts flying filled the air, kicking up locks of Tristan's hair and shredding a few pieces of their clothes.

"Come on!" Joane shouted, stepping out into the open to raise her weapon. "We need to move!" She hoped Tristan understood what she was trying to say: *Leave them behind.* If she did, she didn't listen, because she continued to haul Orion along even as a bolt caught her in the shoulder. Joane shouted in protest, traced the bolt's path, and saw one of the soldiers perched on an upper walkway. She aimed the weapon with cold, silent efficiency and fired without hesitation. The soldier hadn't finished reloading their boltgun before the silver projectile hit them, and they fell backwards off the grated path, slamming into a parked skimship before sliding to the floor, unmoving. "Tris!" Joane shouted, trying to urge her forward with the strength of her voice alone.

Another bolt skimmed past the woman's face, cutting open a clean cut underneath her eye, inches away from being a fatal shot. Joane walked out further and screamed, firing blindly in the direction of the shot. When she heard the whistle of three bolts pass her from different directions, she knew she'd successfully drawn the attackers to her. "Get yourselves on board," she hissed at the pair, shoving them forward roughly. She saw Tristan stumble, but didn't have time to worry anymore. She was busy backing up, hunching her back to make herself a smaller target and firing back at whoever seemed to be shooting at her. She breathed a sigh of relief when she saw Tristan reach the Darling's shadow and cower against the hull. The moment of respite was cut short when a bolt cut across the front of her thigh, causing Joane to fall to one knee. She immediately whirled, saw a figure on the floor approaching her, and fired. The soldier dropped wordlessly; Joane tried to leap forward for their gun, but the pain in both of her legs turned it into more of a fast crawl. She dropped her now-empty weapon in favor of the guard's weapon, rolled onto her back, and traded shots with a soldier high up near the top level of the hangar.

To her shock, her bolt managed to clip the sniper's shoulder and carry them backwards off the platform they were on. Still, their final shot pierced her left arm, passing clear through her bicep and sticking there. Joane fell back with the momentum and bit back a scream. Her eyes flicked over to see Tristan pulling Orion's barely-conscious form up the ramp, and Joane smiled. Her escape plan might just work, even if she wouldn't live to see it. Still, she'd done her part, and she was satisfied with that. *Not yet*, she reminded herself, *not until they're away.* The blood pouring from her wounds made her want to protest, to give in to the darkness creeping at the edge of her vision. But when she watched Tristan moving up the ramp, her eyes nervously darting around the interior, she knew she could keep fighting.

Tristan's eyes found her, and even across the wide space of the hangar, Joane could feel the sharp green eyes lock with hers. "Come on!" she mouthed, waving a hand.

Joane gave her a weak smile, fighting back tears that she hadn't expected. She shook her head. "Take off!" she shouted hoarsely. The words seemed to take all the air from Tris's lungs, because her response was nothing but a few mouthed words: *Not without you.* "Go!" Joane yelled over the incessant sound of bolts slamming into the ground around her. Tristan wasted a few more seconds looking at her, which Joane knew she shouldn't be doing. Still, she was thankful for every moment she could see her. She tried to stretch each second as far as she could, committing Tris's form to her memory even more than she already had. She loathed the fact that so much of their time together had been spent in anger, with manufactured arguments and imaginary slights against one another. As Joane lay there, bleeding and fading out of consciousness, she wished for nothing more than a chance to go back and do things differently.

Despite it all, if Tris's face was the last one she saw, she thought, she could die happy. But Tris wouldn't leave. Joane wanted to scream at her when she saw the woman push Orion into the ship and take a step back down the ramp, already nocking an arrow into her crossbow. Even as the blood poured out of her body, Joane felt rage filling her. Logically, tactically, it made no sense. Joane knew that, and she suspected Tristan knew that too. For all her stubbornness, Tristan wasn't a complete idiot when it came to these things. She'd made it. She had important information about the missing planets, she had a witness, she was *hurt*. Despite all of that, though, Tristan Ninomae was walking away from her ship, her green eyes set with fierce determination. Joane heard heavy footfalls as one of the heavily armored soldiers entered her darkening view. It charged at Tristan, one of those glowing hammers raised up high above its head.

Tristan, who didn't like to hurt people and had killed less than a handful in her entire life, didn't hesitate. She whirled towards the figure, brought her crossbow up in a single-hand grip, and released a bolt directly into her attacker's neck. The dart stuck there, and the figure stumbled, dropping the hammer as its hands went to its throat. Tristan paid the dying person no mind and darted forward, reloading almost absentmindedly as she did so. Joane watched with bated breath as shots whizzed past her, a few even shearing off a few locks of her wavy black hair.

After an eternity of near-misses, Tristan dropped into a slide against Joane and scooped her up under her arm in a single motion. "Don't you ever pull something like this again," Tristan's voice was barely audible over the din of shots around them. Joane was in too much pain and shock to argue at the moment as she felt herself hauled to her feet.

"Why…didn't…you go?" Joane gasped out with each step. She heard Tristan's crossbow fire, followed by the sound of another body hitting the floor. Were they actually going to make it?

"You know damn well why," Tristan said without thinking. Joane had no idea how far they had made it; she didn't have the strength to lift her head and see. When the ground underneath suddenly became Darling's familiar ramp, she let out a breath of relief. Within an instant, she was once again in the corridors that had been both home and not home at all for so many years. Tristan slammed the grip of her crossbow against the panel by the door. The sound of bolts hissing through the air immediately changed to bolts slamming against Darling's hull.

"I'll be right back," Tristan murmured as she lowered Joane into a sitting position against the wall. "Neither of you die."

"No promises," Joane said with a weak smile. Tristan met her eyes and the pair froze for a second. Joane tried to pick out what it was she saw hiding behind the sparkling in Tristan's eyes, but couldn't pinpoint the emotion. She sucked her breath in when Tris suddenly cupped her face in her hands. All the snark and humor she'd come to expect from her old friend was gone.

"I mean it," she said. Tristan hesitated for a second longer, her lips pursing and opening slightly, but she seemed to forget what she wanted to say and ran off without another word. Joane let herself collapse against the wall, trying not to focus on the several open wounds across her body. Taking stock of things, she didn't seem to be bleeding that badly. If Tristan managed to get them out of this mess, there was a decent chance she'd pull through. For now, at least, she thought. With the Consortium after them, there weren't many places in the universe to hide.

Her eyes drifted over to the other figure leaning against her wall. Orion was fully unconscious now, which Joane didn't blame them for. Most of the damage had to have been internal, but from the looks of the hit they'd taken, there was a lot of it. She didn't have high hopes for the spindly senator to pull through. The fact that they were there, however, gave Joane a bit of comfort. Obviously, it wasn't the *entire* Consortium running whatever conspiracy was going on. Secondly, the assholes following them might not want to just blow their ship out of the void if there was a senator on board. Those kinds of things tended to get people talking. Thirdly, she was bleeding a lot now, actually. Wait, that wasn't helpful, Joane thought hazily.

She felt the distant thrumming of Darling's engines as if she was underwater. The thud of Tristan flooding all the power she could into them came to her distantly as she fought to stay awake. She pushed the drowsiness back with all the strength she could muster. Something about the look in Tris's eyes when she'd left her. She'd risked her life and the mission to get Joane onboard; the least she could do was stay alive for five more minutes. She kept herself focused by waiting for the sudden blast of heat of the ship exploding. It never came. After a few minutes of Darling moving quickly and performing a few intense maneuvers that Joane felt in the bottom of her stomach, there was a sound like a series of curtailed explosions that pushed Joane and Orion against the wall.

Tristan must have activated the Redshift drive again, sending Darling on a random course halfway across the universe faster than a Solan body was ever meant to go. Joane made a note to tell Tristan that the drive would be damaged if it had to perform a long jump so soon after the last one, but the force of inertia on her was so great that she lost consciousness before she got back.

# Chapter 14
## Voyage of the Maybe-Not-So-Damned

TRISTAN found herself checking the readouts of the Redshift drive almost constantly. The onboard computer assured her that it was functioning properly, that the maintenance she and Joane had done was effective preparation for a second jump, and the course she'd plotted while flying away from Cygnus hadn't sent them hurtling towards any asteroid fields or errant black holes. The only time she managed to tear her eyes away from the monitor was when she was checking on her patients. Joane had been simple, all Tristan had to do was pull a few bolts out, stitch up the wounds, and inject a few hemosynthesis tablets into her arm to replace the blood loss. The hardest part was forcing herself to look away from her face every time she went to check her vitals. She kept seeing that weak smile Joane had given her while bleeding out on the deck of her ship and remembering the way it had somehow cut through all the chaos of that moment to remind Tristan just how hard and fast she was falling for her.

When did that even happen? Tristan asked herself that constantly, the same question rattling around in the back of her mind. Try as she might, she couldn't stop thinking about it; she couldn't stop thinking about her. It was useless, she tried to tell herself, Joane had made it pretty clear after their night together that nothing had really happened between them. They'd just been comforting each other on what may have been their last night alive. Tristan told herself that a lot, but it didn't change the way they fit in one another's arms and the way her usually stoic heart jumped into her throat whenever Joane groaned in her sleep and shifted slightly under the covers.

Tristan also wasn't sure when her bedroom had become the medbay of her ship. She made a mental note to clean out Ahsha's room and convert it if they ever made it out of this mess. Joane and Orion were both currently lying in her bed, hooked up to a few vital monitors and some breathing equipment in Orion's case. The senator had been a lot closer of a shave than Joane was. Tristan was by no means a doctor, but she knew that most people wouldn't have been able to save them like she had. Orion's chest cavity had almost entirely caved in on itself, not a single rib was fully intact, and both lungs had been punctured in several locations. The only reason Tristan had the equipment on board was because of some work she'd done in the Junos cluster a few months back, when a space station's atmosphere generator had burst and a few hundred people had been put through depressurization. In the confusion of the situation, she'd forgotten to return the "person inflater" she'd been lent to help. There was a better, more scientific name for the device that looked and acted like an air pump, but Tristan had completely forgotten it. The device had kept Orion's body oxygenated long enough for her to sort out the bone fragments and seal up both their lungs. Some calcium putty in the right places and some bone growth supplements later, Orion was also on the way to recovering.

It had been close to a day since their narrow escape from the medical facility at Cygnus. Tristan assumed that the Consortium had loaded the ship with trackers she had no way of detecting on her scanners, and hadn't had time to do a thorough search of the ship's interior to begin deactivating them. On the off chance that they hadn't had time, there was no way they could predict where Tristan had sent them with the Redshift drive, mostly because Tristan didn't fully know herself. With Consortium fighters buzzing around her, she hadn't had a ton of time to carefully plot out a trajectory and endpoint to the journey. She had simply pushed the drive as far as it could go: about two weeks of continuous faster-than-light travel. If she wanted to sit down and do the math, she could probably plot their destination, but there were more important things on her mind. Namely, she had to stare at a screen and an unconscious woman she was falling in love with. She was very busy.

As she sat in the pilot's chair, nervously watching fuel readings on the screen in front of her, a gentle chime from another screen called out to her. Her eyes darted over and read the message in a split second. Joane's vitals indicated that she was beginning to come back to consciousness. Tristan breathed a sigh of relief, but her chest almost immediately tightened back up. She didn't want to continue thinking about the mess they were in alone, but if Joane was awake, it meant Tristan could continue making a fool of herself to her. She sighed. Better sooner rather than later. She was worried she might start talking to the two unconscious people in her bed if she'd been forced to endure everything alone for much longer.

Tristan stood up from the chair a bit shakily, not fully able to keep her nerves at bay. She went to the kitchen and prepared another glass of artificial sowfruit juice, which she brought into her room and set down on the nightstand on Joane's side.

Joane was in the process of groggily blinking her eyes slowly, making a series of guttural groans that seemed to mean her painkillers were wearing off. Tristan pulled up a small foldable chair she'd found on a shelf somewhere and sat down, patiently watching Joane tossing and turning. After a few minutes, her eyes opened wide, blinked a few times, then stayed open. She let out a pained noise as she picked her head up from the pillow, rubbing the bandage around her left arm.

Tristan found herself smiling despite herself as she watched Joane wake up, something she hadn't had the chance to see yet. It was strange and endearing to see her like this, fresh and rested, without her tough attitude and stern expression set in place just yet. Eventually, Joane's gaze fell on Tristan and she offered a tired smile and nod that made Tristan suddenly aware of how she was sitting and how messy her hair probably was.

"Morning, sleepyhead," she tried to say casually. "How are you feeling?"

Joane looked down at her body then slowly back up at Tristan. "I got shot yesterday."

"You did."

"A lot."

"Yeah." Joane reached out to grab the glass on the table, which took a bit of effort and more than a few winces on her part. Something told Tristan that she wasn't supposed to try and help.

"Where are we?" Joane asked after downing the entire glass, washing a bit of the sleepy huskiness out of her voice.

Tristan walked over and took the empty glass out of Joane's hand. She looked thankful, but didn't say anything.

"In a Redshift," Tristan explained. "Other than that, I don't really know. You've been out for about seventeen hours."

"Orion?" she asked, raising an eyebrow. Tristan pointed with her chin to the other side of the bed. Joane turned and started when she realized they were in the bed with her. "Are they going to make it?"

"As far as I can tell," Tristan said with a shrug. She didn't bother whispering. If Orion was going to wake up, it wouldn't be for quite some time. "It's weird, actually. I haven't seen an injury like theirs since…well, it's almost like voidburn. You know, when folks are coming back in from a spacewalk and their airlock pressurizes too quickly? It's like they took an entire atmosphere worth of gravity to the chest."

"It was a big hammer," Joane pointed out. Tristan nodded. "Still, tech like that is new to me. What about you?"

"I haven't seen anything like it, no." It felt good to talk business with Joane. She got all the comfort of her voice and her presence without any of the uncomfortable topics hanging over them. "Gravity manipulation on something like this shouldn't be possible."

Joane was quiet for some time while she absently brushed strands of brown hair out of her face. She grimaced a few times and tensed a few parts of her body that were still hurting. Tristan thought about getting her more painkillers, but she didn't want her to go back to sleep just yet. Finally, she found the thought she was looking for and spoke up.

"If they can control gravity on something that small, what's to say they can't control it on something big? Something really, really big."

"What are you thinking?" Tristan asked.

"I'm thinking that I want to know just how much data we still have from Ahsha's ship," Joane said, almost to herself. Tristan's eyes immediately lit up and she put a hand down the front of her shirt, fishing wildly for the pockets she'd sewn into the inside of the shirt. "Uh, Tris? Is now the time?"

Tristan didn't hear her because she was too busy pulling a small, thin data drive out and brandishing it in front of her. "We've got everything that was on the computer," she said, a bit surprised that the drive hadn't been stolen from her while she was unconscious. Joane's face slowly broke into a smile as she reached out and wrapped her hand around the drive. Tristan felt the warmth of Joane's fingers brushing against hers and froze up, smiling despite herself.

"I've got an idea," Joane said. "Help me up, we've got work to do."

*     *     *

TRISTAN watched Joane work through the mountain of unorganized and haphazardly labeled files Ahsha had allowed to pile up in her ship's hard drive. She helped where she could, but found herself wondering if some of the titles attached to files were genuine words or a random jumble of letters Ahsha had slapped out in a moment of frustration. Either way, she couldn't bring herself to focus much. With most of the adrenaline from the attack passed, it was all she could do to stop thinking of the night the two of them had spent together. That wasn't like her, Tristan knew that. In all her years out in the universe, she had never had more than a passing fancy for any woman. There were moments she remembered fondly, but none like what she felt when she watched the line of Joane's jaw or studied the way her brow furrowed as she examined another paper.

Still, she managed to not be obvious about her staring, as far as she knew. Joane seemed more preoccupied with sorting through potential life-saving information to give her much mind, anyway. Not that Joane had paid her *any* mind since they'd arrived in the Cygnus system. Tristan scolded herself for the thought. The Consortium was bearing down on them, they were probably marked for death in every system in the galactic cluster, there was a dying senator in her bed, and Tristan was focused on the girl not paying her any attention. It was childish. More than that, it was frustrating. She needed to think pragmatically and help find a way out of this mess, if one even existed. She swiped a finger across her datapad, dismissing a thorough deconstruction of the Zydralan biology and onto a description of interplanetary meteorological patterns. Her eyes opened a bit wider at one of the words hiding among the pretentiously wordy abstract.

"Joane," she called out. The woman lowered her own datapad and looked up expectantly. Tristan had figured out over the past few hours it was best not to meet her eyes, or she would forget what she was going to say. "Got another one. They talk about gravity fields surrounding planets and their satellites."

"Send it over," Joane said with a nod. Tristan tapped an icon in the top corner of the document and sent a copy to the datapad plugged into Darling's dashboard. The ship's computer immediately began scrubbing through the file for any mention of gravitational force, the void, black holes, and transportation. It was a rudimentary system, both women knew that. Still, it was faster than picking through whatever organizational nightmare Ahsha had left behind. Tristan was about to move on to the next file when she heard Joane let out a heavy sigh. She immediately looked up at her, cocking an eyebrow quizzically. "Tris, let's take a break," she said, sliding her datapad across the floor towards the console. She stood up slowly, pushing herself off the cold metal floor of Darling's bridge with some effort. Tristan took a few quick glances at the bandages visible across Joane's body. The bleeding hadn't completely stopped yet, she noted.

Instead of heading out of the bridge, Joane stuck her hands into the pockets of her jacket and leaned back against the wall, turning her head towards the viewport. There was nothing to see, of course. With the ship moving at faster-than-light speeds, no visible light had time to reach the ship before it passed by. They might as well have been floating in empty space. "We should talk about what happened," she finally said. Tristan felt her mouth go dry. Her legs went numb in a strange way that could only come from a place of absolute terror and excitement mixing together.

"O-Of course, Joane," she said, clambering to her feet and taking a nervous step forward. "Whatever...you want." Joane turned back slowly to her, then dropped her eyes to the floor.

"You need to be more careful with what you say."

The numbness in Tristan's legs nearly won over as she fought to keep her balance. She fought it by freezing in place, trying to ponder what exactly Joane had just said. "I-I don't, what?"

"I don't know how long I was out, at the station near Cygnus," Joane explained, "but it sounded like you and that senator had been having quite the chat while I was out."

*Oh*, Tristan realized. Joane hadn't wanted to talk about their "last" night together. Of course not. There was business to attend to. Joane didn't give her a chance to respond.

"I don't think I should have to say how dangerous that is. Whatever you may or may not think you know about them, they're still a part of a government that wants us *very* dead. You can't just go around spilling every secret or plan that you've got."

"That isn't what happened," Tristan blurted out lamely. It was all she could muster in the moment.

Joane clearly wasn't going to let her off easily. "Go on then," she said, shrugging with her hands still firmly in her pockets. "Tell me what *did* happen, Tris, so I can figure out how screwed we are."

Tristan threw her arms out to the side and shook her head in disbelief. "It's not like I gave them everything," she said angrily. "I just...I had a feeling. Orion is Cygnus's senator. All they want is to find their planet. I told them we were looking for it, and that we were going to figure it out, that's all."

"Did you mention Ahsha? Her ship? Whatever she might've been studying? Any theories?" Joane pressed. Tristan shook her head feverishly, earning a nod of slightly less annoyed approval from her friend. "Good. From now on, it might be a good idea not to run your mouth to government officials if I'm not there. I thought you were smarter than this." She didn't need to finish the thought.

Tristan felt like she'd been slapped. "I'm not a child, Joane," she shot back, feeling a blush rising in her cheeks. "I've been out in the Void dealing with people — good and bad — for years; I know how to read people. Yeah, I trusted the senator, and guess what, I was right! Because they're laid up in the bed right now because the actual bad guys tried to kill them with us."

"And what if you'd been wrong?"

Tristan let Joane's question hang in the air for a moment. In all honesty, she had no idea. If Senator…Regille, if she remembered correctly, had been the one she'd been talking to and not Orion. They probably would've both been shot there and then in those flimsy hospital beds. Instead, they would get to zip across a few galaxies for two weeks and probably be vaporized not long after the Redshift ended. That whole "way out of this mess" still wasn't coming to her.

"Did you seriously not think about that?" Joane asked, with more venom than Tristan was used to slipping into her voice. In a moment, it was six years ago again. The two of them were at each other's throats over some inconsequential thing while Ahsha sat off to the side, watching with mild amusement and more than a bit of judgment, occasionally peppering in a remark or comment that kept the argument fueled for hours. Something about it felt familiar, almost comfortable, but the sting in her chest quickly stamped that feeling out.

"Who put you in charge of who we do and do not trust?" Tristan replied, deflecting from the question. Joane pinched the bridge of her nose.

"No one! We *agreed* not to trust anyone! You and I actually agreed on something for once in our lives, and you're arguing because *you* decided to break that agreement! You can't just call an audible like that without my input, Tris."

"Oh, so now we're respecting each other's choices?" Tristan half-shouted back, not knowing what to do except yell.

"The hell are you talking about?" Joane asked, her tone lowering in confusion.

She steadied herself, taking a deep, shaky breath. "Why did you run out there?" Tristan asked. It had been hard to fully process in the moment, but the images of Joane running out into the line of fire, taking several bolts for her, and lying on the ground covered in her own blood was as burned into Tristan's mind as the memory of her pressed against her body with her hands entwined in her hair. "You could've died back there."

Joane went silent for a bit, her eyes cloudy and unfocused. Tristan was reminded that she'd definitely suffered a concussion when she hit the deck of Ahsha's ship no more than three days ago. "You weren't going to make it," she said finally, her voice far away and softer than Tristan had heard in ages. "You were going to...I couldn't just watch...I wasn't going to leave you behind. Why did you come back for me? You had made it out, you had the drive, you had the senator."

Tristan took another shaky step forward. "Joane...you," she paused, starting to get lost in those crystal blue eyes again.

*Damn it, focus,* she told herself. "You aren't allowed to die for me, okay?"

Joane opened her mouth to respond, but another voice answered. "Patient vital signs lowering, cause for alarm," an automated voice blared out from the console. Both women turned to look at the blinking red light, then remembered the unconscious senator in the bedroom.

"Shit," they both said in unison and took off running for the door. In an instant, the argument, the anger, the moment of wanting to say more than they had, had passed, replaced with the same familiar sense of urgency that was possibly the only thing keeping them running at this point.

# Chapter 15
## The Gravity of the Situation

ORION Masenna didn't have dreams in the traditional sense. Instead, it felt like they were semi-conscious of every moment of pain their body felt while their mind hung in an empty, maddening void of blood and screaming. Of course, that was far from the case, and the memory of that existential pain had already begun to fade by the time consciousness came back to them.

Even on the faintest edge of awareness, Orion knew something was terribly wrong. When they were ten, only a few years before they stopped going by their birth name, they crashed a hover-cruiser into a river. They'd broken a rib, both legs, and their left arm in one efficient somersault into the shallow water and nearly drowned before being rushed to the hospital. That pain was nothing compared to the searing, burning ache that filled their entire body now. It made them want to cry out; if not for help, then just to let the universe know how they felt. It made them want to retreat back to the relative peace of unconsciousness.

Unfortunately, no relief came. Instead, they found their eyes opening against their will and were immediately greeted by the sight of a dark-skinned Solan woman with sandy brown hair descending to about her jawline. She was propped in a chair close to the bed, flipping through some haphazardly stacked papers resting on her lap. Orion reached out a hand, or they at least tried to. Somehow, reaching out for help turned into them weakly mumbling a sound like a deflating warblerfly. The woman's ears perked up and she looked away from her work to glance at Orion. "Holy shit," she said in a monotone voice that Orion believed might have been sarcasm. "You actually pulled through. Sit tight for a minute."

Orion's entire body was too sore for them to even follow the woman with their eyes as she stood and disappeared from view. They heard the fading of footsteps, followed by a door sliding open and closed in rapid succession. They were alone, now, they figured. It gave them a moment to sort through the last few things they remembered before now. They'd been at...lunch? No, they'd been planning on lunch, that was it. But then the two women on the ship had been brought in, the ones that had slipped through the shield blockade. They had wanted to meet with them, to make sure they were okay. Then the one started talking about finding Cygnus-4, and then Senator Regille had been there. Senator Regille. He was an older senator from a cluster that Orion couldn't remember at the moment. Orion didn't even know why they knew them. They certainly hadn't met many of the countless senators in the Consortium, and even fewer knew them. What had happened then? It got fuzzy then. Orion was...falling? Flying? They were bleeding, they remembered that part at least.

Something about it made them start to breathe faster, and breathing made everything hurt worse. They gritted their teeth and let out a growl of pain as their chest rose and fell in quick succession, feeling like something was holding up their ribcage with each movement. Something was definitely wrong.

Finally, the woman returned, clutching what looked like a wide syringe in her hand. "Don't go freaking out on me just yet, senator," she said, the last word dripping with spiteful sarcasm. "That comes *after* the needle." She plucked the cap off the syringe and put a hand on Orion's arm to hold it still. The prick of the needle was nothing compared to the searing pain in their lungs. Soon though, that pain began to fade too. Their breathing slowed, and the fog began clearing from their mind. Unfortunately, that meant they remembered everything from the station, from the hammer that had nearly punched a hole through their chest to the sight of Dr. Toscana lying dead on the ground. A new kind of pain tore through Orion.

"What- what did you give me?" they asked, staring at the needle and marveling at how hoarse their voice had gone. The woman slid the empty syringe into a pocket on her brown leather jacket and sat gracefully back on her chair, never taking her eyes off Orion as she did so.

"It's a pain suppressant," she explained. "And a bit of an energy boost so you can talk to me for a few minutes before you knock back out."

"What do you want?" Orion groaned, their fuzzy recollection of the past few days solidifying as their mind focused. With the weight of agony completely dissolving from their chest, they tried to push themselves into an upright position. What followed the motion wasn't pain, but a deep sense of discomfort as their ribcage seemed to flex and bend as they moved. They let out all the breath in their newly sealed lungs in a high-pitched yelp and collapsed back onto the bed. The woman twitched as if she wanted to reach out but thought better of it and remained seated.

"You're still healing," she explained as Orion's chest fell and rose rapidly. They were acutely aware now that whatever medicine they'd been given was keeping them awake at a time when their body desperately needed to be asleep. "Chest cavities don't fix themselves overnight."

"No, I don't think they do," Orion agreed, trying to calm themselves down. "Where...where are we?"

The woman shrugged, a few thin strands of brown hair brushing across her jaw as she did. "I have no idea. I'd say you could look out a window, but at the speed we're going there isn't much to see. I'd say to ask the pilot, but she doesn't know either. All I can say for sure is that you're on our ship and you're alive. Not safe, of course, because none of us are, but alive. Now, if you enjoy being alive, I suggest you be as helpful as possible so we actually have a chance of surviving this mess."

"Yes," Orion choked out. "Of course, whatever you need. Oh, Stars, what a mess. How did this happen?"

The lady sat back in her chair, a faint smile creeping onto her lips. There was no kindness in it. "You took my first question right out of my mouth. Let me rephrase: Cygnus-4 disappeared. Is there any reason in your mind that anyone might have *wanted* that to happen?"

"No," Orion said with conviction. They'd already asked and answered that question a thousand times in the weeks since Cygnus-4 vanished. Reporters, scientists, astronomists, panicked civilians, themselves; it was the question on everyone's mind anytime a vanishing happened: Why? "It wasn't any sort of production world, just a rural habitation planet. The crops we grew were all used to sustain the population. We're a small, simple system. We don't have any weapons or rare resources. Outsiders used to say that the only worthwhile thing about Cygnus is the people there."

"Good people?" the woman asked, raising an eyebrow.

"The best people I've ever met," Orion said with conviction. Not like they had many people to compare. They'd only left Cygnus a few times for in-person meetings with the local cluster's Consortium representatives.

"That's nice," she said, clearly uninterested. "Next question: You, who are you?"

Orion blinked a few times, trying to remember. It felt odd, but this situation felt so alien, so impossible for them to be in, that they for a moment struggled to remember who exactly they really were. This was a place for an action hero or some sort of super spy, not a backwater planet's junior senator. "My name is Orion," they said finally. "Orion Masenna. I thought I had already introduced myself." A few memories from that awful day came running back. "You, yes, you're…Joane?"

The woman, Joane, shot him a look, and something in her blue eyes reminded Orion so much of a dagger pointed at their chest that they fell quiet. She pulled a small silver datapad out of her dark brown jacket and began tapping at the keys in silence. While she did, Orion focused on their surroundings. The room was dark, save for some red lights set where the floor met the wall. He heard and felt the hum of a ship's engines all around them, but it sounded odd. Deep Void flights were usually calm and gentle, but the thrum of these engines reminded them of flying through a thunderstorm. After a moment, the glass screen of the datapad shifted, and Orion saw a backwards image of themselves with a wall of text next to it.

"If you're just going to read my Consortium dossier, could I go back to sleep? Everything hurts, and I'm tired," they asked. Joane's eyes flicked up from the screen and met theirs.

"Says you're a recent addition to the Consortium, but that you campaigned five times before you finally got the seat." Orion inclined their head slightly and sighed.

"Yes," they admitted. "It's not easy for a young person to get into politics."

"Sounds like you really wanted to be in charge of your system," Joane responded, glaring at them the entire time. "You seem very drawn to power."

Orion stammered, trying to recover from the verbal slap the woman just delivered as the effects of the stimulant began to wear off. They could feel their body getting more and more sluggish, drawing them back towards the void of sleep. At least the pain was going away, too. "It's not power I'm drawn to. I wanted to *help* my people, to-to raise them up from being some backwater system. The old guard were perfectly happy to let our people be shut out from the rest of the universe, but I did something they never could bring themselves to do."

"And what was that?"

"I looked up," Orion said, the fire and passion that had guided them so many times during their campaign was beginning to burn inside them even as the painkillers dulled their senses. "I saw a sky full of stars and I knew that Cygnus could be more than it was. We are living in an age where the entire universe can be traveled in weeks, and we were hiding in our quiet little solar system. People, Joane, aren't meant to be isolated. Every species, every sentient individual, thrives better in a group. I dedicated my life to my people, and when the incumbent senator finally decided not to run for re-election, I got my chance to bring Cygnus to the universe, and then Cygnus-4 and every person on it vanished. No, Joane, I am not drawn to power, and if this is what power looks like, I can safely say I don't care for it."

Joane had set her face into an unreadable scowl, a look Orion had come to recognize during their time with the Consortium. She'd make a good senator, they thought, but didn't dare to say so out loud. She seemed to consider their words for a second and let out a small, satisfied huff. "I had more questions, but your rant there cut into your time. Get some sleep, don't die, and be ready to talk more when you wake up."

"Has anyone ever told you that you have a terrible bedside manner?" Orion asked, settling back into the surprisingly comfortable pillows as Joane stood and pocketed her datapad. To Orion's surprise, she broke into a smile

"They have, as a matter of fact," she said, turning to walk away. Orion was unconscious before she left the room.

# Chapter 16
## Business Before Pleasure

TRISTAN was waiting in the cockpit for Joane to get done interrogating the half-dead senator in her bed. As she sat sideways in the pilot's chair, her legs tossed haphazardly over the armrest and her head tilting backwards to read a nearby console upside down, she considered the strangeness of her life now. Not that her life prior to this had been at all boring or standard, of course. In the few years since she'd left her homeworld, Tristan had probably forgotten about more planets than an average person would visit in their lifetime. Still, the past few weeks had seen her life turn from adventure to bizarre horror. Tristan Ninomae, wanted by the Consortium Government of the Known Universe, dead or alive. By the time the Redshift ended, her face would probably be on nearly every holo-screen in the universe. She'd been a lot of things in her time, but being an enemy of the state was uncharted territory for her. She continued overthinking until she heard the cockpit door hiss open behind her and the sound of Joane's careful footsteps entering.

Immediately, Tristan sat up, throwing her legs off the armrest and into a normal sitting position so she could spin the chair towards the other woman. Joane watched her as the chair twisted too far, and Tristan had to stop it with one foot on the floor before slowly correcting the angle. "Hard at work, I see,"

Joane said with a smirk. Tristan wasn't sure if it was meant to be a genuine smile, but it stung nonetheless.

"I'm running diagnostics," she explained, jerking a thumb at the pilot's console behind her. "The computer doesn't work as well in a redshift, so it's taking longer than usual. How's the hostage?"

Joane narrowed her eyes and frowned at her. "The *liability* is sleeping. They didn't have much of anything helpful to say, just typical political buzzword bullshit." Tristan watched Joane's face settle into a mask and knew that Orion must have said something that she was turning around in her mind, examining it from every angle. She pulled out her datapad, flipping the display so the information appeared on the back of the glass screen towards Tristan. "Story seems to check out, though. Orion Masenna is a recently elected senator for the Cygnus system. I can't find anything odd in their records that could make them seem corrupt, but that doesn't mean they aren't."

Tristan crossed the cockpit and took the datapad, examining the page. The image of the senator was a far cry from the bedridden, broken person they were now. Hell, the picture barely looked like how Orion had looked on the relief station. There, they'd been shaken, their hands constantly moving with nervous energy and eyes wide open like they hadn't slept in days. This picture was of an idealist young upstart, smiling and waving at a crowd of cheering supporters. "So, are you satisfied?"

Joane took the datapad back and shook her head. "I'm not." Tristan nodded; of course she wasn't. "We're in deep here, Tris. We aren't going to get far if we start trusting the wrong people."

"Do you trust *me*?" Tristan blurted out, the question coming into her mind and leaving her mouth at almost the same moment. Joane blinked a few times, confusion written across her features.

"What kind of a question is that?"

"What kind of an *answer* was that?"

"Of course I trust you, Tris," Joane said, looking hurt. "You and Ahsha are about the only people in the universe that I don't have doubts about right now." *Ahsha.* So much had happened that Tristan had almost forgotten the reason they were even in this mess to begin with. "I need to know you understand the difference between *you* and someone who is a part of the government that just tried to kill us. The fact that you aren't more cautious about them worries me."

Tristan pinched the bridge of her nose and closed her eyes, trying and failing to bite back her irritation. "Joane, I know you and Ahsha think I'm some tunnel-crawling cave rat from an ass-backwards hunk of rock that can barely be called a planet, but I know a bit about who and who not to trust. That's practically all I'm good for to the two of you, aside from chauffeuring you across the universe."

"Tris, I never-"

"No." Tristan was surprised at the forcefulness of her own voice. "Listen, with that strategic, rational, logical, infuriating brain of yours. What seems more likely to you: that every member of the entire universe's government is part of some scheme to make planets vanish and they decided to throw someone at us to gain our trust and stab us in the back instead of just blowing up our ship the second we hit the system, or that maybe some of the government are part of some secret corruption…thing that the rest of them don't know about?"

Joane didn't answer right away; she simply stared at Tristan, mouth slightly open and eyes boring into hers. She took an imperceptibly small step towards Tristan, but the space between them was far, far wider. "I-I'm sorry," was all Joane could manage. "Tris, that isn't what I thought, ever, truly. You're right, of course, I don't disagree with you in the slightest. The entire Consortium couldn't be involved in this, that would be a conspiracy on a scale too large to hold up. However, I just need to make sure we can trust this Orion person to help us, because even if the entire Consortium isn't involved, those that are could easily concoct some story to get the whole of them after us."

Tristan wished she believed her, she wanted nothing more to laugh it off like an ill-timed joke. She couldn't though. She'd spent years watching Ahsha and Joane shut her out of meetings once the technical topics started, her remarks and suggestions ignored and dismissed. Ahsha thought she was smarter than both of them, but Joane at least had been a collaborator. Tristan had been a glorified intern. Maybe they never said it out loud, but she'd felt it. It'd eaten away at her, slowly but surely. "Forget it," she tried to say, unconvincingly. "When they wake up we can ask more questions and figure something out. I'm going to check my diagnostics." She turned away from Joane, but a hand shot out and grabbed her wrist, holding her in place with a grip so tight it almost hurt.

Joane pulled lightly, urging Tristan to turn. She gritted her teeth. *Don't do it,* she told herself, *don't give in.* She turned, cursing herself even as she did so. "Tris," she said emphatically. Tristan stepped forward, her face mere inches from Joane's. She brought her free hand up to rest against her jawline. They were so close, Tristan thought, it would be so easy to lean in and kiss her again. To kiss her again the way she'd been wanting to kiss her again since the first kiss they shared. The way she was worried she would want to kiss her for the rest of her life. *No,* she reminded herself, *you're mad at her.*

"Joane, you don't have to," she said, a nice comfortable middle ground between slapping her and kissing her. "It's been a stressful few days; I'm just saying whatever pops into my head. You know me."

"That doesn't mean you didn't say it," Joane pressed, her grip still tight around Tristan's arm. "I have a lot to apologize for, I know that."

"We all do," Tristan said, trying to force her voice to stay steady. "But not now."

"We might not have many more chances."

Tristan wanted to scream. Why would Joane be forcing this issue when she refused to talk about the night before Cygnus? Why couldn't she let this of all things go and focus on the feelings that were eating Tristan from the inside out. Had it been nothing to her? Some sort of last comfort shared between two people who thought they were doomed? Was that what it actually was? It couldn't have been; not to her at least. She still remembered the way her lips had tingled when she woke up the next morning, how her heart raced in a way it never did when she thought about the several other women she'd shared that bed with.

"I...always admired you, Tristan," Joane said slowly, haltingly, like she was dragging the words out of a well. "I have no love for my childhood, but I'm not so blind as to pretend it wasn't safe or comfortable. When I met you, I saw that you had lived through the exact opposite, but you were so much stronger for it. There was a resilience about you, a toughness that wasn't cold. You didn't fall prey to bitterness or despair, and I thought that was amazing. You have a level of wisdom that I could only aspire to, and I never meant to make you feel small or insignificant."

Stars above, how she wanted to forgive her. To brush everything aside and try to pretend again like they had before. It was no use though, she thought. "Whether you meant it or not, Joane, it still happened. And I don't know how much of it was you and how much was Ahsha twisting things like she did, but sometimes I don't know if I care, because you let it happen. We all did; hell, I let her turn me against you just as much as she turned you. I can't blame her for everything because I feel like somewhere, deep down, we were all just waiting for a reason to jump at each other's throats.

"More than that, you're wrong about me. I *am* bitter. I'm bitter that I was born on a lightless rock slowly spinning its way towards oblivion with no prospects of my own, and the minute I thought I had a ticket out, my only two friends in the universe both started treating me like a piece of hull scrap. And I finally decided to try and make something of myself to prove that I could, but who should come strutting back into my life but the two of you, dragging me into another insane scheme that'll probably get me killed a lot slower and more painful than any tunnel spider back home would've.

"But do you know what's worse, Joane? What's worse than all of that? It's that I'm in this situation: stuck on a ship with you and half a Consortium senator; I'm an enemy of the state and basically waiting to get blasted out of the Void the second we show our faces anywhere and I can't find it in me to stay mad at you. I have tried so damn hard to hate you two, and I just can't do it. I still feel sick thinking about the way things were and yet here I am, by your side, hoping we get out of this because I can't stand to see you hurt."

A silence fell over the cockpit, the stillness of the moment all the more palpable with the heavy thrum of the Redshift engines shaking the cabin. The air felt heavy with tension, and Tristan realized that she was trembling as a few tears began to leak from her eyes. Joane was stuck in place, trying to formulate words that would mean anything. Tristan couldn't stand it any longer, the crushing weight of the closeness between them. It was like weights tied to her shoulders, hooked to a carrier craft, and then shot through a Fastlane. She didn't lean in, though. She yanked her wrist out of Joane's grip, a sudden fast motion that caught the other woman off guard. Joane didn't make another grab for her. Tristan waited a moment, then another before realizing she was wasting her time waiting for a response. She scoffed in exasperation and shouldered past her and through the cockpit door. She heard a ding from her captain's console: the diagnostics report was finished, and right on time for her to leave, too. She slammed a fist against the console on the opposite side of the doorway, and the cockpit door slid down with frustrating slowness.

She took off for her room, listening to the rhythmic clack of her shoes against the floor as she tried and failed to fight back tears.

# *Chapter 17*
## Plotting Courses

THE sound of the cockpit door sliding into place with a decisive thunk jolted Joane out of her stupor. She was alone in Darling's cockpit with nothing but her thoughts of guilt and disgust- at Ahsha and herself. She half-walked, half-stumbled to Tris's chair and fell into it, burying her face in her hands. The numerous wounds across her body that were still healing screamed in protest, forcing her to adjust in the chair even as she let out a muffled yell of frustration. She wanted to yell louder, until her throat was scratched and her voice as hoarse as a rusted engine capsule, but didn't want Tris to hear. What had she done? All her careful thinking, her planning, her understanding of the world around her, and yet Tristan seemed to evade her understanding. She was an enigma to her, a woman made of contradictions and mysteries that both irritated and fascinated her to no end, like a puzzle sphere with no clear solution.

She dug her fingertips into the skin of her face until it hurt, feeling the small pulls where stray bits of hair got caught in her hands. She didn't have time for all this, she knew that. And yet, it was seemingly all she could think about. Tristan's mix of warmth and coldness, the way she opened and shut her heart like an automatic shutter with a busted motor. Every time she opened her mouth, Joane wasn't sure which version of her old friend she would get. Why now, at the most dangerous point in her life, did she decide to take leave of her senses? To fall for a woman who saw her as a cruel footnote in her life, a source of nothing but misery and pain that still festered to this day. Maybe Tristan had been right; she'd gotten out, broken free from under Ahsha's thumb, only for Joane to drag her back in. What kind of friend did that make her? What kind of person?

She'd never stopped to feel guilty in the time since Tristan left. She hadn't had any reason to. At the time, Tris had been a thieving, lying drug addict who plundered their coffers and stole their ship, leaving them stranded on a city world with hardly enough money for a holobooth call. At least, that's what Ahsha had told her. There was no telling how much, if any, of it was true. In the past few weeks, Joane's life had been turned upside down in so many different ways that she could scarcely remember what she believed anymore. The further they went, the tighter the noose around her neck grew, the more she doubted she'd ever have a chance to find out what had ever been real.

Maybe she didn't deserve answers. She'd seen the hurt in Tristan's eyes. That wasn't the kind of hurt that came from one ill-received remark; it was years and years of pain boiling over. If they, by some miracle, survived this, Tristan didn't owe Joane a word. Conversely, Joane owed her a cargo hold's worth of credits and a lifetime's worth of apologies, not that either would change what happened. She wanted to be forgiven, she knew that much, but a part of her wasn't sure if she deserved it. She thought about how easily she'd let Ahsha manipulate her against her best friend, how she had never stood up for Tristan or herself. How could she, though? Ahsha had rescued

Joane as much as she had rescued Tristan. She sighed, thinking back to that day years ago when Ahsha had come to her planet and changed her life forever.

*It was the middle of summer, and Joane Cordelle was taking a walk around the grounds of her family estate so that the local populace would see her, happy and carefree, smiling politely and demurely as she strode across the family manor's grounds. It was a cool spring day on Earth, the sky a gentle eggshell blue above, dotted with wispy white clouds that made lazy paths through the air. Beyond them, Sol glared down from its Derevian Cage, the condensed Red Giant held back by the sphere of black metal that served as the last line of defense keeping humanity's first homeworld from becoming a smoldering lump of magma. On some days, the vents in the Cage glowed a deeper, angrier red, and Joane would think of the Solus Cultists preaching in the town square, declaring the Cage an abomination of the natural order. The star was trying to die, after all, but with the gargantuan device locked in place, feeding hydrogen and containing Sol's expansion, it could theoretically languish as a Red Giant for trillions of years. When she was young, Joane would have nightmares of the Cage cracking open and feeling the pure, unfiltered heat of humankind's first Sun against her skin. Today though, the vents were so calm as to appear almost orange instead of their usual scarlet, and the air was cool and pleasant, so Joane went for a walk without a thought towards Sol.*

*The Cordelle manor was situated on a hill just outside of the city of Marseille, so Joane could look down into the city as she walked, thinking about all the people going about their lives in the urban sprawl below her. Earth, and the entire Sol system, had long ago shed any semblance of labor or production. The birthplace of the universe's* most prominent species was now a vacation destination, each planet full of luxury and relaxation for those who could afford it. Only a select few called it home, some of the richest and most established families in the known universe. Families like the Cordelles. The family had established itself so long ago that no one truly knew where the fortune originated from, but they had diversified enough that the Cordelles were big names in almost every business imaginable. With that money, they had built this manor in Marseille, supposedly the origin of the first Cordelle millions of years ago. It was something to be extremely proud of, her father Alois told her.

Joane would always nod to her father politely, as she'd been taught. To her, the manor was lonely. So few interesting things ever happened within the grand walls, but whenever she found her way down to the city proper, she always came back with interesting stories to tell her favorite members of the staff. Father often told her not to waste her time descending to the streets of Marseille, insisting it was dangerous to mingle with the tourists and pilgrims. On days when his mood was particularly unagreeable, he even forbade it, sending one of the guards with her on her walk to ensure that she didn't stray from the path. Father was shut into his office that day, so Joane was able to slip outside without having to weather a barrage of questions. As she passed through the magnolia garden, brushing through the oranges and pinks of the blossoms, a ship caught her eye. It wasn't the luxurious, sleek void-yachts that usually touched down in Marseille, nor was it a heavy-duty cargo hauling ship. This was a small, blocky, chunk of a ship, with its in-atmo engines trailing a cloud of black smoke and sputtering as it came down towards the city's hangar.

Joane watched it for a bit, curiosity beginning to grow in her mind. Once the ship was out of sight, and that spark in her chest grew into a small, smoldering flame, she made her way towards the estate's twin golden gates.

"Going somewhere, Miss?" The guard perched at the small watchtower asked. His voice was good-natured enough, but there was a hint of a deeper question there.

Joane tried to recall the man's name, but he was one of the staff she never paid much mind to. "Just into town," she said with sufficient vagueness. "My father gave me permission to go visit the shops."

He nodded and threw open the gate, knowing his station well enough not to speak more than necessary to Alois Cordelle's daughter. The hinges and motors hummed as the two gates opened outwards, and Joane stepped through them as soon as there was enough space to fit her body through. Once she passed beyond the bounds of the manor, it was as if a gravity shackle had been taken off her shoulders, and the Cordelle name fell away. With the weight gone, she broke into a run, her dirty blonde hair whipping in the wind behind her.

On a normal day, Joane would've made her way carefully through the streets of Marseille, peeking into shops and cafes to watch and analyze all the different sorts of people in them. On that day, though, Joane had her sights set on only one thing. She didn't spend a lot of time around the hangar. The constant stream of ships arriving and departing meant that there was always a loud, crushing throng of people there. It made it hard to pick out a few unique individuals and try to figure them out when everyone was going somewhere in a hurry, shoving past one another like rapids in a stream. It seemed today was no exception when Joane arrived, out of breath from running through the massive city but exhilarated and full of energy. A family walked past her, nearly running over her foot with their luggage. She let out a scoff, loud enough for them to hear, but they didn't seem to pay her any mind. That was one of the issues with leaving the manor; she shed all the privileges that her name usually offered in favor of anonymity. Still, she would rather have to shoulder her way through a crowd than be hounded by people seeking to ogle an heiress. The crowds were lighter at this point in the day, thankfully, so she was able to carve a path through the hangar easily enough, heading for the arrivals platform. She wasn't sure exactly how she'd find the owner of the strange ugly ship, but she was sure someone willing to fly such an eyesore would stick out on Earth.

And, of course, she was right. In the long line of arrival jetty docks, nestled between bays housing two beautiful starliners, was the ship, dwarfed by both of them in size and grandeur alike. Joane made her way to a bench in front of the starliners, cutting her way past a tourist headed for the same bench. She tried to tune out the din of conversation, intercom announcements, and shuttle engines and focus on the ship. It was, as she had already seen, hideous. Clearly not built for any sort of aesthetic purposes, it almost didn't seem to be built for practical ones either. It was closer to a prefab house like the staff slept in with four rockets welded to the back than an actual space faring vessel. Carbon scoring and plasma burns pitted the ship's hull, and the still-cooling engines had a small cloud of smoke still pouring from them.

After a quick scan of the ship, Joane turned her attention to the dock around it. Standing on the long jetty to the left of the ship, there was a Marseille traffic coordinator, flanked by two Consortium peace officers in bright blue vests, speaking to a single figure that Joane instantly realized had to be the pilot. They were gesturing wildly, speaking loudly with no regard for propriety or decorum, wearing plain, uncomfortable looking clothes and standing next to two heavy briefcases. Their face was sharp and angular, like the skin had been pulled tight over a skull with exaggerated proportions. They were possibly from a planet where the inhabitants lived high in the atmosphere, Joane figured, examining the way their cheekbones cut a decisive profile across their face. Their black hair was trimmed and clean, but completely untouched by any sort of stylistic hands. They looked, for all intents and purposes, like a normal person, which on Earth was about the strangest thing they could be.

Joane moved closer to the ruckus, trying to pick up pieces of the conversation over the overlapping sounds around her. She heard the pilot first, with the other voices coming into focus gradually.

"-visiting the planet on dispensation from the Neptune University Astronomics Campus, I have full legal right to be here," they were saying with a clipped, stern voice that came off as both unhinged and perfectly measured at the same time. Joane smirked. However polite and officious the pilot may have been acting, she could tell they were moments away from losing their temper. There was a murmur from the coordination officer before the pilot spoke again. "Yes, obviously I have signed authorization, I wouldn't have gotten past the defense grid without it. The papers are on board if you need to hold them to believe they're real, but the transmission in your system should have the codes already."

Joane stepped closer, pretending to examine a map of the hangar. They were in Arrivals Bay J7, she noted, nodding to herself as if she was looking for something on the map. From here, she could barely pick up the other voices. "That may be so, ma'am, but we can't have you parked here for three days just for some scientific…dispensation. This is a high foot traffic area, and we get hundreds of flights in here every day. If we have to lock up one of our bays for your ship, it'll cause backups that could cost the line a lot of time and a lot of money."

"Your bottom line isn't my problem, I'm afraid," the pilot said. "I came here to study the geological shift patterns of Earth's tectonic plates since the Pangeal Restructuring Infrastructure was installed, not the goings-on of some second-rate receiving hangar."

"Ms. Reindare-"

"I think you'll find that my title is Doctor, Officer," the pilot said, her neck twisting to face the officer that had spoken so fast Joane thought she may have dislocated a vertebrae.

"Doctor Reindare," she corrected. "There are plenty of ship storage facilities outside Marseille that would be happy to hold your ship while you conduct your research."

"The Consortium Office of Marseille has a lovely impound lot, if you want something closer," the other officer suggested. The doctor's face shifted from measured contempt to a furious scowl.

"Oh, is that so?" she said, her voice growing higher as she spoke. "Perhaps you would like to park my ship there? I'm sure the dean of the University would be very curious to know why Neptunian property was seized by two jumped-up beat cops because of what they think is a parking violation."

Joane knew a conversation heading south when she heard one. If this continued, the woman was going to get herself thrown out of the hangar or led away in shackles. While this normally wouldn't concern her, that flame of curiosity still simmered inside her. Something was drawing her to this eccentric, plain scientist. She was already concocting an idea of how she would explain this to her father as she approached the arguing group, holding her shoulders back and her chin high to appear as formal as possible.

"Excuse me?" she said as she approached, putting on an air of nonchalance but lacing it with the authority her status brought her. "I couldn't help but overhear the situation at hand, and was wondering if I might offer a bit of help?"

The officers turned toward her, and their eyes all widened with realization. The pilot, Dr. Reindare, had no such look upon her face. She reminded Joane of her father when he was conducting a business deal, her eyes jittering back and forth as she analyzed the new variable in the situation. Joane wondered what her assumptions were, and if she knew that Joane had sized her up before she'd taken a step towards the conversation.

"Ma'am," the female officer said, taking her hat off and nodding formally. "You needn't concern yourself with this, just a simple misunderstanding with parking regulations. We've got it all under control."

"On the contrary, officer," Joane said, "the Cordelles have long concerned themselves with the importance of scientific development and the furthering of knowledge. I know my father would be very interested in helping this visiting scientist."

Dr. Reindare squinted at her a bit, a faint smile playing at the corner of her mouth. "Your father's support," she said slowly, emphasizing the words carefully, "is greatly appreciated by myself and the academic institutions of Sol. What help were you wishing to offer?"

"My estate has a sizable hangar of its own. I'm sure it will be able to comfortably house your ship for the duration of your stay here on Earth, as a token of the Cordelle family's appreciation." The officers were glancing back and forth at one another, trading glances and shrugs as the two young women conversed. "Would you find this agreeable, doctor?"

"I could be convinced," she said casually. "It sounds like a much more efficiently run station than this hangar." The officers' frowns grew deeper, but Joane only offered a wry smile.

"We have a state-of-the art facility, I assure you," she responded with gravitas. "If you would follow me to the estate so we can arrange a spot in the hangar for you, I can guarantee that your ship will be undisturbed until your return. Correct?" Joane shot a glance at the officers and raised an eyebrow.

"Of course, ma'am," they said in unison, straightening. Joane gave them a courteous smile that didn't reach her eyes. Joane led the scientist away, heading for the nearest exit as the officers began speaking animatedly to each other. Dr. Reindare had the two heavy metal briefcases under each arm.

"It's a pleasure to make your acquaintance," Joane said as they walked towards the exit in tandem. "I'm sure you have a wealth of stories to share. Joane Cordelle."

The doctor didn't return the nicety, but gave her a curt nod. "Dr. Ahsha Reindare." Joane didn't know it then, but her life's trajectory had just changed.

# Chapter 18
## Bad Cop, Sad Cop

TRISTAN wished the doors on this ship could slam. After pounding her fist against the wall panel so hard it made the bottom of her hand sore, it merely slid into place with a hiss of hydraulics. The sound of her head hitting the door as she leaned against it was louder than it closing. She let it hold her weight for a moment, her back pressed against the firm metal as she hoped Joane wouldn't try to follow her. After a moment, she put her head in her hands and let out a single, pathetic sob. Stars, she needed a good cry. Of course, she couldn't have that because there was an unconscious senator in her bed, and the woman making her cry was in the cockpit. It wasn't like she could throw on a vacsuit and do a quick spacewalk either, not at Redshift speeds. That would be a pretty spectacular way to kill herself, she thought. Whatever was left of her after the inertia was done with her would probably be scattered across a few million miles of void. The Tristan Nebula, she thought darkly.

She needed a private place to feel sorry for herself, but there was nowhere private on this ship. *Her* ship, and she couldn't go anywhere she knew she wouldn't be disturbed. After a few more sobs wracked her body, she decided to head to her room. Orion wouldn't be waking up for a few hours if Joane gave them the good painkillers. She walked quickly through the halls, stepping heavily to make sure Joane could hear her footsteps receding and have an idea of where she was. Did Tristan want her to follow, or stay away? She didn't know. She didn't know anything anymore. Joane was just a swirling vortex of conflicting feelings in her mind, and it was driving her up the wall. Tristan had always been good *with* people, she knew how to talk to them, cozy up, and make friends. Joane, meanwhile, was good *at* people. She was an analyst first and foremost, always picking apart everyone they met the instant she saw them. Tristan was jealous of her for that. She wished she could glance over Joane's features and see exactly how she operated, what she was thinking, and what her next move might be instead of just how sharp her jawline was and the way her hair fell into her eyes.

Somehow, she made it to her room on autopilot, barely seeing through the tears swimming in her eyes. She tapped in the code, and almost walked into the door when the red light shone and the alarm sounded at her. She let out a frustrated groan and wiped her eyes before trying again, and this time the door chimed and slid open easily. She stepped into her room, taking in the sight of Orion splayed out on her bed. The skeletal brace in their chest was obviously making progress, but their chest still wasn't rising and falling the way it normally should. The heavy bruises around their eyes had faded slightly, but it still looked like they lost a bar fight, and badly.

"You awake?" she asked, her voice deeper and choked with her crying. Orion's hand twitched, but they continued to sleep, open-mouthed and clearly deeply unconscious. She sighed and walked over to the chair Joane had brought in to interrogate the senator and collapsed into it. It was one of the dining chairs from the ship's kitchen, so it wasn't terribly comfortable. Tristan curled into it, planting her feet on the floor and her elbows on her knees before putting her head down and grasping the top of her head with her hands. Then, she let herself cry out every feeling she'd been stifling since Joane had sat down at her booth at the Drunken Duck. She cried for a long time, cursing herself for being so open with Joane while cursing herself for not telling Joane more. She was confused and angry and tired and there were still holes in her legs where she'd been shot not two days ago. She was exhausted, but she knew if she fell asleep, she would dream of that damn tunnel back home, so she fought to stay awake. It was better to suffer her feelings in the real world than go back to that awful dark hole in the ground. Unfortunately for her, her body had other ideas. Even as she tried to fight harder, she felt herself drifting off, the soreness of her chest and shoulders easing as her muscles relaxed and she felt her mind drifting and losing focus.

She had been right about the dream. The last time she had this dream, Joane had been there with her, taking her hand and lifting her to her feet. They had walked together, hand in hand, and Tristan hadn't worried about the engines in the distance. She'd been happy. This time, she was just as alone as she'd ever been.

She wasn't sure how long she'd been walking in the dream before a soft voice filled the tunnel. As soon as she realized that the voice wasn't part of the dream, she realized that she was, in fact, dreaming, and the rocks and stone around her fell away. She bolted upright, almost falling out of her chair as she gasped, taking deep breaths to try and steady herself as her senses came back to her. When the voice came again, she understood the words.

"Ma'am, are you alright?" it was saying. She sucked in another deep breath and let it out quickly, looking wildly for the source. There was Orion, not entirely sitting up but not lying down and certainly awake. Their eyes were bruised and ugly, but the green in them shone with awareness and focus and a little bit of concern.

"Must have nodded off," she said hoarsely, glancing over at the clock display on the wall. Time was hard to keep track of during space travel, and it was almost impossible to do so while in a Redshift. Some ancient Solan philosopher had once said that moving at the speed of light meant you experienced less time than someone moving slower, or something like that. While Redshifting was much faster than the speed of light, the theory was still true, in a way. Thankfully, scientists a lot smarter than Tristan had long ago designed Temporal Dilation Inhibitors so that they wouldn't come out of the Redshift to find that several years had passed and more planets had gone missing. Tristan wasn't sure when she fell asleep, but by her estimate, it had been about four hours. She groaned, leaning forward and feeling the ache in her chest from crying so hard earlier.

"You've been crying," Orion pointed out. Their voice was strained, like they were trying to speak and hold their breath at the same time.

"No I haven't," Tristan said, immediately sniffling. *Damn it.*

"What were you definitely not crying about?" they asked, seeming genuine in that political way that made Tristan doubt how genuine they were.

"What's it matter to you?"

"Well, it's been a difficult few days; I wouldn't mind having a conversation that doesn't feel like an interrogation or a string of barely concealed threats," they explained. "From what I can remember, you seem more like the 'good cop' between you and your partner."

"'Partners,'" Tristan muttered sarcastically, the word tasting bitter in her mouth. "Just because I'm not interrogating you doesn't mean I trust you either, Senator."

Orion nodded, closing their eyes and settling into the pillows stacked behind their head. "I can't blame you, honestly," they sighed. "It seems like the two of you have had quite the journey, and what reason would you have to trust anyone from the Consortium right now? However, I can't help but notice that I'm still alive, so you must have decided not to kill me yet. That means I prefer you all a lot more than some of my colleagues at the moment."

Tristan gave a small laugh. "How are you feeling, by the way?"

"Awful," Orion said, gesturing to their chest.

"Understandable," Tristan said. "I would give you more painkillers, but your body probably can't handle that much more of a dose." Orion looked saddened, but nodded.

"It's alright," they muttered. "I wouldn't mind being awake for a bit anyways. I need time to process everything that's happened."

Tristan scoffed. "Well, that's the first sleep I've gotten in two days and let me just say, I haven't been able to process anything."

"That's not very comforting," Orion said. They were silent for a while, then a shadow passed across their face. "The doctor, Dr. Toscana, did she really…" The look on Tristan's face must've been all the answer Orion needed, because their face looked even more stricken than before, something Tristan didn't think was possible. Their bottom lip trembled, and Tristan figured they might have cried if they could manage it. "She…she was there to help people."

"I'm sorry," was all Tristan could manage. "We tried to help, but we were lucky even to get you out of there."

"I know," Orion said, their voice dripping with sadness. "I know, and I do appreciate it. I just…don't understand."

"That seems to be the standard around here, welcome to the party," Tristan said. "We're trying to figure it out as best we can, so if you come up with anything about the people who tried to kill us, we'd really appreciate it."

Orion fell silent again, slowly wracking their brain and giving the occasional wince as a tinge of pain flashed across their features. "The man with the soldiers, his name is…Regille. Argus Regille. He's a senator from a few sectors over; I've only met him in passing a few times, but he didn't seem to like me that much. He seemed like the standard old guard politician, an inoffensive bureaucrat just looking to maintain his position. I have no idea why he would…do what he did."

"I don't suppose you know anyone who would?" Orion shook their head, unsurprisingly. "What about other relief stations, have there been any sort of attacks like what happened at Cygnus?" She wasn't as good of an interrogator as Joane, but she could still draw information out of someone like ore out of a rock.

"No, there were no attacks, except…" Orion trailed off, staring at the far wall for a moment. "Oh no."

"Oh no?"

"I've spoken to some representatives from the other vanished worlds. We've formed a sort of half-committee, half-support group. Senator Mertes from the Lalande sector, one of the relief outposts in her region was apparently destroyed by a 'localized gravitational anomaly' that didn't register at any other location in the area." Orion was looking at their hands. "Do you think that…"

"It's possible," Tristan said. "Right now, it wouldn't be a bad idea to question everything we think we know."

"I need to speak to the others in the group," Orion said, scrambling. "If you would help me to the communications center of the ship, I can try and reach out to the frequency, maybe we can-" They were trying to move, throwing the covers back to slowly twist out of the bed, when Tristan stood up and tried to settle them back down. Joane had already given her hell for speaking to Orion; she shuddered to think what she might say if Tristan let Orion start making calls across the universe. She was no doctor, but she remembered the way a skeletal brace felt and knew if they tried to move too much it could collapse.

"Alright, alright, listen," she said, darting around to Orion's side of the bed and gently easing them back down. "I like where your head's at, but there are a few problems. First of all, we have absolutely no idea who we can trust right now, so any sort of communication is a bad idea. I know you didn't do anything wrong, and neither did we. However, for the time being, we may or may not be fugitives of the Consortium, so we need to act like it. Secondly, even if it were a good idea, we're in a Redshift right now, so the communications system isn't even working."

"A Redshift? I thought Redshift drives were dangerous! And illegal!"

Tristan shrugged. "You're alive right now," she pointed out, "so you've lived a lot longer than you would have without one." Orion swallowed hard and nodded quietly.

"Understandable, however, I really think that we need to let people know what's happening. I have a-" Their hand went to their chest and found only bandages. "Where's my jacket?" Tristan pointed to the other side of the bed, where it had been haphazardly thrown as she tried to stabilize both them and Joane. Orion reached for it, letting out a high-pitched whine as their arm stretched for the gray sleeve. After a minute of struggling, they managed to find the breast pocket of the coat and fished out a small device, designed to look like the silver and blue wings of the Consortium. "This," they explained, "is a senator's badge. It allows me to activate a signal in an emergency situation that alerts every Consortium senator across the universe if I set it to. The vanishings are a universal problem; if Senator Regille or others are causing them, that information *needs* to be made public."

There was something hidden under Orion's expression as they brandished the badge. It was something Tristan had caught a brief glimpse of when her and Joane had been in the medical bay aboard the relief station. Orion, for all their confusion and naivety, was missing a planet. Joane had her doubts, and she was entitled to them, but Tristan could tell that above all else, Orion was loyal to their people. If there was someone responsible for what had happened, they wanted, no, *needed* to see them brought to justice. Tristan examined the badge and considered their options. Alerting the entire Consortium meant that everyone on Regille's side would know they were onto them, but it also meant that everyone else would know too. It was just a question of how many people would be on their side once everything came out. "That's a risk, senator," she said. "If you do that, you put a target on your back. You have no way of knowing how many friends you'll have left in the Consortium, or how many of them will even believe you."

Orion glanced at the badge, then curled their fingers around it slowly. They looked afraid, lost, and unsure, but they set their jaw in place and shook their head. "It's a risk I have to take. There's already a target on my back anyways. If it helps us find Cygnus and the other planets; no matter what happens before then, it'll be worth it."

"You'll need to talk it over with Joane first, I think," Tristan said. "Because it'll be putting us in more danger, too. We're trying to find the vanished worlds too, but it might be safer to lay low until we have something more concrete than the word of a junior senator. No offense."

"None taken," Orion said, looking offended. "I suppose you're right, though. We don't have much evidence besides the giant bruise on my chest and our word. I should ask though, who are the two of you, really? What part do you play in all of this?"

Tristan sighed, taking a step back to prop one foot against the wall and lean her head back. What part did she have to play? She was just a wanderer, and Joane was just a mercenary, and they were supposed to take down a government conspiracy? It was hard to fathom how she had gone from Joane paying her to help find Ahsha to an enemy of the state running for her life within a month, but here she was. "A…former colleague of Joane and myself was investigating the vanishings. She apparently thought Cygnus-4 would be the next planet to vanish, so she went there to study it. Apparently, she was right, because she vanished right along with it."

"Your friend knew Cygnus was going to vanish? Did she say how she knew?"

"My *former colleague*," Tristan stressed the words, "did not. She never was fond of explaining her ideas to people she thought she was smarter than. *If* she's alive, and *if* we can find her, I'd be happy to ask her about it once I get done slapping her across the face."

Orion ignored the last part of Tristan's sentence, turning their face away as thoughts visibly crossed their face. They mouthed a few words to themselves before finally speaking again. "Miss Ninomae, there are *countless* planets in the universe. Twenty-seven of them have vanished in the past year, something unheard of. Until now, people have believed that the vanishings were completely random. Unless your friend made an incalculably lucky guess, she figured out some connection between the vanishings and was able to predict the next one, meaning they can't be random."

"I understand what you're saying," Tristan responded. "If they aren't random, we can predict the next one, and maybe find a way to stop it." Orion shook their head.

"No. Well, yes, but that's not what I mean. If the vanishings aren't random, that means there is a reason those twenty-seven planets vanished. In all of this, there is one thing that everyone wants to know. Some people think the planets are being moved, some think they've been destroyed, some creative types even think they've moved to another dimension. One thing all those people don't claim to know, though, is *why?* The person you're looking for may just know. If we find her, we can explain the vanishings. She very well may be the key to solving all of this."

Tristan chuckled a bit despite the seriousness of the situation. "Well, if she were here to hear you say that, she would be insufferably pleased with herself. Unfortunately, or fortunately, depending on how well you know her, Ahsha isn't here right now. So, until we find your planet, we won't know why."

Orion's face fell, and their shoulders sank in dejection. "So it's still hopeless, then? No answers, no steps closer, just leads too far away because we don't have the missing link."

"We might," Tristan said, trying not to sound too hopeful. She didn't want to give Orion false hope just to bring them down again. "We have the data drives from Ahsha's ship, and she was monitoring just about every reading she could from Cygnus and the other vanished worlds' gravity wells. Joane started talking about an idea she had earlier, but I'm not sure if she's still working through the data. There's a chance that we cobble together some sort of answer that could point us in Cygnus' direction. It's a lot to sift through; it could take days to find what we're looking for."

"Do we have days?" Orion asked. "The Consortium is after us; planets could be vanishing as we speak!"

"It's not a question of *if*, I'm afraid," Tristan said, gesturing towards the back of the room. "Hear that Redshift drive? I plotted the longest straight course I could to get us as far away from Cygnus as I could without throwing us into a star or crashing into an asteroid. Once you start a Redshift, the computer takes over. If I tried to take us out of it now, the inertial dampeners would fail and the ship would tear itself apart faster than you can blink."

"So you're saying we're trapped."

"In a way," Tristan conceded, "but at the same time, we're as close to safe as we could possibly be right now. We're going far too fast to track or follow, and even if they know what direction we're moving, they don't know how far we'll go before the shift ends and we're back at voidpace. Of course, once we get to that point, any trackers your people put on my ship will start pinging again, and who knows how long we'll have before they're on our asses again."

Orion swallowed. "Your ship was logged," they said. "None of the engineers said they installed a tracker, but like you said, it's time to start doubting everything. How long until the shift ends?"

"It's been about two days since we left Cygnus," Tristan began, pausing when she saw Orion's eyes widen. "So about a week and a half. That's enough time for me to try and find any trackers on the inside of the ship, but there may be untraceable ones on the hull outside that I won't be able to find until I can leave the ship and check for myself."

Orion put their head in their hands and groaned, long strands of brown hair falling past their fingers. "Two weeks?" they asked, incredulous. "We have no idea what's going on back in the Cygnus system, or anywhere else for that matter, and we're supposed to just sit here for two weeks?"

"Joane and I already had to do it once. Consortium ships were trailing us on the way to Cygnus, and it was our only option." It was strange to think that the anxiety that had filled her during that first Redshift was absent now. Tristan didn't want to be used to all this, but she supposed it was the closest thing her mind had to a coping mechanism right now. She had so many things going through her mind that there simply wasn't room for the dread of waiting just yet.

"How did you even pass the time?" Orion breathed. "Just waiting and not knowing…I don't know how to manage." Tristan nodded in understanding. She tried to think about how they'd managed the first Redshift. Mostly, they'd kept each other busy, trying to think of plans for every possible outcome, running repairs, remembering better times.

"Can you repair a ship?" she asked, already knowing the answer. Orion shook their head sadly, like she expected. "Do you drink?"

"Not very often."

"Well, get ready for that to change," she said, trying to give them a warm smile as she did. Their grimace implied that it didn't have the desired effect. "Listen, don't strain yourself too much. After all, your ribs are still growing back together. Right now, just try to rest and we'll let you know what we find out when we can."

"I don't know if I can rest right now, Miss Ninomae," they said lamely.

"First of all, call me Tristan," she interjected. She sighed. She didn't want to go back to the cockpit to see what Joane was up to; Tristan wasn't ready to face her again so soon after her last outburst. However, if she didn't placate Orion, she had a feeling they would run her up the wall. "If it will make you feel better, I will go check on what Joane is working on. I'll explain everything we talked about, and see if she's found anything out, and then we can all have a nice chat over some dinner. That sound good?"

"It's about as good as I could hope for right now," Orion said with a shrug. "I am starving." Tristan was halfway out the door when she remembered herself and turned back.

"About that, no solid foods until the brace is done setting," she said, wincing apologetically. "If your stomach expands too quickly, it could distend your ribs or even re-break them."

"*Re-break them?*" Orion asked, putting a hand to their chest. Tristan smiled slyly at the look of horror on their face.

"Gotcha," she laughed.

Orion looked stricken as they processed the joke. "And here I was thinking you were the nice one." Tristan could tell, even with their strained voice, they were trying to make a joke. She laughed a bit and walked out the door, leaving it open behind her. *Oh no*, she thought, *I like them*. It would hurt all the more if they didn't make it out of this.

# Chapter 19
## Chopping Off Loose Ends

ARGUS Regille watched the primary relief platform for the Cygnus system implode on itself, the energy generation facilities erupting into blue flames as the rest of the large station crumpled like a ball of paper preparing to be unceremoniously tossed into a waste bin. As he looked up from his desk to stare out the window of his personal craft, he took a moment to appreciate the power at work. A few conveniently placed gravity well generators, some structural supports weakened just slightly, and *voila*, a tragic, unpredictable accident that would consume all the evidence that he and the others had ever been there. All evidence, that was, except for one pesky senator and the two women who had orchestrated their escape. The blue flames of void-harnessed fuel sputtered quickly in the vacuum, but not before they tore through half of the wreckage, incinerating enough of the bodies and filling the space with enough dark matter radiation to render any investigation into the collapse a futile effort. Cygnus' relief station would be left to drift, sucked into the gravity well left behind by its planet, and pulverized into atoms. Argus took a moment to think of the people on the station, however many there may have been, drifting lifelessly through the cold void. Regrettable, yes, but necessary. The issue of Orion Masenna was of far greater concern to him at the moment. Satisfied that the station had been completely obliterated, he returned his gaze to the desk and the datapad concealed under a panel of Eridian mahogany wood.

He took the featureless black stylus out of the pad and twirled it between his fingers, absentmindedly fidgeting as he tried to prepare his message. He would have to prepare several official, carefully worded addresses today, and this was the one he was dreading the most. He would have to prepare a letter to the Consortium, expressing his sadness at the tragedy of the Cygnus-4 relief station's destruction and the death of Senator Masenna. There would also be a letter addressed to the Vanished Worlds Relief Subcommittee, explaining how he was overseeing a shipment of medical supplies to the sector when the accident occurred. That one would have to be drafted extremely carefully, with just enough truths sprinkled in to be irrefutable in the event his presence in the system drew any unwanted questions. This one, however, was not just to his colleagues, but his *allies*. How would he explain the loose ends he had failed to tie up with an entire regiment of troops under his command?

For a time, he had considered lying. It could be done. The station was gone, and the nosy group had vanished. Perhaps they would be of no more trouble. No evidence would be needed either way to prove their deaths if their lives didn't throw any wrenches into the plan. However, Regille knew it would be folly. If they turned up again, if they grew even *closer* to the truth, his attempt to cover up the failure would only draw more ire from his allies. No. He was respected, he was capable, and most importantly, he was *established*. He had been a part of this since the beginning, one small, easily managed blunder wouldn't be enough to see him thrown out. He just had to be more careful and not allow any more mistakes.

The door to his private quarters chimed twice in quick succession, followed by a brief silence, and a third, longer chime. Out of habit, Regille powered down the datapad and slid the panel of his desk back over it, concealing the device. Once it slid into place, he cleared his throat and called out. "Come in." The ship's onboard computer read his voice, and the door split in half vertically before sliding open to reveal one of the blackguard soldiers. Regille quickly glanced at their left shoulder pauldron, where he saw three orange, gently glowing stripes.

"Captain," he said, acknowledging the highest ranking member of the regiment he had brought to Cygnus. "Thank you for meeting with me."

The captain inclined his head as he entered, his face invisible behind the curves of his jet black helmet. "Of course, Senator," his voice was muffled and slightly modulated to conceal his identity. "I just finished my debriefing with the rest of my soldiers that survived the incursion."

*Incursion.* Regille sneered at the word, and the captain must have seen it too, because he straightened ever so slightly more. Regille could almost feel the sweat on the back of the man's neck; he could sense the slight tremor of the man's hands as he stood and waited for his answer. *Good,* he thought, *let him feel a fraction of the weight his men have laid on my shoulders.* "Incursion," he repeated, rolling the word over his lips, testing the sound of it. "One senator and two unremarkable civilians. I would like to know what planet you're from, because obviously our worlds have different definitions of the word, Captain."

"Senator, I only meant-"

"No," Regille said, holding up a hand slowly to silence the man. "That won't be necessary. I did not request you here for an explanation, nor excuses. Tell me, Captain, how their ship was allowed to escape the system? You all are outfitted with some of the finest equipment available, and those two women were able to not only waltz out of the station while carrying Senator Masenna, but they also killed several of your men in the process. I monitored security camera footage from the station, I've read the after-action report, and I've spoken to the medical technicians treating the wounded. I know all about what happened back there, Captain. You are simply here to help me understand why."

The captain swallowed so hard that Regille could hear it through his helmet, and kept his gaze focused on the wall behind the senator as he spoke. "Senator, the women were able to seize the equipment from some of our soldiers. With the gravity-propelled launchers, they were able to pierce our body armor and cause meaningful damage in a way they would not have been able to with conventional pressurized-air weapons." He paused, waited. Regille steepled his fingers and took a moment to breathe. He supposed that was at least a testament to the effectiveness of their equipment, which hadn't seen much extended use just yet. Still, if it could be so easily commandeered and turned against them…that would be a problem for the tech department to figure out, he supposed.

"Very well," he said with a sigh. That was probably the most satisfying answer he was going to get during this conversation. "That doesn't explain how they were able to fight through an entire regiment of similarly armed soldiers. They were wounded civilians, Captain, not hardened soldiers. I struggle to understand how they survived to make it to their ship."

The captain, surprisingly, seemed to perk up slightly at this. "As a matter of fact, Senator, I received a dossier on the two women we encountered earlier." He pulled a small datastick out a container on his armor and placed it on the desk. Regille took it, examining the simple silver and blue design of the device, and retrieved his hidden datapad once again. It wouldn't go well if this datastick appeared on the access logs for his officially issued and monitored Consortium datapad. Instead, he inserted the stick into the concealed datapad, setting it off to the side while scrolling information filled the screen, followed by images of the two women. He didn't bother looking closely at the moment. "These are the two women spotted recently in the Waning Crescent Nebula?" he surmised. The captain nodded, and Regille swore. He had hoped against hope that this was all merely a coincidence. No one was supposed to notice a pattern, no one was supposed to look into the vanishings, no one was supposed to get this close. Argus knew just how much danger these two could mean for the whole operation. They needed to be dealt with, and soon.

Regille rubbed his brow for a moment, biting his tongue to try and bring his mind into focus. Too many variables, too many problems, too many loose ends. How he wished everything was as simple as the pulverized station outside his window: a large, slow problem he could crush into nothingness and forget about. It was the smaller problems, those ones that slipped through his fingers, that were the true cause for alarm. "Lastly, Captain, and then you can go," he said. "Explain one more thing to me. These women boarded their craft, which I requested disabled. They were able to take off and exit the station, despite most of the regiment being present in the hangar at the time. They were then able to fly away from the station, evaded our fighters, and then...what? I ordered a tracker placed on the hull of their ship, and every time I check the signal, I receive no pings whatsoever. Was the ship destroyed in the chase, and you simply decided to wait to tell me? Because if you wanted to make it a pleasant surprise, Captain, you should know that I do not care for surprises."

To prove his point, Regille spun a monitor on his desk to face the captain, showing the tracking signal history of the device planted on the crimson and white starship that had been impounded. For nearly fourteen hours, it had remained stationary in the station's hangar, then a brief log of motion, followed by nothingness.

"Senator, my pilots all reported that the ship engaged a Redshift drive before they could successfully eliminate the target. The ship in question was clearly heavily modified for speed and durability, and it clearly has an exceptional pilot."

"Exceptional pilot, yes," Argus grumbled. "I thought we had hired the most exceptional pilots there were. A Redshift drive, you say? So, there's a decent chance they've catapulted themselves into an asteroid belt somewhere and we won't be hearing from them again. I wish I could be that optimistic, Captain, truly, but this line of work does not *have* a margin of error."

"I understand, Senator," he said lamely, clearly at a loss for words. "This was a…unique situation. It won't happen again, I assure you." Regille nodded, and slowly pushed himself up from his desk. A small pain in his back pulsed as he did so, and he grimaced a bit. He was far from a young man, but that pain reappearing meant he was overworked and overstressed.

"May I show you something, Captain?" he asked, walking slowly and deliberately towards the window. The captain wordlessly approached and stood by Senator Regille's side as he gestured to the curved, tinted window and the view beyond. The flames of Cygnus-4's relief station had died by now, replaced by a tangle of dull gray metal cast in strange shadows by the distant sun. "Impressive, isn't it? The power that has been given to us. I had them wait to destroy the station until your troops had time to collect themselves and any more loose ends on board had been dealt with, because I wanted you to see and to understand the magnitude of what it is you and I are a part of." Regille knew that the Captain was more than aware of their power, but that was not the lesson here. "I had them wait, Captain. Fail me again, and I will not extend such consideration to you and your soldiers."

"Yes sir," he said, his voice small and hushed underneath the imposing mask. Regille smiled, knowing that the message was received.

"You are dismissed. Return to your men and inform them that we will be returning to Eden's Cradle to regroup and decide how best to proceed."

The captain turned to look at the Senator. "Senator, the Cradle?" Regille was already back at his desk, preparing to examine the data that had been brought to him. He looked up, gazing at where he guessed the captain's eyes might be hidden.

"Of course, Captain," he said warmly. "At times like this, the best thing one can do is go home."

# Chapter 20
## A Perfectly Normal Dinner, Under The Circumstances

TRISTAN made her way to the cockpit slowly, rubbing sleep out of her eyes as she did. A few strands of her long black hair had fallen into disarray while she tossed and turned in the uncomfortable chair, and a knot of tension had formed somewhere in the middle of her lower back. She was sure she had had less pleasant naps in her past, but none came to mind at the moment. Eventually, she stumbled her way to the bridge and found herself before the cockpit door. She took a moment to steady herself, bracing for the inevitable confrontation with Joane. Would she try to apologize again? Would she be angry at her for keeping things bottled up? Or would she ignore the conversation entirely like so many others from the trip? Part of Tristan hoped it would be the latter, but another part of her was tired of sweeping things under the rug.

It was like the knot in her back, just endless tension driving her slowly mad. She knew it would hurt, but she knew it would ache incessantly until someone dug their knuckles into the sore spot and worked out the muscle until the knot was gone. Tristan sighed and pressed the control switch; better now than later. The door slid open to reveal an empty room, and a mixture of relief and disappointment washed over her. *Stars, what did she want?*

The pilot's chair sat empty, and a screen on the console was slowly pulsing white to display the diagnostics that had finished hours ago. Tristan crossed the cabin, looking left and right to make sure Joane wasn't sitting in one of the corner stations. Once she was sure she was alone, she tapped the blinking screen and brought the diagnostic readouts into view. Tristan scanned them for a few minutes, skimming past less important systems and focusing on things that actually mattered in the moment. She didn't like what she saw, but there wasn't much she could do about it at the moment. Any in-flight repairs she could make would be limited, and she doubted some of the damage could be fixed without visiting an actual repair facility.

Disappointing as the news was, the current Redshift seemed to be holding steady, and their life support was functioning at optimal levels. That meant they still had time to plan their next move, so she tried to focus on that. Planning their next move was a three-person job now. Orion had become just as much a part of this as her and Joane, whether or not anyone was happy about it, and that meant they deserved a say in the plan. She knew Joane wouldn't be pleased, but she would see reason eventually. At least, Tristan hoped she would. The woman was unpredictable, like a tunnel back home without any support struts. Sure, it was safer than a natural cavern, but you could never be sure of when it might collapse on you. *Oh well,* she thought, *nothing I'm not used to at this point.*

If Joane wasn't in the cockpit, she was most likely in her old room, situated somewhere atop the mountain of old and discarded clothes Tristan had stored there once she'd taken Darling as her own. Tristan made her way through the ship, stubbing her toes against boxes that had moved from places they hadn't moved in months. She shuddered, thinking about those masked Consortium soldiers on board her ship, shuffling their way through and rearranging her space. It was like walking through a maze she'd mastered over time, but suddenly the walls had shifted and the old paths she used to take lead to nothing but dead ends. It made her feel strange, like the ship that had become her home wasn't the same anymore. It didn't feel entirely like home anymore, and she couldn't quite shake that feeling.

Eventually, she found her way to Joane's door, which was closed like usual. She brought up a fist, swallowed hard, and rapped on the door a few times. She bit down on her lower lip and held her breath until she heard a gentle shuffling, followed by uneven steps on soft ground. The steps came to a stop, there was a brief pause, and the door slowly slid open, allowing a stray scarf to tumble out into the hallway. Tristan locked eyes with Joane, giving her an uneasy smile. Joane blinked slowly in response, her hair wild and unkempt, her blue eyes tired and heavy. Her jacket was half-unzipped, revealing the blue shirt underneath. It wasn't fair, Tristan thought, why did she get to wake up looking so good?

"Tris," Joane said, rubbing her eyes with the back of her hand. "Do you have any idea what time it is?" Tristan slipped her hands into her pockets and shifted her weight back and forth, cringing a bit.

"I actually don't," she admitted, watching Joane stifle a yawn. "I fell asleep for a while."

"Yeah, figures," Joane mumbled with a yawn. "I don't really know either, because of the whole...thing, but I know

I've been asleep for about forty-five minutes. The last time we talked was about…seven hours ago."

*Damn it.* She must have misread the clock when she woke up. "Shit, Joane, I'm sorry," she said, stumbling over her words. "I didn't mean to wake you up; I just wanted to see if you were hungry and able to maybe…talk about what happens next?" She waited for a moment while Joane straightened and yawned, covering her mouth with her hand. Tristan found herself staring at one strand of mostly-blond hair that was sticking almost straight up. She fought the urge to reach up and brush it down with her fingers, knowing it wouldn't be right. Her staring was interrupted by Joane's eyes going wide as she exclaimed.

"Tris!" she yelped, the drowsiness vanishing from her face. "Right, yes, I'm awake, I remember. I figured something out! I was reading through the files from Ahsha's ship and I think I have something!"

"Something good?" Tristan asked apprehensively and a bit caught off guard by Joane's sudden outburst of energy.

"Yes? No? Maybe!" Joane said rapidly, turning her body to let Tristan see into the room. There were datapads and folders of physical paper strewn in a rough circle around a pile of jackets and pants, with a Joane-sized dent in the middle of them. "I've been reading them for about six hours," Joane explained, "and I think I finally have an idea of how they're moving the planets."

"That's good news," Tristan surmised. In all honesty, she wasn't sure if the "how" was the most important question to answer right now, but more answers meant more understanding, which was something they sorely needed at the moment. "Listen, I want to hear everything, but if you're okay with it, I want Orion to be there too. They deserve to hear this too, don't you think?"

Joane stared at her for a bit, her manic expression replaced by one of gentle confusion. "I...just woke up, Tris. What?"

"I know, I know," Tristan held up her hands. "You don't trust them, but I do. We talked a little bit, and I think they may be able to help us. More importantly, we can help them. We may be up shit creek, but at least we're all in the same ship."

"I don't think that analogy makes sense," Joane said, crossing her arms. She blinked slowly. "Then again, I just woke up, so that might just be me. Tris, trusting them could mean the difference between us living or dying. If you're wrong about this..."

"You're right, Joane. Trusting them could mean the difference. What if we need them?" Joane kept her arms crossed, leaning against the doorframe and eyeing Tristan up and down. She glanced down the ship's hallways as she mulled it over for a moment. Tristan couldn't take the silence. "Do you trust me?"

"Of course," Joane said immediately. There wasn't an ounce of hesitation in her voice. "I told you that already."

"Then trust me," Tristan said, stepping closer and looking up into Joane's eyes. "Please." She was doing it again, trying to close the distance between, to offer Joane another chance to step forward into her arms.

She didn't take it. Instead, she dropped her arms to her sides. "Okay," she said, tossing her head back. "I trust you.

Give me a few minutes to wake up and collect the data I need; I'll meet you both in your room and we'll all talk."

"Alright," Tristan said, brightening. She was a bit surprised Joane was going along with this so easily. She needed to catch her right after she woke up more often. "Have you eaten? Because we haven't."

Joane looked back into her room and the nest of papers and tablets strewn across the floor, as if trying to remember. "No," she said finally. "I haven't. I'd really like to."

"Good to know we're all starving," Tristan said. "I'll get something whipped up by the time you're ready."

Joane smiled sleepily and began to reach for the door controls. "These dinners just get weirder and weirder, don't they?" She closed the door before Tristan could answer.

*      *      *

IT took about ten minutes for Tristan to pull together a simple meal for three, consisting mostly of rehydrated rice noodles with a few small strips of protein flavored like Andalarian chicken split between the three plates in a simple, tangy sauce. It was far from a luxurious meal, but it smelled decently appetizing and reminded Tristan of the meals they used to share on Darling when the money was running a bit tight. She arranged the plates on a hover tray that bobbed just slightly in the air next to her, then bent to retrieve a glass of wine from the cabinet. Unfortunately, one of the people who had raided her ship had been too clumsy with the cabinet with all her glasses in it, because it was currently lying facedown on the floor, surrounded by a few piles of crystal dust. Tristan shrugged it off and tucked the bottle under her arm; she was far past the point of worrying about germs. As she walked the gently floating tray back to her room, she took a moment to chuckle at the idea of her serving this meal to a Consortium Senator. She wondered if she could convince them that the protein strips were genuine meat. She smiled to herself as she let go of the tray, leaving it hanging in the air while she typed in the passcode to the room. The door slid open, and there was Orion, sitting up in bed looking a bit more alert than when she'd left.

"Oh good, you're alive," she said as she brought the food in.

"I seem to be," Orion said, their voice still weak and raspy, but more cheerful than she'd expected. She supposed politicians learned to pretend to be chipper early on in their careers. "Where is your mean friend?"

Tristan let out a laugh, surprising herself. "She's getting ready; apparently I was out for longer than I thought, because she'd just gone to bed after a long research session."

"So she'll be extra pleased to see me?" Orion asked, eyes going a bit wide. Tristan waved them off as she approached the bed. She hooked her foot around one of the legs of the chair she'd slept in and dragged it over to the bed. Her room wasn't furnished for sharing meals, but she could manage in a pinch.

"Don't worry about Joane too much. Sure, she's not very friendly when you first meet her, but she warms up to people eventually."

"And when does that happen?"

"I'll let you know." Tristan laughed as she grabbed two of the plates off the tray, setting them on the side of the bed, and pushed the tray towards Orion. "Don't get sauce on my sheets, alright? I've already had to wash enough blood out of them in the past few weeks."

Orion caught the tray weakly and situated it close to their chest. They picked up a fork and tentatively poked at the protein strips. Just as Tristan expected, they looked a bit reluctant. "What is it?" they asked, stirring the sauce further into the noodles.

"It's what we had," Tristan said with a shrug. "I know, I know, probably far from a catered parlor room ball with the rest of your Senator friends, but we do have wine!" Orion smiled at her, spinning their fork through the noodles.

"You know, Tristan," they said. "I'm a *junior* senator. I'm not so out of touch that I can't enjoy a simple meal. Especially now, when I'm fairly sure I could eat just about anything." They took a bite of the noodles, though Tristan noticed them avoiding the protein stick. "Hm," Orion remarked once they'd swallowed. "It's...oddly familiar. Reminds me of the dinners I had when I was away at college and had to throw something together with what I had left in the fridge."

Tristan began cutting her fake chicken with the side of her fork, taking the comment in stride. "My cooking being compared to a desperate college student's? That's high praise, Senator."

Orion didn't respond immediately, because they were busy shoveling another forkful into their mouth. They took a moment, wiping their mouth delicately with the back of their hand. It was a humorous mix, Tristan noticed, the decorum of a practiced politician mixed with a person who hadn't eaten in days. "I didn't say it didn't taste good!" they finally said. "In fact, I find myself quite nostalgic for this type of food sometimes. High class dinners surrounded by stuffed-shirts and pretentious colleagues get tiring after a while."

Tristan smirked and glared at them from under her eyebrows. "Oh yes, my deepest sympathies to you, being forced to eat all that delicious food while surrounded by other rich people."

Orion sighed, setting down their fork dramatically. "Keep in mind, one of those other rich people tried to have me killed recently. They aren't exactly good company to keep." Tristan gave them a nod of acknowledgement. "Besides, I mean it. When I was in college, or on the campaign trail eating Necessity meals, it wasn't necessarily comfortable but it felt like I was *doing* something. I was making progress, working towards a goal. Ever since I got elected, and especially in the past month, I've just been…drifting in cold Void."

"Carving new caverns?" Tristan said, tasting a bite of the noodles. She had to admit, Orion wasn't terribly wrong. It had the taste of a meal cobbled together with whatever the chef had left in their pantry. However, it only tasted that way because it was cobbled together with whatever she had left in the pantry.

"Pardon?" Orion asked, testing a small bite of the protein bar. They chewed slowly, clearly put off by the soft, chewy texture of it, but they swallowed nonetheless.

"Oh, just a saying from back home," she explained. "It meant you were putting all your energy into slow, tedious work and not making any progress."

Orion considered it for a moment. "Rude, but not unfair," they said with a sigh. "Where are you from, by the way? Here we are, jetting across the universe together and I barely know the two of you."

"It's been a bit too busy for introductions, I guess," Tristan said with a dismissive shrug. "I'm not really from anywhere, just a hunk of rock so insignificant the Consortium didn't feel like giving it an actual name."

"You're from one of the Hollow Worlds?" they surmised, something odd flashing across their face. Tristan couldn't read it precisely, but they clearly stopped themselves from saying whatever it was that was on their mind.

"Uhm, yes," she said, narrowing her eyes. She had to remember she was talking to a politician. Easy-going and vulnerable as they might be, they had to know when to hide just enough of the truth. "I don't care for the title, but that's what it is."

"My apologies," they amended. "So, you consider it your home?" The question startled Tristan. She didn't think about it much, mostly because thinking about the planet she was born on filled her with dread. Still, her family was from there. She was born and raised there. She may have tried to escape that planet the second she had a chance to, but she didn't know if she could say she hated it.

"I...I think I did," she answered finally, tapping her fork against her food as she spoke, "but I don't anymore. Darling is the closest thing I have to a home now."

"Is that what you call Joane?" Orion said with a kind smile, causing Tristan's eyes to shoot open. She wordlessly reached for the wine glass and tore the cork out with her nails.

The pain of it stung, but she ignored it, tilting the bottle back and taking a deep swig of the dark purple wine. She swallowed hard, feeling the gentle tinge of alcohol on her tongue and wishing it was something stronger. She held out the bottle to Orion, who glanced around for a glance before uneasily grabbing the neck of the bottle.

"No," Tristan said, shaking her head so hard that waves of hair passed in front of her eyes. "Joane and I aren't...we don't...Darling is the ship's name; that's my darling."

"Ah," Orion said, watching Tristan's face curiously. "Well, I didn't expect to be eating my own foot for dinner tonight, but here I am." They gave her an uneasy smile. "I apologize, I didn't mean to assume; it's just that you two...well, never mind. On the subject of Joane, though, what about her? What corner of the universe does she call home?"

"Here and there," came a sudden voice from the hallway. There was Joane, looking refreshed and put together, her jacket zipped up and her hair laying down like normal. Tristan had to admit she missed the authentic nature of how she'd looked fresh out of bed. She was leaning against the doorway, and she wondered just how much of the conversation she had heard. Orion looked over at her, obviously surprised.

"Oh!" they said, trying to sound cheerful. Tristan saw their grip on their fork tighten slightly. "Why don't you join us? Your friend has prepared a lovely meal."

"Is that sarcasm?" Joane asked, looking at Tristan. Tristan gave a shrug.

"It's nothing special, but we do have wine." Joane perked up at that. As if on cue, Orion took a sip of the wine and quickly came away coughing. They began inspecting the label as they tried to clear their throat while Joane and Tristan rolled their eyes at one another. She came into the room, accepting a plate from Tristan with a smile and nod before sitting as far away from Orion as she could manage on the bed. She tore into her food, avoiding looking at either of them. They ate in silence for a few minutes, the bottle of wine slowly being passed around between the three of them. Once the silence had gotten sufficiently awkward, Joane set her fork down, covering her mouth with one hand while she finished a bite of the false chicken.

"This is delicious, Tris," she said. "Thank you." Tristan let her fork dip slightly in her hand, looking up at her with confusion. She stammered a bit, trying to remember the right response.

"Oh, of course," Orion chimed in. "Thank you, Tristan. It's quite good."

"You're both welcome," Tristan managed, enjoying the feeling of gratitude. It had been a while since she'd been genuinely thanked for a meal, and it made warm feelings spread through her chest. "It isn't my best work, but I try."

"What does your best work look like, if I may ask?" Orion said, setting their empty plate down on the tray and leaning back into the pillows.

"Oh, let's see," Tristan said, mirroring the motion and leaning back in her chair. "Joane? What do you think?"

Joane chewed ponderously for a few seconds, then smiled as the memory came to her. "Those butter-glazed tubers from Andromedae-7," she said. "With that blend of 'secret spices' that you refused to tell us about."

Tristan remembered it fondly. She had to hand it to Joane; they had been delicious. The secret spice blend, she remembered, was every spice they had in storage. She was beginning to think she did her best work when she didn't think her meals through and just tossed things together. "That was the first meal Ahsha admitted to liking, you know," Tristan said. "She came to me afterwards and asked me to make it again sometime."

"Really?" Joane said. Tristan nodded smugly. "She never did that for my cooking."

"Well, it was about the only approval I ever got out of her," Tristan scoffed. "I swear sometimes, I've met rocks less stony than that woman."

"I assume you're talking about your *'former colleague?'*" Orion piped up, mimicking Tristan's emphasis. Joane, who was taking a drink from the bottle, jerked forward and nearly spit the wine onto the bed as she fought back a laugh. Tristan leaned forward and snatched the bottle from her hand and took a vindictive swig.

"If that was supposed to be me, Senator," she said, pointing a finger at them, "I'll toss you out the airlock. And you, too." She narrowed her eyes at Joane, who was still laughing.

The other woman took a moment to collect herself. "Oh come on, Tris, that was spot on!" They both knew it wasn't, but Tristan couldn't stop herself from cracking a smile. It was good to see Joane laugh; she didn't do that often.

"To answer your question, dick, yes. Ahsha Reindare, Doctor of Astronomy, Astral Geography, Inter-galactic meteorology, and about five other things that she'd talk your ear off about if you so much as mention it."

"She sounds like a piece of work," Orion said, raising an eyebrow at Joane. "Tristan was telling me a bit about your past relationship earlier." Joane crossed her arms and settled in, having finished her meal as well.

"Ahsha is…a complicated woman," Joane explained to them, pausing to find the right words. "She's an intellectual, not a people person. Obviously, she's far from perfect-"

"She told you I was a drug addict who stole your money and the ship," Tristan interjected. Orion's mouth dropped open in shock.

"She did what?" they asked, but Joane and Tristan both waved a hand as if to say, *it's a long story.*

"In all fairness," Joane said. "You *did* take the ship. As for…the rest of it, I know she has a lot to answer for. When we find her, she will; I'll make sure of it." There was an edge to her voice, an anger simmering beneath the surface of her calm exterior that made Tristan, for some reason, actually believe her for once. "There's a lot I have to say to that woman."

"Well, you'll have to get in line," Tristan muttered after taking a heavy drink. She wished the wine would go ahead and take effect. She could feel a sort of lightness in her brain, but not nearly enough to dive into the past just yet. She only passed the bottle to Orion reluctantly. "I've got some new dents in my ship and in *me* because of her latest stunt."

"Surely it hasn't been all bad?" Joane asked, some sarcasm in her voice, but Tristan picked up on a more genuine question hiding beneath the surface. She was crossing her arms, drawing into herself and hesitating as she spoke, drawing Tristan's eyes to her face. She took a moment to stare at her, the angle of her jaw, the set of her shoulders, the still-messy hair. She found her breath catching a bit and collected herself.

"Far from it," she said, her voice almost a whisper. Joane stared back in silence, chewing her bottom lip in thought as they gazed into each other's eyes.

Orion looked back and forth between the two, their mouth a thin line of confusion. "Uhm, ladies? I would offer to give you a moment alone, but I…can't walk." Joane immediately blushed and looked away from Tristan, who mirrored the motion as she felt her own face turn a dark, slate gray. She cleared her throat for a solid few seconds.

"Joane, I believe you had done some research earlier, and you wanted to tell us about it?" she said loudly, looking up for just a moment to stare daggers at the Senator. They gave her the smallest, almost imperceptible, most insufferably smug shrug she had ever seen.

"Why yes, Tristan," Joane said, her voice cold and formal. "I have very important findings and research that I wanted to share with you all." She pulled her datapad out of the side pocket of her jacket and pointed the top of it at the far wall, where it projected a simple blue holographic display. There was a large circle in the middle of the display, surrounded by 5 thin circles with heavier dots arranged somewhere on each line. Joane tapped another button, and the 5 smaller circles began to move, following the path of their lines at a steady pace. A small numerical display showed the galactic standard date about a week before Cygnus-4 vanished. "Senator, this might seem familiar to you, but this is the

Cygnus solar system," Joane began. "According to planetary mapping data that Ahsha acquired from an observatory on Cygnus-4, the orbits and revolutions of every planet in the system were proceeding on their normal trajectory immediately before the vanishing." She clicked another button and the circles began moving faster until the counter displayed the date and time of the vanishing. Sure enough, as Cygnus-4 was moving across the line, the circle representing it disappeared. "Now, Ahsha has gathered some basic information on Cygnus-4. By that, I mean she could probably write an atlas of the planet's history and defining characteristics. Can either of you tell me what might make Cygnus-4 special?"

"It has the highest number of population centers of any planet in the system," Orion pointed out, a sad edge to their voice. Tristan turned away from the graph to see them staring at the spot where Cygnus-4's dot had been. Their eyes had gone glassy.

"Yes," Joane agreed. "But not what I'm looking for. What else? Look at what you see here." Tristan leaned forward, pushing herself out of the chair slowly and taking a step towards the display hanging in the air. She examined the space where Cygnus had been, then glanced over at each of the other planets in turn. *Think like Ahsha*, she told herself. *Wait, no.* She was smart enough to figure this out, she knew it. She saw it, even as the thought crossed her mind.

"Moons," she said, holding a hand up to the display. Her fingers crossed through the hologram displaying a miniscule orbit around Cygnus-2. "Every planet in the system has at least one moon, but not Cygnus-4." She looked back at

Joane, the blue light of the hologram reflecting across her face. Joane was smiling at her, her eyes shining with delight.

"Bingo," she said, glancing over her shoulder at Orion. "I did some digging, and believe it or not, out of all twenty-seven vanished worlds, not a single one of them has a moon."

"I'm not sure how this helps us," Orion began. "Yes, it's a connection between the planets, but to what end?"

"Gravity," Tristan said, still staring at where Cygnus-4's orbit was. She made a fist and placed it in the spot where it vanished. "That's what you said, right Joane? They're manipulating gravity to move the planets." She dragged her fist outward, away from the sun, crossing the orbit of Cygnus-5, which was conveniently on the other side of the star.

"Exactly," Joane continued, pressing another button and advancing the clock a few days. "Ahsha's ship kept taking readings after the vanishings, and it noticed anomalies- very small anomalies, but they are there- in the orbits of Cygnus-3 and 1." The two dots that had been closest to Cygnus-4 shifted on the graph, ever so slightly, as they watched. Both of them shifted just barely out of their paths, before settling back into a routine path. "Imperceptible to most graphing software," Joane explained, "and the people on the ground wouldn't notice it either, save maybe some strange tidal shifts."

"What do the moons have to do with it, though?" Orion asked.

Joane turned to them. "It's funny you should ask, because I was thinking about something you said, Senator. You said that people thrive together; it got me thinking about bonds and closeness and all of that. That's when I made the connection: every planet that has vanished has been alone. I looked at system maps at that time of all twenty-seven vanishings, and I found this." She tapped a few more buttons, and the image of Cygnus shrunk, while more maps filled the space around it. After a moment of buffering, 27 solar systems glowing different colors hung in the air of Tristan's room, casting shadows and strange lights around them. Then, in each one of them, a light blinked out, one by one. "You can check me if you like, and Ahsha would probably say you should because it's the closest thing we have to peer review right now. Every vanished planet was orbitally isolated. No moons, and no planets close enough in their revolution cycles to have any noticeable anomalies in their orbit."

Tristan stepped back until she was leaning against the wall. She was no longer watching the diagrams, but the woman in her bed, gesturing animatedly as she explained her thoughts. Not long ago, Tristan would have laughed her off as a conspiracy theorist. Hell, she *had* done that not long ago. Now, she was following the path, connecting the dots as Joane laid them out and coming to her own conclusions. She saw the glimmering in Joane's eyes and recognized the feeling. She recognized it because she felt it too: something she hadn't felt in a long time. It was hope. Genuine, tangible hope that they were getting somewhere with this. "They're using gravity waves of some kind to pull these planets out of their orbits," she spoke up, trying to snap the puzzle pieces together. "But they're picking planets that are far enough away from anything else because it would be obvious if the neighboring planets started getting yanked out of their orbits."

"Yes!" Joane said, hopping to her feet. "Because if you have data on gravitational anomalies affecting orbits..." She jabbed a finger at the hologram of Cygnus. "…You can reverse engineer that data to find out where gravity's pull is coming from." She clicked furiously on her datapad's screen like an eager convention speaker, and a dotted line emerged from Cygnus-3 and 1, towards the space where Cygnus-4 had been. "And once you have that, you have this." She pressed one last button, and a dotted line emerged from Cygnus-4's location and exited the system.

"We know which direction it went," Orion said, a smile creeping onto their face. The magnitude of this was starting to dawn on them too. "And because gravity is a straight pull, there wouldn't be any deviations from this path?"

Joane nodded. "I'm not a scientist," she said, a bit of cautious doubt in her voice, "but this path is my direct estimate. If we had all the time in the universe, we could go to Cygnus, follow that line, and eventually, find your planet. Unfortunately, we don't have billions of years on our hands."

"But?" Tristan said, her voice rising hopefully.

"But, there are 26 other systems we can check. Two more sets of data would be nice, but if we can get readings on gravity waves like this in even one more system, we can plot those lines on the universal map, and figure out where they intersect."

"And that's where the planets will be," Orion finished the thought, then fell back with a soft laugh.

"Holy shit, Joane," Tristan said, breathless. "This is…amazing." Joane smiled at her from across the room as a green hologram drifted past her face, highlighting her cheekbones and the line of her jaw.

"It's a start," she agreed. "I know we're all sick of Redshifts, but I figure once we leave the current one, we'll point ourselves at whichever system is closest and jump there. Tristan, if you want to look through the navigational computer, we might be able to go ahead and have a destination picked out. That way, we spend as little time on their scanners as possible."

Tristan found herself cringing as she remembered the diagnostic scans from earlier. She shifted her weight to her right foot, kissing her teeth as she prepared to ruin the positive energy in the room. "About that," she said, and Joane visibly deflated the moment she saw her face. Tristan hated having to take her smile away from her. "Darling's got a top of the line Redshift drive. In fact, it's technically souped up above the legal limit of modifications and enhancements. Sorry, Senator. Unfortunately, there's a reason most ships don't even bother installing a drive anymore. If you use it too often without giving it a chance to cool off and cycle the equipment, it'll corrode the whole device.

"You see, FTL travel is powered by a special kind of extremely unstable, volatile fuel made from standard propulsion fuel mixed with a species of bacteria that harnesses and stores ultraviolet radiation like food. Essentially, they eat starlight and keep it wrapped up inside their cell membranes. The Redshift drive delivers a highly concentrated energy beam to the cells as it burns the fuel, and releases the condensed energy of nuclear fusion as a means of hurling the ship forward. If I can be totally honest, it's a miracle it does anything but blow up the second you turn it on. The issue is, it's not a perfect process that creates a really corrosive byproduct that the drive needs time to flush out of the system. Time that we didn't give it.

"Right now, the drive is still working fine. Keeping us at this pace is a lot easier and requires less fuel than reaching the speed we're moving at. As far as I can tell, the drive is going to function perfectly normally for the rest of this trip. That's as far as the good news goes. Because we've already burnt most of the fuel we need for the shift, the drive has the bulk of the buildup it's going to get. But because it's still active, the drive can't enter the cleaning mode to prevent the corrosive byproduct from eating it from the inside. In the absolute best case scenario, we're going to not be able to use the drive for weeks while it tries to reset itself. In the worst case, it burns out not long after we leave the shift, and we have to get a new drive all together."

"No more Redshifts?" Joane asked, her voice a frightening monotone.

"Not until we get a chance to do repairs," Tristan said with a nod. "Even if the drive doesn't melt, if we fire it again before the cleaning is finished, it'll probably rupture in transit and kill us all anyway."

Orion put their head in their hands. "So, how are we going to stay mobile?" Joane continued. "If we show up at a Fastlane gate, the Consortium officers there will clock us immediately and blow us to atoms. If we try to go Voidpace, we'll never leave whatever galaxy we land in."

"Look, I know it isn't ideal," Tristan said, rubbing her eyebrows and dragging her hand down her face. "But there isn't a lot I can do. As for travel, I know a few tricks. We can maybe disguise our ship's signature and sneak through."

"That's *if* the Consortium has a bounty out for your ship," Orion pointed out. "We still don't know the full situation."

"The Consortium will be looking for us," Joane said immediately, glaring at the Senator. "There's no way they won't be. They wanted us dead at Waning Crescent, they wanted us dead at Cygnus, and they'll want us dead wherever we end up next."

"We might not have the entire Consortium trying to kill us," Tristan reminded her, calling back to her earlier conversations. "Not all of them are involved in this."

"No, but the ones that are probably made up some story about two insane women who kidnapped or killed a Cygnan Senator and attacked a relief facility. I think that will get quite the hunt stirred up, don't you two?" Joane looked back and forth between them expectantly, and Tristan had to admit she saw her point of view. A good enough lie from a trusted authority figure could turn every officer and citizen against them. "If it's one thing I've learned," Joane continued, "it's that people don't want the truth, they want answers. You have to dig in the mud for the truth. They'd rather turn and accept the first answer that's offered to them, then act like they dug it out and washed it off themselves. Ask yourselves, if you didn't know everything you know right now, which story would you be most likely to believe?"

Tristan inclined her head a bit. "I mean, I've never really had a lot of trust in the Consortium," she said, "but you're right. I told Orion, if they've made us fugitives, we have to act like fugitives."

"Or," Orion said, producing the same silver and blue badge from before, "we set the record straight." Tristan watched Joane's face as Orion launched into an explanation of the badge and how they could use it to signal the Consortium senate, trying to figure out what was going through her friend's head. The dancing lights in the room made it difficult to focus, but Joane's expression seemed like it had been carved from stone. She was motionless, her eyes set in place in a way that most people would see as boredom, but Tristan knew that Joane was laser-focused on every word. Orion continued on, explaining their idea to call for all their allies in the Consortium, expose the truth of Senator Regille and whoever he may be working with, and shut down the operation through proper legal means. It was idealistic, to say the least, but Tristan couldn't help but daydream up a future where fixing this problem could be so simple.

Finally, Orion paused for breath, visibly tired from the long-winded explanation. How tragic, Tristan thought, for a politician to lose their ability to give long speeches. She imagined it felt like losing an arm to Orion. Joane took a moment before her statuesque pose broke and she let out a long, uneven sigh. "I can't begin to tell you just how bad of an idea using that would be," she said. "Alerting this…Regille to show exactly how much we know? Broadcasting our location on an open channel to the entire universe? It's…ridiculous."

Tristan nodded sadly. She figured it would go this way.

"Miss Cordelia," Orion implored, still using the fake name she'd given them days ago. "We are three people against a group of unknown size. We all almost lost our lives just trying to escape the system. Whoever Argus is working with, they have the power to make planets disappear as if they'd never been there in the first place. It's not just that I think we don't have to face this alone; we *can't* face it alone."

"We were doing just fine when it was just the two of us," Joane sniped back. Tristan pursed her lips and wished that she hadn't brought wine to this dinner, seeing the way it loosened their tongues.

"You were captured almost immediately!" Orion said. "By doctors! Working for me! And I wasn't even looking for you!" The room went silent. Tristan watched Joane's frown and furrowed brow, waiting for her to explode. She took half a step forward towards her.

"We've made progress here, everyone," she tried to say gently. "We know what we're looking for, and we have a path forward. We've had worse odds than this, and we have almost two weeks to think of how to deal with this. Maybe we call this a successful first step, go to bed, and come back in the morning with fresher, *cooler* heads." By the time she'd finished speaking, she was at the edge of the bed, standing between Joane and Orion and twisting her neck to look at each of them in turn. Joane's expression softened while Orion's dropped into the picture of exhaustion.

"Fine," they both said at once.

"Good," Tristan said, shocked that it had worked at all. She pulled a small bottle of pills out of her pants pocket and set it on the nightstand next to Orion. "You've been drinking, so you wait until that's out of your system, or these painkillers *will* kill you, do you understand?" Orion stared at the bottle, then back at Tristan, and nodded in fear. "Alright, sleep tight." She jerked a shoulder at Joane as she made for the door, and she heard the sounds of Joane's footsteps following her. In a moment, the soft sound of her steps on carpet matched Tris's heavier thumps on the metal hallway outside. She waited for the hiss of her door closing before turning back to Joane. She spun faster than she'd meant to, causing a spike of dizziness that made her stumble a bit. Joane looked briefly amused, but her face quickly settled into a business-like expression.

"Why'd you tell Orion they couldn't take the painkillers yet?" she asked, "You and I both know you were lying."

"They need time to think and digest everything," Tristan explained, leading her away from the door. "I think they could be a lot of help to us in figuring this out, but they can't be constantly doped up on meds. Besides, we've been getting hurt a *lot* lately. I'm trying to save as much medicine as I can."

"Smart," Joane conceded. "You really think they'll be useful? I'm not even talking about them betraying us anymore, I mean them actually being of any help to us."

"A Consortium senator is a Consortium senator," Tristan pointed out as they walked side by side through the narrow hallway, only a few inches of space separating their shoulders. "That means access to people, information, and money." Joane gave her a nod of understanding. "Plus," she continued, brushing a strand of hair behind her ear. "It's not like I'm built for this kind of work either, and I've managed not to slow you down too badly so far."

"Tris," Joane began, turning her body to face her. Tristan cursed under her breath as they both stopped in place. She'd said too much, she realized, and here came the inevitable confrontation. "You're so much more than you give yourself credit for. You're wise, personable, insightful. You're an extraordinary pilot and not a bad fighter either, both of which have saved my life several times already. I-" she seemed to catch herself, swallowed hard, and gave a small shake of her head before speaking again. "I'm glad you're here."

Tristan wondered for a moment what Joane may have wanted to say instead, but thought better than to delude herself. She was an adult, she told herself, there was no use wasting time on daydreams and wild hopes. On the other hand, here they were. Tristan could take the first step, open herself up to Joane in a way she hadn't even when they'd had sex together the night before they were supposed to die. If she'd known then that she would still be here now, that it wasn't their last chance, would it have been different? Would they have had the sense not to throw years of arguments and tension to the side? As she stepped closer to her friend in the hallway, feeling the heavy thrum of Darling's engines in her ribcage matching with the beat of her heart, she knew she wouldn't change a thing. She wanted to ask, stars above, how she wished she could just *ask*. She wanted to grab Joane by the shoulders and scream at her, "What did it mean to you? Are you dying the same slow death that I am?" She wasn't that kind of woman, though.

"Thank you, Joane," she said eventually, unable to meet her eyes. "It's just, all this. You here, us looking for Ahsha, it all feels so familiar. It's bringing up a lot of…old memories."

"I understand," Joane said. "It's weird for me, too. Sometimes it feels so much like old times, but sometimes…it doesn't."

"Well put," Tristan said, unable to stop the sarcasm from pouring out of her. It was like her immediate, instinctual defense mechanism. Joane chuckled weakly, punching Tristan on the upper arm not lightly enough to not hurt.

"Shut it," she grumbled, and Tristan found herself laughing, her chest suddenly feeling tight. *Make me*, Tristan wanted to say. She paused, maybe the wine had affected her more than she thought.

"It was a good night," Tristan said, trying to signal an end to the conversation. "Sorry for waking you up so early, but I think we made a lot of progress, don't you?"

Joane nodded. As if Tristan had reminded her that she was tired, she bit back a yawn and scratched the side of her face. "I'm going to go back to my floor nest," she mumbled. "What about you? I can't imagine you're wanting to share the bed with the senator, are you?"

Tristan scoffed and started walking down the hall. Joane followed her as they made their way through the U-shaped loop, pausing at the door to the cockpit. "Same place I always sleep," she explained, jerking a thumb at the door behind her. "The pilot's chair reclines. It's pretty comfortable."

"Tris," Joane said, sounding disappointed in her. "You're going to sleep in a chair until Orion is up on their feet? Why not sleep in Ahsha's old room?" Tristan gave a sarcastic laugh.

"Well, Joane, if you think your room looks bad, you don't even want to look at Ahsha's. I threw all the crap I didn't want or need in there. It's probably a fire hazard at this point, but I've got it entirely sealed off. I couldn't get into that room if I wanted to. Besides, it's fine, most of the time I sleep in the cockpit anyway. I really only use the bedroom when I-" She caught herself.

Joane stiffened, crossing her arms across her chest. "Have to do in-flight surgery on a hostage Consortium senator?" she said quickly, trying to ease the tension.

Tristan faked a laugh and leaned against the door. "Believe it or not, it happens more than you'd think." Joane glanced sideways down either end of the hall, around the stacks of crates and boxes lining either side of the curve.

"One time is more than I'd think," she said. They were quiet for a bit, shuffling their weight back and forth. Darling's lights had dimmed in some attempt to keep a normal time schedule going on board during the Redshift. Tristan, having spent most of the day catching up on sleep, didn't feel at all tired. Finally, Joane broke the silence. "Still, curled up in that old chair can't be good for your back, which you very recently hurt, if you remember." Joane didn't have to tell her twice. The recency of the bolts from Cygnus made the pain stick out more in her mind, but the dull ache in her leg and head were still very much there. She missed that time long ago when there wasn't some part of her that was always hurting. "Look, I'm going to fall asleep on the pile of clothes because it's the best sleep I've had in months; if you want to just shove all the clothes onto the bed to make you room you can have it."

Tristan kept her face level while her mind collapsed in on itself like the black hole that her home planet orbited. "Joane, I wouldn't want to make you uncomfortable," she said with a small shake of her head, a slight hint of a question hidden in her voice. "You can't tell me sleeping in a chair is bad for my back and then go sleep on my scarves."

"Don't doubt how comfortable my nest is," Joane said indignantly, "and you won't. There's no reason that two friends can't share a room for a night without it being weird or…anything."

"Yeah, of course," Tristan said, trying to sound casual even though she never thought hearing Joane call her a friend would have the same sting of her pulse knife being plunged into her chest. "I mean, yeah, obviously, yeah. It's fine. If you don't mind, I wouldn't mind an actual bed. I don't snore or anything."

"I know," Joane said, before realizing what she'd said and letting out an exasperated sigh. Tristan decided not to point it out and just let it drop. "We should go to bed," she said, her voice dripping with exhaustion. Tristan nodded and turned away from the cockpit door, following Joane back to her open bedroom. For some reason, her heart was in her throat as she stepped across the threshold. She'd been in here plenty of times to store things here and move stuff around, but she'd never slept in Joane's bed. She'd never spent the night in this room, let alone spent the night in here *with* Joane. It would be fine, she told herself. She'll have her part of the room, and she would just sleep on the bed and try to get out of the room before Joane could wake up.

Tristan stepped over to the bed, finding a pile of mostly pants and heavier jackets waiting for her. "Sorry," Joane said as she climbed back into the nest on the floor. "I found everything scratchy or with buttons on it and tossed it over there."

"Oh, it's fine," Tristan said, her voice squeaking for some reason as she tried to shove the pile off to the side of the single bed. There wasn't much room for her already, but she had to practically spoon the mound of clothes to keep herself from sliding off. "Thank you, Joane, for…a lot of stuff." As she looked up at her, Joane was beginning the process of settling in. She kicked off her shoes, went to unzip her jacket, and apparently thought better of it before lying down fully clothed. Tristan was already in a t-shirt and simple lounge pants from her nap, so she didn't need to worry about getting comfortable. She thought about offering to close her eyes, turn away, or even step out for a while, but she knew drawing attention would just make the moment all the more uncomfortable. Joane grabbed a large, authentic woolen blanket that Tristan had accepted as payment for ferrying a grain shipment from some farmers seven months ago and wrapped herself in it before settling down into the nest. Tristan smiled at the back of her head, seeing her all rolled up like a kid in a sleeping bag made her heart feel warm. "I just want you to know, I'm sorry for the way things happened." Tristan wasn't sure what she was apologizing for, but she meant it. Was she talking about the night they'd spent together? Was it the way she'd left? Was it the predicament they were in now? She had no clue. Maybe she was sorry for it all.

"It's alright," Joane said, not turning to face her. The drowsiness in her voice was palpable, so Tristan decided not to try and continue the conversation. It was better just to let her sleep. And so, there she lay, wide awake, staring at the bundle of fabric that was the woman she was falling for, wishing to close the distance between them and knowing she couldn't. She watched Joane's shoulders rise and fall under the blanket until they fell into a slow, calming rhythm, and the sound of her breath could just be heard over the engines running.

"Are you asleep?" Tristan asked after what may have been an hour. "Joane?" She waited for a while, but Joane didn't respond or even move. "It meant everything to me." She rolled over to stare at the ceiling, listening to her ship humming beneath her and hoping she would have a chance to say those words to Joane's face before something else went wrong that she couldn't fix. It took a long time, but the droning of the engines eventually drowned out the storm of thoughts in her mind and dragged her into an uneasy, but dreamless, sleep.

# Chapter 21
## The Math Checks Out

JOANE was curled up in her nest of coats and sweaters, slowly trying to fall asleep and resisting the urge to call Tristan over to her, when she heard it. "Are you asleep?" Tristan asked her, and for whatever reason, be it curiosity or anxiety, she didn't respond. "Joane?"

She waited with baited breath, unsure of what Tristan might do or say. She was always unpredictable that way; it both excited and confused Joane. Finally, barely audible over the engines and muffled by the blanket. "It meant everything to me."

Shit. Shit, shit, *shit*. Her nails dug into the blanket, threatening to tear the wool apart. She wanted to stand up, throw the blanket off, and whirl on the woman in the bed. She had to have misheard her, right? There was no way she'd heard that from Tristan the womanizer, who had brought dozens of women back to the ship when they'd been traveling together. Tris who laughed about all of her past flings and could never remember some of their names. Why would that Tris have gotten sappy all of a sudden, and why did it have to be for her? No, she told herself, she must've been hearing things.

*Wishful thinking*, a voice in her head said, and she bit back a curse at herself. She couldn't afford to ponder it, she told herself. There was too much at stake. Their lives were on the line, when it had been like this with Ahsha, it had always fallen to Joane to find a way out for them all. It was no different now, and she couldn't afford to be falling for someone she could barely stand to think about not a month prior. She tried to shake the thoughts swimming in her mind unsuccessfully, and didn't sleep for a long time after that.

*     *     *

JOANE woke up first, even though the clock on the nightstand said it was fairly late in what amounted to morning. Time was strange in the Redshift, so Joane ignored the poor approximation of Consortium standard time and instead read the smaller, crimson numbers below the larger display. Beside them, in script almost too small to read at this distance, read "Hours until Redshift completion." She did the quick math in her head and surmised that there were now a little under ten days until they returned to voidpace travel. Ten days to think of a plan to evade the Consortium without a Redshift drive, on a ship that was almost certainly bugged in a way they would never be able to detect, with a highly recognizable public figure and two likely fugitives. She let out a sigh as sleep left her. It hadn't all been a dream, after all. She found herself thinking that same thought every morning since she'd received Ahsha's message, always hoping for a brief second as her consciousness swam from dreams to reality.

She turned over, shucking off the blanket that had been comforting when she had gone to sleep. By now, it was just stuffy and constricting. As she dropped it, she remembered that she'd also slept in her clothes, which were sticky and uncomfortable with sweat now. Finally, Joane saw the shape partially hidden under a blanket and remembered the final moments of the night before, inviting Tris into her bedroom like it was some sort of high-school slumber party.

*It meant everything to me.* The words rang in her mind like an alarm bell, driving the last bit of sleep from her mind and forcing her back to complete alertness. She wondered for a moment if it had been a dream, but no. It felt all too real in her mind. Words she never thought she'd hear Tristan say. Words that forced her to wonder just how much that night had meant to her. She hadn't given it much thought since then; it had been easier to shut her mind down and focus on the tasks at hand. Now, though, she had two weeks ahead of her to think about it, and she was afraid she already knew the answer. Tristan Ninomae, the heartless thief, the womanizer, the one who abandoned her with Ahsha. Tristan Ninomae, who was none of those things. Tristan who had risked her life to save a cargo shuttle without so much as a second thought. Tristan who came back for Joane when she'd been bleeding out on that hangar floor. Tristan whose lips and hands had felt so much gentler than Joane had expected.

She took a half step towards the bed, watching her as she did. Her gray skin darkened as she slept, some sort of evolutionary camouflage meant to mimic the dark stone of her homeworld. Her hair was, to put it kindly, a nightmare. It was like a hopelessly tangled net that Joane could only barely see her face poking through. Her mouth was hanging open as she lay on her side, facing the wall, but she never snored. Joane found herself sitting down on the bed next to her, settling carefully into what little space remained on the bed. Gingerly, painfully slowly, she moved a strand of Tris's black hair out of her face, allowing her a better view of her face.

Joane had always known Tristan was pretty. She'd known since the day they met all those years ago. Sleeping, though, with all the tension gone from her brow and the guarded expression gone from her face, it was easy to see just how beautiful Tristan was. Joane wished she'd seen it earlier, but she was afraid the time had passed. What use was sentimentality to them now? The power of love wasn't going to find Ahsha, or return the missing planets. It wasn't going to save them. She lowered her hand to Tristan's shoulder and shook it gently. "Tris," she whispered, trying to whisper and keep her voice soft at the same time.

Tristan jerked awake, her green eyes slamming open as her face hardened and snapped to alertness in an instant. The peaceful look on her face was gone, replaced by wild confusion. She made a short noise, almost like a panicked bark, as she rolled over to look up at Joane. Her expression softened slightly, but only just slightly, when she realized it was her. "Mm?" was all she could manage.

"Can I borrow some clothes?" Joane asked softly. "I need to wash mine." Tristan sleepily nodded in the affirmative. Joane smiled, thinking that Tristan probably wouldn't remember this conversation later. "Get some rest, alright? I'm going to go take a look at our navigational data."

Tris nodded again, her eyes glossy and unfocused. She curled into a ball, facing Joane this time, and was immediately back to sleep. Joane slowly, almost reluctantly pulled her hand back from Tris's shoulder, then hesitated a second before leaning down and giving her a swift kiss on the forehead. It was barely anything, just a soft brush of her lips across her hair-strewn face, but it made Joane's heart sing and her stomach turn itself inside out. She got out of the bed quickly, unsure if she had accidentally woken Tris up. She didn't wait around to see; she hastily grabbed some of Tris' clothes from the closet and headed to the showers.

*  *  *

JOANE spent a while checking and rechecking the Redshift trajectory estimates that Darling's navigational computer had made. The cockpit was quiet and empty, which gave her time to work uninterrupted. It was slow, tedious work, but she didn't mind it. Each possible trajectory had to be followed through with orbit projections to make sure they weren't going to pass through any dense asteroid fields or planetary bodies, then a probable endpoint could be calculated. It allowed Joane to turn the emotional part of her brain off and focus on the work, even though she occasionally gave a passing thought to the fact that Tris' clothes smelled so much like her, like cinnamon and other warm spices. The smell enveloped her just like the long, black cloak did: warmly and softly, making the tough synth leather pilot's chair feel a bit more comfortable to sit in as she scanned through the console screens before her. Every now and then, when the lights of the screens made her eyes sore and the text before her began to swim across the glass screen, she would blink hard and look up at the viewport. Every time, she saw nothing but blackness, and tried to convince herself that she wasn't just floating through an endless void. They were moving, she reminded herself, just so quickly that any light from the passing stars couldn't reach them before they were gone. Still, it was unnerving in a purgatorial way.

Most of the potential trajectories the computer had prepared for her were far from ideal. Tris hadn't had enough time to program the usual safeguards for a Redshift, so there were plenty of chances that they'd leave the shift in the middle of nowhere, weeks or perhaps even months from the nearest populated galaxy. Worse than that, they would have to hope Darling's shields would hold up if they passed through any dense clouds of space vapor or solid bodies. If they didn't, well, they wouldn't have much time to worry about it. In a cruel bit of irony, a lot of the trajectories took them past one of the solar systems where a planet had vanished a few months ago: Cetea-9 in the Messier Nebula.

While she was in the middle of her work, the cockpit door hissed open behind her, interrupting her concentration. She began turning the chair around, expecting to see Tris coming to throw her out of her chair, but instead saw Orion stepping through. "Captain Ninomae, I was just-" they began to say, then stopped once Joane's face came into view. "Oh, my apologies." It was clear Orion was afraid of her, which Joane didn't mind. Tris had asked her to trust them, and Joane did. Trust, however, was a long way away from friendship. Dinner with them had been nice, but it would be a long time before she would consider them a friend. "Joane, good morning," they said. "I saw the coat and the pilot's chair and I thought…nevermind."

Joane gestured to her own clothes, draped over her usual chair at the weapons platform. The self-cleaning nanomachines embedded in the fabric were in the process of washing the garments, making the outfit shake slightly. "Captain Ninomae," she said, chuckling internally at the formality of the title, "let me borrow a coat while I washed my clothes. Speaking of which, yours are clean if you feel well enough to be on your feet." Orion was currently shirtless, wrapped in the silk sheet from Tristan's bed like some sort of luxurious robe. They looked like a spa attendee more than a fugitive. They reddened and drew the blanket closer around themself.

"I'll have to go grab those, thank you," they said. "In truth, I'm not sure I feel well enough to be walking, but I was getting so restless I think I stopped caring."

"Were you hoping to find something?" she asked impatiently, looking over her shoulder at the console, eager to get back to work.

"No," they said casually, strolling forward into the room. "Just trying to familiarize myself with the vessel. Tris said it was called The Darling?"

"Just Darling," Joane corrected almost immediately. They'd all corrected so many people during their time traveling together, except Ahsha, who only ever referred to it as "the ship." She never considered it as much of a home as she and Tris had.

"Darling," Orion echoed. "It's a very nice ship. A little bit…crowded."

"Tris is a bit of a hoarder," Joane agreed. "Just don't go around touching stuff. I'm not liable for whatever happens to you if you break something."

"Does that not bother you?" Orion asked, their voice sounding genuinely curious.

Joane let out a long sigh. She wanted to be working, not thinking about Tris. "I don't live on the ship," she explained. "This little trip has been the first time I've seen Darling in three years."

"Three years?" Orion said. Joane was getting tired of hearing her own words echoed back at her. "I thought you and Tristan were-"

Joane stepped forward and pointed a finger at them forcefully before they could continue. "Whatever assumptions you have about me, *Senator*, they're wrong," she bit her tongue, but not quick enough to stop the outburst. She sighed and rubbed her eyes, trying to relax her shoulders. "We're not together. We're not partners. We're barely friends. We worked for Ahsha years ago, then we went our separate ways. That's it." Orion was quiet for a while, a strange sort of look flashing across their face. Joane realized with horror that they were trying to figure her out, and it seemed to be working. She'd grown used to Orion as the ineffectual bedsore Tris had insisted on bringing along that she'd forgotten they were a professional politician.

"You two seem quite close for 'barely friends,'" they said in a more measured, deeper voice than they'd been speaking with since the attack. Their lungs must have nearly healed fully by now. "Tristan speaks fondly of you."

"It isn't your place to tell me what she says behind my back," Joane said defensively, a bit of panic rising in her chest. After Tris's whispered confession last night, Joane didn't want to know more about what Tris said when she thought Joane wouldn't hear.

"I'm just trying to understand you," they said placatingly, holding up their hands, palms out. "Not to mention, you are wearing her clothes. You'll have to forgive my confusion."

"I'll have to do nothing of the sort," Joane said, wondering if she had made a mistake not throwing them out of the airlock when she had the chance. She didn't need someone picking apart her brain now, of all times.

"I can tell when I've hit a nerve," Orion said, failing to suppress a smile. "I'm sorry."

"Are you?"

"A little bit." Joane rolled her eyes at the senator.

"I'm working," she said, gesturing to the console, "Do you want to help?" Orion's shit-eating grin shifted to one of eagerness.

"Absolutely!" they said, reminding Joane of a Corian Bird Pup. "However I can."

Joane returned the smile with a chipper tone in her voice. "Good, leave," she said, watching Orion's smile vanish.

"Joane, I know you don't think very highly of me," they said, "but if you're just scanning navigational data, I'm pretty sure I can help cut down on the time." Joane squeezed her eyes shut for a few moments before answering.

"Okay, go for it. But go to that station." She pointed at the seldom used navigational station. Even when Darling had a full crew, they almost never touched the console. "Just, don't touch anything that actually controls the ship. If Tristan finds out we touched anything but the database, she'll throw us out the airlock, jump out after us, and beat us to death."

"You're a strange woman," Orion said, moving past her to the console. They didn't bother leaving to retrieve their clothes, apparently satisfied with their makeshift silken cape. They began tapping at the small keyboard, accessing the same set of trajectory files that Joane had pulled up on the main console.

"You're one to talk," she grumbled. She sighed, not wanting to admit that she was thankful for help churning through the hundreds of barely different possible trajectories they were on. "Start at the bottom of the list, I'll work my way down, and we can meet in the middle."

Orion gave her a thumbs up, and she rolled her eyes as they both got to work. She began scanning a new trajectory, which ended oddly close to the Andromeda-Milky Way twin galaxies. A short ride from her home planet, she observed, though not without a bit of distaste. Sol-3 was an ancient history to her and to all those with Solan ancestry, history she was eager to put behind her. The trajectory seemed mostly viable, save for a brief skip through a cloud of dust left behind by a dead asteroid.

"So, how long have you and Tristan known each other?" Orion asked, suddenly, not turning in their chair. Joane stared daggers at the back of their head.

"If I don't answer, are you just going to keep asking?" she asked, receiving a simple nod in response. She groaned, but knew this would probably be the easiest question to answer. "I met Tris about eight years ago, Ahsha hired her while we were refueling on her home planet. She was eager for a way offworld, and we needed muscle and a pilot."

"I thought you were the muscle?"

Joane chuckled. "I am. And so is she. If you ever meet Ahsha Reindare, you'll understand why we needed a lot of muscle to balance out her attitude. She was always talking us into fights she couldn't talk her way out of. I think I've only met one person I think she could beat in a fight."

Orion tilted their head slightly, still focusing on the menial work in front of them. "Who is that?" they asked. Joane was silent. "Oh. It's me, isn't it?"

"You are smart, Senator," she said, sorting the Solan trajectory into the 'finished' section of the document. Once she had a range of every viable trajectory, they could prepare flight plans for each one and be prepared for wherever they ended up.

"You know, you can just call me Orion," they said. "I've probably been reported either dead or a fugitive by now, so I doubt they're keeping my office empty and waiting for me. Speaking of nicknames, why do you call her 'Tris?'"

By the Singularity, they never stopped asking questions. "Her friends call her Tris," she explained curtly.

"I thought you said you were barely friends?" Orion's voice was chipper and casual.

"Do you ever shut up?" Joane asked, grabbing the sides of her head in frustration. "We were friends, and we're working together now, and we're trying to be friendly for the time being."

"But you still care for each other." Joane froze, whirling towards Orion and scowling at them fiercely. They seemed to feel her eyes bearing down on them finally and turned to face her. "Joane, I know you don't care for politicians, and I can't help what I am. I know people; I know how to understand the dynamics at play in any relationship. It's been a long time for me, but I know what being in love feels like."

"I am *not* in love with Tris," she spat forcefully, eagerly, like she was trying to convince both of them. Orion held up their hands placatingly.

"I apologize. It was a poor choice of words," they conceded. "However, whatever you may feel about her, I believe Tristan has feelings for you. Have you considered the possibility?"

"Whatever Tris feels about me is her business," Joane said, shutting down her emotions to the best of her ability. She was working through the data faster and faster now, mindlessly checking the straight paths of their Redshift and crossing out any options that ended in their death. She wished the computer worked fast enough to calculate their location in real time during the Shift, but they were moving so quickly that it couldn't possibly triangulate their position. "I've got a job to do, and I find that having as few distractions as possible helps me do that."

"I perfectly understand; I'm just worried that perhaps you're letting your feelings distract you more than you let on." Orion had no idea how dangerously close they were to being punched. "Oh, by the way, what does 'Unexpected Slowdown' mean?"

"*What?*" was all Joane had time to say before the entire ship lurched, groaning like an oceanic vessel running aground suddenly. She jolted forward, slamming her torso against the console and bouncing back into the pilot's chair, all the wind knocked out of her. She looked out of the viewscreen, and the endless, impenetrable blackness flashed for a brief moment. There, for just a moment, was a point of red light that streaked into a line and was gone. It was brief, and at the furthest end of the visible spectrum, but it was still light. That meant Darling was slowing down, more than a week before the Redshift was supposed to. Something was deathly, horribly wrong. She coughed and wheezed as the ship groaned under the weight of inertia. Hauling herself out of the chair into a sitting position took almost all of her strength. Orion, who had buckled their seatbelt to read through navigation charts for some reason, had fared much better than her. "Go get Tris," she managed, her voice straining to be heard over the rumble of the engines.

"What's happening?" Orion asked, the smug analytical look gone from their face. "Turbulence?"

"We're in space, dipshit," Joane spat, not bothering to worry about being polite in what could very easily be her last moments. "Go get the pilot!"

# Chapter 22
## Murphy's Law Was Never Disproven

ORION struggled to pull themself from the chair. It was hard to fathom just how quickly everything had gone entirely wrong. Moments ago, they'd been trying to figure out a way to get through to Joane. Now, the ship sounded like it was shaking itself apart, the bulkheads straining under some force they couldn't see. Being attacked at the relief station had been frightening, but it had been random, unexpected, and they had blacked out quickly. This time, they were painfully alert as everything came crashing down around them. This was worse than before; it was terrifying.

Whatever inertial dampeners Darling had installed were clearly not enough to handle whatever was happening, which was about the most Orion could hope to understand. If they could just get to Tristan, she would know what was happening and maybe, hopefully, how to ensure they all survived. With a grunt of effort and pain from their still-healing ribs, they managed to get to their feet, bracing against the wall as the ship started to spin.

"Joane, are you alright?" they asked, looking over at the woman hunched over the pilot's console.

"I'm fine!" she yelled, punching at buttons and clearly panicking just as much as Orion was. "Just go!" Orion tried to pick up the pace, but the second they tried to run the shaking of the ship became too much and they fell face first to the floor.

It took them a long time, too long, to rise to their feet, panting and sweating from the effort. Their lungs weren't working the way they were supposed to. Everything felt sluggish and slow. Orion didn't want to die like this. It wasn't fair. They struggled into an odd sort of crawling posture and scurried towards the door. They managed to reach up for the control panel, catching a glimpse of Joane activating the control sphere as they did.

"Can you fly this thing?" they asked over their shoulder as the door slid open with a slow grinding sound.

"No!" Joane said, her voice devoid of any sarcasm, "so go get the goddamn pilot!" Orion swallowed hard and halfway threw themselves out of the room into the hallway, howling as their shoulder slammed into a corner.

"Tristan!" they yelled at the top of their lungs, hoping she might hear. They doubted it. If the racket from the ship hadn't woken her up, a few shouts probably wouldn't do it. To their surprise, almost as soon as the word left their lips, Tristan's gray face rounded the corner, running at almost full speed down the hall.

"What did you people do to my ship?" she yelled, green eyes wild and hair going in every direction. There was a small bit of dried drool coming from one corner of her mouth.

"We didn't do anything!" Joane answered from inside the cockpit. "Something's wrong!"

"I figured that much," Tristan said to herself as she shouldered past Orion into the cockpit. "Strap in, both of you. This is going to get a lot worse before it gets better." Orion stumbled in after her, trying to crawl back towards the navigation station without falling over again. Their head was still ringing from the first impact.

"What exactly is this?" they asked, slowly making their way, bracing against the wall of the room as they went. Tristan made her way to the pilot's console, gingerly touching a bloody scrape on Joane's forehead before pushing her aside. If Tristan leaned down and placed the briefest of kisses against Joane's lips before pushing her away, it was none of Orion's business.

"Do you want a short answer, or a long answer?" Tristan asked as she yanked the control sphere out of the air and began strapping herself into the pilot's chair. More and more pinpricks of lights were appearing in the viewport, still passing by impossibly fast but becoming more and more noticeable.

"Would I understand the long answer?" Orion asked.

"Probably not," Tristan said, her face set into a heavy snarl as she began wrestling with the controls, "and you might not live long enough to hear it. Short answer: it's really fucking bad."

Orion nodded, gripping the armrests of their chair. *Really fucking bad.* They had figured that much, but hearing the seasoned pilot say it out loud didn't help to soothe their anxiety. Joane had stumbled into a seat, one hand on her forehead, the other brushing her lips with her fingertips. "Tris," she said, trying to keep her voice steady. "How can we help?" *We,* she said. Orion wasn't sure they could do much of anything to help here, but it was nice to be included.

Tristan seemed to rack her brain for a bit, looking over the console as she tapped in commands with her free hand. The lights in the viewport were no longer just red. There were faint tracings of scarlet, orange, and even yellow. "The navigational records," Tristan responded, her voice frantic. "Were we passing by any large gravity wells? Supergiants, black holes, even a really big planet, anything?"

Orion watched the two of them shouting back and forth to one another over the rumble of the ship and the complete understanding that passed between them. For "barely friends," they seemed remarkably effective together. Joane's face turned thoughtful for a moment, then dropped. "Shit, yes," she said. "The Cetea system." The name rang with familiarity in Orion's mind. Cetea. Senator Eradon Murvac and his own vanished world.

"The gravity well from Cetea-9," they said, their voice too hushed to be heard in the chaos. Tristan seemed to understand, however. She nodded grimly.

"Wherever we are, whatever it is," she said, bracing herself against the back of her chair, "it's pulling us out of the Redshift. The inertial dampeners aren't built for something like this, and neither are the shields. If I can fire the engines at the right moment and keep the shields up, we *might* survive the slowdown. I...I'm very sorry."

"Don't apologize for something that hasn't happened yet," Joane's voice came through, making Tristan jolt. Orion had never seen so much intensity from the woman, even when she'd threatened them only a few minutes ago. "Tris. You are the best damn pilot I've ever met. I don't care if you think you can do this; I know you can." Tristan looked at her, and something wordless passed between the two of them. Orion, despite all the time they spent learning to read people, couldn't quite put a finger on it. They only hoped Joane's words had gotten through to Tristan.

Apparently they had. The pilot straightened, clutching the control sphere so hard her knuckles turned from gray to a chalky-white. Orion saw her green eyes shining like twin beacons under her dark hair. There was…a ferocity about her, like a cornered animal that had suddenly decided to fight its way to safety. *Oh,* Orion thought as they realized, *they're both crazy.*

"Alright, Darling," Tristan said with a low, almost hungry growl. "Dance for me."

She pulled the sphere towards her body, and Orion lurched in their chair as Darling's eight engines all fired at once, their reverse thrust a negligible counter to the forward momentum they had. Through the viewport, the shields flashed a brilliant blue around the ship, even though they hadn't hit anything solid. Even traveling through vacuum, the sudden slowing of the craft was as much of a threat as any asteroid in their path. A deep red light filled the cockpit and warning alarms sounded as Orion heard a muffled crash from the starboard side of the ship. Or was it the port? The left side, they finally decided.

"Minor hull damage," Joane reported, fiddling with the controls at her own station.

"How minor?" Tristan asked, her brow furrowed and her eyes focused. She wasn't looking at the console, the screens, or any of the numerous warning lights across the cabin. Orion could see that the only things Tristan Ninomae was watching were the stars coming into focus outside. They swallowed back their fear, trying to remain confident in their pilot. She'd flown them out of a tight spot once before, surely this would be no different.

"Just focus on what you're doing," Joane insisted. "I'm getting the fire suppression systems going now."

Tristan nodded slightly, a motion only Orion saw. She slowly began twisting the control sphere, almost curling it towards her wrist as she kept it pulled back towards her elbow. Through the failing inertial dampeners, Orion felt the ship tilt and turn on its axis, the engines shifting downward to start the ship into a sort of slow circular pattern. Orion felt like they were back on one of the spinning carnival rides they'd thrown up on as a child, or the space travel prep courses they'd thrown up on as an adult. Everything was spinning back and forth at speeds that no sentient being was meant to feel. "Joane, can you seal the cockpit's atmosphere?" Tristan called.

She didn't need to explain what would happen if the cabin depressurized. Orion didn't know much about piloting a starship, but they knew enough about depressurization to wonder why every compartment hadn't already been sealed. Joane yelled an affirmative and began keying commands into the console furiously. Orion heard the cockpit door slam closed with more force than it usually had, followed by the harsh sound of air hissing as the airlock sealed.

"If I can just," Tristan grunted, wrestling with the control sphere as she fought to keep twisting it. Orion heard Darling's engines fighting against her, straining under the effort to keep firing backwards as the Redshift drive powered down. "Need to get us into a spin, then we'll centrifuge while the Drive tires itself out."

"And what happens to us while that happens?" Orion called out, knowing how effective centrifuges were at separating organic matter from itself.

"I'm working on that," Tristan said honestly. The sphere slipped from her hand for an instant, rocketing back into place over the console and spinning wildly. She swore as the ship's engines went back to their forward position and Darling hurled forward through the vacuum. The shield's flared again, brighter this time as they struggled to keep the hull from tearing apart. Tristan snatched the sphere out of the air like an annoying insect and yanked it down with both hands. When she pulled it backwards, resting the sphere against her abdomen, it sent the ship into a series of backwards somersaults as it careened "downwards" through the directionless expanse of space. Honestly, Orion wasn't sure what direction they were moving without any sort of visible reference point. Whatever way they were going didn't matter, they still squeezed their eyes shut and tried to hold down last night's dinner.

With each turn of the ship, though, Orion heard the hull shaking, threatening to buckle. The noise from the engines was profoundly wrong, sounding more like howling, wounded animals than pieces of fine-tuned machinery. The rapidly spinning viewport made it impossible to see the pinpricks of light clearly, but Orion did see a brief flash of blue from the shields before they faded completely.

"Yes!" Tristan shouted as the sound of the dying shield generator filled the ship.

Orion stared at her with wonder as she smiled with relief. "How is that good news?" they asked, hesitant to hear the answer.

Tristan responded by flipping open a glass case on her console with a now-glowing blue button underneath. "This is going to hurt, but it's our best shot. Brace!" She pounded her fist against the button, then immediately let go of the control sphere and shrank into her captain's chair, her face set into a grimace. Orion tightened the seatbelt around their waist and dug their fingernails into the synthleather seat so hard it threatened to tear the covering apart. They were about to press their head against the back of the chair when inertia did so for them, the movement so quick that they immediately felt light-headed.

The second Tristan hit the button, everything went dark. Orion thought they'd died instantly, and that the afterlife was just an eternal sense of vertigo. Then, the room was lit up by a bright, solid blue glow through the viewport. The shields were back, full of power and shining brightly enough to illuminate the entire room. Orion saw Tristan and Joane similarly pushed back in their seats, and that's when Orion realized that they couldn't hear the engines anymore. In fact, they could hear nothing but the abnormally loud hum of the shield generator, like a swarm of angry bees.

They careened freely for one second, two, three, and just as the glow of the shields began to flicker, Tristan pushed herself forward and slapped the blue button again. Within an instant, the hum died down to a roar and the sound of the voidpace engines activating filled the ship. Orion watched Tristan reach out for the floating control sphere, just barely getting the tips of her fingers around the multi-faceted device and pulling it harshly. The shields flared so bright that they glowed white for a second, and then vanished. Then, Orion saw the lines of light grow shorter and shorter, then saw bits of green, blue, and purple emerging in the viewport. The short lines began to congeal into the shapes of stars and the clouds of color into a nebula. Someone in the cockpit was screaming. It was probably Orion, but it could've been all of them. They shot forward like an arrow from a bolt gun, even though the engines were firing in the exact opposite direction. The clouds of a nebula were passing them at breakneck speeds, and then a thick line of blue light condensed into a large dot on the viewport: a star they were dangerously close to. In truth, they were millions of miles away from it, but with their current speed and lack of shields, getting much closer would destroy their ship in an instant. Tristan made a startled noise and yanked the control sphere to the left, making the ship tumble violently to the side, away from the rapidly approaching sun. All three passengers moved with the motion, tossed around like ragdolls as the ship whirled through space.

Orion tried to grab on to the armrests tighter, to anchor themselves in place, to make something feel still even as the entire universe pivoted around them. They needed some sort of equilibrium, a constant, something to keep the nausea and panic at bay for just a little bit longer. To their horror, though, they felt their grip loosening, and the edges of their vision going dark. It was too much. Entirely too much. Were they having a heart attack? Some sort of stress-induced aneurysm? Orion had no idea, but it only made the panic worse.

They fell to the edge of consciousness, brought back momentarily by a loud bang from the back of the ship. Tristan grunted, said through gritted teeth, "Joane?"

"We've lost one of the engines," Joane reported, her own voice sounding foggy and unfocused. "I don't…know…how much more…" She trailed off, and Orion saw through half-lidded eyes as Tristan's head whipped towards each of her passengers for the briefest of moments before turning back to the viewport.

"Both of you stay with me, you understand?" she yelled. "It's just a few G's, nothing we haven't all felt before. Like riding a rollercoaster, right?" She twisted her wrist backwards, tilting the nose of the ship up and pulling Darling into a U-turn that pointed them away from the star. Orion felt the harness on the chair struggling to hold them in place. All they saw was a curtain formed of their long brown hair as it fell into their eyes.

"I don't like rollercoasters," Orion tried to say, but all that came out was a groan and the inevitable release of vomit and bile from their stomach. Tristan growled, a panicked noise of frustration and pain.

"If we make it out of this, Orion," she yelled, trying to shake them out of their stupor, "you're cleaning that up, you understand me?" Orion wondered if her words would be the last thing they ever heard, and then the blackness swallowed their vision and there was finally stillness.

# Chapter 23
## It's Pronounced Mes-see-ay

TRISTAN thought she could only have one dream, but when the G's finally knocked her unconscious, she believed she discovered a new one. She was floating, gliding through an ocean of blue and purple water that glowed softly around her, waves of color rippling across her body as she hung there, drifting but never drowning. It was strange that she wasn't drowning. There were no oceans on her home planet, but Tristan had been in enough pools and lakes to know that it wasn't supposed to feel like this. The water was supposed to be heavy; it was supposed to press against her ribs and head. Her eyes and lungs were supposed to burn; she was supposed to panic, to thrash her body around and race for the surface. None of that happened in the dream.

Because while she was floating, Tristan wasn't underwater. She wasn't even dreaming. As clarity returned to her and she regained some control of her senses, she took in the sight of her cockpit around her. Anything that hadn't been tied down securely was floating freely through the space, hanging completely still or gently spinning and knocking into other objects. The lights were dark, and the room was cast in a dim light by the distant sun's light refracting through the Messier nebula. She blinked a few times, trying to make her vision focus while her head continued to swim. She groaned, and the sound rattled around her skull like a drum. She winced quietly;

wondering if the G-forces of their deceleration had permanently damaged her eardrums.

It occurred to her that if she was in pain, she was still alive. That was good. Surprising, but good. The last thing Tristan remembered was trying to turn Darling away from Cetea's cold blue sun, then the mix of acceleration, deceleration, and directional shifts hit her like a wave and she'd collapsed. She let out a deep sigh of relief. She was alive, which meant the ship was alright, which meant Joane and Orion would be alright too.

*Shit.* She twisted her head to the side, feeling soreness in her neck as she moved. Another pleasant reminder that she was very alive. She saw Orion first, vomit stains down the front of the satin sheet draped over their body, hair wild and swept back from their face. Their eyes were closed, but after a moment of careful watching, Tristan saw their chest rising and falling gently. Satisfied that she could get to yell at them for ruining her sheets, she whirled around to face Joane.

Joane had, not surprisingly, also vomited. Tristan remembered just how much her friend hated entering Fastlanes, and whatever insane stunt she had just pulled must have been a thousand times worse for her. She felt a pang of guilt for hurting them, but reminded herself that they were extremely, incomprehensibly lucky to still be alive right now. Joane had shown so much faith in her, when she'd reached for the control sphere with shaking fingers, the only thoughts in her mind being regrets about things she should've said sooner. The second Tristan had understood the situation, she pretended she was already dead, as if that made it easier. She'd been doing that since the Consortium ships had attacked them in the Waning Crescent. Hell, she'd been doing that for most of her life, a dead woman walking, just trying to eke out a few more days, hours, seconds of life before the ceiling came down on her head. Somehow, even that line of thinking didn't make facing the end any more manageable.

She pushed her hair back from her face, batting the loose strands aside in the gravity-free environment. The gravity was off. That explained the floating, she realized, her ability to think coming back slowly. She looked down and noticed that her seatbelt had snapped, probably in that last maneuver, and she was now freely floating through the cockpit. She touched a finger to her lips and found that she, thankfully, had not vomited at any point. At least not all of her cooking had gone to waste. By now, she was closer to the ceiling than the floor, so she slowly shifted her body until she was able to get her feet on the ceiling and kick her way down to the console. She grabbed the arm of her chair, holding herself there with one hand while she began inspecting the state of the ship.

The power array had overloaded itself trying to keep the shields up, so only the most essential systems remained operational. That explained the lights and the gravity well enough, and thankfully the life support and shields were functioning. She had worried about the shield generator being completely burned out, which would've meant that the ship would slowly cook under the heat of any nearby stars and background radiation. Yet another improbable bit of luck keeping them alive, she supposed. She distantly remembered Joane saying something about the engines before she passed out, so she looked for any reports on that part of the ship. Apparently, three of the engines had sustained significant enough damage to require professional service before they would fire again. Tristan cursed and slapped the console. That would slow them down significantly. She didn't even bother looking at the Redshift diagnostics, knowing that whatever she saw would be upsetting.

She took a look outside through the viewport. They were rotating slowly, still carrying momentum from the series of wild spins Tristan had thrown them into in an attempt to slow them down. Cetea wasn't visible at the moment, but Tristan caught a slight glimpse of the reason they'd been pulled out of the Redshift. Tristan pushed herself up and over the console, drifting up to the glass and pressing a hand against it to steady herself. She floated there for a moment, gazing out into the expanse of the Messier Nebula. There, maybe half a Solan AU away, were the remains of Cetea-9. It was the furthest planet in its system from the star, surrounded by a set of dazzling white rings. Now, the rings hung empty in space, their planet having vanished months ago. Tristan examined the rings, wondering why they hadn't been affected by the gravitational forces that had pulled the planet away. She supposed that, rather than orbiting the planet, they were now orbiting the gravity well that hung in its place. Beautiful as the rings were, without a planet in the middle it was unnerving.

"Unnerving, isn't it?" a voice said, echoing Tristan's thoughts. She yelped and pulled back from the windscreen to see Joane hovering next to her against the viewport.

"Don't scare me like that," Tristan hissed. "How long have you been awake?" She turned back to the view, her heart rate elevated. The anxiety of their escape from the Redshift clearly not all gone just yet.

"I woke up when you punched the ship and called her a bitch," Joane explained, pushing herself closer to the window and taking up a spot right next to Tristan. Joane's breath was visible, Tristan realized, suddenly noticing that the heat had also lowered in the cabin significantly. "You should be nicer to Darling, you know."

"She knows I didn't mean it," Tristan said casually, though she found herself stroking the glass a little more apologetically and felt silly for it. "Are you okay?"

Joane took a moment to look down at herself, at Tristan's clothes on her body. "I feel like I threw up," she said numbly, "but I don't remember throwing up."

"You did," she assured her. "In my clothes, too." Joane grimaced apologetically. Tristan smiled, but her teeth began to chatter as the cold set into her bones and she started to shiver.

Joane noticed and hugged her arms a little tighter around her body. "I'd offer you my jacket, but I'm already wearing yours. Plus, you know," she gestured to the stains on the front of Tristan's black coat. As if on cue, Joane's brown synthetic leather jacket drifted by, its arms splayed out wildly like some ghostly figure was wearing it and dancing around the ship. Joane snatched it out of the air, then kicked over to drape it around Tristan's shoulders. She felt strange accepting it, but she grabbed it and held it closed over her body, enjoying the slight warmth it offered her. As they drew closer in the weightlessness of the cockpit, drifting painfully close, Tristan found herself looking at Joane's forehead, and the angry smudge of red at the edge of her hairline.

"You're still bleeding," she said, raising a hand to inspect the wound. Joane winced when Tristan's fingers parted her dirty blonde hair to inspect the cut, letting a few droplets of blood float away from her forehead. Tristan flashed back to seeing the wound when she'd ran into the cockpit to find Joane there, leaning helplessly over the console. She remembered running to her, touching it gently, ushering Joane out of the way so she could take her place as pilot. She remembered kissing her, just for a moment, when she thought they'd be dead within a minute.

Stars above, she had kissed her. And now Joane was pulling her jacket over Tristan's shoulders, her strong hands holding them both steady against the backdrop of the vanished world's glowing rings, with the nebula filling the void behind them. Her entire body buzzed, every nerve on edge. The thrill of surviving against all odds filled her, made her want to grab Joane's hands and pull her close. To kiss her and kiss her until that was the only thing she could think about, until it was the only thing that mattered.

"Joane," she said breathlessly. On her lips, the name was a plea, an admission, every one of her desires, hopes, and fears poured out into a single syllable laden with every bit of adoration she could muster. "You believed in me." It was all she could manage.

"You proved me right," Joane said, still holding Tristan there. Had they drifted there by chance, or did Joane mean for her fingertips to brush against Tristan's as they hung there, staring intently at each other? Her face looked so soft, so open, so vulnerable in a way Tristan couldn't remember ever seeing before now. Then, a shadow passed across her eyes, and Tristan almost whimpered in protest when she watched Joane's face harden into that same, business-like expression. "We're not safe here. If the Consortium bugged the ship, they'll know where we are soon enough. We need to find a way out of this system, or a hiding place, or something."

"Right," Tristan said, letting Joane's hand slip away from her own. She forced her eyes to turn back to the vanished world outside. "This could be good, though," she pointed out. "We needed readings from another vanished world, and here we are."

Joane nodded, her gaze lingering on Tristan's face for a few seconds more before turning to watch the empty rings with her. "We'll have to make it quick. Can you get out there to look for trackers while I set up the equipment we need to get a reading? It'll take a few hours, but once it's done we have to go."

"It'll be a few hours before the power cycles back on and the engines start working again," Tristan added. They weren't going anywhere for a while. A childish, selfish part of her mind thought that meant they had plenty of time to enjoy this unsettling, beautiful view in each other's arms, but she knew Joane better than that. She shrugged off her jacket and pushed backward from the viewport, heading towards the back of the room.

"Whenever Orion wakes up, have them clean the cockpit," she said over her shoulder. "And try not to be five feet up when the gravity comes back on." Joane gave her a smile and a nod as she reached the door, now unpressurized and unsealed. Tristan returned the smile, feeling a heartache deeper and more excruciating than the pounding in her head.

*        *        *

IT didn't take long to find the tracker. Darling wasn't a large ship, and the Consortium clearly hadn't been worried about being subtle with the placement. It was tucked just in front of the third starboard engine, which had burned out during the Redshift disaster. Tristan plucked the large black disc, about the size of a grav-frisbee, from the hull after disabling the mag-lock that had fastened it there. Not content to simply let it float into the void, she grasped it as tightly as she could and walked across the hull towards Darling's stubby wing.

It was hard to hold anything while wearing a vacsuit. The translucent clear projection of atmosphere around her melded enough to let her hold an object, but the seal never broke around anything unless she fiddled with the projector on her back to extend the range of the field. For now, Tristan was keeping the field contoured to her body, with her hair tucked back into a tight ponytail and stuffed down the back of her shirt. It was uncomfortable, but getting ice crystals and background radiation in her hair would have been a lot worse. The shields were up, keeping the worst of the void away from the ship, but she didn't want to risk it. She stepped towards the edge of the wing, feeling the satisfying thunk as her mag-boots locked in place against the hull, and cocked her arm back. She squinted, trying to focus on the distant sun through the glare of its light. Thankfully, they were far enough away that it didn't blind her instantly, but it did make it hard to see. She twisted her body like she was throwing a spear and hurled the disc, which went spinning off, through the shield, and hurtled through space at a steady, constant velocity.

If she'd thrown it right, Cetea's star would eventually catch it with its gravity and pull it in to be devoured by the cold blue dwarf star, but Tristan doubted it would be anytime soon. Still, it gave her a bit of peace to spite the Consortium in some small way. She watched it go, until the black metal projectile was indistinguishable from the blackness of space, and turned back to her search. More than one tracker was redundant and wasteful, but she didn't want to risk underestimating the Consortium. They clearly hadn't gotten this far by being clumsy or careless. She found no more trackers, but did find a buckled hull plate on the starboard side of the ship, through which she could barely see one of the cargo bays. Everything inside was covered in soot and ash, which had then been covered by a layer of ice.

She cursed as she reached for the toolkit strapped to her belt. She remembered Joane mentioning hull damage during the fiasco; this must've been it. The oxygen rich atmosphere must've ignited when the hull plate sparked and tore itself loose, then froze over once the decompression took hold. She couldn't remember what she'd been storing in that room, but it was certainly worthless now. Once Tristan patched up the hull, she would have to spend time repressurizing the room before she could examine what was left. She got to work, yanking the bent metal back into place with pliers and knocking out dents with a hammer. She felt sweat trickling down the back of her neck, a few droplets managing to break free of the vacsuit and drift off into space. It was a long process, and Tristan wasn't sure how long exactly it was taking. Still, they couldn't go anywhere until the power came on, so she had plenty of time to seal the breach. It was a simple enough fix once the hull plate had been flattened out, using a laser welder to heat the inside of the bulkhead, then flash-fusing it to the other side of the hole with an electric current. Once that was done to the best of her ability, she sprayed it with patching agent, aerosolized metal that coated the patched hole and sank into place before hardening to the strength of steel alloy. With the hull breach closed, she refastened the crimson hull panel and pulled herself back onto the top part of the ship. She took deep breaths as she lay out on the hull, not being used to heavy repair work after spending so much time just waiting onboard the ship. It felt good though, finding a problem that she could fix and then fixing it. It was simple and made sense, unlike everything else.

*Here we go*, she thought, and before she could stop herself she was thinking about Joane again. Floating there, feeling weightless in more ways than one, Joane's arms around her shoulders and staring into those pale blue eyes…Tristan cursed herself for not just kissing her. She had never been shy about kissing, or anything, for that matter. She'd loved women before, or at least she thought she had at the time. Never had she felt so completely undone by someone, though. It was like there was a loose thread on her somewhere that Joane had pulled and pulled until Tristan was unraveled, a useless pile of string. She brought her hand up to her face, watching the crackle of the vacsuit as the seal met itself before merging to allow her hand through it. She touched her lips ponderously; they were still abuzz from the momentary kiss they'd shared. Just one, Tristan thought, she wanted to kiss her when she didn't think it would be her last chance to do so. After a moment, she felt a few vibrations in the hull.

"I thought I'd find you here."

The voice was muffled, reaching Tristan like her head was underwater. She didn't startle when she heard it; instead, she shifted her knees up towards her chest and let out a sigh. If she focused, she could see the carbon dioxide she exhaled pass through her vacsuit in a small, thin cloud. It drifted up and away from Darling's hull, dissipating rapidly in the endless blackness of the Void. She didn't turn her head away from her view of the Messier Nebula, but her eyes lowered as she listened to the soft thuds of footsteps approaching her.

In a few moments, Tristan could feel Joane standing to her right, awkwardly. She could see the edge of her legs, surrounded by her own vacsuit. Tristan waved a hand in exasperation. "Sit," she said, her voice coming out choked and strained. She hadn't spoken aloud since she'd left the ship hours ago, she realized, as she cleared her throat.

Joane obliged slowly, favoring an old injury in her left leg as she folded herself into a comfortable position on Darling's crimson hull. There was a series of scuffs and thumps as Joane tried to tuck her good leg under her body while stretching out the other, all while keeping her magnetic anchors engaged to the hull. "Find any trackers?" Joane asked, always focused on business. Tristan nodded wordlessly. Joane didn't seem surprised. "I saw that the hull breach had been sealed, so I went ahead and started the repressurization. What's keeping you out here?"

Tris finally turned to look at the woman sitting a few feet away. "I came out here for some peace and quiet, actually," she deadpanned. If Joane wanted to be professional, Tristan could do that, even if she couldn't meet her eyes.

Joane nodded in acknowledgement, but stayed where she was. "Orion woke up a while ago," she continued. "They were very apologetic about the cabin and wanted me to give you their sincerest thanks for not condemning them to a cold, awful death in the void. They said the cockpit would be as clean as the day the ship was built by the time the engines are ready to go."

Tristan chuckled a bit, despite herself. She forced her smile down. "Good," she said curtly. "And the gravitational readings?" Joane seemed to watch her closely, taking a few moments before responding.

"I had Darling's sensor array working on it," Joane said. "I'm not Ahsha, so I can only hope I calibrated it right. We'll know in a few hours when we plot the charts and try to find wherever the planets were headed. The rings on Cetea-9 make it a lot easier, it's hard to see now but there would've been some level of disturbance when the vanishing happened, which should be a lot easier to plot than planetary orbits."

Tristan tuned her out, staring up at Cetea, several million miles away, barely bigger than any of the other stars she could see. It was a cold star, one that had long burnt out of its main sequence, but instead of collapsing into a black hole or fizzling out as a white dwarf, it had gone cold, drawing in the gasses in the nebula and turning a bright blue color as it fought to keep itself burning for just a few more billion years.

It was hard to make out from this far away, but Tristan could barely see a small white flare shoot up from the star, a column of fire blasting its way away from the surface and reaching out for the void in an instant. It wasn't long before the inevitable, crushing gravity of the small star seized the hopeful band of flame and yanked it back down, forming a band of light that quickly shrunk down back to the surface.

Tristan had never seen a fully emergent solar flare, though she longed to watch one before she died. The thought of watching a little bit of starlight break off from a seemingly inescapable object and shoot out into the void, bringing light to some distant edge of the system. The idea of it filled her with…something she couldn't describe.

"Tris," Joane said forcefully, yanking her out of her melodramatic thoughts. Tristan reluctantly turned to face her, swallowing hard in preparation. When she looked back, Joane was looking at her like she hadn't turned away from her for a second. It made Tristan fight back a blush, even though her cheeks were already flushed from the effort of her repair job. She suddenly felt self-conscious about her hair, oddly tucked into her collar, though she wasn't sure why. She also wasn't sure why looking at Joane was a lot like stargazing. Her eyes fixated on all the smallest details, all at once. The way her dirty blonde hair fell past her cheekbones, the way her vacsuit's pale blue light reflected in her eyes, almost the exact same color as the hardlight. "We should talk."

Tristan forced herself to look into her eyes, despite how much it hurt, how hard it was not to look away. "Yeah," she admitted. She turned her body, which wasn't an easy motion when her feet were magnetized to Darling's hull.

"You kissed me," Joane said, like she was reading off a weather report. It was so clinical, so monotone, so unremarkable. Tristan lowered her gaze to Darling's hull. She saw Joane's hand, protected by the suit, resting against the deep red metal. Her mind wandered to a distant memory of the two of them arguing with Ahsha, all of them drunk and laughing, about how much their ship needed a custom paint job. *"If we're going to be the best damn field researchers in the universe,"* they had said to her, *"we need to work on branding. People need to know us when they see us."* Ahsha had vehemently refused, of course, so the next time she took a few days to herself to do some study on some atmospheric pressure shift or something similarly interesting, the two of them had hijacked the ship and had it painted anyway. When Ahsha had found out, she'd been furious, launched into a diatribe about docking their pay, leaving them on the most barren asteroid she could find, and reverting the "garish" paint job the first chance she got. For all her talk though, Darling had kept the same coat of paint since that day.

Tristan let her own hand fall to the hull, brushing across the smooth metal surface. Their fingertips were only a few inches apart. "I did," she said, not willing to admit more than that just yet. She wouldn't make a fool of herself until she could adequately judge Joane's reaction. Joane was quiet for a long time while Tristan tried as hard as possible to keep her eyes aimed at the hull. If she dared meet Joane's eyes…she wasn't sure what she'd say or do.

After what felt like an eternity of silence, Joane pulled her hand away from the hull and gestured to the view in front of them. She cleared her throat awkwardly and waved her arm. "I'm glad you still do this," she said, her voice stilted and strange. "I remember the first time we did an orbit around a star after Ahsha hired you. You looked like a kid in a candy store."

Tristan smiled despite herself. She followed Joane's gesture back to the star, trying to remember what her life had been like back home. It felt like a thousand years ago, but so strangely familiar that she sunk back into it with ease.

*It had been only a few weeks since they'd left the Hollow World with Tristan onboard. Darling, though they didn't call the ship that just yet, was cycling engine charge buildup, so they'd waited for a day in the middle of a small, out of the way solar system somewhere in the Old Andromeda Nebula. The first time Tristan saw the star through Darling's curved viewport, she'd stood frozen in place for minutes, her eyes and mouth both wide open. She didn't remember entirely, but she thought she may have even shed a tear. It would've been justified; growing up in the crag tunnels of a Hollow World meant Tristan had scarcely seen the night sky her entire life, let alone a star up close. All she'd had were glimpses of her system's black hole, a yawning mouth of unceasing hunger and destruction, surrounded by a corona of orange light that haloed out around the singularity. It was all that remained of what had once been her home planet's sun, and within a few hundred thousand years, it was going to swallow her home with it. For most of her life, Tristan had expected that her ultimate fate resided beyond the event horizon of that singularity. She would have carved out a short, uneventful, brutal life in the tunnels of her home before something got the better of her, and then her bones would have waited patiently for the black hole to swallow them up. She'd spent so many nights awake, lying on her stiff, small cot, staring down the endless tunnels and trying to imagine what it would feel like to fall into a black hole's gravity well. That's the life she would've lived, were it not for Ahsha Reindare and Joane Cordelle.*

"Ahsha almost had to drag you back inside so we could leave," Joane mused, filling the silence that had fallen over them while Tristan was lost in her memories. "We all sat out here for an hour watching the Star burn before-"

"Joane," Tristan cut her off, reaching out and grabbing her hand. "You aren't good at beating around the bush. Just say what you need to say." Joane stammered a bit, fell silent, and then took a deep breath.

"What's happening here, Tris?" she asked, her voice soft and uncertain. "What are we doing?"

"I have no idea," Tristan said honestly, her eyes focused on their hands and the way their vacsuit seals sparked against each other. "I shouldn't have kissed you like that, without your permission. I'm sorry."

"Please don't be sorry for that," Joane whispered hoarsely, desperation in her voice. "I don't want you to regret it." Warmth flowed through Tristan's body, making the blush in her cheeks grow even darker. She had to say something. Something smart and witty, clever and suave, the way she usually did when she was with a beautiful woman.

"I can't stop thinking about you," she said finally, all dumb honesty and rushed words. She almost slapped herself as soon as the words left her, but there was no going back. "Even before we slept together, just being around you again is…it's tearing me apart. I spent three years on my own with Darling, and I thought that was all I needed. A ship and a home, all in one. But I forgot, Joane. I forgot that you and Ahsha were my home, too. I see you now and it's like…everything's different but exactly the same somehow."

Joane was quiet for a long time, so long that Tristan felt stupid. So stupid. "I…I don't know how this happened," she said finally. Tristan didn't say anything, but she nodded in agreement. She doubted she'd ever really know. Something about it felt inevitable, like their destinies were always going to lead them here, to this Nebula, holding hands and pouring out feelings like flushing the buildup from a power coil. "I don't even know what to call…*this*. Do you?"

"Ahsha would call it a frivolous distraction tangentially related to the completion of the mission at hand," Tristan muttered, trying to joke as she fought back a sniffle. She didn't want to cry in space, it was an awkward mess as tears either filled the inside of the vacsuit or drifted off into the void.

"It's like she's here with us right now," Joane said, trying to match her tone, "but she isn't. We're the only ones here, Tris. I…I have to know how you feel."

*I would tell you if I knew*, she wanted to say, but she would've been lying. She knew, deep down, that she had made up her mind about Joane a long time ago. It was when they'd stood in the cockpit together, arguing after they had nearly kissed while working on the engine, when their confused feelings had crashed against each other like asteroids on a collision course. She'd seen Joane, really seen her, for the first time ever, and she had known in that instant exactly how she felt. Everything since then, the anger, the bitterness, the avoiding her, it had been real, but she had focused on it to keep the truth suppressed. There was an old Solan adage, warped by translations and changed over time: No one can hear you scream in space. Here, under Darling's shield, there was only one person in the universe who could hear her. It just so happened to be the hardest person in the universe to admit it to.

But she did. "I'm in love with you, Joane." She expected the words to feel heavy in her mouth. To come out awkwardly or with some grand, graceful tone. Instead, she said it with a sureness and certainty that she'd been missing for weeks. "I don't know when I fell in love with you, but I only just realized it recently. I don't know how to explain it or rationalize it or condense my emotions down into some neat and tidy little capsule to study and pick apart piece by piece, but I know that much. And I know that I could try to stop loving you, and believe me, I have, but it would be a waste of time."

She could feel Joane's eyes on her, but she didn't want to look up, didn't want to risk seeing that same, stony look on her face. It might kill her, she thought without an ounce of irony. Still, Joane's hand had tightened on hers to the point that, even through the two vacsuits, she could feel Joane's nails against her palm. Her hand was shaking, and it took Tris a moment to realize that she was too. She was panicked and shivering like a lost kitten, all because she told someone how she felt, how pathetic. How annoying. How exciting. She reached her free hand to her back and fiddled with the suit projector, expanding the seal to envelop the both of them and make it thin enough for her hand to pass through Joane's. The heat controls in the suits meant her hand was warm, despite the biting, unforgiving cold of the void that surrounded them. "You're not saying anything, Joane," Tristan said, never taking her eyes off their interlocked hands.

"I don't know what I'd say."

Tristan swallowed hard, dread and regret settling in her stomach like she'd just swallowed a particularly large stone. "Please," she asked. "I just told you…everything. Please don't make me even more of a fool by not being honest with me."

"I'm not as good at this as you are," Joane said softly, voice quivering weakly. She tightened her grip on Tristan's hand, like she was afraid if she let go she might slip away and float away from the hull. Tristan squeezed her hand back, trying to ground her in some small way. "I don't know…how."

"Can you try? For me?" Tristan begged. Tears began to fall from her eyes of their own volition. She was such an idiot. Why did she have to beg for honesty and openness from her? It wasn't fair. She heard Joane trying to form words, starting sentences and stopping them just as quickly.

Finally, she found the words. "It meant everything to me, too," she said, and Tristan immediately understood. Drew in a breath. Pulled her hand away from Joane to bury her face in her palms. She felt the blush in her entire face and wanted to scream.

"You heard that," she said, squeezing her eyes shut even though her fingers blocked everything.

"I did," Joane answered quietly.

"Fuck."

"I should've said something then," Joane went on. Tristan felt her hand on her shoulder and shook her head in response, disbelief and embarrassment overwhelming her. She thought about disengaging her mag-boots and jumping off the ship, following the tracker disc towards Cetea's star. "I was just…surprised. I needed to think and process it."

Tristan let out a long, pained groan. "You weren't supposed to hear that," she said. "It was stupid and sappy and I was *drunk*."

"You didn't mean it?" Joane's voice sounded wary, defensive.

"Of course I meant it," she corrected. "Damn it, Joane. By the Singularity, I just feel so stupid." Immediately, Joane's grip on her shoulder grew more firm, and the woman pulled herself closer, until they were pressed against one another. Tristan felt the tingle of her suit for only a moment before her seal expanded to cover them both. Finally, Tristan looked up at Joane again, pulling her face away from her hands slowly and fearfully. Joane was smiling at her, but it was a sad, aching smile.

"I'm the one who's being stupid," she said, whispering despite the fact that they were alone, like she didn't want to risk the sound of her words escaping into the void. "I wish I could put everything I'm thinking into words like you."

"Then forget about what you're thinking," Tristan said, leaning forward until all she could see was Joane's face. It was a view to rival the nebula around them. No star in the universe could have possibly shined brighter than her eyes did in that moment. "Tell me what you're *feeling*. Stop thinking so damn much and just feel; I won't interrupt."

Joane sucked in a deep breath as she tried to steady herself for a few moments. The hand on Tristan's shoulder flexed a few times. She brought her own hand up and covered it, holding it firmly in place. She knew how calloused and rough Joane's palms were, but the backs of her hands were soft and smooth. "Tristan Ninomae, you are…like a black hole to me. A singularity all your own. I'm like a ship adrift, dead in the void. You have such a gravity to you that I am useless to try and escape. I can feel the weight of it threatening to crush me, even now. The pull of it could tear me in two, but it wouldn't matter because you'd still be pulling me in. I know I passed the Event Horizon a long time ago, and it's just a matter before I'm sucked in completely. And I have no idea what is going to happen to me when you do.

"And, Tris, I'm terrified. I've been scared before. Of dying, of losing people, of a lot of things. This is different, though, because now I'm scared of *myself*. I've never not known myself like this before. I try to unravel how I feel, but I just get more tangled up. All of this mess around us, all these problems to solve, and the only thing that I have no answers for is how I feel about you. I can't get you out of my head, I lose sleep because I stare at the ceiling and think about you, I can barely look you in the eye and still get a sentence out.

"But I don't know if I deserve to say I love you. After everything that happened between us, after I dragged you into this hell — I almost got you killed and still might — How could I do something like that to someone and still say I love them?"

Tristan put her hand up to Joane's face, caressing the line of her strong jaw with the softest touch she could manage. "Joane, it isn't up to you to decide what you deserve to feel. If I didn't think you could love me, I wouldn't have let myself fall for you. I wouldn't have kissed you that time in the cabin, or earlier. I can't say that you didn't hurt me, or that I can completely forget the things that happened, but I'm sick of holding on to that pain. I want to forgive you, Joane. And I can't believe I'm saying this, but I want to forgive Ahsha, too.

"I do forgive you. I don't care if you think you deserve it. I don't care if you forgive me. I mean, I do care. I just mean…you don't have to; I'm far from innocent." They both fell silent for a long time, just holding each other quietly and waiting for the other to gather the courage to speak. Tristan was aware that she was wasting time. Eventually, the scans would be done, or the engines would power up, or the people chasing them would show up and kill them. She hadn't gotten this far by being cautious, and she'd already made a fool of herself once this conversation. There didn't seem to be much reason to start hesitating now. "Would you kiss me right now if I asked you to?" she asked, her voice falling into a whisper.

Joane looked startled, but she didn't pull back or away. "Why don't you ask me and find out?"

Tristan bit back a smile. "Because I don't know if you want to kiss me or not."

Joane's hand left Tristan's shoulder and moved to the back of her neck, slipping beneath her braid and dancing across the sensitive skin just above her shoulders. She tried and failed to repress the shiver that moved up and down her spine as Joane's fingertips moved tenderly across her skin. "I won't kiss you if I don't want to," she promised.

"Will you kiss me?" Tristan asked, utterly debasing herself. She wasn't used to being on this side of the equation, needing someone's touch so madly, so deeply, that she would resort to begging for it. And yet, here she was. And yet, Joane's hand went from tender to firm as it gripped the back of her neck and pulled her in. And yet, she let her pull her in, a soft whimper escaping her lips as she drifted towards her. And yet.

The kiss itself was…cautious. They hadn't learned how to kiss one another in a way that wasn't fueled by desperate, blind passion or immediate fear of death. Joane had, thankfully, brushed her teeth since they arrived in the Messier Nebula, and she still tasted of sharp, cold mint. Tristan's hands fell to Joane's waist, grabbing fistfuls of her jacket and holding her firmly in place, like a tether tying them both to one another. It was exactly the kiss Tristan had wanted, the closest thing to a moment of true peace she had felt in far too long. At that moment, everything was alright. She was safe, she was at peace, she was *happy*. She found herself smiling through the kiss, fighting to keep her lips in place against Joane's. Joane felt her smile and returned it before her lips parted against Tristan's, a wordless question that she answered immediately by letting Joane into her mouth hungrily. She let out a gasp as she felt Joane's other hand snake around her waist, yanking her closer until they were fully pressed against each other, rolling over one another against Darling's hull.

After a kiss that lasted an eternity but still wasn't enough for her, Tristan had to pull back to draw a breath from her oxygen supply. She looked up at Joane, who was perched above her, keeping her arms straight to give Tristan space despite her entire body lying on top of her. Joane's mouth hung open, her eyes unfocused but full of admiration and affection. Her auburn and blonde hair fell past her face in wild strands, and her copper cheeks were flushed.

"Orion is going to wonder about us," Joane said, suppressing a laugh. Tristan reached up and put her arms around Joane's neck and pulled her back down towards her.

"Let them wonder," she said, before kissing her again.

# Chapter 24
## It Was Nice While It Lasted

ARGUS Regille stood at the window of his private quarters, hands clasped behind his back, standing perfectly still and formal despite being the only person in the room. Character was what one did when no one was watching, after all. He didn't need to look over his shoulder to know that every item in his onboard office was perfectly straightened, dusted, and in its exact place. The thought was the only thing that gave him a measure of peace. He gazed out at Eden's Cradle, marveling at the culmination of all their years of work. It was still unfinished, imperfect, but already it was…magnificent. Argus wasn't one to exaggerate, but he found himself thinking that one day the Cradle would be seen as the greatest achievement of sentient life. From the first Solans fighting to escape their atmosphere, to the first Redshift drives, to the Wayfaring Stations, to this. It would be ready soon, and it *would* be ready. The work was going to be finished, he told himself. No one, not even Senator Masenna and his two cronies could stop it now. The tide of progress was as total and unrelenting as a singularity.

Blue light from the Cradle bathed his face and accentuated the shadows of his old, withered features. It was the only light for millions, no, billions, of light years. Supervoids were convenient hiding spots, but they were terribly dark and not at all pleasant. The Void, what was once just called "space" by the first starbound species, wasn't normal here. Neither "void" or "space" were technically correct terms, for there was always a presence of something. Background radiation, trace elements, even antimatter filled even the darkest corners of space. The Supervoid wasn't any different, there was just…less. Less than physicists and astronomers could understand. There were no theories or explanations for why or how these low-density regions existed, they simply did. The subject, like the regions themselves, was avoided, its edges skirted and ignored to the best of everyone's ability. It made it the perfect place for a construction as ambitious as this.

The message to the others had gone…as expected. He was admonished for his carelessness, and instructed to make sure no further errors were made. No disciplinary action was to be taken for now, but they made it clear that such forgiveness was a one-time offer. He had received a letter of thanks from the Cygnan Relief Group for his remarks on their tragically lost Senator, which he kept for reasons he couldn't quite explain. He'd spent the next few days researching the two women who had been at Cygnus, the two women who had slipped through his fingers through sheer dumb luck.

Joane Cordelle and Tristan Ninomae. He sneered to himself as he stared at the window, unable to repress his annoyance at them. He couldn't fathom for the longest time why or how a disgraced Solan heiress and a philanthropic Hollow mercenary had ended up stumbling across the few breadcrumbs they had been clumsy enough to leave behind and let it lead them so close to the truth. Then, he had found it: the stem from which the thorns in his side had grown. The connection had come in the strangest of places, a picture that recognized their two faces from a scientific journal. They were at a beneficiaries gala, five years ago, both looking mildly bored and annoyed to be surrounded by upper class individuals and intellectuals, flanking the connective tissue between them and the Cradle: Dr. Ahsha Reindare.

Argus began to pace as he went over it again in his mind, walking back and forth before the floor-to-ceiling viewport. Dr. Reindare was imminent in her field; Argus had even read some of her works on gravitational science in preparation for the work he was now so close to seeing completed. Unfortunately, like too many scientists, she had been too damn smart for her own good. He hadn't met the scientist personally — he was much too busy for that — but his colleagues spoke about her as if she was quite the handful. Perhaps it was time to meet with the famed Doctor and have a conversation about her employees.

He was on his way back to his desk, ready to hail the Cradle and have them prepare Reindare to meet with him, when the signal light flashed with an incoming message. He hummed in curiosity and sent the message through. The Captain's voice came through, barely masking his elation. "Senator Regille," he said. "We've got a ping on their tracker, they emerged from the Redshift in the Messier Nebula, inside the Cetea system."

Cetea-9. How odd. The idea troubled him. They had gone straight from Cygnus to another one of the "vanished" worlds. What could they possibly have pieced together, he wondered to himself. Still, this was good news. Whatever they knew, whatever they thought they had figured out, whatever their plans to stand in his way, he had them now.

"Send a wing of fighters," he said, keeping his voice measured and the hatred tamped down, deep in his chest. "Don't leave *anything* behind."

# Chapter 25
## Break Time's Over

TRISTAN left Joane after they got back inside the ship, heading off to the engine compartment to work on the three engines they'd lost leaving the Redshift. It made her ache to watch her leave, but she reminded herself who she was and the job she had to do. She could be mushy later; right now they were on borrowed time. She made her way to the cockpit, dodging fallen stacks of boxes and storage crates as she went. The artificial gravity had come back on while they were outside the ship, but nothing in the ship had been properly tied down, so it had spent a few hours drifting freely before collapsing all at once. Joane hadn't thought it was possible, but Darling was even more of a mess now than it was before. At one point, her foot caught on a particularly heavy crate she hadn't been paying attention to. She managed to avoid falling entirely, but the crate fell over and spilled its contents out onto the floor. It was full of picture frames of all makes and sizes. Metal alloys, holographic displays, and synth wood. One in particular caught Joane's eye. It was resting atop her foot, a simple physical photograph held by a reddish brown frame which had broken in half when it hit the ground. She paused for a moment, her mission be damned, and bent down to pick up the photo.

She rubbed her thumb across the flimsy photo paper, clearing the dust off the three smiling faces in the photo. It was them. Her, Tristan, and Ahsha. It was the photo that had sat by her bedside for years, the photo that had been missing when she boarded Darling. "You kept it," she whispered to herself, smiling like an idiot and shaking her head. She sighed happily. "Full of surprises." She folded the photo into a neat square, tucked into her pocket, then continued on her way to the cockpit.

When the door opened, the smell of cleaning chemicals hit her like a steel beam to the face. She made a face as she walked in, and was met by the Senator almost immediately.

Orion had finally decided to put their clothes back on, and the image of a Consortium senator in their finest official garments scrubbing the floor of a ship was odd, to say the least. They gave her an uneasy, embarrassed smile. "Miss Cordelia," they said. "I hate to say this, but it seems like I may have thrown up twice during the unpleasantness, but I'm done cleaning up the worst of it. I'm just scrubbing the floor to make myself useful."

Joane swallowed hard, remembering the harsh taste of bile that had been in her mouth when she woke up. Oh well, she thought, what they didn't know wouldn't hurt. "Thank you, Orion," she said. "Tris will be pleased, it looks lovely."

"Speaking of Tristan," Orion said, leaning back onto their knees and pushing a sweaty lock of hair out of their face. "You went to fetch her from the hull forty-five minutes ago." Joane nodded curtly, not giving them an inch. "Your jacket is buttoned wrong."

"What?" Joane hissed, looking down and checking herself. She had been so careful to make sure she was well put together on her way back into the ship. She pawed at her jacket, inspecting the buttons, and found each one of them was properly affixed to cover the fully closed zipper.

"Gotcha," Orion said with a grin as they went back to scrubbing. Joane frowned.

"I suppose you think you're real clever for that," she said with a heavy sigh. Orion laughed goodnaturedly, and she rolled her eyes, fighting back a smile. She didn't want to let herself like the senator like Tris had.

"A bit, yes," they said. "If it makes you feel any better, I knew before you came back in. This hull isn't entirely soundproof, you know." Joane's face went red, with shame or rage she wasn't quite sure. "Have you two admitted your feelings for one another or is it back to normal now?"

Joane glared at them as she approached the console, checking for the gravitational scanner. "I don't really know," she found herself admitting against her will. Hell, what was it about Orion that made her want to admit things to them? "You didn't do anything stupid while I was gone, did you?"

Orion set down the wide scrubbing brush and pushed themselves to their feet with only a slight bit of struggle. They still needed to take a deep breath after getting up, but they had come a long way from their injury in just a few days. "You know, it's the strangest thing, I *was* going to do something stupid, but came to find someone had stolen my badge." Joane smirked, reached into her jacket's inner pocket, and pulled out Orion's blue and silver badge. Orion nodded, unsurprised, and crossed their arms. "Did you know that stealing from a Consortium official is a serious offense?"

Joane laughed. "Didn't you say, Orion, that you've probably lost your credentials by now, whether you're dead or a criminal? Also, I'm glad to know I was right not to trust you with this thing."

Orion sighed and held out their hand, palm up. Joane looked down at their hand, back up at Orion's face, and pulled the badge away. "It's mine," they said petulantly. "I'm not going to initiate a call or anything, I only meant to send a ping on my unique frequency to let people know I'm not dead." Joane rolled her eyes. It was like trying to paint a fence during a hurricane with them. By the time she got done, everything she'd started out with had been washed away.

"And let Regille and his allies know our exact location?"

"Well, I figured they were tracing our ship, so once we left the Redshift, they should have known where we were almost instantly. Wouldn't you rather everyone know where we are instead of just the people trying to kill us?" Joane paused for a moment, hefting the dense badge in her hand as she let herself consider the thought.

"It's dangerous," she said. "You seem to trust your allies a great deal, but I don't. We're all part of the Consortium, Orion, and those silver wings have never done anything to lift me up."

"I'm not going to try and take it from you," Orion said, as if she'd ever considered that as a real threat. "I won't argue. If you think we've got enough time to avoid the ones after us, then very well." Their face suddenly went very grave, eyes serious and dialed into an intense focus. Orion took a few steps forward, and Joane pocketed the badge as they approached. The sterile cleanliness of the chemicals in the air, the Consortium uniform bearing down on her, it was a suffocating feeling she knew all too well. "I would rather not die in obscurity, Miss Cordelia. When my time comes, I would like to know that the truth of my death will be known. Don't you?"

She stared up at them, eyes locked. "Take a step back, Masenna," she commanded, her voice shockingly level. She was relieved when they did as she asked; she didn't want to have to hit them.

"Are you alright?" they asked in that annoying way they did where it was hard to tell if they were being genuine or just political.

"I'm trying to work," she said pointedly, dodging the question neatly. "Here we are." She tapped the screen of the console and swiped her fingers upward, sending the data to a hologram projector set in the top of it. A rough image of the rings outside and Cetea-9's gravity well emerged in the air, then expanded to include Cetea-5's orbit, the closest planet that had been on the same side of the system's star when the vanishing happened. Joane muttered to herself, talking through the data she was looking for as she worked, and Orion watched her quietly. She hadn't originally picked Cetea as a good system to check for gravitational anomalies. Many of the other ones had planets far closer in their orbits to the vanishings, and she'd thought it would've been easier to get noticeable readings from them. Cetea-9's rings, however, made the work infinitely easier. The rings themselves were unchanged to the naked eye and most standard scans. All of the large clumps of ice and stone that orbited the planet had stayed in place, a fact that surprised Joane. Whatever device they were using to move the planets was so precise it had been able to move an entire world without affecting the patterns of its rings only a few hundred thousand miles away. The density of the rings, though, had changed ever so slightly. The clouds of dust spread throughout the rings had shifted with the force of gravity, pulled toward the location of the waves. If Joane looked very, very closely, a process that would've been silly to anyone who didn't know what they knew about the vanishings, she could see the pattern. After maybe an hour of closer scans, she had it: the clouds in the ring were pulled ever so slightly towards a point, then away at that point, they moved away from the system. She spent a while checking Cetea-5's orbit as well, just to be as sure as she possibly could, and confirmed her rudimentary calculations. It took a lot of fiddling with the computer's graphing ability, but she had some practice from her presentation the other night. She got done drawing her best approximation of Cetea-9's flight path just as the cockpit door slid open behind her.

In walked Tris, her cloak missing, engine grease and oil staining her simple white undershirt, hands, and face. Her hair was still pulled back in a braid behind her back, and the imprint of a face shield was still evident around her eyes. She looked winded, but not too disappointed in the work she'd been doing.

"Well, I got two of the engines working," she said, wiping her hands on an old, almost entirely blackened rag. It did almost nothing, so she tossed the rag over her shoulder back into the hopeless mess that made up the ship's common area. "Do we have good news?"

"We have great news," Joane said after taking a moment to drink in Tris's appearance. She turned to the holomap projection behind her, swiping the data from Cetea-5 into the graph. The graph went pixelated for a second, and then a bright red line appeared in the middle of the gravity well of Cetea-9, pointing towards the edge of the system. Joane twisted a knob on the console, zooming the map out to show most of the known universe. From another point a few regions to the universal south, there was another line representing Cygnus-4's path. The lines both projected on their paths, neatly dodging any galaxies or standalone planets, then eventually met and passed one another. Joane raised her finger and pointed at the spot where they met. "There you are," she said, grinning wildly. Ahsha would've been proud of her, she thought. Ahsha would've figured it out sooner and more exactly, but she hoped that when they found her, she'd appreciate the work they'd done.

Orion and Tristan approached the map, inspecting the point where the two lines intersected. There was nothing of note there, no system that had opposed the Consortium or site of some great historical significance. In fact, there was almost nothing at all there. It was a massive hole in the void, even more sparse than the usual mind-boggling distance between galaxies and the solar systems spread throughout them. For billions, trillions of miles, there was nothing. No planets, no stars, not even a cloud of dust left over from something that had been there eons ago and since crumbled. Most of the locations on universal maps bore additional details, such as when they were inducted into the Consortium, population, and the cosmic weather patterns common to that area. This area, though, was labeled with nothing but a name: The Hesperides Supervoid.

"I don't understand," Orion said. "It's a Void, things aren't supposed to go into Voids, and they hardly ever come out."

"Well, planets aren't supposed to move," Tris offered with a shrug. "People aren't supposed to move faster than light, and so on and so forth."

"It's a good place to hide something," Joane said, crossing her arms. She felt winded for some reason. Adrenaline was coursing through her as she stared at the intersection between the two lines.

"That's like saying the inside of an engine makes for a great storage compartment," Orion countered. "I know enough about Supervoids to know that people avoid them for a reason. No artificial planets or city stations are set up in them for a reason. Space is…wrong inside them. It's colder, emptier." Joane couldn't help but nod. She knew the stories, the warnings, the old wives tales mixed with just enough fact to keep all but the dumbest adventurers from straying too close to the borders of the dozen or so true Supervoids. Ahsha had once expressed a desire to visit the Piscean Void, and it had been the one time Tris and her had been able to talk her out of something. If something was bad enough to turn even Ahsha Reindare away…it made Joane's stomach turn.

"Look, they aren't just throwing these planets into a Void so they can disappear," Tris spoke up. "They've got to be doing something with them, otherwise they'd just pull them into a black hole or blow them up and save a lot of time. So, clearly, they've found a way to navigate it safely, and all we have to do is…find out how they do it."

"Easily done, I assume," Orion said sarcastically. Tristan clasped her hands together.

"Look, it's not like we don't have time to think about it. Until the Redshift drive is done flushing itself out, we're not going anywhere fast without a Fastlane. And we can't use a Fastlane because the three of us are enemies of the state," she said. "All we can do now is get out of the way, find a hiding spot, and if we're lucky, we won't have to worry about anyone finding us."

As if the universe heard Tris speaking, the fabric of space rippled just slightly, a few thousand feet away. Then, like an imitation of Cetea-9's rings, a white circle cut itself into view, a spinning point of light that curved around into a gossamer thin line that began to glow with shimmering blue and green. The point traveled around the afterimage of its own light, growing brighter and brighter. Then, another point of light joined it, following just behind the first one. Then another, and another, until the whole circle was full of the glowing dots, shining so brightly that the glare made them impossible to distinguish. The space inside the circle began to shimmer and ripple, like water on the surface of a lake being disturbed. The black void background gave way to the white glare, which took on its own, silvery glow.

"Shit," they all said in unison. Each of them knew what a Fastlane looked like. With Cetea plagued by gravitational anomalies, the Wayfaring Stations had all been shut down, which could only mean one thing. They'd been found. Tris ran for the console, punching the button to deploy the control sphere. Joane stepped aside without being asked.

"Fighting or running?" she asked as the sphere in Tris's hand began to hum, and the functioning engines at the back of the ship burst to life, thrumming weakly.

Tris stared at the circle for a moment, watched several sharp, angular shapes materialize in the glow, black silhouettes against the almost blinding light. Consortium Wing Fighters. Joane counted the shapes to the best of her ability — there were at least three — and turned back to her pilot. Her face was ashen and grim as she stared at the power readouts for the engines.

"We can't run," she reported simply. Joane nodded. The Redshift had made their decision for them. Here, crippled and alone, with nowhere close enough to even think about hiding, there was only one option. She didn't need to wait for Tris to tell her to turn around and jump into the weapons systems deck.

"What can we do?" Joane asked, diverting as much power as she could to the weak ion cannons and warming them up. She tried to leave the engines, shields, and life support alone, even as the lights around them dimmed.

"I can keep them off of us for a while," Tris said confidently as she curled her fingers around the control sphere. "What can you do?"

Joane glanced at the viewport. The Fastlane was still open, and five ships were now clearly visible, closing on them quickly. They were here to kill them. They'd tried to kill them at Cygnus. The system in front of her chimed as Darling's rudimentary weapons activated. She deployed the trigger and looked back to the targeting screen, taking in a direct view of the field from cameras mounted near the ion cannons.

"Whatever I need to do," she said, her voice even and steady. She knew Tris didn't like hurting people. Joane didn't care for it, but she knew what she had to do. If she lived to see the other side of this, she didn't expect to lose any sleep over the pilots of the Wing fighters. Tris looked at her for a second, set her face into a stern, focused frown, and punched the control sphere forward.

Darling bucked and jolted as it shot forward, nebulous clouds passing by and framing the attacking ships. "Uh, Tristan?" Orion said, panicked. "I can't help but notice we're moving *towards* the fighters, when I personally think moving *away* might be a better-"

"We're going to have to fight this eventually, Senator," Tris cut them off, glancing downward to flick a few switches on her captain's console. She was standing up, control sphere in one hand, the other switching between bracing herself and activating subsystems Joane didn't even begin to understand. "I'd rather get things started now instead of letting them chase us halfway to the edge of the system."

"It's suicide!" Orion countered. Joane responded by unleashing her first shot at the Wing in the middle of the formation. The bolt of blue energy thrummed and crackled as it shot through the void, arcs of electricity igniting a small portion of the nebula into a green flame that quickly fizzled. The Wing moved oddly, its four hooked, bird-like wings spinning on an axis around the ship's long, angular body as it darted to the right, allowing the bolt to pass by it harmlessly before dissipating behind it. It quickly, smoothly, slid back into formation with the others.

She never expected the shot to hit. It was a trade, the first two tokens sacrificed in a game of keras. Information for information. The Wings knew what weapons they had at their disposal, and Joane knew just how maneuverable their ships were. She mentally prepared herself to lead her shots, predict the movements of the fighters, something that was difficult in atmosphere and nigh impossible in void. There was no air resistance here, hardly any inertia. Any of these ships could turn on a dime and be a thousand meters away before she could blink. Luckily, she had a few tricks up her sleeve.

After the attack at the Waning Crescent, Joane had realized just how lacking Darling's weapons were. There wasn't a way to install any salvo launchers or javelin propellers while traveling, but she'd made a few modifications that she hoped would trip them up. "Straight ahead, Tris," she called out, placing her hand on a shining new lever affixed to her station. "Trust me?"

"Straight ahead, banking to starboard at 200 yards," Tris reported, authoritative and calm. She didn't even know what Joane was planning to do, but she was on board fully. Joane gave a wry smile; they were more in sync now than they had ever been. The Wing fighters spread out, the edges of the wings glowing with white and blue energy that pulsed up the length of each strut. It became so bright that the ships began to glow with radiance, like the many-winged angels from Solan myths and architecture. Joane kept her eyes fixed on the lead ship, the one she'd fired at. She charged the ion cannons, knowing that it would dodge out of the way as soon as they detected a discharge of energy from the coils. It would never come, though.

They closed, and closed, until the Wings on the edge of the formation had to spin around to still point their weapons at Darling, who never slowed. "They're going to hit us!" Orion cried.

"The shields will hold," Tris assured them. "We can take a few hits." Then, she turned towards Joane and reminded her, "A *few* hits."

"I know," she said, her sweaty hand clenching the lever tighter and tighter. She had to wait until the very last moment. If what she did didn't work, or left them vulnerable, this battle was going to end very quickly. 500 yards. 400. 300. 250.

The Wings all unleashed their shots at once, long bands of spinning, whirling energy singing through the void, filling the cockpit with light as they danced across the energy shields, shaking the ship. The lights flared brightly for a moment from the charge, but quickly dimmed. Twenty shots in total, almost all of them direct hits, and they were still alive. Joane said a quick thank-you to Darling, and pulled the lever. The energy was still fizzling across the shield when a section of the projected energy, about the size of an escape pod, shot forward from the uniform bubble, moving forward through space as if it had been fired from a cannon.

It flew forward, visible only because of the light from the Wing's attack, and slammed directly into the fighter in front of them. Projected energy shields didn't play well with one another. They were designed to prevent collision with anything outside a ship, be that asteroids, projectiles, or other ships. Ship-to-ship collisions were exceedingly rare. Space was big, and the intelligence of controls and proximity warning systems meant that most of the time, collisions were intentional. When they happened, the energy shields usually flared up and repelled one another with such force that the ships would be sent hundreds of miles off course. When a section of energy shield was fired like a weapon, however, that's when it got messy.

Tris had already veered away, yanking the sphere to the left just as she'd planned, pulling away from the Wing at the last possible second. Joane didn't see what happened next, but she heard the tearing of energy, the crumpling of Core Steel, and the implosion of the ship's shield projector. The concussive force of the explosion hit them a second later, sending the ship careening wildly along their path. Darling's nose tilted and turned wildly, offering them a brief glimpse of several views through the viewport, but Tris quickly righted them and turned back to the squadron awaiting them. The four remaining Wings were circling around in a dramatic, admittedly beautiful formation, moving more like an elaborate flock of birds than actual spaceships. Floating nearby was the scattered, shredded remnants of the first fighter.

"Re-routing shields," Tris said, her voice triumphant. Joane smiled, thrilled that her idea had worked at all. Still, the front shields were down, which was a dangerous situation to be in, and pulling shields from anywhere else on the ship would just leave that location vulnerable until enough power came back. Their shields shimmered faintly as they closed the hole in their defenses, even as the Wings began to prepare another volley. "I'm guessing you want me to dodge these?" Tris asked.

"If you don't mind," Joane said sarcastically, letting her white-knuckled fingers slip from the lever. She doubted that trick would work again.

Tris gave her a devilish smile, her teeth visible just barely through her parted lips. "Whatever you say, Joane," she said, her voice husky as she ducked and weaved in a shaky line towards their attackers.

"Flirting? Now?" Orion yelled, doubled over in their chair. They looked like they wanted to vomit again. "Is this really the best time?"

Joane looked at Orion, then took a hand off the trigger handle to fish something out of her pocket. "Hey, Senator," she said, tossing the object across the cockpit. Orion, surprisingly, caught it without much trouble, gazing at the Consortium badge she'd tossed them. They looked at it, shock written across their face, a question forming on their lips. "I want people to know what happened here." They nodded and flipped a panel open on the back of the badge, fidgeting with tiny buttons and keys.

"You're sure about that?" Tris asked, making a noise of effort as she banked to the side, sending Darling into a roll as the first Wing fired its four shots. The bands whipped towards them, end over end, and Tris bent her wrist forward, throwing them under the path of the shots and pulling up to be level again in one fluid motion.

"No," Joane said, yanking the trigger to return fire at the Wing. She let the bolt go, but the Wing rotated its central hull section, pulling the wings into a vertical position and dancing away from the attack. "But I think we're in enough trouble already. What's a little bit more?"

Tris nodded and pulled the ship's nose upward, arcing between two of the Wings and forcing them to bank out the way. Arcs of energy from their wings were grazing the ship over and over again, the shields flaring up with too much intensity each time for any degree of comfort. The ion cannon wasn't going to be killing any of these ships, Joane knew that much. She ran through the catalog of "weapons" she'd prepared on the ship, and an idea began to form in her mind. "Tris, get us between two of the Wings, directly in the middle."

Tris grunted as a shot caught the back of the ship, pitching her forward into the console. Tristan pulled the sphere to the right, then back, reversing the engines until the Wing soared past her and back into formation with the others. After a moment, she kicked the engines back into forward motion, chasing the formation despite the fact that they could easily outpace them. "They're going to pick us apart," Tris said, "and more of them will be here soon. If anyone has any good ideas, feel free to speak up before I go with my bad idea."

Orion had apparently finished activating their badge, and was now busy pressing one button furiously, over and over with a dogged intensity. "Every member of the Consortium knows where I am now," they said helpfully, tapping the button over and over again. "They're probably very irritated by the pinging."

"Let's just hope someone's listening," Joane said, firing another shot at the Wings. The beam flew past the back left section of one of the ships, causing its wing assembly to rotate wildly as it veered away from the shot. The other three fighters continued to bear down on them, their wings filling with energy once more. Despite the chaos of the battle, they refused to do anything but attack in perfect synchronization. It was...frustrating. It meant maneuvers like the one they were about to try meant taking hits from not just one of the Wings, but nearly all of them at once. Even with Tristan's flying throwing them around in their chairs, the shields were rapidly running out of power. A Consortium Wing fighter was equipped with four of the strongest hard light beam projectors on and off the market. They could cut clean through a decently sized asteroid without much resistance, so they would make short work of Darling's hull if the projector failed.

One of the beams skimmed off the top of the hull, forcing the energy shield to buckle and dent down to the hull, throwing them all off balance for a moment. Tris screamed and nearly lost her balance, but caught herself and threw the ship into a wild turn with the momentum. The squadron passed them by as the ship finally righted itself and began moving under its own power. Joane watched the viewport, and slammed her hand down onto a button the instant the fighters passed them by, only a few dozen feet away from their viewport. They'd been trying to show off, keep them scared, and force them to make a mistake. What they didn't know, however, was that Joane had deployed the ship's magnetic landing gear during their initial pass. As her palm hit the button hard enough to make her hand sting, twin tractor beams fired out from the back landing gear. With an inaudible rending of Core Steel and the visible fluttering of the fighters' engines, two of the Wings were pulled into a trail behind Darling as it rocketed forward, dragging them backwards and towards the rear of the ship. Joane checked a rear camera display on her station and saw the two ships, their wings turning wildly as they fought to escape the magnetic pull of the lock with their voidpace thrusters. She took a breath to steady herself, and twisted two identical knobs toward one another, reorienting the tractor beams towards an intersecting path.

The fireball of the Wings impacting one another shook Darling again, but the ship quickly left the tangle of metal and flame behind and circled around to face the two remaining ships. Joane wondered what their pilots were thinking. How could they, trained pilots flying the best-equipped and maintained ships in the universe, being picked off by a single civilian vessel? She realized she'd been breathing hard since the Wings had emerged. The Consortium had underestimated them every step of the way; let them see where that got them.

The final ships went into a synchronized loop, separating for a moment before turning back and approaching them side by side. Joane craned her neck to look out the viewport, and saw the ship on their right still trailing blue sparks from the ion shot that had grazed it. Joane felt an idea forming in her mind as she sent another charge to the ion cannon. She pointed the struggling ship out to Tris. "Bank towards that one," she said. "I can end this."

She saw a concerned look move across Tris's face, but she nodded anyway. They knew there were only two ways for this fight to end: with them dead, or the Wings destroyed. It was unsavory, but it made perfect sense to Joane. Eight bolts of energy flew toward them, and Tris fought to evade as many as possible without throwing off their flight path. There was a sound like glass shattering all around them, and Joane saw the fading blue light of their shields out of the corner of her eye. No more shields, she thought in passing, but never took her eye off the screen. This was going to be her only shot, she wasn't going to lose her focus. A bead of sweat from her forehead trickled down into her eye, and she shut it, squinting the other eye at the screen and trying to shut out everything but the view from the cannon. She preemptively rotated the cannon towards the back of Darling, catching a glimpse of the wreckage of the two Wing fighters.

"Bank at 150," Joane called out, unable to stop her voice from shaking.

"We can't risk that," Tris said immediately. "Without the shields, if we hit them-"

"Without the shields, we can't take another hit! Bank at 150!" Joane was holding the trigger tightly, her knuckles sore and twitching with intensity. She hoped she hadn't doomed them.

"400 meters," Tris said steadily, the control sphere resting in the crook of her arm like she had a baseball in a headlock. Her other hand was on the sphere too, each finger perched onto one of the tiny sides. The hesitation in her voice was evident. "300. 250. 200. Now!" She wrenched her arm and pushed the sphere with her hand at the same time, pulling it out of the gravity beam and executing a turn so sharp Joane heard the bulkheads groan with effort, like the ship wanted to tear itself in half. She only stayed in place in her seat because of the tightness of her restraints. She heard Orion make a choked noise, followed by Tris grunting and the sound of someone hitting the floor. She tuned it out, all background noise. She waited for the moment, a moment that would be so brief, so fleeting, that the pilots wouldn't know if it passed without incident. As Darling flew away at a sudden ninety degree angle, the two would turn to follow them and prepare another volley. For a moment, they would be flying not side-by-side, where an ion shot would be nothing but an annoyance to the ship it hit. They would be flying with one ship in front, and they had banked to put the damaged, less maneuverable ship in the path of their weapon. Joane saw the tip of the ship's nose appear in the edge of the frame and squeezed the trigger with every bit of strength she had, even before the rest of the ship came into view. It was hard to see past the flash of blue on the screen and the distortion as the ion shot briefly impaired the camera, but the crippled ship had no time to dodge the shot at such a close range. The bolt hit home, square on the ship's nose, rippling across its surface and disabling it entirely. Shields, engines, and weapons all went dark as it began to drift freely for just a moment.

Then, the other ship finished its turn. The Wings had been in perfect synch for the entire fight, so the pilot had expected its partner to have already shifted into position. Instead, as the last ship came around, pushing itself back to combat speed, it found a ship dead in the void mere yards away from it. It bucked to the side and spun its central axis frantically, but the fastest ship in the universe was only so fast. Its right wings caught the side of the disabled ship, shearing through the hull as the undamaged ship's shield projector flared brightly, rapidly failing under the horrible scraping and tearing impact. Its own wings rapidly tore themselves free, pulling most of the ship's central section with it. Joane watched through the camera display as both of their pursuers crumpled into one another and ejected their atmospheres into space, their cabin's depressurizing with a violent stream of oxygen releasing into the void.

"We're clear, time to move," she cheered, turning back to Tris. Her breath caught in her throat once she saw her. Tris was doubled over the console, still trying to pick herself up from the floor. There was blood on her arm, blood on her shirt, and blood on her forehead. "Tris," Joane said, horrified, "Are you-"

"Just winded," Tris said, her voice straining out of her like air leaking from a pierced oxygen tank. "That was a good shot." She hauled herself up, letting the control sphere slip out of her hand. It zipped back into place, hovering a foot from the console as she took a few deep breaths. "I'm going to put some cushions on this console if we keep bashing our heads on this thing," she said, gesturing to the bloodstain on the edge of the console. She looked up at the viewport, and the smile she'd forced onto her face vanished.

Joane followed her gaze to see the still-open Fastlane whirling a few thousand yards away, and another squadron of Wing fighters emerging from it. They spread out into a similar arrangement of five ships, their wings growing with fierce energy. The cockpit was silent. They'd barely survived the first wave, and that was clearly just the beginning of what they could throw at them. Joane let out a breath and sent another charge to the ion cannon, but an error message appeared on her targeting screen: *Action canceled by Pilot*. She looked over her shoulder at Tris, who was staring at the approaching ships with a grim look on her face. "Are we surrendering?" Orion asked. It wasn't entirely a bad option, Joane found herself thinking. They were outnumbered, underequipped, and already on their last legs. If she thought their hunters would ever consider mercy, she might have suggested the option herself.

"Something like that," Tris murmured, flipping a few switches. The lights overhead shut off with a heavy electrical hum, so the only source of light remaining in the cabin was the glowing nebula around them. Joane struggled to pick out Tris's features in the dark, highlighted and cast in soft purples, vibrant blues, and a distant spot of white from the Fastlane. The light was reflecting in her eyes, making them look almost sea-green. "We want answers, right?"

"Tris, what are you thinking?" Joane asked apprehensively, but her mind was already at work, weighing their options. She knew what Tris was about to say before the words left her mouth, because it was the only idea that made any sense.

"We've got to get to the bottom of this," she said. The Wing fighters were getting closer. She reached up and snatched the control sphere with a scowl. Darling's engines roared in response, flaring to life. "One way or another. Orion, get ready to ping your friends again, because we're going straight to the source." Her eyes were dead set on the Fastlane, still shimmering. She didn't wait for Orion's response, gunning it towards the encroaching group of fighters. Joane wondered if the shields had recharged enough to take a few shots as they made a mad dash for the Lane, but a quick glance at the screen in front of her showed that the shield projector had been switched off. *Insufficient power allocation*, read the display. Joane keyed a command to check the entire system. Just as she'd expected, Tris had put every bit of power the ship had into their engines, even lowering the life support system's priority. By the Singularity, she loved that woman. She slid her hand off the trigger handle, held tight to her seat, and prayed that her faith in her pilot wasn't misplaced.

# Chapter 26
## Eden's Cradle

TRISTAN hoped Joane and Orion's faith in her wasn't misplaced. As Darling rocketed forward, her working engines blazing with every bit of power she could afford to give them, she began weaving the nose of the ship, cutting odd shapes through the void as the Wings closed in on her. Cutting the shields to power the engines was an insane gamble, made even more insane by the fact that even going for the Fastlane was a bigger gamble. She was rolling dice at the highest stakes table in the universe, and she'd never had particularly good luck when it came to dice. She had to admit, the plan was driven almost as much by curiosity as anything else. She figured their odds of survival were about even on either side of the Fastlane, but she *had* to know. Where were these people coming from? Who were they? She'd come too far, risked too much, and fought too damn hard to die without seeing the full picture. And so, she pushed her ship, her home, into a squadron of Consortium ships.

*"Tristan, you're a fine pilot,"* Ahsha's voice in her head. She gritted her teeth, swung her head to the side to get the hair out of her face. *"But you're far too reckless. Don't forget whose ship this is."*

Beams of light heading her way. Each one of them whirling and spinning along wild trajectories, burning the nebula around them as they sought out her ship. Tristan pulled the sphere downwards, almost back into the console port. Darling dipped, and she felt her stomach rise into her throat as beams hurled past. She bent her wrist to the side, and Darling spun on her axis, turning into a knife edge angle to dodge a pair of beams that just barely missed her port wing. She didn't see them, but knew that there were two more just above them. She made a complicated gesture with the sphere, pulling Darling's nose up while reversing the thrusters so that the back of the ship continued moving downward while she readjusted their course. She heard a screech of light tearing through metal, and the loss of atmosphere in a chamber far away, but she'd already sealed the cockpit and depleted the life support everywhere but here. A red light began blinking on her console, but she ignored it. Her engines were still running, and her heart was still beating. All that mattered was that she kept flying.

*"You get on that ship, Tristan Ninomae."* No, not her, not now. The voice she heard so rarely in her mind that she thought she'd forgotten it, but there it was. As Tristan ducked and dodged and weaved her ship, an extension of her soul, towards the Fastlane, she heard her mother's voice. *"You get on that ship and go see what a real star looks like. You go see all the light in this universe, but don't forget to show it just how much light is inside you."*

Her mother, dead under a pile of rocks drifting towards a Black Hole somewhere back home, who had only ever wanted a better life for her. Tristan hoped she could see her now. A blast tore through the ship, a hard light shot that she was never going to dodge. She fell against the console, hitting the exact same spot on her hip that she'd hit earlier. Her breath left her all at once, but she braced an elbow on the console and pushed the control sphere forward, ever forward. The Fastlane was a few hundred yards away; the Wings were closing on her, looping around to finish them off, but they were *so fucking close.*

"I'm coming home, Ma," she said to no one in particular. It was impossible to hear her voice over the roar of the engines, the screaming of alarms, the crackle of energy passing them by. She wasn't even really sure if she'd said the words, or just felt them in the deepest part of her being. She pushed with everything she had, every dirty trick she'd learned dodging pirates and blockades, every maneuver that strained Darling's bulkheads that didn't break them, while a chorus of voices in her head urged her on.

Another blast hit them, taking the edge of the starboard wing. One of the warning lights went dark; whatever room had depressurized was now completely gone, so the system didn't have to worry about it anymore. They were slowing down, the thought came to her from a thousand miles away. The engine closest to the edge of the wing must've gone down in the shot. She keyed a few commands, overloaded the engine's internal reactor, and released it from the ship. It was a risky move, but she couldn't seem to stop taking risks lately. She didn't wonder if the engine's detonation caught any of the Wings in its blast; she only hoped it would distract them for a few seconds longer. The Fastlane was straight ahead, glowing and glimmering with pale, unnatural light. Tristan remembered for a second that looking into a Fastlane was strictly warned against, but she wasn't about to lower the blinders now. If she could survive this, she could see the horrors of dimensional reality being bent and twisted to the point of snapping for a few moments. If she could survive this. She yanked the control sphere to the left, and Darling banked to allow a spray of beams past them. One of them went into the Fastlane, causing Tristan to wonder if the reinforcements on their way may have just taken friendly fire. The thought made her wonder about meeting another squadron of ships in the Fastlane, and what might happen if they were to collide. It was no use thinking about it now, because they were nearly there. There was no time now to dodge a volley, no time to maneuver or weave a pattern into the flight path. Straight on to the end, Tristan told herself, putting all her weight behind her fist and punching the sphere forward. The remaining engines fired everything they had in one tremendous burst, sending Darling rocketing upward, angling into the gaping maw of the Fastlane. As soon as the nose of the ship passed the threshold, it was like the Lane grabbed them and yanked them the rest of the way into the portal. There was a sound, a roar so all-encompassing and ear-splitting that it made the ship shake, and they were inside the Fastlane. Tristan fell to her knees as soon as the light — no, it wasn't light, it was an absence — hit her eyes. She slapped wildly at the console, and didn't reopen her eyes until she heard the shutters lock into place.

It took her a minute to realize she was alive. Over the rush of the Fastlane outside like water pouring over a bad holocall line, she could hear her ragged, uneven breaths.

She was on the floor, her back pressed against the edge of her console, covered in sweat. After a moment, she realized she was still holding the sphere. It took some effort to make her fingers open, but when they did, the sphere zipped back into place, before the gravity current pulled it back into the socket.

"Is everyone...okay?" she asked, her voice labored and tired. She felt like she'd just outran a tunnel spider.

"Did anyone else just see...everything?" Orion sounded weak and terrified, but alive. Tristan allowed herself a brief smile.

"You could've been a stunt pilot in another life," Joane said, similarly winded and awestruck.

"Hey, don't spoil my retirement plan," Tristan grumbled, trying to push herself off the ground and struggling. Somewhere along the way, her knees had locked and subsequently turned to jelly. She got to a half-standing position before falling again with a heavy sigh. It took her vision a few seconds to clear, and when it did, there were two hands outstretched in front of her. She looked up into the faces of Joane and Orion, both there waiting to help her up. She smiled shakily and grabbed them both, and together they helped haul her up. Tristan looked at them each in turn, but froze when she saw Orion's face.

They looked haunted, almost like they'd aged years in a few seconds. Their eyes had gone from a pale green to one so dark it almost looked black. Pinpricks of white showed through in the irises, like stars burned into their eyes. For a moment, it was like they were looking past her, staring wistfully at the closed shutters and the Fastlane roiling behind them. Then, they blinked hard and focused, putting on an uneasy smile. The patterns of stars in their eyes had shifted.

"Orion," she began, her voice trailing off into a horrified whisper.

"I'm...alright," they said, but they didn't seem to believe what they were saying. "Just...dizzy. You are an amazing pilot, Captain Ninomae. It seems like I owe you my life once again."

"Hey," she said, trying to keep her voice light as she clapped them on the shoulder. It took them a second to focus on her eyes. She forced herself to stare back at the twin voids of starlight that bored into her face, ethereal and strange but still Orion. "My friends call me Tris, understand?"

Their mouth twitched into a slightly more genuine smile. Tristan thought she saw a few tears gathering at the corner of their eyes, but they blinked again and they were gone, replaced by a new pattern of constellations. "Thank you, Tris." They slipped away from her, her hand slipping off their shoulder weakly as they returned to their seat. She watched Orion move oddly then rest their head in their hands. She wanted to approach them, to ask what they'd seen, to help, but then Joane's hand was on her shoulder, turning her around and pulling her in. Tristan was taller than her, but she found herself stumbling into her grasp, resting her head on Joane's shoulder and pressing her face into the crook of her neck. Joane's arms held her steady as they clung to each other, the weight of the fight crashing down on them both at the same time.

"You did so good," they both said in unison, then shared a tearful laugh. Tristan made herself pull back; she wasn't sure how much time they had. She sniffled hard, trying to gather her voice and her thoughts at the same time.

"This isn't over," she said with conviction. "It nearly is, but we can't stop just yet. There's a light at the end of this tunnel, and we're almost there. If we work together, we're going to make it there, I know it."

"I don't think that metaphor means the same thing on Cygnus as it does on the Hollow Worlds," Orion mumbled. Tristan nodded at the back of Orion's head, her concern growing with every second.

"Orion, do you still have your badge?" she asked, trying to be as gentle as possible. "Once we leave the Lane, we need to ping wherever we are, because odds are they're going to be on us pretty quick. If we could get some backup there, that would go a long way."

"Of course, Tris," Orion said, holding up the badge and rotating it in the light, watching the way the light reflected off the edges of the wings. "Funny little thing. You know, I dreamt of having one of these things since I was a child...I didn't dream of this part."

"Orion-" Tristan said, taking a step toward them. Joane stopped her, and when Tristan turned towards her, she gave a small shake of her head. She knew the expression on Joane's face. *There's nothing to be done right now*, it said. Tristan nodded grimly, hoping she hadn't doomed her new friend to madness. "Okay," she said, taking a moment to steady herself. The hits Darling had taken meant the Fastlane was playing hell with the ship's systems. The shields had automatically begun recharging once Tristan had stopped bypassing the safety failsafes manually every few seconds, but in a weakened state that barely managed to hold together, let alone keep out the turbulent shaking of the Fastlane. "We don't know how long we have, and we don't know where we're going. We have no idea what to expect, but that doesn't mean we can't have a plan. Joane, this Fastlane had to come from a Wayfaring Station. The Wings back there probably followed us back through, but it's gonna spit us out first. If we can charge up the ion cannon, do you think you can disable the gate before they can come through?"

Joane mulled it over for a second, chewing the side of her cuticle before giving a brief nod. Tristan took one moment to think of the pilots of those ships, who would either be torn apart by the Fastlane collapsing on them, their bodies lost in a space that wasn't quite real, or trapped in that semi-dimensional space until they went mad. She had no idea what would happen; nor did anyone else in the universe. Whatever fate awaited them, she knew pitying them was foolish. They wouldn't extend the same consideration to her, but all the same, she did.

"Okay, the rest of the ship isn't breathable right now, but I've got a spare vacsuit in the cabin. I'll fetch two more and some weapons for you all, because odds are we're going to have to fight. Orion?" She waited for a response, but they only turned and stared at her blankly for a second. "Can you use a weapon?"

Orion laughed a bit, their voice wispy and faraway. Tristan shook her head, popping open the compartment under her console and strapping the vacsuit disc onto her back. "Joane, see what you can do for them; I'll be back."

"Aye, Captain," Joane said, moving across to kneel down in front of Orion, who was still looking at the floor, dazed. With a rush of air, Tristan's vacsuit formed around her and locked into place, and she made her way into the small makeshift airlock in the hallway. She'd had to turn the gravity off again during the battle, so everything in the ship was floating freely through the air like a dense fog of junk she had to push her way through to get to Darling's loading bay. The vacsuits, thankfully, hadn't been damaged too badly in the battle, so she unhooked two from the charging station, easily hefting the heavy discs under her arm in the weightless environment.

She searched the ship as thoroughly as she thought she might have time for, but Fastlane travel times were always a rough estimate at best. She picked her way through memory after memory of the things she'd collected, the places she'd gone, and the people she'd helped. Though each one gave her a pang of nostalgia that warmed her heart and calmed her nerves, she couldn't help but wish she'd collected more guns in her time. In the end, she found nothing but a few more bolts for her own hand crossbow. She knew Joane could handle herself with her pulse knife, and odds were they would just end up seizing those odd, gravity-powered weapons from back at Cygnus. Tristan remembered the hammer that took Orion off their feet, sent them flying across the room, and broke all of their ribs without missing a beat. She wanted one of those.

After twenty minutes of hopeless searching, she floated her way back to the cockpit and let herself back in. Orion was still slumped forward in their chair and Joane was shining a penlight from a small first-aid kit into their eyes. "How's it going?" she asked them both. Joane whirled around to give her a worried look as Orion's face slowly rose to meet her gaze.

Joane stood up, clicked off the penlight, and jogged over to Tris, taking one of the vacsuits and sliding it between her shoulder blades. She leaned in close, keeping her voice hushed. "I have no idea what's wrong with them," she reported, a grim edge to her voice. "I closed my eyes when we went into the Fastlane, so I don't know…whatever they saw did a number on them. Did you…?"

Tristan shook her head. The flash of…whatever she'd seen had been impossibly brief, but even then it had seared her retinas and threatened to overwhelm her. "Just a moment; I'm okay. Where do you even take someone for this?"

"I don't know," Joane said with a defeated shrug, "but I can guess we aren't on our way."

"I'm not so useless, you know," Orion said, their voice rising to nearly a normal volume for the first time. "Well, no more useless than usual. I have the badge; I can make the call. That's all I was ever going to do." Tristan gave them a steady nod and knelt down in front of them to offer a vacsuit. They accepted it with careful hands, adjusting it into place methodically and carefully. "I think I'm going to see Cygnus again. How exciting is that?" Tristan paused, fighting back a shake in her lower lip. She clapped her hand on their shoulder and gave them the warmest smile she could muster.

"I'm sure it's beautiful, Orion. I can't wait to see it." Orion said nothing but turned around to face the empty shutters. They seemed to be imagining whatever was outside them. Tristan rose slowly, wringing her hands as she turned back to Joane. "I didn't find any weapons," she said weakly. "If they come after Darling, though, it won't matter. They'll blow us into dust before we can get the power allocation set back to normal. I've got maybe five engines left, and the shield projector is only working at forty percent capacity. May as well be dead in the void."

"Do you still have the lander?" Joane asked, crossing her arms in thought.

"I...do, what are you thinking?" Tristan responded, raising an eyebrow. Joane had a haunted look on her face that Tristan knew meant she wasn't going to like whatever she said next.

"You're not going to like this, but I have an idea," Joane said.

Tristan didn't like it.

*     *     *


IT took forty-five minutes to reach the end of the Fastlane. Tristan spent the time preparing the shuttle, making sure the hatches were ready to unlock all while floating above the floor and trying to keep her untied hair out of her face. She was thankful for the solitude while Joane watched the ship's controls and the weapons. She let herself cry all she needed to, because as soon as the plan went into motion, she needed to be focused. She wished Joane could teach her how to shut down the part of her brain that felt so much. Once she had triple-checked the release mechanism, she turned back down the hallway, taking deep, heavy breaths as she pushed her way through her home. She'd been prepared to give it all for this; the Consortium hadn't given them much choice in the matter. She hadn't considered this, though. She was the captain; this was her ship. It wasn't *right*, but it was necessary.

She made her way into the cockpit slowly, wordlessly, and took her place behind the captain's console. Joane, seated at the weapon's bay, glanced sideways at her as she approached. There was regret written into every inch of her face. "If there was another way…" she began.

"There isn't." Tristan was shocked at how steady her voice was. "When we leave the Fastlane, you take the shot then get Orion to the lander. I'll get everything keyed up and meet you there."

"You'll be there, right?" Joane demanded, eyes boring into Tristan's face. "I'm not leaving without you in that lander, Tris. You have my word on that." Tristan let out a long sigh, not wanting to admit that she had been considering it. They needed her, though. Ahsha needed her. And whoever was behind this needed a swift kick in the shin.

"I'll be there," Tristan said simply. It was all she could manage. A klaxon blared the second she finished her sentence, and Tristan drew a shaky breath. They were there, wherever "there" was.

There was a sound like glass tearing in half, and the thud of the remaining engines died down to a normal, voidpace level as the Fastlane released them back into proper reality. Tristan opened the shutters, and Orion flinched for a moment before they saw the blackness of the void waiting behind them. Tristan heard the ion cannon fire, and somewhere Joane confirmed that the Fastlane gate behind them was closing. She didn't hear it entirely, though, because she was too busy focusing on the space station laid out before it.

No, "space station" wasn't the proper word for it. A space station was large, yes, but generally no bigger than a medium sized moon. This was a construction on a scale that took Tristan a few moments to truly appreciate it. What she thought was a cold blue star in the distance was, in fact, a massive, roiling cloud of pure, arcing energy dancing across a sphere larger than a main stage star. It was like a model of a solar system, but at an exact scale. No wonder they had gone to the middle of the Hesperides supervoid to hide the thing; it would've been the easiest thing in the universe to find literally anywhere else. There was an ovoid disc of silver metal surrounding the false star, a patchwork of panels and bare machinery. There were struts and connections clearly unfinished between sections of the disc, but for the most part, it was a perfectly smooth disc that must have been millions of miles in diameter.

Well, it would've been perfectly smooth, if not for the horrible sights in the circles cut into the disc. In the hollowed section closest to the "sun," there was what looked like a world that had endured the brunt of a supernova. It was little more than a lump of magma and cooling volcanic rock, the tectonic plates coming apart slowly as the cold of the void hardened the exposed mantle. The casing around the planet glowed the same brilliant blue as the sun, and several hundred-thousand mile wide channels directed the energy from the planet towards the center of the system. On the other side of the sun, the second closest planet had met a similar fate, but more of the magma was still burning across the dying world. At least a dozen worlds were housed in similar zones, the rings around them fainter and fainter the further they were from the sun. As they got further away, the planets looked healthier, too, with water and forests visible on some of the ones locked into place. Tristan's eyes went to the edge of the disc, where she saw a massive semicircle of glass, the open side facing outwards like they were offering a hug. Resting in their grasp was a planet, and the other half of the circle was being slowly guided into place by what must have been a fleet of construction vessels.

Orion was on their feet in an instant, running to the viewport and pointing wildly.

"Cygnus," they said forcefully, even as they hunched forward. "Cygnus! We found it!"

"Welcome home, Senator," Tristan said, a bitter smile on her lips. Even as she said the words, she was tilting Darling towards the nearest power line. How polite of whoever built this to leave the channels so open and visible. "Both of you, to the shuttle."

Joane ran to the viewport, grabbing Orion by the shoulders, and half dragged them towards the door. "I meant what I said, Tris. I'm not leaving without you," she called out as the airlock door hissed closed.

When she was sure they were gone, Tristan let out a sigh and slumped her shoulders. She ran her hand over the control sphere, stroking it like a beloved pet. "It was a hell of a ride, Darling," she said to the ship. "Thank you."

Her fingers danced across the keys one last time, and she heard the distant hum of the Redshift drive firing up. It would fire, but it would tear the drive apart, starting a chain reaction that would ignite every drop of fuel onboard the ship. Darling had been her home, and now Tristan was lining up the nose of the ship like it was a missile. She set the vector for the glowing blue power tunnel, took one last look out the viewport, and shut down the gravity current. The sphere went limp in her hand, deceptively heavy for its small size. She ran through the halls as fast as she could, aware that there may be a group of fighters on their way towards them right now. She didn't have time to slow down, to look into her room one last time, to pick up any final mementos, or to even shed a tear for every memory, good and bad, that she'd lived in this ship.

She reached the lander, a small, cramped thing that was barely more than an escape pod with an engine strapped to it. Joane was already at the controls, and she slammed a lever home the moment Tristan crossed the threshold. Tristan watched through the clearsteel panel that slid shut, as the release boosters fired and sent them sailing away from Darling's hull.

She hung there, in the void, engines spinning up and glowing with a radiance like nothing Tristan had ever seen. The Redshift engines were shining with power and ready. The only thing that wasn't ready…was her.

She felt a hand on her shoulder, recognizing Joane's steady grip without having to turn around. "She was my home, too," she said. "If you want me to-"

Tristan pressed one side of the control sphere still clutched in her grip. In one instant, Darling was there, and then she wasn't, just a red line of light and speed pointed directly at the machine below them. The afterimage of the ship vanished, leaving nothing but empty space. The three of them approached the front viewport, then shielded their eyes as a second, smaller sun blossomed into existence in the middle of the power line. Every planet set into the device suddenly cast another shadow across the almost endless expanse of metal, and shrapnel and wreckage flew upward like a wave crashing against a rock.

"Think they noticed?" Tristan asked.

# Chapter 27
## Unannounced Houseguests

ARGUS Regille watched out the window of his office. He steepled his fingers under his chin and glared with a burning hatred he didn't know he was capable of feeling. He thought his heart might beat right out of his chest with the intensity of the breaths he was drawing. Outside, he watched Eden's Cradle burning, blue lights dimming and secondary explosions rising from the now useless section of the construction. This could mean weeks, months, *years* of repairs before the engine was ready to be put to use. They would need to secure yet another planet to prepare enough power to move forward. More and more setbacks, roadblocks, moving backwards, when they were so close. He almost couldn't believe it.

His computer system was chiming, an emergency alert from Senator Orion Masenna. It pinged several different messages: Senator in distress, senator under attack, danger, requesting assistance. He moved to his desk, grabbed the pair of metal wings that he pinned to his lapel whenever he made a public appearance, and threw it at the window as hard as he could. Both the badge and the window went undamaged, but it made him feel better all the same. The badge pinned to his chest currently began to light up too, an angry, orange light glowing from within the black circle. He sighed and plucked it from his shirt, brought it to his mouth, and answered the call.

He wanted to ignore it, but he knew that would just lead to more punishment.

"Regille," he said, his voice small. The voice coming through the badge, meant to evoke the image of a black hole, was heavily distorted to mask the speaker's identity, just in case his office had been bugged. Regille knew exactly who he was speaking to, but didn't dare say their name.

"What," the voice said, deep and sent through so many filters it was barely recognizable, "is going on out there?"

"I don't know," Regille said. "Something came through the Fastlane, and then…"

"Your *target*, Regille!" it corrected. "Your target evaded you once again, and the Cradle is in flames! We have given you so much to take down these three civilians. How can you be expected to move worlds, Regille, if you can't stop these three nobodies?"

"I can stop them!" he protested, stepping nervously to the window. He didn't know what to do with his hands. There had to be a way, some way to remedy this. "I can. I swear, they won't last the hour."

"Someone is going to die today, Regille," the voice said. "Make sure it's them." Before he could respond, the line went dead, leaving Regille alone with the sound of Orion's incessant pinging. It was all falling apart, but maybe, just maybe, he could contain it. As if he could find a bandage big enough to fix the hole that had just been torn through his life's work. His ship's pilot came over the intercom, their voice panicked and strained.

"Senator, the Cradle is under attack! Shall I move us to a safe distance?" Regille stared at the flames burning out rapidly, but the electrical explosions still blooming upward from the crater.

"Negative, pilot," he said after taking a moment to consider it. "Bring the *Ladon* into an intercept course with the light craft that jettisoned from the ship before it was destroyed. I would very much like to deal with our guests *personally*."

# Chapter 28
## Answers

THE lander moved at a decent pace towards the disc below them, the explosion looming in the distance as they made their way for the station. A fireball the size of a large moon drifted outwards from the station, carrying wreckage across the disc and casting strange shadows across the glistening silver panels. Joane, at the control yoke of the lander, piloted it carefully but quickly, keeping one eye on the radar beacon on the rudimentary console in front of her. She thought about offering the controls to Tris, but one look at her sitting in the back of the lander, cradling the control sphere in both hands, staring blankly, told Joane that she wasn't in any shape to pilot them yet.

"We're being hailed," Orion said in that calm, wistful tone they'd taken on since the Fastlane. "Should we… answer it?"

Joane frowned, trying to sort out the logic behind the move. They had to know where the lander was, so they weren't trying to triangulate the location. Any virus that could be transmitted through a commlink wouldn't be able to harm the rudimentary ship in any meaningful way. "Send it through, let's hear what these pricks have to say."

Orion clicked the blinking blue button on the wall of the lander, and a tinny voice came through the small speaker above it. "Greetings, intruders," an old, masculine voice hissed, dripping with resentment and bitterness, "May I be the first to welcome you to Eden's Cradle." It took a moment, but Joane recognized the voice as Argus Regille. He went on. "It seems you are…less than appreciative of the wonder of creation stretched out before you. I imagine I already know, but courtesy demands me ask, to whom do I have the displeasure of speaking?"

Joane rolled her eyes, never looking away from the window. She never thought the end of her life would come at the hands of someone who said things like "to whom."

"Regille, this is Senator Masenna," Orion said, clicking the button to transmit their voice through. "I have…gazed upon many horrors recently, but this is…something else entirely. What have you done here?"

"Ah, Orion," Argus said, his voice biting and venomous. "You sound like you've made a quick recovery. What good news. I imagine you all want answers. Well, never fear. The Unbounded Progenitors will be more than happy to answer any and all questions you may have face to face. All I ask is that you meet me at the coordinates I'm transmitting to you now, and to stop blowing holes in the machine that will save the universe."

"What assurance do we have that you won't simply blow our shuttle to dust as we approach?" Orion asked cautiously.

"Assurance?" Argus responded. "Why should I offer you any assurance after what you've done to the Cradle?"

"And why should we meet with you?" Joane piped up. "I've never been fond of negotiating with planet killers."

The line was silent for a long minute as they continued to descend towards the disc. The idea of trying to find Ahsha somewhere on the facility was daunting, if not entirely impossible. She might not even still be there. A data point appeared on her radar screen, landing coordinates. They pulsed once, twice, before Argus spoke again.

"You want answers. You want to see your friend," he sneered. "Go there and you will receive both. Try to land anywhere else, try to leave the station, try to stall, and I will have your shuttle dusted before you can close your shutters." The line went dead, leaving them in silence. Joane glanced down at the data point.

"It's a trap," she muttered matter-of-factly. She didn't have to ask; she knew beyond a shadow of a doubt.

"Most likely," Orion said, their finger brushing across the comms button. "He didn't seem to offer us much in the way of alternatives, unfortunately."

"If we go there, we might be able to take him down," Tristan pointed out, like it was the only thing that mattered. "I wouldn't mind putting a bolt between that creep's eyes."

"That probably won't stop this," Joane countered. "There's no way he's the only one behind this, or even that high on the food chain of what's going on with these…Progenitors."

"I didn't say anything about stopping them," Tristan said, climbing to her feet. She had to stoop slightly to not scrape her head against the ceiling, but she still managed to look menacing as she slid the bolt home in her hand crossbow. "I said we can stop *him*. He's tried to kill us all personally by now, why don't we return the favor?"

Joane looked over at Orion, expecting them to be green in the face at the prospect of killing for a reason as petty as revenge. Instead, they seemed resolute and determined. "If it's an option," was all they said. Joane gave a quiet nod and tilted the shuttle towards the coordinates she'd received.

*      *      *

IT was no easy task flying the dinky little shuttle through the low-density space of the supervoid. Every twitch of the engine sent the ship rocketing wildly in whatever direction she'd accidentally nudged the control yoke. Despite that, she managed to guide her ship to a small raised section of the flat, seemingly featureless metal that, as they approached, stretched to cover the entire horizon. The section was the size of a few large office buildings, stretching hundreds of stories above the disc and connecting with what looked like half a dozen factory-like facilities that were seemingly connected to one of the distant power channels. As luck would have it, the planet looming over them, a few hundred thousand miles away and hovering in the grasp of the station, was Cygnus-4. After a bit of scraping from the minimal landing gear the shuttle possessed, they activated their vacsuits and unsealed the hatch, stepping out onto the surface of "Eden's Cradle."

As they approached the sprawling facility, Orion's neck was craned upward at their planet, slowly being fitted for its terrible fate. Their eyes looked less glassy than they had, like anger and righteous indignation had brought some of their focus back. "We all agree not to trust a word this slimeball says, right?" Tris asked, earning a nod from Joane as she checked her pulse knife.

Orion looked over at her for a moment, ponderously, and said, "Of course we shouldn't trust him. He's a politician, after all." Tris and Orion shared a chuckle, and eventually Joane couldn't help but join in, even though she could feel her hands shaking.

As they approached the facility, the shapes of guards in those same jet black suits of armor began to appear, patrolling between the buildings, watching doors, and peering through windows. They were obviously trying to make a show of being stealthy, but really wanted the three of them to know they were being watched. Joane didn't draw her weapon, but kept a hand on its holster. Tris drew her hand crossbow and checked the air canisters affixed to it. They walked up to an ostentatious looking skyscraper, the only building with two of the guards flanking the entrance. Their faces were hidden behind a skull-like sheet of reflective black metal. Both of them held what looked like segmented javelins, with a few sections of the outer plating floating free from the weapon, suspended by some form of gravity manipulation. They turned to face them as they approached the door, and Joane paused, glancing at them in turn.

She reached slowly for the doorknob while Tris held her crossbow casually, but ready to aim in an instant. The guards made no move to stop them as she pulled the door open and stepped inside. They stepped into a small airlock that pressurized as soon as the door swung shut, then through into the lobby of what could've been any Consortium office building, except for the dozens of heavily armored soldiers standing in strategic locations around the room. Joane felt like a caged Sillian Grubhunter.

"Well, don't just stand there letting all the good air out, come and sit with us!" a voice rang out, drawing their attention to the center of the room. There were a few long, luxurious couches of black leather arranged in a square around a silver and blue circular table emblazoned with the Consortium Wings. Sitting on one of the couches, arms draped over the back of the cushions and casually clutching a glass of wine, was Senator Argus Regille. A few feet to his left, curled up into a ball and breathing shallowly, was the emaciated and beaten form of Doctor Ahsha Reindare.

They'd found her. "Ahsha," Joane whispered breathlessly, taking a step forward involuntarily. Tris took a step forward with her and stuck her arm out across her chest to slow her down.

"We have to be smart about this," Tris said in a harsh whisper. Joane took a moment, swallowed a deep breath, and nodded thankfully. The trio walked forward slowly, eyeing the room as they did. There were no windows in the lobby, and only one set of two elevators in the back of the room, nestled in a small hallway with three guards blocking that section of the room. Joane glanced over her shoulder to see two of the guards take up positions in front of the airlock door. It was increasingly hard to think of a situation where she made it out of this room alive.

"Doctor," Regille said forcefully, shoving the barely moving woman on the couch with his free hand. "It seems your hypothesis was correct, your associates *have* come for you." Ahsha jolted slightly at the touch, reacting viscerally and with more emotion than Joane had ever seen from her. When Ahsha sat up, it struck her just how long it had taken for them to reach her. Her blonde hair was tattered, uneven, and dirty with grease. Her eyes were bedraggled with more bags under them than she'd seen when Ahsha had stayed awake for two weeks straight on nothing but stims to finish a t-test analysis. She was still wearing her usual lab coat, but it was torn to shreds at the bottom and was covered in smudges that must've been driving her insane. Her face, neck, and the visible parts of her forearms were covered in bruises.

Still, Ahsha managed a tight, judgemental huff when she saw the three of them. "It certainly…took you long enough," she said with some effort. The effort of pushing herself up seemed to overtake her, and she slumped back against the cushions, gasping.

"Ahsha," Tris said, her voice as even as the edge of a blade. "You look as good as you always do. What the hell have you done to her?" The last sentence was aimed at Regille, and despite the sarcasm of her remark to Ahsha, Joane could hear the rage in Tris's tone.

"Believe me when I say," Argus said, holding up his palms placatingly, "I did nothing to your friend here. In fact, today is the first time I've had the pleasure of meeting the Cradle's own troublemaker. She's garnered quite a reputation among the Unbound for her…willfulness."

"You haven't changed, have you, Ahsha?" Tris asked, looking at the scientist. Ahsha looked at Tris, her hazel eyes searching the woman's face.

"Tristan Ninomae," she said. "I didn't expect you to come, truthfully. Joane I had some measure of...hope for, but not you."

"Well, don't sound too disappointed," Tris said, striding up to the couch and throwing herself down on it, leaning back against the cushions with an intensity that gave Joane pause until she saw what she was doing. She made her way to the other side of the couch and mirrored the motion, gesturing for Orion to sit between them. They did so slowly, cautiously, glancing around the room slowly.

"You promised answers, Senator," Joane said, glaring at the man sitting next to her old friend. "Do you have an explanation planned or are we just supposed to start asking questions?"

"'Senator,'" Argus said with a chuckle. "It's such a small title, for a big group of small people with small ideas. Please, call me Progenitor Regille."

"I'm not doing that," Tris said casually. "It sounds stupid and pretentious." In response, the guards around the room cocked and raised their boltguns in unison. Tris grimaced and swore under her breath.

Regille waved a finger in the air and the guards lowered their weapons, but only slightly. He looked at Tris, then Orion, then Joane. "Hopefully you understand the situation a bit more clearly now. I am not offering information as a trade for anything. I am not bargaining. You all, I'm afraid, have lost. I simply felt that you've earned some...clarity as to the grander purpose your deaths will serve."

Ahsha scoffed indignantly, and Regille leaned over and smacked her with the back of his wizened hand. She fell back down to the cushions with a groan. Joane wanted to leap to her feet, but knew that it wasn't the right time. She had to wait, to be patient for the right moment, if there ever was one. The three of them were silent for a while, until finally, Orion was the first to speak. "The planets. Why did you take them? Was there a reason, or was it just…happenstance?"

"Ah, that's a very good question, Orion," Regille said with a chuckle, before pausing for a moment. "Have you…changed? You seem a touch more insightful since we last met. Maybe that hammer knocked something loose in you?" Regille laughed, but Orion's face was stony and unmoving.

"Answer the question."

Regille's laughter quieted, settling into a businesslike expression of focus. "Truthfully, it was a matter of convenience. The movement of the planets involved a series of gravity well generators so advanced and proprietary that, if I may, no one in this room is smart enough to fully comprehend."

"Untrue," Ahsha interjected, earning another slap from Regille.

"We chose planets close to the edge of their systems with no satellites and stable tectonics to allow them to survive the movement and subsequent Fastlane travel without breaking apart," Regille continued. "And yes, we use Fastlanes to transport them most of the way, once we get the planet far enough out of the way for the energy signature to be hidden from their sister worlds."

"What happened to the people on those planets?" Joane asked, her foot tense against the floor. She pushed, just a bit, and felt the front legs of the couch lift just slightly.

"They were informed of the purpose of their…upheaval. For obvious reasons we couldn't let them go, but there are housing facilities on the Cradle to keep them and allow them to contribute to the work. In fact, many of the workers building this station are citizens of the vanished worlds who accepted our offer."

"And those who don't?" she pressed, but she was afraid she knew the answer already.

Regille gave her a pleasant smile that made her blood run cold. "Well, what kind of people would we be if we ripped those people away from their homes?" Joane tried to keep her face level as she remembered the worlds reduced to roiling masses of magma and broken stone.

"How many people have died for this…thing?" she asked, the horror slipping into her voice involuntarily. Her grip tightened on her dagger.

Regille only shrugged. "We didn't exactly take a headcount. It will be a small number compared to how many lives will be allowed to flourish because of their sacrifice."

"Now tell them," Ahsha struggled to pick herself up yet again on shaking arms, "what it is you're doing here. You'll like this next part; this is where it gets truly interesting."

"Quiet, you," Regille said, pulling his hand back to hit her again. "You aren't part of this. You're here so that we can rid ourselves of four problems all at once." Before he could strike, Tris pulled the crossbow onto her lap and aimed it at Regille's neck. The guards stepped forward and raised their weapons, but Tris didn't react.

"You may have a small army pointing guns at me, Progenitor," she said evenly, "but it only takes one gun to kill a man." She gestured with the weapon pointed at him. "They can put as many bolts in me as they want, but I can still pull this trigger. And you'll be dead. Answer Ahsha's question, if you don't mind." Ahsha glanced over at Tris, a bit of surprise dancing across her bruised face.

"Finally, someone asking the important questions," Regille said. Joane saw the faintest beads of sweat trickling down from his shock of white-gray hair. "Though, Miss Ninomae, I wish you wouldn't point that weapon at me. It's awfully rude, considering that we are neighbors and all."

"Beg pardon?" Tris asked, and Orion leaned over slightly.

"I meant to tell you," they began, but Argus cut them off.

"I am *your* senator, Tristan," he said with a dramatic wave of his arms. "On that pathetic little body of bureaucrats, I represent the supercluster containing your Hollow World and the black hole it orbits." He let the information hang in the air, grinning devilishly at the gray-skinned woman lounging on the couch. His smile faded as Tris's expression never changed.

"If you thought that was going to make me want to shoot you *less*," she said, "I have to disappoint you again, Argus. The question. Now."

Regille straightened and gave a short, angry huff. "Very well. As you all know, there are…boundaries to the known universe. Not just physical boundaries beyond which matter struggles to maintain its composure, but boundaries of time and decay. Stars burn out every day, despite every sun-feeder and Derevian Cage we may employ, there is a limited amount of energy available in the universe, and some of it is lost every day. Eventually, the stars will burn out, the universe will turn cold and dark, and everything will die. The walls of the universe, with no energy pushing against them, will collapse inward and crush every last atom down until this universe is returned to the Singularity that birthed it.

"What if I told you, though, that it didn't have to end this way? That sentient life could create its own Eden? That we have the power in our minds to defy the inevitable end? With the Cradle, we can push back the walls of our universe, expand it artificially and generate a new form of energy that will allow for the formation of entirely new stars, planets, and everlasting life. We can stop the procession of time, of entropy itself, with these engines. Think of it, Tristan, no more planets left orbiting the dead husks of stars. Miss Cordelle, your dynasty could continue on into eternity. Orion, given enough time, even your pathetic little system might even have a chance to make something of itself. The Unbound Progenitors are on a mission to *save* the universe, and you have the audacity to stand in our way?"

"By killing billions," Joane deadpanned.

Regille shrugged again. "The work is harsh and cruel, but it must be done. Don't think I haven't considered the blood on my hands, Miss Cordelle, but I've run the numbers. Ask your scientist friend, the math checks out." Joane looked at Ahsha, who had her eyes on the floor. She recognized that look, but she wasn't used to seeing such pensiveness on Ahsha's face.

"Don't you tell me you believe this nonsense," she begged. Ahsha looked up at her, seemingly offended that she would suggest such a thing.

"Come now, Joane, do you think so little of me?" she said with as much sarcasm as she could muster. "The idea is completely untested, it operates on unproven theory, and most importantly, it is driven by a belief in a force entirely unscientific and false."

Regille laughed. "That is where you are wrong, Doctor," he said, relishing the moment. "It feels good to say that to you."

"Amen."

"Tris!" Joane hissed at her.

"Have the three of you ever heard of gaiaformulaic energy?" Regille continued like the interruption hadn't happened. "The 'song of the planets,' as more romantic types used to call it?" He waited for a moment, glancing at the three of them before continuing. "It was hypothesized a long time ago as a type of invisible, unseen energy that gathers within planets. Habitable worlds of plenty were said to be rich with it, blessed with a strong soul that preserved their skies and their seas. Most scientists didn't support the theory, but some visionaries began looking into it. Lo and behold, the Unbound Progenitors found that this energy is very, very real, and it exists within every world. Not only does it exist, it is an energy so pure and so powerful it can be used to create things thought impossible even by today's great standards. A Fastlane can cut a hole through reality, yes, but with the Cradle, we can expand reality into whatever we wish. If a few worlds have to give up their souls for the soul of the universe, then...so be it."

"I'll believe it when I see it," Ahsha spat.

"We've seen it, Ahsha," Tris said matter-of-factly, her eyes haunted and rageful. "They're...tearing those planets apart to harness whatever that energy is."

"That's impossible, Tris," Ahsha said dismissively. "I know you aren't a learned woman, but you have to understand-"

"Ahsha," Joane half-shouted, drawing every pair of eyes in the room to her. "Tris is right. We've all seen it. Now isn't the time to argue." Ahsha's cracked lips tightened into a thin line as she stared into Joane's eyes like she was a particularly intriguing equation.

"As a matter of fact," Regille said after a pause. "Now *is* the time to argue. I would hate for you all to leave anything unsaid. I'm running out of time before I need to get back to my colleagues, and so, it might be time to make peace with yourselves."

"How are you harnessing this 'energy?'" Joane asked, an idea brewing in her mind. It was unlikely to ever work, but they needed a next step in the event they made it out of this room with their lives.

"Still talking business, Miss Cordelle?" Regille said with an impressed shake of his head. Her stomach churned at the mention of her family name. "You would make your father proud. Refineries, like the facility attached to this processing center, use a variety of ingenious machines inspired by the gravitational pull of black holes to shake up the tectonics of a world, harness the energy, and transfer it to the central hub for storage and eventual use. I would offer you a tour of the facility, but I really must be going." He waved a hand at his guards, and they raised their weapons.

"Ready for this?" Tris asked, her leg tensing.

"Ready for what?" Orion said, a soft tinge of panic in their voice.

"Ready," Joane said, and kicked backwards. A dozen guards fired at them at once while Tris and Joane kicked the couch backwards, tipping over and spilling them out behind it. Several of the bolts went wide or sank into the metal bottom of the couch, but the guards by the door still had a clean shot. Tris let out a grunt of pain as one bolt nicked her thigh, and Joane felt a pulse of electricity as the bolt meant for her clipped her shoulder and scraped off the vacsuit disc on her back. Tris wasted no time sending a bolt into the two guards behind them. One stuck into the guard's armor, causing them to stumble but not fall, while the other took a bolt directly under their helmet. They fell with a distorted yell, muffled by the sound of pressurized gas releasing from the helmet. Joane saw the first guard fall, dropping their long bolt-rifle as they fell. She gritted her teeth and bolted out from the cover of the couch and ran for the fallen weapon, keeping as low to the ground as she could.

"Shoot them! What are you all doing?" Regille was screaming as she ran, the measured calmness in his voice replaced by blind, mad rage. Joane heard bolts singing past her ears, she felt tears open in her clothes, cuts across her skin, the pings of bolts hitting her vacsuit projector. None of them were enough to stop her from dropping into a slide, scooping up the weapon, and whirling around to send a shot through the faceplate of the wounded guard. They fell with a choked noise, but Joane simply ducked behind the body of the massive armored figure as bolts continued to volley her way. She counted the shots, but quickly found that the guards were staggering their reloads to cover one another, while she only had one shot left in her weapon.

"Joane!" Tris yelled, but she couldn't see her. She only heard her crossbow fire, and saw one of the guards stumble into view, carried slightly forward by the momentum of the small bolt stuck in the back of his arm. He was hefting one of those massive gravity hammers over his head, now off balance but very much still coming her way. Joane, on her back, had nowhere to go. She twisted her arms uncomfortably as she tried to find a shot, and by the singularity, she found it. The long bolt sank into the soldier's stomach, causing them to freeze with the hammer still held high. Joane took the opportunity to spring to her feet, drawing her knife as she did so. It sang with electricity as she sank it into the figure's neck, twisting the blade until she felt them go limp and drop the weapon.

She wrenched the knife free, aware of the remaining guards rapidly closing on her, and used the momentum of the motion to roll towards the first guard she'd shot. She seized their weapon, giving her two more shots to work with. Unfortunately, a guard to her left had a lucky shot on her as she moved, and she felt a bolt sink into her calf. She screamed in protest, but she didn't feel any broken bones. She sent a shot back at him, but the pain clouded her vision and the bolt flew towards the back of the room. One of her eyes followed the motion, catching a glimpse of Regille dragging a struggling Ahsha towards the elevator. Oh no you don't, she thought, and prepared to fire her last shot at Regille, even as several guns prepared to fire at her. She took the shot, just barely missing

Regille's head and clipping the top of his ear. He yelped and ducked down, two of the guards noticing and moving to cover their leader's escape.

Joane dropped the empty bolt-gun and drew her knife as she dove for the closest guard, the one who had shot her in the leg. He sent another shot into her side, which sent blinding white pain through her entire body, but she didn't let herself slow. She heard Tris yell and watched her leave the safety of the couch, leaping for the fallen hammer on the floor.

Joane's guard was lowering their gun to draw the long segmented spear off their back, but it was too late. She was on them in a moment, slitting their throat with a quick, ugly slice from her weapon. For good measure, she plunged the blade into where she thought their eye might be and left it there, letting electricity arc across the expressionless helmet as they fell. She took the staff from their hand, giving it a twirl to test the shockingly heavy weight.

She heard a bolt rifle click behind her, and turned her head to the side just long enough to see a guard standing a few feet behind her, having just finished reloading his weapon and lining up a shot. And then, with a blur of orange energy, the guard was gone, hurtling towards the center of the room and slamming into the couch they had tipped over at the beginning of the fight. And there was Tris, clutching a gravity hammer with both hands and breathing hard as the head of the weapon clicked and shifted and hummed with power.

"You gotta try this," she said, a fire in her eyes. Joane smiled at her, then ducked to the side, trying to make her profile as small as possible as more bolts zipped past her.

"Maybe later, Regille is getting away with Ahsha."

"I saw," Tris said, letting the head of the hammer fall to fire her hand crossbow at one of the two remaining guards on their side of the room. They took the bolt in their shoulder without acknowledging the impact, drew a staff of their own, and charged forward.

Joane leapt forward, trying to remember the few times in her life when she'd trained with a bo staff. She hadn't been good at it, but what was a staff but a long, blunt dagger that you held with two hands? She threw her first strike at the middle of the weapon, which seemed to lack the gravity field from the ends of the weapon. The guard simply stepped onto his back foot, pivoted away, and then closed the gap with a strike that nearly took Joane's jaw off her face before she leaned away. Joane twisted her grip to bring the staff into a vertical position, then swung the uppermost end at her opponent's head. They batted it aside with the end of their own weapon, and the gravitational shockwave sent them both skidding backwards across the polished brown tiles.

As she skidded to a halt, she saw Tris hiding behind a pillar, exchanging what fire she could with the guards on the other side of the room who hadn't closed the distance just yet. They were seemingly satisfied to pick them off, slowly but surely. Two bolts caught the pillar Tris was leaning around, and a third skimmed her arm, causing a small spray of blood to spill to the floor. Joane was about to run at the firing line, but she felt herself pulled back across the floor against her will. A few feet away, the guard with the staff identical to hers was twisting the handle of their weapon, and the upright end of the staff was glowing brighter with orange lights, and Joane felt herself being yanked towards it. As she slid across the slick floor, she saw one of the other guards approaching casually, their black armor seemingly unaffected by the gravity well. This one, hefting one of the hammers, simply waited for her to be pulled into the path of the weapon.

Joane tried to fight the pull, but it was like steering away from a black hole after crossing the event horizon. She had no purchase, no leverage, nothing to grab hold of. Unless, she thought, glancing down at her own staff. Finding the adjustable sections of the grip, she twisted the opposite direction of her opponent, and found the weapon growing lighter, almost weightless in her grip.

She didn't need time to think about the physics of it; she leapt forward with a suddenness and a ferocity that caught both guards unaware. As she swung the staff at the hammer-wielding guard, she twisted the section the opposite direction, generating a gravity well at the head of the staff. They didn't even have a chance to raise their hammer before the staff collided with their head, and it would have sent them sailing across the room if not for the force of gravity keeping their helmet molded to the weapon. Joane lowered the gravity's strength, and their cracked helmet dropped to the ground along with the rest of their body as she turned to face the last guard. They looked down frantically, moving to turn off their gravity well.

Joane leaned into the pull, letting it guide the momentum of her swing into their stomach, then over the back of their head when they doubled over from the impact. The metal made a sound like glass shattering when it hit the floor, and suddenly Joane was standing alone with no cover. The guards across the room all turned towards her, until a bolt suddenly appeared in one of their necks. They fell, sputtering and groaning through the voice modulator in their helmet.

Joane didn't need to look at Tris to know the woman had just saved her life, again. Instead, she dropped to the ground, picked up a bolt rifle from one of the fallen guards, and fired twice from one knee. The first shot hit the guard to the left in the stomach, causing a flare of electricity to break out across their armor. Joane winced when she saw them stumble but not fall, sending her next shot clean through their chest. The force of the weapon carried them backwards off their feet and to the ground.

She quickly shifted her aim to the last soldier in the room still on their feet, but the boltgun clicked with a decisive emptiness when she pulled the trigger. She swore; her luck had finally, finally run out, at the very end. She curled around as the shot came, trying to protect as many of her organs as possible by turning her back to the shot. She heard a hollow thunk, followed by a small stab of pain and warmth in her back, but mostly she felt the shock of her vacsuit's battery rupturing under the force of the bolt. She fell to the ground, convulsing, clutching the empty weapon against her will as her muscles all revolted at once. She wondered if she would even be able to feel the next shot.

# Chapter 29
## Breaking Promises

TRISTAN watched Joane fall in slow motion, electricity arcing around her body like a cage and throwing her to the polished floor. The pain of the cuts and bruises across her body was instantly forgotten, replaced by a tireless, furious desperation. She left the safety of her cover, already knowing she was too late to do anything. Her crossbow was empty, and all she had was a giant hammer to stop the soldier ten feet away from pulling a trigger. They were already lining up the shot with Joane's prone form, standing like a statue, immutable and unmovable from their course. Still, Tristan charged, her legs pounding the hotel-lobby tile as she hefted the weapon above her head with all the strength she could muster. It would do no good, she thought. If she was lucky, the guard would turn to her, put her down in one shot, then finish off Joane. If she was unlucky, she would have to watch them kill Joane first, then her.

Fate, it would seem, had other plans. Because just as the soldier was about to pull the trigger, their faceless blank helmet pointed directly at Joane, there was a blur of motion in the corner of Tristan's vision, and a bolt scraped through the soldier's kneecap. They stumbled, just slightly, and the shot fired into the overturned couch. Before they could readjust, Tristan was on them, her hammer coming down in a heavy overhead swing with a furious roar. The soldier folded neatly to the floor in a heap and didn't move again, and the room was quiet, save for the quiet trickling of the large decorative fountain and Tristan's wild, panicked breathing.

She spun around to take in the scene. Nearly a dozen dead guards, pools of blood of all different colors, Joane slowly breaking herself out of an electroshock induced stupor, and Orion, holding a boltgun and looking utterly amazed by themselves while vapor rose from the firing chamber.

Tristan nearly dropped her hammer in gratitude and relief. "Nice shot, Senator," she said, giving them a thumbs up as they both ran to where Joane lay on the floor.

"I have literally never fired a weapon in my life," Orion responded. "But they were going to…you both would've…" They were on their knees at Joane's side, inspecting the tears in her clothes and the dots of static still dancing along her hair. Tristan grabbed their arm to steady them, drawing their attention.

"Hey," she said. "Thank you. We're not done yet, though." Orion looked tired, but nodded. Of course they weren't done yet. "Regille got out, did you see where he took Ahsha?"

"He went that way," Orion said, pointing towards the elevators. Tristan nodded, trying to think her way through everything even as she held Joane's jaw and tried to rouse her back to consciousness. Her blue eyes were rolling back and forth, dazed but not entirely unfocused or glazed over. Tris saw the vacsuit disc on her back, still sparking from the bolt protruding from it, a thin trickle of blood escaping down the two-foot shaft of the projectile. Without pausing to consider it, Tristan pulled the broken, useless vacsuit off Joane's back, removed her own, and swapped them out. As she tightened the straps of the functional projector onto Joane, one thought ran through her mind. *Keep her safe, keep her safe, keep her safe.*

"Come on, come on," she urged, tracing her thumb across Joane's cheek. It left a trail of brackish blood across her tawny complexion, which she tried to smudge away. She didn't even know if it was her blood or not.

"Tris," Joane said, blinking hard a few times as her eyes swam across her features. She gave her a weak smile, and Tristan caught the smell of singed hair. "Are we dead yet?"

"Nope," she said, trying to help her up unsteadily. They'd both taken a fair share of hits in the fight, and the loss of blood was starting to hit them. Tristan swayed back and forth as she got to her feet, leaning her weight against the handle of her new hammer and letting the gravity generator keep her upright. "Regille has Ahsha."

"He's probably heading for a hangar somewhere," Joane reasoned, examining the state of chaos they'd left the room in. She picked up a discarded bolt rifle and a quiver of bolts from one of the guards in a heap at her feet. "We…might be able to catch him, and then we go. Orion, you've signaled the Consortium?" Orion nodded slowly, clutching their own boltgun like a security blanket. Joane looked them up and down but said nothing more to them before continuing. "Good, then they'll be able to put a stop to whatever's happening here. We just need to get Ahsha out, that's what we're here for." Joane steadied herself on the staff she'd taken, looking utterly exhausted but still pushing herself to the back of the room. Tristan didn't miss a beat following her, but Orion stayed still for a moment.

"If I may," they said slowly, turning the weapon over and over in their grip. "I am not here for your friend. I am here for *my* people."

"What are you saying, Orion?" Tris asked, an edge creeping into her voice as she turned to regard them. She found herself pushing Joane behind her with one hand while tightening her grip on the hammer.

"I'm saying," they took a deep breath, not looking at either of them directly but a point somewhere in between them. "I came to help my people, my planet. Cygnus-4 is right here. If there is a way to free my world from its prison; I will pursue it."

Tristan and Joane shared a look. She almost expected Joane to argue, but the woman gave a heavy, determined nod. "You're right, Orion. If we can do something, we will, but we're running out of time, we should move."

Orion, seemingly satisfied, hefted their rifle and moved to follow them to the elevators. Tris jabbed a finger against the button, tapping it as many times as she could and listening to the repeated clicks while Joane scanned the room. No one entered through the airlock, none of the bodies on the floor sprang to life. For the moment, they were alone, but even Tristan could tell something about that felt...wrong. Had it been too easy? Finally, the elevator opened, revealing a stark contrast to the extravagantly comfortable lobby behind them. The elevator was as bare bones as possible, a simple boxy platform encased with steelstone walls and a rudimentary control panel set into one of them. There was no bronze detailing like the rest of the room, nor were there a set of vaulted windows offering views of Eden's Cradle. It had a stale, industrial smell to it, and as the three stepped through, Tristan was reminded of the lifts that traversed half-finished space stations.

"The veneer is pulled away," Orion remarked softly, gazing at the dull red buttons on the control panel. "The skin pulled back and wicked bones revealed." Tristan shot a look over at Joane, who merely shook her head softly. *Now's not the time,* her eyes seemed to say. Tristan hated to admit it, but she was right. They needed to find Regille, get Ahsha back, and get off of this place. She looked at the panel, puzzling over the list of locations the lift could go. Their current location seemed to be "Lobby." Other options included Power Conduit, Planetary Brace, Intake Valve, and one button labeled Harvester Facility/Hangar Access. Her hand moved towards the button, pausing only momentarily to look back at her companions.

"Regille's running scared," she explained. "If there's a hangar, then there will be ships. If he's running, he'll be there. Right?" The two of them nodded quickly, and Tristan slammed her palm against the button. With a sudden, violent hiss of hydraulics, the elevator door slammed shut, locking them inside the dingy box. As soon as the elevator began moving, the lights flickered and shut off, leaving the room lit only by the dim orange glow of Joane and Tristan's weapons. They descended in silence for a while, too full of nervous energy to think of anything to say to one another. Tristan hoped her instinct had been right. After an eternity of waiting, the elevator jolted to a stop, the three of them almost stumbling as the room shook, and then began moving horizontally along a path they couldn't see. It wasn't long before their movement slowed again, and the grinding of brakes filled the room.

Tristan loaded her crossbow, leaning the hammer she'd procured against the side of the elevator and aiming it at the space where the flat gray doors met.

They came to a final, complete stop, and the doors opened.

# Chapter 30
## An Unraveling

ARGUS Regille led Ahsha through the halls of the harvesting facility. The half-conscious scientist slowed him down, but with enough force and a pistol pressed against the small of her back, she managed to carry herself forward decently well. He moved through the facility quickly, shoving past workers that looked up from their assigned stations to gawk at him as he passed. Occasionally, he would pause to shift his weapon towards them, usually convincing them to focus on their work. Everywhere he went, he saw pulsing blue energy glowing through conduits in the ceiling, the floors, and the walls. That precious, universe-reshaping gaiaformulaic energy was still flowing. There was a chance to save this; there had to be. Even if the Consortium arrived in full force, perhaps the Cradle could fight them off, relocate the station, or negotiate a peace. There was always a way out, he reasoned. He pushed the thoughts out of his mind. Right now, the only way out he needed to be thinking of was his own. The Unbound Progenitors would at the very least ostracize him for this, but more than likely he would simply be left behind for the Consortium, or killed to keep him quiet. *No*, he thought, *not after everything.*

He let go of the scientist for a moment, shoving her roughly against an inactive conveyor belt while he reached for his commlink. His pilot picked up the moment he signaled for him to, his voice full of nervous tension.

"Senator?"

"Have the Ladon prepared for launch immediately," he barked. "I want to be clear of the station the second the airlock is closed, do you understand?" He didn't give the pilot time to respond before dropping the comlink and crushing it with his boot. He knew the other Progenitors were hailing him, and he wasn't in the mood to talk. Turning back to Dr. Reindare, he found her gazing around listlessly at the facility buzzing around her, hard at work harvesting the planet locked in the brace a few kilometers away.

"So it's true," she muttered, almost sounding disappointed. "Gaiaformulaic energy? It was supposed to be a fairytale perpetuated by old mystics, but here it is. How does a facility like this even begin to operate?"

"You'll never know," Regille said, backhanding her with the grip of his weapon. She buckled, coughing blood onto the ground and narrowly missing his priceless caraxian leather boots. "Let's move." He grabbed her roughly and began ushering her towards the hangar. "By the time we leave this station, your colleagues will be dead. They probably already are. Some rescuers they turned out to be." He delighted in spitting the words in her ear as he pushed her forward; it was a small victory in his eyes.

"Are you so certain?" Ahsha responded. "Seems to me like you destroyed your one way of contacting the guards you left to execute them. And insofar as you've underestimated them already, who's to say they won't surprise you one more time?"

"It doesn't matter," Regille said, trying to convince himself he was right. "If they've survived, I'll be long gone before they catch up, and you'll be dead on the hangar floor."

It was meant to be a threat, a promise that all her posturing had failed. Ahsha, however, laughed haughtily. "You think they'll come after me? Tristan and Joane hate me, both rightfully so. On top of that, they're both stricken with an impractical amount of nobility. If I had to guess — and I'm rarely wrong — I would say Tristan and Joane plan on finding a way to cripple or perhaps destroy this entire station. All that energy must be funneling through a few power channels, something to house the energy you harvest before sending it through these conduits."

Regille paused, his rapid steps coming to a halt and his grip on the gun tightening. He thought of the harvest centers, the amount of energy housed in those rooms. If one of those were damaged, the Cradle would be…

"It's a shame," Ahsha muttered as if talking to herself. "Soon you'll be gone, known to your betters as the one who ran away when he *could* have saved this station. I imagine anyone who stopped them would be lauded as a hero, enough to forgive any sort of previous failings that might be weighing on their reputation."

Argus tried to steady himself. She was lying, she had to be. Those women had come all this way for her. Except, the way they'd spoken in the processing lobby spoke clearly to some amount of bad blood between them. If he saved the Cradle, he could save himself at the same time. He frowned deeply, set his resolve, and pivoted, grabbing Reindare's arm as he did so.

"Don't try to think you can talk your way out of this," he hissed. "I'm not letting you take one step out of my sight. Congratulations, doctor, you've bought yourself a few minutes to ponder the beauty of this facility." He dragged her backwards, towards the nearest Harvest Intake Room.

# Chapter 31
## In The Belly of the Beast

THE doors slid open. Tris fired her crossbow, but the bolt simply hit the wall ten feet away and stuck there. The hallway in front of them was empty, stretching out to the left about twenty feet to a corner, and ending in a wall of solid dark gray metal to the right. Joane stepped out into the dim hallway, keeping her boltgun raised as steadily as she could manage it with her shaky hands. She could feel it: she was losing steam and fast. If they didn't find Ahsha and a ride out soon, she wasn't sure how much longer she could push herself.

"It's clear," she mumbled, keeping her weapon trained on the corner as the others followed her out of the elevator. "You all hear that?" The two of them craned their necks and focused, and soon enough they all heard it: the sound of machinery, heavy and industrial, coming from nearby. It made her nerves stand on end, but nothing about this station felt natural to her. There was nowhere to go towards the sound, so Joane took an uneasy step forward. In a few moments, she felt Tris next to her and only then noticed that she'd been leaning against the wall, leaving a trail of blood behind her. She forced herself to keep her eyes forward, even as she felt Tris staring at her, trying to draw her attention. She couldn't let herself slow down to reassure her that she was okay, because she wasn't sure she could keep moving if she did.

"Joane," Tris finally said, demanding an answer. Joane swore under her breath. Never in her life had she let someone stop her in her tracks with a single word, but here she was, turning to face Tris in the darkness of the hallway. "Tell me you're going to be okay."

Joane wanted to tell her to stop worrying, that she was fine, to focus on the job they came here to do. But something about her brown eyes peering into hers, so dark in the low light they were almost black…she couldn't bring herself to lie. "Tris, please. Let's just move."

"She's right," Orion spoke up, a surprising amount of intensity in their voice. "Too many souls are calling out for us." They didn't wait for a response and trudged on forward, ready to leave the two women behind if need be. Joane followed, leaning on Tris's arm more than she wanted to, but the help was welcome. They caught up to Orion after a few paces, close to the corner. Even in their fervor, they were still nursing several broken ribs and whatever the Fastlane had done to them. By the time they rounded a corner, they were walking in unison again, until they turned and came face to face with a man holding a gun. Orion froze, too stunned to lift their gun, while Tris and Joane reached for their gravity weapons. Joane knew they'd reacted too late to stop the man. By the time her or Tris reached him, he would've fired a shot, maybe even two, and it would be over. Shockingly, even as their weapons hummed to life, the man dropped his gun and stared at them with a look of awe on his face.

"Senator Masenna?" he breathed, like he'd seen a ghost. "They told us you died in the relocation."

Orion lowered their gun, taking an uneasy step forward. It was only then that Joane saw the similarities. The wide, dark eyes, the slightest green tint to the skin, the heavy set of their shoulders. This was a Cygnan, just like Orion. "Are you hurt?" Orion asked, all the force gone from their voice. The man shook his head.

"No, Senator, no more than most. After what happened, after they took the planet, those people in the armor came to us. They said we could either stay on the planet or work on the station. I...I didn't want to help them, but I had to...they offered to bring my family."

"You bear no blame for this, my friend," Orion said, placing a hand on the man's shoulder. "We're here to help you, all of you. The Consortium is coming to help. This ends today, and if I have any say over it, Cygnus-4 will be free within the cycle. Now, the facility, how many guards are there?"

Joane looked past the conversation to the room beyond. The hallway ended in a grated platform connected to a wide lift, which lowered down into a sprawling, massive room full of servers, breakers, and other equipment she could only guess the purpose of. Everywhere she looked though, she saw clear pipes glowing brightly with that electric blue light, the gaiaformulaic energy being harvested from Cygnus-4. "There are no guards, Senator, someone called them all away a few hours ago, back to the processing lobby. We thought they may have transferred more workers over from another facility."

Tris glanced at Joane. "They really laid out the welcome mat for us."

Joane shook her head. "It doesn't make sense, why would there be so few guards in the facility? An organization with this much power should have more manpower to spare."

The man turned to look at her. "This isn't the only harvesting facility for Cygnus. There could be…hundreds, thousands of 'em. And besides, most of the guards are down on the surface, trying to keep the rest of the population in line. It wouldn't do us much good to fight anyways, there aren't any ships in the hangar most days, and none big enough for all of us."

"There will be soon," Orion assured him. "What's your name, friend?"

"Rhoth," he said, "Rhoth Vanrashan."

"Rhoth," Orion repeated. "Gather everyone you can find, get them towards the hangar. Wait for us if you can, but if you have to, and there's a ship to take, you do. We're going to put a stop to this one way or another."

Rhoth shook his head. "You didn't give up on us, Senator; there's no way in hell we'd give up on you." Orion hesitated, then clasped the man's hand firmly and nodded.

"Rhoth, have you seen anyone come through here? An old man leading a woman in a lab coat? She would've looked a little roughed up?" Joane asked, straining to get the words out without stopping to take a breath.

He jammed a finger over his shoulder. "I don't know why they were, but yeah. They stopped for a bit, then headed for one of the housing rooms. You just follow the white signs and-"

"Great, thanks," Joane said, pushing herself off the wall and into a weak half-jog. "Come on!" There was no time to waste, she told herself, she could feel everything coming to a head. Blood was roaring in her ears, her heart was pounding, every muscle in her body hurt but she didn't care. Tris and Orion were there, matching her pace and moving along with her. Vaguely, she saw Orion fiddling with their badge before shoving it back into their shirt pocket, but she didn't think much of it. They ran through the room, past belts and bays of different machines none of them had ever seen before. Workers, all looking downtrodden and exhausted, looking up to watch them pass, and Joane heard the murmurs as Orion was recognized by almost all of them.

"Look," Tris said, sounding winded as they ran. She was pointing at a bit of purplish blood on the ground, an uneven, fresh splatter. Joane vaguely remembered that Ahsha came from a species with purple blood. She looked at Tris, who nodded in silent confirmation. "We're going the right way." They ran on, more and more, further into the facility until the cavernous room gave way to a 10-foot wide service hallway, lined with occasional discarded carts and toolboxes. The white signs bolted haphazardly to the walls and ceilings pointed them towards "Housing Unit 36," through a maze of other stations and sub-facilities that seemed to drag on eternally. Joane had forgotten how long they were running by the time they heard the nearby roar of machinery, like the sound of a vacuum constantly on inside their heads. Joane clicked her staff on as they neared a heavy silver door, featureless except for the corrugations in the steel. There was a keypad by the door, but it had been left oddly ajar, keeping the locking mechanism from activating. As Joane glanced at the recessed door, she noticed that it was actually a condensed form of airlock, or perhaps a quarantine measure for whatever was inside the room. It would be so painfully ironic to get to the final step only to be melted by radiation or decompressed by a vacuum.

Still, she found herself approaching the slightly open door, trying to peer inside without exposing herself to whoever was waiting for them. Try as she might, she only saw a wall of monitors and readouts stretching around the circular room, and pipes lining the walls and jutting out towards the middle of the room, connected to something bright that she couldn't quite get a look at. She wondered how many guards might be waiting in there for them, how many reinforcements Regille may have directed here. It was possible she might be dead on the ground before the door even opened all the way. She was tired of waiting, though. This had gone on for too damn long. Joane took a step back, twisted her staff to increase the weight of its swing, and delivered a sideways blow to the heavy door.

It swung open like a screen door in a hurricane, and Joane waited for the barrage of bolts to come through. None did, so she barrelled through the door, her staff raised and ready.

# Chapter 31
## Equivalent Exchange

TRISTAN followed Joane into the room without hesitation, her hammer dragging behind in one hand and her crossbow raised in the other. The room they entered was, for the most part, quite unassuming. The walls were only about thirty feet high, made of simple gray metal and joined with ugly bolts and exposed support beams. Almost every part of this station, Tristan realized, was unfinished. A patchwork job they were frantically trying to finish even as they began their work. It made her smile to think of them being the wrench in their already haphazard plans. Despite the rudimentary construction, the tech in the room was top of the line. Computers and monitors lined every inch of the room's circumference, displaying huge amounts of data that was too small to pick up on as it moved. The larger graphs, which seemed to be power levels and integrity measures, showed green readings. It could've been a standard Consortium monitoring station, if not for the massive glowing white crystal standing in the middle of the room. It was braced in the center of the floor, but the actual structure reached almost to the ceiling. There were pipes all over the surface of the crystal, bolted in place by heavy metal rings. Most of the pipes connected to wider, clear pipes that glowed with the same blue energy they'd seen throughout the station, but one pointed diagonally, then widened into a clear glass window. Through the bright glow behind the glass, almost impossible to see with the glare, Tristan caught a glimpse of Cygnus-4's surface miles above them.

"Beautiful, isn't it?" a voice trilled. "Always makes you stop to marvel at it for a moment." The three of them shifted their focus from the glowing energy-housing crystal to the floor in front of it, where Senator Argus Regille held Ahsha by the arm, holding her like a shield between himself and them. "And this crystal holds just a fraction of the power Cygnus-4 will give us. Each world we harvest here at the Cradle contributes amounts of power that are inconceivable compared to the scales we use now."

"I'm about sick and tired of listening to you talk," Tristan said, leveling her crossbow at the Senator. "Hand over the doctor, before this gets uglier."

"Still so shortsighted?" Ahsha called, even as the gun pressed into her back. "You've come all this way, just to turn your head away from answers? From the truth?" Tristan narrowed her eyes at Ahsha, ready to yell back at the woman for old times' sake, but she realized something important. When she spoke, Ahsha wasn't looking at her. She was looking past her, peering over her shoulder at Orion. Her eyebrows furrowed when she said the word *truth*, the slightest emphasis slipping into her voice. Tristan bit her tongue. *Always the smartest person in the room*, she thought, frustrated and impressed all at once. She only hoped Orion understood Ahsha's mannerisms on intuition.

"Your colleague is right, Ninomae," Regille said, gesturing behind him at the crystal. "There is a whole new universe, boundless and eternal, being crafted here. And you would smash it with a hammer?"

"You've lost, Regille," Joane said, stepping forward into the room. Unconsciously, the three of them were spreading out. Joane moved to the left, Tristan to the right, and Orion back at the doors. Argus's weapon swayed between the three of them, but his grip on the gun was shaky and uneven. "The Consortium knows where you are. I don't care how many Senators you have on your side; the body won't let this continue. And once this reaches the public? Forget about it. You're done, all of you. You drop the gun and come with us peacefully and maybe, just *maybe* you might get out of prison at some point before you die."

Regille's face turned into a scowl, then morphed into a smirk. "You take us for fools? The Unbound Progenitors were wise enough to cover all of our tracks. Not a single nail can be traced back to any of us. Even if the Cradle falls, we simply disappear, lay low for a while, and begin anew. You fools have given your lives for nothing but a delay."

"It is the smallest moon that loses its orbit first," Orion said, pointing limply at Regille. "You have failed too many times, Argus. Do you truly think you will be allowed to walk away, by us or by your co-conspirators?"

Regille seemed, for a moment, truly stumped. The veneer of snide confidence fell away, and Tristan realized the man was truly scared. All his bluster and pride was as much to convince himself as it was for them. "I-I still have a chance. When I kill the four of you and save this station, they'll reinstate me, obviously! And even if they don't, I can disappear. No one could prove my involvement, not definitively."

"Except for the four of us," Tristan pointed out with a dismissive wave of her crossbow. "Your plan is full of holes, like you're about to be."

"Your petty threats belie your limited view of the situation as always, Tristan," Ahsha bellowed loudly, even though they were barely fifteen feet apart. "Senator Argus Regille has no plans to let us leave this station alive. He'll kill us all to maintain the secrecy of this station and his connection to these 'Unbound Progenitors,' isn't that right?"

"Indeed, you should listen to your colleague," Regille said, forcing Tristan to stifle a chuckle. "It would help you accept the reality of your situation."

"I'm not accepting a word out of your mouth, Senator," Joane spat. "And Ahsha, watch your mouth. Tristan and I traced Cygnus-4's path halfway across the universe looking for you. We figured out how to follow the paths the planets take by measuring the gravitational effects the moving had on nearby objects, and we figured it out together. Once you know what to look for, it doesn't take a high profile scientist to figure out where the planets are going; anyone could do it with some basic data collection."

"Absolutely right, dear," Tristan continued. "Imagine that, Argus, all your hard work and secret planning, foiled by two nobodies with some gravitational surveys and a map. After that, it wasn't hard to find out where you all were hiding. Something like this could only be hidden in the middle of a supervoid like the Hesperides. I'm guessing you've got more Cradles hiding out in the other empty spaces across the void."

"No, Eden's Cradle is the only one of its kind," Argus spat bitterly. "Still in its infancy, too. And whatever disruption you've caused today may cause us to have to begin again. For all your talk about 'blood on our hands,' you have ensured that the people on those worlds have died for nothing!"

"Dear?" Ahsha mused, tilting her head. "Perplexing." Tristan felt her face redden. Was that really worth focusing on right now?

"We didn't kill those people, Senator Regille," Tristan said forcefully, projecting her voice as loud as she could. "You and the Unseen Progenitors did. All for a fairytale."

"Gaiaformulaic energy is not a fairytale! Your colleague here is right about one thing, Ninomae, you are a small-minded *fool*," Argus yelled, leveling the gun at her. "How emblematic of the rest of my constituents. Small people with small ideas, living small lives. When we expand this universe to its new horizons, perhaps I shall let your hollow world fall into the mouth of its black hole. Then, there will be no one left to remember you! You and the rest of your pathetic friends."

Tristan raised an eyebrow. "Are all your little clubmates this unhinged, or is it just a you thing?"

"You irritate me," Argus deadpanned. Ahsha chuckled.

"You get used to it," Ahsha muttered under her breath. Tristan didn't have the energy to fire back with a snide remark of her own.

"I don't have to get used to it, Doctor," Argus responded, jerking Ahsha into an upright position. "Because now, I'm going to be rid of all four of you, all of my problems will wash away, and I will leave this station a free man."

It was Orion who spoke first, taking a tentative step forward. "Are you sure about that, Senator?" they asked, casually clipping the badge from their chest and brandishing it. Tristan chanced a glance to the side and saw a small blue light glimmering at the corner of the badge. Regille's face fell, while Ahsha's lit up with smug satisfaction. Tristan found herself grinning devilishly, despite her exhaustion.

"Is that-" Argus began, but his voice trailed off. Orion nodded calmly.

"An open channel," Orion explained, flipping the badge over and returning it to their chest, "Every Consortium vessel approaching this station — several of them, by the way — just heard you admit to everything and boosted it to the outlying sectors near the supervoid, who will then boost it further, and further, and so on and so forth."

"In other words," Joane began, steadying herself on her staff.

"You lose," Tristan finished. No one spoke for a moment, the room filled instead with the hum of the crystal and the endless droning of the factory. In the distance, Tristan thought she heard shouts and cries from the workers rising up. The soreness in her arm overtook her, and she lowered her weapon in triumph. Argus looked tired, old, and frightened.

"Ah," the Progenitor said quietly, looking at the floor. He took a glance over his shoulder at the crystal, then looked back at Senator Masenna. "Oh, well." Without another word, he raised the pistol and fired. Everything happened too quickly. Tristan saw the weapon fire, saw the bolt leave the weapon, but there was no time to do anything to stop it. Before she could raise her own weapon, the bolt caught Orion in the center of their chest and they fell back, the air escaping their lungs in one shocked gasp.

Orion hit the floor hard, the back of their skull impacting the dull gray metal with a heavy thud. "Orion!" she heard herself scream, the cry overlapping with Joane's own. She saw the other woman running towards the fallen senator as blood began to pool around their body.

Without thinking, Tristan raised her weapon and fired a shot at Regille, aware that there was every chance in the world that she could hit Ahsha. Thankfully, her automatic aim held true, and her bolt caught Argus's gun, sending it spinning away to the corner of the room. In an instant, she was charging the pair of them, the hammer dragging along the floor behind her as she screamed with a defiant rage. Regille cowered behind Ahsha, but the scientist drew what little strength she had into herself and drove her elbow into the old man's stomach. He groaned and stumbled, allowing Ahsha to slip below his grip and roll away just as Tris jumped into the air, her roar growing louder as the hammer arced above her head, then swung down into a sideways swing.

Argus Regille made a funny noise when the hammer hit his side, like a balloon full of bones popping. He went sailing away with the momentum, landing in a heap a few feet away then lying still. Tristan felt dizzy, her head swam as she looked at the two senators lying on the ground. Joane was crouched by Orion, having already pulled the bolt from their chest and pressing her hands to the wound. The dried blood on her hands was mixing with fresh, sickeningly bright red blood. "Are they…?" Tristan asked, stepping forward.

Joane shook her head. "They're breathing, but...not much. We need to get them out of here."

"Who is this again?" Ahsha said, climbing to her feet and crossing her arms with all-too-familiar pragmatism. "Shouldn't we be focused on disabling this station, or escaping?"

"Ahsha," Tristan said, another horrible idea forming in the back of her mind. "We just flew halfway across the universe for you, and we wouldn't have gotten here without them. So I suggest you put one of those doctorates of yours to work and get them out of here, *alive*."

Ahsha Reindare took a step towards Tristan, eyeing her up and down slowly. "You've...changed, Tristan, but much of you remains the same. Perhaps my skills would be better suited to disabling this power station."

Tristan stumbled forward, her eyes cast downward as she caught herself on Ahsha's shoulder. As she leaned in to whisper in her old employer's ear, she made sure Joane couldn't see her lips moving; Joane would never go through with the plan if she knew what Tristan had in mind. After a moment, she pulled away and wrapped her knuckles around the hammer. "Do this for me," she begged. "Just once." Ahsha was silent for a minute, studying her with a newfound curiosity, like Tristan had just walked into the room for the first time.

"Very well," she said reluctantly. "This station, for all its misguidedness, is a miracle of engineering. It's almost a shame."

"Whatever you say, doc," Tris said, ushering Ahsha towards the other two. Ahsha began speaking to Joane and lifting Orion between the two of them. Tristan watched them go, catching a glimpse of Joane's worried eyes frantically searching Orion's face for signs of life as they left the room. Joane never looked back at her, and Tristan found herself glad for it. She was sure her resolve would crumble if she looked into her face.

In a few moments, the three of them crossed into the airlock, which sealed and pressurized with a heavy mechanical thud. Tristan Ninomae swallowed hard and hefted her hammer.

"Don't...don't," came a weak voice from her right. She looked over to see Regille, his torso oddly caved in, trying to crawl his way towards her. "You'll damage this station irreparably."

Tristan sighed heavily. "Aren't you tired of talking?" she asked.

"We are saving the universe here, Ninomae," he struggled out. "You would have it all fade into nothing? All our lives...your life, will mean nothing. Your name will be forgotten from history. Are you so content to be nothing?"

Tristan looked up at the airlock, where she could just see Joane's head through the window. She turned towards her, and her heart melted. She thought of growing up on the Hollow World, believing her life would amount to exactly what Argus was saying to her now. She remembered being found by Joane and Ahsha, and the opportunity they'd brought with them. All the years she'd wasted, Tristan thought, at her friends' throats. All the anger, the fighting, the time she'd spent away from them, on her own with nothing but a ship that was dust now. She remembered the feeling of Joane's arms around her, her lips against hers. There was so much she would change if she could go back, so much she would fix.

"Those people out there are gonna make it," Tristan said. Joane was saying something to her, but it was inaudible through the glass. She was pounding on the glass with her fist, and Ahsha was behind her, still supporting Orion on her shoulder. She gave them all a weak smile. "They're going to tell people what I did today. I'm not *nothing*, Argus. I'm Tristan Ninomae, the woman who's about to save this world." She lifted the head of the hammer off the ground, tensing all the muscles in her arms.

"You fool!" Argus yelled desperately.

"Eh," she said, "the nickname could use some work." She gave herself one more moment to remember Joane's smile, her voice, her kiss. Then, she swung the hammer at the crystal.

# Chapter 32
## Sunset Over The Event Horizon

JOANE and Ahsha set Orion on the ground outside the airlock, tearing open their ruined, bloodsoaked jacket to inspect the wound. It had been a clean shot, so the flesh wasn't torn or damaged, but the small hole was right in the middle of their chest, and the blood pouring from the wound made it hard to inspect. Joane looked up, scanning the walls. "Ahsha, where's that medpack you said you saw on the way in?"

She turned her gaze back to the woman she'd flown across the universe looking for, only to see a dark expression clouding her face. "I must have been mistaken," she said. "There isn't one here. We should get them to the hangar; we can procure a ship and find medical supplies onboard."

Joane knew when she was being lied to. If there was one thing she'd learned in the past few weeks, it was that. Ahsha was lying to her, not for the first time. But why? "We're not going anywhere without Tris," she said, standing up and craning her neck over her shoulder. "You can go look for a medpack; I'll tend to Orion and wait for her to finish disabling the power station."

"Joane, it would be best-"

"I don't care, Ahsha," she hissed out, her voice raised. The doctor almost fell back, stunned by the ferocity in Joane's face. Obviously she hadn't been expecting Joane to start defying her all of a sudden. "I'm not leaving her, and you aren't either. Whatever happens to Tris, happens to all of us. Do you understand that? You're not in charge here, not anymore. I don't care what you say, how you twist your words, what lies you sprinkle in; I'm not going anywhere."

Ahsha didn't raise her hands from Orion's chest. Joane faintly realized they were both putting pressure on the wound. It was possibly too much pressure, since Orion's ribs had just recently finished healing. When Ahsha looked at her, there was an uncharacteristic softness in her eyes. "She asked me to get you out." Joane had to admit, it was the most convincing thing she could've said in the moment. "Tristan plans to disable the power system…permanently. Perhaps inelegantly. She…asked me to make sure you were away. I figured I owed her at least a favor for the role she played in my rescue."

Joane immediately staggered to her feet, her back pressed against the heavy airlock door. "No," she breathed out, like a silent wish. "Tell me you're lying. Now." Ahsha got to her feet slowly, pulling Orion up with their arm around her shoulders. She said nothing. Joane turned back to the window, peering in at Tristan. She was looking at them all, a small smile passed across her face, even as tears slid down her gray cheeks. "Tris!" Joane screamed, pounding her fist against the glass even though she knew she wouldn't hear her. "Don't do this!"

When Tris swung her hammer at the crystal, all the sound in the universe fell away. It was like watching the events in slow motion, or on a screen while in a vacuum. The glowing head of the weapon hit the massive crystal, and immediately the cracks began to splinter up the face of it, glowing and sparking with raging blue energy. Red warning lights filled the space around Tristan as she followed through on the swing, tearing through the crystal completely. Power surged from it, the cables, the walls, everywhere. Tris's hair was blown fiercely by the wind, but she stayed stuck to the floor as the room came apart, explosions of blue light beginning to shred the ceiling and walls as the crystal imploded on itself. Through the gaps forming in the walls, Joane saw the blackness of Void outside. The atmosphere in the room began to rush out of the holes forming, sucking the fire and the energy out into the nothingness. Tristan's vacsuit tried to activate automatically, but only a spray of sparks emerged from the damaged device. *Her* vacsuit, Joane realized in horror, Tris had switched them out in the lobby. She watched the woman she'd flown across the universe with float gently into the air, her hair tossed around as gravity abandoned her, then the crystal exploded, and everything vanished in a cloud of white light. Sound came back to Joane in a rush as the station rumbled, the lights flickered, and she screamed with every last bit of breath she had in her lungs. Her heart ached, it raged, it felt like it would come apart. They'd been so close, so painfully close to making it out.

A spray of electric sparks covered the three of them as the electric grid backfired with the surge of power. She flinched down, then immediately pressed her face to the window again. There was…nothing. No Tris, No Argus, no crystal. Just some wreckage spiraling off into the void, and the distant view of a chain reaction from the detonation. She wondered just how much damage Tris had just done to the Cradle. Joane hoped it would take the whole damn place apart at the seams. She didn't want a single rivet to survive. "Joane, we need to leave!" Ahsha yelled over the groaning of the hallway. "If you want your friend here to live, we need to get them medical attention. Tristan wanted to do this for you so you could escape, are you going to deny her that?" Joane wasn't sure if Ahsha was being genuine or just trying to save her own skin. She didn't care.

"Yes I am," Joane said, her face set with determination. She thought back to the relief station in Cygnus. Tristan had come back for her, refusing to leave her behind to an undignified death on a hangar floor. She'd risked the mission, her life, everything, for her. Not for a moment did Joane consider doing anything but going after her. "Get to the hangar, get yourself a ship, and save them. Come back for us if you want, or save yourselves. Do what you want."

"What are you even going to do?" Ahsha asked, incredulously. Joane opened the airlock, which remained operational, thankfully. She stepped in and activated her vacsuit as the doors began to close. A small atmosphere formed around her.

"Something stupid, probably," she shrugged, and then the airlock sealed, depressurized, and hurled her out into the void. Even with the personal atmosphere around her, she felt the cold against her skin. It made goosebumps pop up under her jacket sleeves, but she pushed past the chill and looked up at the cloud of wreckage drifting away from her. It was moving too quickly for her to swim her way through the emptiness to it, she realized. She cursed, looking around for any sort of propulsion device. The wall was too far away to push off from, but she still had her gravity staff. She inspected the device, looking anywhere for a helpful knob or dial labeled "gravity push" or anything similar. Predictably, she found nothing. Had she just killed herself for no reason? Had she just rejected Tris's last ditch effort to save them all without taking a moment to prepare herself for a rescue? When did she become this stupid?

As despair set in, luckily, a piece of the wall gave out and began drifting away from the structure, right towards her. Joane angled herself towards it, preparing her staff and looking back at the cloud. She would have one impossible shot at this. If she failed, she would send herself hurtling into an endless vacuum until her vacsuit battery gave out. If she failed differently, she would splatter across a piece of random wreckage before she could do anything heroic at all. None of these images were helpful as she guided her aim, with the staff tucked against her side. As the panel drifted just within range, she pulled back, then jabbed the staff forward with all the force she could manage. With a roar of effort that only she could hear, Joane Cordelle pushed backward, somersaulted end over end with the momentum of the push. Moving in a vacuum was tricky. There was no gravity to slow her momentum, so she hurtled towards the cloud with the same, unchanging velocity. *Too fast*, she thought as the pieces of sheared metal came into view. She bounced off a few of them, tiny plates of wall or scattered computer bits pounding against the walls of her suit. She tried to use a few of them to slow down, but until she was well within the cloud of debris, she had no luck slowing down. As she drifted, bouncing off the shattered room and climbing over chunks of ruined crystal, she looked around hopelessly. How could one little room create so many chunks of metal? It would be impossible to find Tristan in this, she knew that. She'd been coasting on luck for weeks, though, why would it give out now? She unclipped her pulse knife from her belt, set the radial pulse setting to its maximum distance, and held it over her head as she perched against a half-melted housing unit. She held her breath, sharpened her vision, and activated the pulse. Void was a bad conductor of electricity. In fact, it didn't conduct electricity, but she hoped the gathered hunks of metal would be enough to bounce the charge off each other. She just needed to see one specific glint, one tiny light, and she'd have a chance to save her. And then, glimmering like the last star on a cloudy night, there it was. A flare from Tris's broken vacsuit, a pale blue spark from the broken machinery. Joane let out a sob of relief, but the work wasn't done. Tristan was there, and when she focused, she could see the shape of her. Burnt, bent, and floating weightless in the void, her vacsuit a pale, useless shield from the vacuum. Crystals of ice were already forming on her hardy gray skin. Joane didn't waste a moment. She tensed her legs and pushed off her perch, hurtling towards Tris with all the force she could muster. The woman grew larger and larger in her vision, until she was there, within arm's reach.

Joane reached out and seized her by her scarf, pulling her into her arms and holding onto her like a lifeline. She chanced a second to press one hand to her back, extending the range of the vacsuit atmosphere to encompass as much of Tris as she could fit in the lowest density setting. She felt the air growing thinner and thinner, but she didn't care. She was dizzy enough already not to notice. She put a hand to Tris's cold, cold face, brushing ice from her cheek and pressing their bodies together with as much force as she could muster. "Please, please," she cried, begging the universe for one more miracle. "Please don't leave me."

For a minute, there was nothing. Joane drifted through a cloud of dust and debris with what might as well have been a corpse. She wept, clinging onto Tris's back with all her might. She remembered drifting in the cabin with her after the Redshift, their hands brushing gently. And then, outside on Darling's hull, their vacsuits buzzing against one another as they held each other. Tris's hair was flying out behind her now, dancing in the void like she was underwater. Slowly, so imperceptibly as to make Joane think she was seeing things, Tris' eyes began to flutter. Then, they opened, and Joane stared into them with a relief and joy in her heart she didn't know how to express.

"Joane?" she croaked, her voice hoarse and broken from the decompression.

"I'm not letting you go," Joane said, aware of how wild her voice sounded. "You aren't getting away from me that easily." Tristan didn't have the energy left to smile at her, but Joane felt her arms slowly wrapping around her back, solidifying the connection between them. Her breaths were shallow and slow, but they were there. Tris was breathing. Joane was breathing. Despite everything, they were alive. They were together. That was all that mattered.

"Good," Tris said weakly, her eyes sparkling. "Because you still owe me some money." Joane found herself laughing, even though the joke wasn't funny. She laughed and laughed until tears spilled down her face and her fingers shook against Tris's back. After a while, she heard Tris trying to laugh through the pain in her lungs. They drifted together, sharing the limited air for as long as it would last them. Joane tried to think of what would happen next, but she was running out of ideas, and she didn't care. Surrounded by the torn shreds of metal, lit from below by the blue glow of the artificial sun of Eden's Cradle, Joane was content to hang in the vacuum forever.

She caught a glimpse through her tears of Cygnus, miles and miles below her. There was a black spot on the unfinished ring surrounding the planet where the power station had been destroyed. Following the lines of blue light, she saw that the destruction had indeed spread across the entire array. Eden's Cradle was far too large to see if they'd damaged any other sections, but the massive power conduit around Cygnus had dimmed, and in the distance, she could barely make out fires coming from what must have been other power stations caught in a chain reaction.

"We did it," she whispered, her head pressed against Tris' shoulder, who nodded carefully.

"Look," Tris responded a few moments later, and Joane craned her aching neck around to look at where Tris had indicated with a weak point of her chin. There, emerging from several Fastlanes, thousands of miles away, were a swarm of Consortium Wing Fighters, guiding mobile relief stations and freighters of all kinds. "Looks like someone was listening." Joane nodded, satisfied. Even if they didn't make it, the Consortium, the *true* Consortium, would learn the truth of this place. They would stop the Progenitors, rescue the people here, and maybe even save some of the remaining planets resting in the Cradle. Joane imagined Fastlanes opening all around the artificial systems, the universe-spanning government bringing its forces to bear on this cult and its sickening machine. It wouldn't bring anyone back, but she hoped it gave the dead some measure of peace to know that their killers would be brought to justice. She took a deep breath, and found herself coughing. The oxygen in their miniature atmosphere was growing stale. Soon, the air would grow poisonous, and they would lapse into unconsciousness, clasping each other in a death grip as they spun through the Void endlessly.

"Tris," she said, her voice weak. She pulled back to look the woman in the face, one last time. Understanding was written across her features.

"It's okay," Tristan said, blinking slowly. "I'm…I'm glad you're here." It was then that Joane felt, rather than heard, a rumbling through the Void. Something was shaking the emptiness, driving a thrumming beat through the cloud of metal around them. She looked around them frantically, trying to figure out what was happening. Then, she saw it, as the darkness closed in at the edges of her vision. There was a ship, plated in gold and carried aloft by four massive engines glowing with gaiaformulaic energy at the corners of its hull. The cockpit jutted out from the body of the ship like the neck of some massive creature bearing down on them. Joane thought maybe she was hallucinating, but Tristan seemed to see it too.

They gaped at the vessel, minds spinning as they tried to understand what was happening, and who was rescuing them. Then, an entryway ramp dropped from the belly of the ship and a figure descending through the projected energy shield. It was Orion, sporting a glowing bandage across their chest and surrounded by a bright vacsuit. They waved with as much enthusiasm as they could muster, then pointed to their shoulder. Joane saw nothing on their jacket, then glanced down at her own shoulder. There, tucked into the pocket of her jacket, was Orion's badge, pinging away. She grinned. Those silver wings had finally lifted her up, she thought. The realization hit her then, that she *wasn't* going to die here. For once, there was the promise of safety. The promise of tomorrow. They'd fought and fought and fought, and somehow they'd survived.

She looked back at Tristan, who was already staring at her. As the ship coasted ever closer, a wordless agreement passed between them and they pulled each other closer. As the Cradle burned below them and the last bit of oxygen in their vacsuit dissipated, Joane kissed Tristan gently, softly, and with the promise that this would not be the last one they shared.

# Chapter 33
## New Beginnings

TRISTAN strode towards the cockpit, favoring her left leg. She wasn't sure exactly when she'd hurt it, but that didn't make the pain less real. The hallways of the Ladon were wide and extravagant, dotted with alcoves sporting beautiful stone statues and other icons of wealth. In the hours since their escape from Eden's Cradle, it hadn't taken much to discover that this ship, the Ladon, had indeed been Argus Regille's former craft. Tristan didn't think he'd have much to say about them commandeering it, and the thought of one final slight against the man who had almost killed them made Tristan chuckle. Consortium senators, even those involved in insane planet-stealing cults, carried a great deal of supplies on their ships. The medical supplies were beyond state-of-the-art, so much so that Tristan barely felt the sting of decompression in her lungs as she reached the cockpit door and keyed the command to slide it open. It opened in four triangular quadrants, sliding neatly into the corners and disappearing. She strode into the cockpit, a massive, pretentious ordeal with a captain's station raised above a lower bank of smaller monitoring and piloting stations.

Sitting at one of the stations, leaning back and evidently fighting off sleep, was Orion Masenna. The medical supplies on board had healed their wound almost immediately, and despite looking a bit pale, they seemed in good spirits. Across the room, already hard at work decrypting the ship's hard drive and the hidden datapads they'd found in Argus's desk, was Ahsha. She was still bruised and beaten up, but her eyes had the same glisten of intelligence and hypervigilance Tristan had spent years of her life staring into. She glanced up at her as she entered, and an odd look of satisfaction passed across her face.

"You're well, I take it?" Ahsha asked professionally, turning away from her work to give Tristan more attention than she'd ever gotten from the woman.

Tristan, startled, gave a small nod. It still hurt to speak, but she gave her a weak smile as she strode to the captain's station. Through the large, outward-pointing slope of the Ladon's viewport, she looked out at Eden's Cradle. Relief Stations had parked close to Cygnus-4 and the other salvageable planets. Though she couldn't see them, Tristan knew that Wing Fighters were everywhere across the station, fighting the Progenitor army and trying to arrest as many fleeing members of the cult that they could. Most of them would escape, if they were even here at the station, Tristan thought. The fight was far from over, but they'd scored a massive victory today and saved at least a dozen planets.

"I'm being contacted by a lot of my colleagues," Orion called out. "Soon enough, I'll have to answer them. We're about to be very popular, I'm afraid." Tristan sighed. The thought of endless questions about the events of the past few weeks made her stomach turn, but Ahsha looked positively giddy. She would be delighted to have a room full of people listening to her prattle on about her findings and how cleverly she had orchestrated the whole operation, no doubt. The door slid open, and the anxiety melted off of Tris' shoulders in waves as Joane stepped through, wearing her same beat-up jacket and a tired, weary smile.

"No one else on board," she confirmed. "Just us and the Cygnans who commandeered the vessel. They're in the communications center, contacting the others." Tris glanced out the viewport, squinting to make out the scattered freighters carrying the Cygnan factory workers that had risen up, overthrown the guards, and taken control of the power stations across the planet. As far as they could tell, Cygnus-4 had entirely been reclaimed by its people in a matter of hours, thanks in no small part to the chaos in the Progenitors' ranks.

"We're about to have company," Orion reported again, and Joane nodded gravely.

"All I want to do is sleep," she groaned, stumbling forward unevenly towards the captain's console. Once there, Tristan wrapped her in a firm, warm embrace and hummed pleasantly against her. "You sure you can't just punch it and get us out of here? We've outrun the Consortium a few times before."

Tristan smiled and patted her on the shoulder. "I think we're done running for a little while," she choked out, and Joane smiled in return before glancing around the cockpit.

"This is a really nice ship," Joane muttered conspiratorially. "I don't think anyone would notice if we…kept it." Tristan laughed. Joane was right, the Ladon was a fine ship, but walking the halls and standing at the captain's console still felt wrong.

"It's not home," she said quietly, running a finger along the console. She slowly pulled Darling's control sphere from her coat pocket, which it had somehow stayed secure in, then set it on the console, clicking it into place where the old control sphere had rested. Joane's hand came into view as Tris stared at the last piece of her ship, and she unfolded a small photo. Tristan gasped when she saw it. It was her, Joane, and Ahsha, all of them smiling for once. It was one of her favorite photos, but she thought it had been lost, along with everything else onboard the ship.

"But it could be," Joane offered, placing the photo into a groove at the back of the station. She stared at the image, the three of them smiling back at her. Tristan looked back at Joane, then at Orion, and finally at Ahsha. How quickly her life could change, she pondered. A chirp came from a nearby computer monitor, reporting that a Consortium vessel was inbound. Soon, the peace of this moment would be broken and they'd be thrown back into the chaotic mess of their lives. For a moment, though, it was just the four of them.

"It could be," Tristan agreed, taking Joane's hand. They prepared to face whatever was coming next the only way they knew how: Together.

# ACKNOWLEDGEMENTS


First and foremost, I have to thank everyone who has ever encouraged me along this journey. From those who simply listened to me ramble about my crazy ideas to those who were with me every step of the way, this book would not exist without you.

Notably, I would like to thank my fiance, Chloe, who stubbornly refused to let me give up on this book when the writer's block seemed insurmountable. From cheering me on to pitching the book to Line by Lion Publications, her steadfast dedication, unconditional support, and genuine love have shaped this story in countless ways.

On that note, I'd like to thank the entire team at Line by Lion Publications. Amanda, who listened to me nervously stumble my way through an elevator pitch for The Vanished Worlds under the sweltering summer heat at the Kentucky Renaissance Faire. Ian, my editor, who was extremely patient with my poor technological capabilities and my addiction to comma splices. Thomas, my cover artist, who endured and translated the sketches of someone who went into writing because he can't draw to save his life.

I would also like to give thanks to Cygnus, the constellation whose name I gave to the Cygnus system. Many of the locations in this novel are named for real astronomical objects; these references and artistic choices were made with the utmost respect for these locations, and no offense is intended to any future or current residents of those locations.

I must also thank my cats, Banshee and Archie, who served as emotional support during long hours of drafting and editing. They also served as distractions by attempting to sit on my keyboard. Archie, you are the most joyous little toasted marshmallow on both sides of the Mississippi. Banshee, you are my personal black hole: devoid of light, inescapable, and you suck.

I would like to offer a final thanks to you, dear reader. Ever since I was sharing my Transformers fanfictions with the rest of my fifth grade class, all I have ever wanted was to share the stories in my mind with the world. By picking up this book you have enabled me to live that dream, and I am eternally grateful.

9 781948 807562